Eliza
and
Silvanus

An 18th Century adventure
over land and sea

by

Graham Rogers

Copyright © 2022 Graham Rogers
All rights reserved.

ISBN: 9798801241449

Foreword

This story has been with me for nearly thirty years. I first came across it whilst I was an education officer working for Dorset LEA at Poole Museum around 1995. I left the museum in 1999 to become a professional storyteller and one of the hundreds of stories I told, over the following twenty years, was this one. Initially, it was the true-life tale of a shipwreck on the Purbeck coast on the 6th of January 1786 but as I told the story, over the years, my fascination with the characters grew until I wanted to know more about them. Eventually, I peeled off the strapline of 'true story' and discovered a world of fiction - and so the novel began.

I already had an interest in 18th-century life, on land and at sea, through family history research. Most of my ancestors, it appears, were labourers. The occasional cooper, carpenter and Royal Marine drummer boy, therefore, garnered extra interest.

This book has been twenty years in creation and ten years in writing and editing, both latter being largely a wintertime activity.

In 2005 Tim **Clare** wrote in the Guardian,

There is an auld axiom beloved of burnt-out English teachers, glamour-impoverished fantasists and a million other drudges seeking to transcend their lives of quiet desperation: everyone has a novel inside them.
This slogan has been appropriated as an article of faith by the amateur writing community, whilst its corollary - as a novelist, you have six-and-a-half billion potential rivals - remains the gravest of

heresies. Like a blind man in a room of ill-positioned rakes, any group indulging in such wilful myopia is doomed to a series of unpleasant collisions with reality.

Tim is probably right, and certainly in my case because my piece of *wilful myopia* is no longer inside me but is out there. I await, with curiosity, any distant reverberations it may provoke from its *doomed ... unpleasant collisions with reality.*

Contents

Foreword		v
Contents		viii
1	Skillet	1
2	Oranges	10
3	Bridge	21
4	Spidez	30
5	Breeches	40
6	Coop	44
7	Jacob	53
8	The Ugly Nymph	66
9	The Devil's Interval	76
10	Shears	89
11	Governess	94
13	There was a Crooked Man	97
12	Sons of Cockcrow	103
14	Lagoon	114
15	The Red Lodge	118
16	Will O' the Wisp	124
17	Minnows	137
18	Porcelain	141
19	Old Woman Lived in a Shoe	145
20	The Sea from the East	151
21	Rising Moon	157
22	Warren Blackmore	163
23	London	177
24	Threadgate	179
25	Beau Dan	188
26	Stars	199
27	Susan	206
28	Ashes	210
29	Punt	214
30	Pottage	220
31	Dogs	227
32	Trial	237
33	Lily	243
34	Mucking Flats	252
35	A Letter from India	260
36	Soup	264

37	Sparrows	269
38	Muffit	275
39	Bucket	281
40	Nawab	287
41	Elishimorta	293
42	Sampson	301
43	Frumenty	305
45	Anchors	333
46	Sheep	339
47	Quarrymen	345
48	Antelope	351
49	Anfin	359
50	Tom	367
51	Bedlamites	373
52	Bladders	377
53	Hair	387
54	Tuppence	391
55	Asylum	395
56	Greedy	403
57	Honey	409
58	Flames	417
59	Witness	421
60	Yawning Grave	423
61	Summer	427
62	Like two nightingales	431
List of Characters		i
Bibliography		viii
The Percy Family		xi

1   Skillet

Sixth of January 1786 – Aboard an Eastindiaman ship bound for India off the Purbeck coast, Dorset.

    Needs must when the Devil's at the helm. Bethany repeated this to herself several times, until it brought a swell of pride in her own determination. Her mother had taught her to stay away from such places as this. Being from the dockside meant that climbing down these steps was against all she had ever learnt. Nevertheless, Bethany told herself, there was no choice but her confidence soon faded as she remembered that anything more than one swig of port always provoked her suppressed vanity. She had found the wine in a corner of the captain's roundhouse and had thought to have just a single mouthful but in the darkness had gulped down half the decanter. Normally, boldness rarely failed her, she seldom needed drink to fortify herself against adversity, but events on this ship, and in this storm, were far from normal, and now time was running out. She waited a moment for the Madeira to warm her blood but she knew this was nothing more than procrastination.
    Drink, it is said, always provokes equivocation but she was on the gundeck of a sinking ship, in the middle of the night, and she needed to act decisively. She took the last few steps to the bottom of the ladder and then hesitated - yet again. Her face was burning and her

heart racing. The ship fell away, dropping a few feet, making her stumble and bringing a wave of water and a flurry of ice-cold wind from out of the darkness. Recognising the stale smell in the air, she put her hand over her mouth to stop herself from retching. It was the stench of tobacco, piss and vomit; the odour of drunken lecherous men. She turned, to run away, but the ship lifted and lurched to one side, and she tripped on her sodden skirt hems, stumbled to her knees and soaked more of her clothing. The ship shuddered back onto the rocks, grinding and splitting its timbers. The freezing water and rolling of the ship beneath her feet made Bethany's stomach feel as though it was squeezing against her lungs, which set her heart pounding. She must carry on and gain control. Taking a deep breath, she continued, the freezing seawater rolling in wavelets over her feet. Passing hammocks hanging between the ship's guns, all swinging in eerie unison, as if synchronised by some unseen controlling mechanism, she felt as though she would be sick at any moment and held onto the nearest hammock, but jumped back when she realised that there was a man in it – a soldier. Was he alive? As if to answer her question, his eyes opened and he grinned, saying,

'Thankee kindly, Molly.' Who's Molly? Was he talking to his last whore? He rolled over as if to go to sleep. And why was he still here? Had he ignored the call of, 'Every man for himself?' Should she tell him that the ship was sinking? But then, perhaps, he had reasoned that if his time had come, the Devil would take him, be he the foremost or hindmost, and that he may as well remain in a warm hammock and let events choose their own path.

Bethany had been here only a few days before, shown around the refitted ship with Eliza, her mistress, on a tour of the ship led by the first mate, Mr Berrington, who happened to be Eliza's, her mistress's, uncle. On that day everywhere had been freshly scrubbed bright and clean. Each deck had hanging pomanders and bunches of lavender. There had been swaggering officers, pristine scarlet-clad soldiers, shanty men, fiddlers, fife players, drummer boys and jigging, forelock-tugging, sailors. It was hard to believe this was the same ship now. What a difference a few days, and this storm, had made. Her nausea had passed and she continued forward. Somehow, she must overcome everything, treat these obstacles as distractions, and finish the task she had set herself.

For three years, until the beginning of this journey, Bethany had been Eliza's governess. As well as teaching her mistress everything Mrs Percy thought her daughter should know; Bethany had tried to keep her young charge out of trouble. But governing Eliza had not been easy. Now Bethany was Eliza's travelling companion and at this moment she was trying to fulfil a plan whereby her mistress might escape this sinking ship with her life. Bethany had become accustomed to placing her mistress's needs before her own – and, anyway, keeping busy with this survival plan she hoped might quell her own fears.

In front, and to her right, was a heap of musical keyboard instruments piled high between two of the ship's great guns. Seawater washed over the lower frameworks. Then she heard a noise, out of place amongst the roaring storm and the groaning timbers of the ship, it was the bleating of sheep. Out of the darkness ahead, emerged three of the animals, two paddling and a lamb swimming along the deck by their side. Seeing Bethany, they turned back. Strange, she thought, in this situation, you would think a plump governess would be the least of their fears.

This area was the soldiers' mess. Was there anything she could use here? Having to walk through deeper water raised her fear of what lay ahead, and made her stomach heave again. She must concentrate on the task, and not let the perils overwhelm her. The mess area had some lanterns, hanging from chains and still illuminated. Bethany searched a vacated hammock and an abandoned kit bag, while, somewhere a drunken sailor sang, interrupting himself, and cursing the Devil, his own luck, and God Almighty, for allowing this calamity to fall upon his back. Bending over to rummage through a soldier's kit, she felt something pushing against her backside. Bethany turned and screamed, being face to face with a grinning soldier. His hand was on her backside. His other held a bottle and was hooked over the hammock ropes. She backed away as far as possible from his leering face, missing front teeth and foul breath, but the ship's gun and mess-table prevented her escape. The soldier's dishevelled red coat hung open and as the ship rolled, he struggled to stay upright and was having difficulty focussing his eyes. One minute he was eyeing Bethany, the next he looked off into the distance, as if searching for someone else. It did not look like this was his first bottle of brandy that night.

"Whoa there! What have we here, then? A lass, looking for a man, I'd say. Yes, Billy, that's what we have here, alright. And ain't that a blessing, to be sure, 'cause don't you happen to find a little time on your hands at present, Billy? Didn't your very own sergeant, not so long ago, say to you, Now, Billy Spraggs, you done your bit on these here pumps for John and Company? Get yourself up above, now, Lad, and on your way help yourself to a bottle, or three, of the captain's brandy. Oh, and be sure to find yourself a whore with hips like the rear end of three-deck Spanish man-o-war. A whore, what needs a good ramming." He tried to make a matching gesture with his hips but almost lost his grip on the hammock and struggled to regain his feet, spilling brandy over Bethany's bonnet. "Well, Sergeant, I got the brandy, pretty quick. But where's your big hipped whore, Billy Spraggs? She's here, Sergeant, right here. Billy Spraggs always does what his sergeant tells him. Now, madam, here I am, and all our prayers is answered."

Bethany had heard that most of the soldiers had jumped ship when first it had hit the rocks, but this one looked too drunk to stand, let alone jump. I could do without this, she thought. How, in the name of Jesus, can I get away from him? Before, in times of crises, sometimes an inner voice surprised her, by speaking up and suggesting a way out of her troubles. Routinely, she put this down to divine intervention, but in this situation, Jesus must have been pressed for time, what with the other two-hundred-and-fifty souls aboard this ship. Luckily, another voice came to her aid, her mother stepped forward to fulfil the need. She must have been sitting in a corner of her daughter's mind, all these years waiting for the moment her advice would be required. Bethany's panic began to peel away as her mother's confident tones reminded her of another drunken man. That time it had been in the backroom of their family inn. The sailor had broken into their room. Bethany – Little Flossy in those days – had been terrified as she watched the drunken man push her mother across the room, but her mother had stayed calm, and had later scolded Bethany. Not for being scared, but for showing the man her fear. 'Never let them see you are afraid of them,' she had said, 'and never turn your back. Wait until the opportunity arises, then hit them with something weighty and, if they're still moving after that, hit them again.' After Bethany had become a governess, she assumed that her mother's advice would never be needed, Bethany having become part of an upper-class family's household. Nevertheless, being in the captain's wealthy family had not saved her from the assault from Eliza's drunken brother. That time she had been caught off guard and had not yet taken to barricading the door to her room each night.

"Not so fast, my lovely cherry top," Bethany said, placing a hand on her hip and a palm in the air between her and the swaying soldier, "anybody would think the ship's sinking."

"I thought it was sinking."

She looked at the soldier: tall, thin, boots, breeches, jacket, all near enough her mistress's size. She could achieve her task down here and quell his unwelcomed ardour all in one fell swoop if only something heavy would come to hand. She needed some time.

"The matter of it is this," she said, "I'll not be fucked by a man with his boots on. Call me fussy, if you like, but that's the way I am. Get them off, and you can have me over this table." The offer instantly wiped away the soldier's lecherous grin and replaced it with a wide-eyed gawky look of surprise. He tried to concentrate while fumbling drunkenly with his boots.

"Give us them here," Bethany said. The soldier sat on the mess table between the hammock and gun, while Bethany stepped over his outstretched leg and he pushed her backside away with his other foot.

Shouting out, Billy asked himself, "Who was the last woman to take your boots off, Billy? Well, that'd be your dear ol' mother, back in County Clare. God bless you, Mother! Your Billy boy's doing just fine ... just fine."

His boots off, Bethany said, "Now your breeches, Billy,"

"What, kicks and all?"

Bethany's mother had felled her attacker while his breeches were around his ankles, making him stagger and fall, ready for the secondary blow. However, this soldier was so drunk, he could barely stand – kicks or no kicks.

"Now your jacket, if you please, and that shirt too. Let's have you as your mother first saw you." He did as Bethany asked and then stood there, naked and to attention, in front of Bethany. He saluted and continued his dialogue with himself,

"Are you ready for action there, Billy Spraggs? Yes, Sir, Sergeant, Billy Spraggs is ready for action, guns loaded and rolled out."

"Close your eyes then, Billy and I'll give you such a sweet kiss to start us off." She looked at him; she was thirty-seven years old, and had never seen a naked man before. The attack by Eliza's brother had been in the dark. He had crawled into her bed and she, not being fully awake, had gone against her mother's advice and turned her back on him to escape. Master Welstan had grabbed her, forced her face down into the pillow and, had his way. She had seen nothing of him. Now, this man, Billy Spraggs, was naked, grinning, eyes shut, standing to attention. Bethany had worked hard to remove traces of her background. If she had completed this voyage to India, her acquired manners would have been sufficient to gain her a good position. Her plans, however, were about to be wrecked, along with this ship, by this ferocious storm.

"Keep those eyes shut tight, now Billy." Now she had a moment to look around for a suitable weapon. Amongst the remains of a meal on the mess table, there were bowls, wooden spoons, a dish of half-eaten stew and a knife. She grabbed the knife but then felt she could not come to terms with stabbing someone, even this soldier. What else could she use? Then she saw it, fallen from the table onto a bench, a heavy cast iron skillet with a wooden handle. Well, thank you, Jesus, for this very small mercy. Two-hundred-and-fifty souls aboard this ship, praying for miracles, and you find time to send Little Flossy a cast iron skillet. Her mother had never trusted to divine providence and had relied upon a copper cudgel, kept under her pillow for such eventualities. Bethany raised the heavy pan above her head, but … he was just a boy, such pale skin under his black hair, lean, bulging muscles, his eyes tight shut, silly drunken grin and his lips puckered awaiting a kiss. Bethany's mother piped up again. 'Do it Flossy; hit him now. The bastard will open his eyes any minute and he will have you and slit your throat by way of thanks.'

'Needs must,' she said to herself, but stopped again. His stupid grin was fading, and tears were running from his screwed-up eyes. He began shaking and sobbing, and cried out,

"We're all going to die, Mama. Captain to smallest nipper, all going to sink to a watery grave and be eaten by the stinking crabs."

He set the bottle on the table and did not appear to notice Bethany holding the skillet high over her head ready to strike. He turned and fell onto the bench, head in his hands, his cries, for a moment, competing with the noise of the raging storm above.

Bethany put the skillet down, picked up the boots, clothes and the bottle of brandy, carefully squeezed behind him as he lay, head on the table. She turned to make her way back towards the ladder but stopped to look down at him. The soldier seemed so fragile, young, pale and weak, now stripped of his uniform and piss-pot bragging. She noticed for the first time the lash marks crisscrossing his backbone and was tempted to run her fingers over the scars. Not much older than her mistress, his sobbing continued. She pulled a blanket from the hammock, draped it over his shoulders and walked off with the bundle of boots and clothes.

2   Oranges

This was his world; he felt at home here. Standing upright on the larboard side of the roundhouse, back against an oak stanchion and arm braced against the beams above; the captain held his head high. It was where on previous voyages he would stand to receive reports from his officers and, following dinner, talk to his officers. When the roundhouse was empty, it was here that he would ponder over decisions he was about to take. Now, despite the situation of despair, hopelessness and fear, he would stand here, as a figurehead of leadership, a beacon of salvation, a buttress of resolution.

The highest deck of an East Indiaman is the poop deck, which is at the stern of the ship. On this ship, immediately beneath that deck, and stretching almost the whole width of the ship, is the captain's cabin, known as the roundhouse. Here were gathered an assortment of over fifty disparate individuals. Even if there was little prospect of rescue, the captain was determined to provide comfort to these souls by enduring as a competent figure of command. Even if all around him: his family, friends, crew and the ship itself, appeared to be falling apart, he would remain unbroken. Yet beneath this resolute mask, hid a distraught man, repeatedly asking himself, how and why all this had come to pass? The ship was sturdy, well tested, had an admirable set of officers, an almost full complement of crew and had recently undergone an extensive refit. Had something failed in his chain of command? Had he made errors? Or was it simply due to a design fault with the new, untested and, as had been proved, poorly constructed, haws-plugs? Designed by the company's naval architects, the haws plugs were meant to keep the sea from entering the ship through the spaces beside the anchor ropes, but in the storm, they had let in an uncontrollable amount of water. Possibly the problems arose from his decision to set sail before Mr Dodds, the ship's carpenter, was aboard. The experienced Mr Dodds may have made a quicker and more efficient effort at rectifying the deficient plugs. Perhaps, the captain thought, he should have been more thorough in his investigation into the disquiet amongst the crew; many had refused to man the pumps. In the end, for all he could tell, it could have been the sheer scale of the storm – in all his years at sea, he had never seen the like: temperatures below freezing, the storm so violent and long-lasting, perhaps it was more than any ship might survive. Maybe, God, in his fury at mankind's omnipresence upon the oceans of the world, had created this storm to rage around the globe, bringing peril to every ship afloat. Captain Percy decided that he would complete the ship's log in the morning, and that he would point out that the unfortunate situation had arisen from, 'a confluence of circumstances. Inwardly, but the feeling was not far below the skin, he felt his anguish was at the point of breaking through. However, he was determined to keep it under control. Although the ship might not be saved, he would navigate a course of salvation for his passengers and crew.

Either side of the captain sat his two young daughters, Eliza and her younger sister, Mary-Ann.

Nearby were his nieces and some other young ladies on a passage to a new life in Asia. The captain was conscious that everyone looked up to him for reassurance. Everyone, that was, except Miss Mansell, who was crying to the heavens for help. Distress had overwhelmed her to such an extent that the captain had ordered his officers to secure her with heavy woollen blankets and straps to prevent her from fleeing into the night. Repeatedly demanding that she should follow the commandments of the Lord and be allowed to walk to France; once restrained, she had descended into fits of screaming. Eventually, as she became exhausted, her cries faded, until another huge wave would hit the ship, when her panic would rise again and her torment renew.

When the ship had struck, many had fled into the roundhouse, hoping for help or consolation from the captain. The purser sat on the ship's chest of gold and silver, the ship's surgeon embraced his medical bag, various crew members and army officers huddled in the shadows, some with wives whom they were attempting to console. Some sat disbelieving, others comforted neighbours, whilst many were on their knees in prayer.

A door opened at the rear of the cabin, letting in an icy blast of sea spray. Those at prayer looked up in a moment of expectation, hoping their prayers had reached the Almighty, and that the arrival of a rescue party was about to be announced, but it was only the captain's eldest daughter's travelling companion, Bethany, carrying a bundle of clothes, followed by the second mate, Mr Congleton with a box of candles. Hope amongst those at prayer soon faded as he busied himself cutting the candles with his pocket knife, lighting and placing them around the cabin. Rather than lifting the spirits of those in the roundhouse, the extra illumination only helped to expose the despair on the faces of everyone and increase the general feeling of inescapable hopelessness.

Having finished with the candles, Mr Congleton, produced several oranges, cut them into slices and offered them around,

"Perhaps, the ladies would care for a little orange, to quench their thirst," he said, offering the fruit to the captain's family and other ladies, but ignoring the Indian soldiers' wives and female servants.

Mr Miller got to his feet and took a piece of orange, saying,

"A word, if you please, Mr Congleton." Then, stepping a few paces to the rear of the roundhouse and away from the other passengers and crew, said, "Sir, although, due to a matter of convenience: I may appear on the ship's muster as a midshipman. You may be aware that I am in fact the captain's daughter's tutor of music. Also, I am charged with the care of the captain's personal cargo of musical keyboard instruments, which are to be sold for considerable profit on arrival at Madras. The day before yesterday, the captain arranged to have these items moved from the lower cargo hold to a safer ..."

"Mr Miller, I fear time is not our ally, please, Sir, your point?"

"Mr Congleton, there is a spinet, a virginal and three folding harpsichords with a total value, on arrival at Madras, of well over one-thousand pounds. These are now on, what I believe you call, the gundeck. I fear they may well be in danger from the moist conditions which prevail in that part of the ship, please, it is imperative that you arrange to bring the keyboards up here."

"Mr Miller, at present I am concerned with the matter of preserving the lives of these ladies. My advice to you, Sir, is abandon anxiety for your musical instruments and look to saving your own life."

Bethany had always imagined that the prospect of impending doom would force her to hide in some dark corner, but now she was faced with the reality of imminent disaster, she felt free of her usual constraints. The captain's sherry, together with some of Billy Spraggs' brandy, seemed to have freed her from the shackles of social etiquette. Consequently, she walked over to the silver tray, still half-full of oranges and said, "Excuse me, Mr Congleton, please, allow me." Then she walked over to the other side of the cabin, where she offered the fruit around. On the floor, in the shadows, sat a delicate young Indian woman, her arms around her knees. She rocked back and forth, chanting a repetitive phrase in a language that Bethany could not understand. The young woman stopped, declined the orange, saying,

"Thank you very much, that is kind of you. Please, you can help us?"

"Yes, of course, if I can," said Bethany, sitting down by the woman's side.

"You ask the captain for us; we get into small boat and go to the land?" The soldier put his arm further around his wife's shoulders,

"Kalinda, that is not possible. All the small boats are gone, swept away. Even if one survived, the sea is too rough." Looking up at Bethany, he said, "I'm sorry Miss, my wife is distraught. It was kind of you to bring the oranges."

Bethany replied, "The captain believes we shall be safe until the break of day, and that with daylight, rescue will arrive."

The woman closed her eyes, continued her chant, but soon broke off again,

"Husband, you are a good man; bringing me here to visit England and your family. You are a soldier of the East India Company; surely your Devayana – your journey – will take you on the path of the sun. I have been bad, horrible. I have offended the Gods by leaving my family against my father's wishes and coming to England with you, my husband. My Devayana will take me along the path of the Moon, and down to the land of darkness." Bethany touched her gently on the wrist and quickly glanced into the soldier's eyes. Then she got up without saying anything further and returned the tray of oranges to Mr Congleton.

"A little orange, Sir?" Mr Congleton asked, offering the captain some. The captain ignored the oranges, leant towards his officer and said, quietly, in his ear,

"Mr Congleton, we should attempt to devise a course of escape for passengers and crew. You have been out on the deck and seen the situation for yourself. Can you see a way forward?"

"I think not, Sir, the situation looks hopeless."

"Then if not for all, is there not a plan we might execute to save the ladies?"

"Maybe, if the ship lasts another six hours, 'til daybreak, and those on shore perhaps have heard our distress gunfire and, in the daylight, they discover our predicament; then they might manage to organise some sort of rescue. Mr Reeve is attempting to cut the bowsprit away and fashion a bridge to the nearby rocks. If he can get across, and manages to scale the cliffs, he might well summon help earlier. Then, with ropes and cradles from the cliff top, a rescue could be effected for the ladies, but with the tide on the turn and soon to be rising, I fear there is no telling what situation Mr Reeve will find on the rocks ashore, or what will befall the ship in the meantime."

"Quite so, Mr Congleton, quite so. Then we shall pray that the ship holds together until the morning and the safe return of Mr Reeve. But then, if Mr Berrington had not been lost overboard, I would have appointed him for this undertaking. Mr Reeve, whose competence I do not question, is ranked, third mate. As second mate, and senior to Mr Reeve, you must undertake the crossing to the shore to raise the alarm."

"Sir, Mr Reeve is the far more agile man than I, being much younger of course, perhaps, the task would be in more capable hands if he were to undertake it?"

"It is a question of seniority, Mr Congleton. You shall head for the shore, while I remain here to comfort and reassure the ladies, passengers and remaining crew. Now, we have our courses charted for the way ahead to seek out assistance; you shall look to the adjacent land and I to the heavens above. Good luck to you, Mr Congleton."

"Bethany," said Eliza, "a companion should be with her mistress, sit here beside me."

"Certainly, Miss."

"Sing for me, Bethany."

"Sing, me Miss? What shall I sing?"

"A suitable hymn, of course. What else?" Bethany obeyed,

"O Thou who comest from above."

Eliza recognised the song and joined in.

Hearing the singing, the captain smiled and felt relieved that his daughter was apparently coming to terms with the situation.

"Kindle that flame of sacred love

upon the altar of my heart."

Eliza stopped singing at the thought of love. The fearful questions that had filled her mind over the past month returned and choked her with tears. Where was he? Her love? What had happened to Silvanus? Had he been hanged as Bethany had said?

"There's a bottle of brandy here Miss," said Bethany, "would you like some?"

"Brandy, Bethany? Certainly not. My father is only ..." Eliza stopped, as another wave thundered over the decks above, replacing her fear for Silvanus with terror for her own predicament. She took the bottle,

"A glass, if you please, Bethany?"

"Put the bottle to your lips, Miss." Eliza did.

"Bethany, what is this? Surely it is not Brandy. I think it must be rum?" Eliza closed her eyes and took another larger swig. When she opened them, her father was standing over her,

"Eliza, what are you doing? How unbecoming of my daughter. Come with me." Eliza wiped the dribble of spirit from her chin and stood up to follow her father.

"Stay close by, Eliza. I fear for your safety when you are out of my sight," said the captain.

"Father, is the ship sinking? It is of comfort to be with you, but, forgive me, should we not attempt to make for the shore and save our lives?"

"I am surprised that you should question your father, and do not forget that I am also your captain." He paused, for a few moments and then added, in a gentler tone, "Believe me, Eliza, I can see salvation ahead, and meanwhile this is the safest place." The captain then turned his attention to others in the roundhouse,

"If you would please be kind enough, ladies and gentlemen? I have just been assured by one of my officers that the ship is holding together well. She is a sturdy vessel, built of the finest English oak. I have instructed my highest-ranking officer to carry out whatever is necessary to reach the shore with a party of men, inform the authorities of our plight and request that they assist in arranging our safe rescue. I have every confidence that he will carry out my orders successfully. With the coming of the new day, those ashore will have become aware of our situation and rescue will be forthcoming. I am confident that all will be well. In the meanwhile, please try not to alarm yourselves unduly."

With the waves and the wind outside, few of the more distant crew and passengers in the roundhouse could make much of the captain's words. However, he continued as loud as was conducive to keeping a reassuring and calming tone,

"May I also add, that in no way should you consider these events have been brought upon your good selves by the wrath of the Almighty because of some transgression of your own. I do not believe that this storm is the work of the Lord. Conversely, its violence and duration suggest that it may very well be the work of the Devil. In which case our prayers will bring the Lord's help, in whichever manner he chooses. If, however, God has sent this fearsome storm, then undoubtedly it is because of my actions and in no way retribution against anyone else. As the Lord said, 'Woe be unto the shepherd that destroys and scatters my sheep.' And, if my memory serves, the passage concludes, 'For I will gather them and bring them unto me and they will fear no more, nor be dismayed.' It is always darkest before the dawn ...

"Despite being at the coasts of dark destruction, deliverance, I am sure, will arrive with the rising of the sun. Let us all remain calm. Let us pray."

Eliza felt comforted by her father's words, but, as if in an angry response, the storm blew even harder, huge waves crashed over the ship, water poured in through cracks in the deck above and soaked the huddled, cowering crew and passengers.

The onslaught shifted the ship from its position on the rocks, the bows slipped further beneath the waves and the upper deck split with a sickening crack from the starboard to the larboard gunwales. Causing Miss Mansell's screams to pierce the night yet again.

3   Bridge

"Father, I fear that waiting here in the dark we shall all soon follow Miss Mansell's example and lose composure. Is it possible," Eliza asked, "that some of us might join the officers and cross to the shore?" The captain said nothing for a while and continued gazing across the roundhouse. Eliza began to wonder after a minute, or so, whether her father had heard her question. But then he sat down on the settle next to her, and said, in as quiet a voice, as he thought might still be heard against the storm outside,

"Eliza, need I remind you that you are a lady, and my daughter," He spoke whilst maintaining a reassuring countenance for his passengers and crew. He continued, "You cannot join the officers. They should be allowed to carry out their work unhindered. Ladies and passengers must stay in the safe confines of the roundhouse. You, as my eldest daughter, should stay by my side. Please behave like a daughter of whom your mother and I can be proud." The captain shifted from beneath a stream of seawater, which had begun pouring from the split timbers above. He then went to help Miss Mansell, who had fallen from her seat and was similarly being drenched with seawater and from which her bonds prevented her escaping. Again, the ship shifted on its rocky perch. While her father was distracted, Eliza took the opportunity to escape his attention, and slip way to the darker side of the roundhouse, where she sat on the deck beside Bethany,

"Have you finished that rum"?

"I still say it is brandy, Miss, but what would a governess, turned travelling companion, know about spirits?" She passed the bottle to Eliza, who drank some,

"I have a confession to make, Bethany."

"You, Miss, confess to me? I'm not a priest."

"Do you believe that our lives are predestined, Bethany."

"Predestined? Could we discuss this later, Miss?"

"I have never discussed the subject with anyone before, Bethany, I have heard the vicar refer to the subject on occasions, which has led me to believe that our lives are all preordained by the Almighty. I should have remembered the fable of the Old Man and Death, and been careful for what I wished."

Bethany said, "Miss, my mother tended to believe that we choose our own paths through this world, and that the better informed we were, the more likely it was that we made good choices. I suppose that I believe the same, Miss. But let's continue this another …"

"I have supposed that prayer can change these preordained paths. I have been praying recently – I could see no other way – I think the Lord has listened to me, and answered my supplications. And therefore, I need to apologise to everyone aboard this ship," Eliza said, "and especially to my poor father."

"Why, Miss? Do you believe that you raised the storm?" asked Bethany.

"Yes, possibly. In some way. Yes, I think the storm could be my responsibility. I think that I have caused it. I was selfish. I should have taken care of what I asked for. In the fable the old man casually asks Death to relieve him of his burden, but he did not expect Death to appear."

"Fables are just stories, Miss. Do you believe it to be possible that your thoughts and prayers could invoke a storm?" asked Bethany.

"Yes, I do. Why else would people pray? I have been asking the Almighty to change my path, and to make something happen, which would prevent me from travelling to India. I wanted to stay here in England and have been pleading that our journey will come to a premature end. Consequently, I believe my prayers brought this disaster upon us all."

"Can you believe that, Miss? Believe that the storm of recent days is not due to happenchance, but is a child of your wishes? Are you sure you have not been influenced by the memory of Shakespeare's Prospero? I seem to remember that you read that not so long ago. If your one mind can foment such disaster, it would seem equally reasonable that two-hundred-and-fifty souls' prayers might counter such a wish and avoid all this torment. Look at all these people, Miss, why would the Almighty listen to you, and not see fit to listen to them? Unless, what you are suggesting is that the Lord gives more attention to the prayers of people like yourself, of high status, than the prayers of these ordinary people."

"Prospero was a magician, he used magic. I was just praying, Bethany. Prospero used magic and that is blasphemous, Bethany."

"Do you think so? God doesn't give a man a snake if he is praying for a fish." Bethany tried to catch her mistress's eye, but Eliza resolutely stared away into the darkness. After some thought Bethany said,

"While we are in the business of unbosoming confidences, I believe it is I who should make an apology to you, Miss."

"What? If it is the matter of you drinking my father's sherry, Bethany …"

"He has enough to go around, Miss. No, it is more serious: if it were not for me, you would not be here; in this perilous situation," said Bethany.

"But what have you to do with the matter?"

"Your mother instructed me to report to her on your behaviour."

"What, how dare you, Bethany?"

"I tried to protect you, but she saw through my evasiveness. Your mother is a very persuasive woman. Eventually, she convinced me that going to India would be in your own best interests. Also, you must remember, Miss, that there was a time when you wanted nothing else but to travel to India. You told me you were going to ride elephants and chase tigers – have you forgotten that?"

"But I was a child then." Eliza tensed; she was shocked and confused. How could Bethany have done such a thing, to spy upon her and tell her mother? Had all that she had thought private been spied upon and related to her mother?

"If there was one person in our household whom I felt I might have trusted," said Eliza, "it would have been you, Bethany."

"I did it for you, Miss. Your mother convinced me that telling her about your behaviour was in your best interest. I reported to her that you had visited the cooper at his camp on Fiddlespit." Eliza could neither speak nor move.

"I am sorry, Miss. Your mother persuaded me that in India you would soon meet a young dashing English officer and forget about your lowly cooper. I never knew his name, and never connected him to the robbery on your way back from London."

"I was there, Bethany, Silvanus was not one of the robbers ... don't you think I would have recognised him?"

"I understand now, Miss, that I was wrong to believe your mother's version of events." Eliza could say nothing, but stared into the darkest corner of the roundhouse, trying to come to terms with this new information about her mother's involvement. While the storm raged outside, there was silence between the two.

A door opened, and a gust of cold wind howled in and around the roundhouse. Mr Reeve, the third mate, arrived, gaining everyone's attention. He went straight to the captain and whispered in his ear. What new information was he delivering to the captain? He turned to take his leave, but one of the passengers scuttled up to him, blocking his exit. It was the man whom Bethany had nicknamed, Crab-like Man, as he always appeared to be walking sideways and seemed to have his eyes set very high in his head. His name was George Schwartz and, speaking with a German accent, had told anyone and everyone who would listen that he was returning to Madras to collect the remaining part of a considerable fortune. As he talked to Mr Reeve, Schwartz continued his sideways movement, encircling the third mate. Mr Reeve had to spin around to keep facing the passenger and hear what it was that the man wanted. Eventually they were near enough to Bethany for her to overhear the pair.

"Mister Reeve, please, I am asking, is there a way to get onto the shore?"

"We have, Sir, engineered a rough bridge," replied Mr Reeve, "built from the remains of the bowsprit. One end is secured to the ship and the other, when I last saw the situation, resting upon a large rock towards the shore. Those that reach the rock may well be safe there, or perhaps might swim or float with the aid of some buoyancy, and reach the foot of the cliffs."

"Thank you, Mister Reeve. Please, would you help me to get my goods together?"

"I am sorry Sir, but my duty is my master and the captain's commands direct me elsewhere." As the two spoke, Mr Reeve tried to get away from Mr Schwartz, who scuttled even faster around the officer.

"My goods are worth much money." Schwartz stood still for a moment, then leant forward and said discretely,

"I will see you well rewarded, Mister Reeve,"

"I cannot, sir. If you wish to attempt the crossing, which I must warn you is precarious in the extreme, then follow me now. With or without your goods."

"Miss," said Bethany, tugging at Eliza's arm, "did you hear that? A bridge. You can save yourself, Miss."

"I would fall off and drown."

"But you can swim."

"How could I swim; the water is far too cold?"

"You swam last Autumn in the sea."

"How do you know that? How ... You were watching us?"

"I wanted to see that you were all right. I went to get help but then decided against it. Then later, when I returned to Fiddlespit, there was no sign of either of you. I assumed you had gone home. So, I returned to the house."

"I shall not swim; my father would never allow it," said Eliza. "Well then, Miss, we'll stay here and trust that God has time to attend to the good captain's prayers and grant that tomorrow night we shall sleep in a bed ashore and not have to be content with a bed on the seafloor."

The captain addressed his passengers again,

"Having just received reports from my third officer, Mr Reeve, I believe that the ship is reasonably sound and will remain a haven for us until daylight. Our earlier gunfire, I do believe, will have attracted attention ashore, and Mr Congleton's arrival there, forthwith, will serve to speed our rescue. I assure you; all will be well. Meanwhile, let us all pray together,
"Our Father who art in Heaven …

Bethany tugged at Eliza's sleeve again.
"Stop that, you forget your place, Bethany," said Eliza.
"Miss, I know a way that I might repay the debt I owe, for wronging you so, but you must swim, as you did in the sea at Fiddlespit."
"As you spied upon me, I am surprised you do not remember that I swam in breeches and a close-fitting jacket. I could not swim in these heavy skirts."
"I have clothes, see?" she showed Eliza her bundle, "Look, soldier's clothes. Please, Miss, put them on."
"Bethany, I shall not. How dare you suggest such a thing?"
After some discussion with the captain, Mr Reeve together with Mr Schwartz encircling him, made his way out of the back of the roundhouse.
Maybe, thought Eliza, I should ignore my father and follow them to see this bridge, but why is everyone not attempting the crossing to the shore? She heard her father's voice faltering. Was his rock-like nature beginning to crumble? She could not bear the thought of her father being in such a situation. How could she leave him now, she wondered, pulling a blanket around her shoulders? Bethany's confession came back to her, like a pain in the pit of her stomach. But then perhaps

her travelling companion was not to blame. No one could withstand her mother's interrogations.

She tried to conjure up pleasant dreams to calm herself, as she had done when a child. She pulled the blanket over her head to shut out the world. Yes, she would stay with her father. It was her duty. In the morning rescue would arrive, and all would be well. She closed her eyes and struggled to blot out her worries by replacing them with comforting memories.

Outside the wind rose in fury and the sleet turned to snow, which then began to freeze to those parts of the masts, spars and rigging, which were not constantly washed clear by the onslaught of the briny waves. Any potential rescue party arriving at the top of the cliff, would have been set into flight by the apparition of a ship's ghostly skeleton, lolling around in the shadows, and as they fled, not one of them would have imagined they were abandoning so many desperate souls.

4   Spidez

September 1783 – The garden of the captain Percy's family home at Fiddlesham in Sussex.

Eliza never felt relaxed indoors, and especially when sitting alone in her classroom facing her governess. Sometime, before Bethany had arrived at Fiddlesham House, Eliza had to contend with a far stricter governess named Kelpwell. In those days, the young girl would try to escape into the gardens, but Kelpwell nearly always tracked her down. During the day, Kelpwell kept her ward confined to the study-room, where the governess would strut up and down, while Eliza pretended to struggle with some problem in maths or grammar. Eliza would pass the time by choosing which creature Kelpwell most resembled. One thing Eliza was sure of was that Kelpwell was bird-like, but which bird? Her solitary nature and cold, calculating walk, suggested the raven family, albeit, one that had recently undergone a strict military training. Kelpwell always dressed in black, wore grey knitted mittens without fingers and when Eliza was on the run, would swoop out of a hedgerow when least expected. That was like the behaviour of a rook, Eliza thought. However, Kelpwell's practice of constantly picking on Eliza and going over the same issues, together with her eerie distress call, 'Eliza, Eliza,' gave the game away; she was, without question, a carrion crow.

Eliza's mother chose Kelpwell, firstly, because of her grim outward appearance; secondly, Kelpwell's conviction that an upbringing should be based on an assumption that, all joy is thinly disguised temptation, and thus, the work of the Devil; and thirdly, Kelpwell was the only candidate who would take the position at the remuneration offered. Eliza's attempted escapes were mostly unsuccessful, and on the few occasions they did succeed, freedom was short-lived. Nonetheless - as is the way of a trapped sparrow seeking the one solitary open window in a conservatory - persistence succeeds. When an escape was successful, Eliza would seek out Esau, the old gardener. It appeared that her governess would not willingly confront men, and when Eliza was with Esau, Kelpwell – along with everyone else – would leave her alone.

Esau fascinated Eliza, mainly because he had always shown great interest in her. He was the closest she had had to a childhood friend. One day, having escaped from supervision, she could smell wood smoke and, in a few moments, had found Esau sitting by the edge of the lake, poking a stick in the embers of a fire that he had lit to burn cut branches. Esau had been the Percy's gardener for so long that the rest of the family took little notice of him. Captain Percy would often remark on the height of the monkey-puzzle tree, the magnificence of the rhododendrons on the path to the sea or the splendour of the lily pads in the lake and Mrs Percy would often charm visitors with the fragrance of the garden roses, the beauty of the hydrangeas or the brilliance of the azalea beds but in their eyes, Esau was just another part of the garden, which in some manner maintained itself. Esau always had the same appearance: ragged brimmed straw hat, sun-wrinkled black face, silver tipped ginger stubbly beard, yellow neckerchief, rusty brown corduroy waistcoat and moss-green breeches. He looked, to Eliza, as though he had himself sprung up in some overlooked part of the garden.

"There you are, Esau. I have come to talk to you?"

"An' there 'e be, Miss. Gooday to 'e. Esau be 'appy to listen to 'e, Miss. Goodness, 'e 'ave grown, since last Esau saw 'e."

"Why do governesses have to make life so difficult?"

"Esau wouldn't truly 'ave an answer to that, Miss; what with Esau never having a governess, himself. How about Miss assists Esau, an' pokes these embers round clay pots? Let's warm up some grub. Now, how comes 'e finds 'e self here, Miss, all lonesome, like?"

"Everyone was too busy watching my sister show off, to see me escape. If Mother hears that you have been talking to me, it will mean trouble for you, Esau?"

"Don't 'e be worrit about Esau, Miss."

"How is it, that my mother never seems to trouble you, Esau?"

"Esau suppose it bees 'cause Esau doos not enter 'er ladyship's window an' 'er ladyship doos not enter Esau's window – not these days, anyways. When Esau first come to Fiddlesham Esau weren't gardener, Esau be a page boy. It being the fashion to 'ave a Blackamoor in big houses in those days. Can 'e imagine that, Miss; Esau in finest blue and gold livery, an' shown off to all visitors as a great curosity? But folks didn't understand young Esau, an' Esau didn't understand folks, 'cause Esau still be speaking an' thinking in 'e words of Esau's Debbonshire family, who Esau grew up with. So, after a few days, Esau be prenticed to gardener. Nowadays many folks don't see Esau; 'cause Esau be in shadows much of time."

"I see you clearly, Esau?"

"Aye, reckon 'e doos, Miss, for 'e have learned 'e ways of colly-bird."

"I beg your pardon, Esau? You told me that the colly-bird's trick was standing still to catch worms?"

"Aye, Miss, but 'e also 'ave 'e way of seeing tiny folk, when tothers see nought. Angel twitching, folks doos call it."

"Angel twitching?"

"Aye, Miss, wouldn't surprise Esau, if 'e could see pigsies."

"I have never seen Pixies; not to my knowledge."

"Well, 'e can only see pigsies when pigsies choose to be seen."

"There are no such things as Pixies, Esau."

"Maybe no, but maybe so, Miss. Now let's leave grub to warm. Come for a look-see over here, Miss." Esau got up from the fire and walked to a thicket of rushes at the lake edge."

"Sit here, Miss. Look, can 'e see them?"

"See what, Pixies? I cannot see anything."

"Near top of rushes, there. Tiny critters, doos 'e see them?"

"Oh yes. They are not Pixies, though. They are tiny spiders?"

"Aye, Miss, spidez is what they look like at moment."

"They are so small," said Eliza, kneeling next to Esau and watching the spiders climb to the top of the rushes.

"What are they doing, Esau?"

"Watch, Miss; hush, and 'e'll learn. Time now for spidez to fly." Esau straightened up, removed a box from his pocket and took out some spectacles. After some fiddling around, he secured them on his nose and sat down on the grass to watch. Each spider, when reaching the top of bullrushes, did the same thing: they would lift one leg after another, as if testing the breeze, and then spin out a silken thread, which was so fine that you could not see it unless the light caught it just right. The thread, carried on the breeze, floated in the air and out over the lake.

"How does such a tiny spider have so much thread inside it?"

"It be a mystery, Miss," said Esau, "as be source of all your questions?"

"Cannot mysteries be solved, Esau."

"Not often, Miss. Esau try to spends Esau's days on bits which ain't mysteries."

When the spider's thread was four or five feet long, the tugging of the silk in the breeze overcame the spider's grip on the bulrush, and the creature let go, flying out across the lake on the end of its silken thread.

"How does it know where it's going?" Eliza asked.

"Don't suppose 'e doos, Miss. Look, 'ere be more spidez climbing up and flying over lake. See, Miss, 'ere soon be a multitude of spidez." Eliza watched as hundreds of threads, each with a spider holding on, floated out over the lake.

"What is happening, what are they doing, Esau?"

"Escaping, Miss. Spidez mothers 'ave too many young 'ns. They can't all be living in 'e same tuffet of grass. those who stays behind doos most likely get themselves eaten by frogs. So they's all getting going, looking for a new place to live. Somewhere better than they be now. Some'll drown, some'll get eaten by frogs, but 'ere be lots of spidez get to tother side of lake. And then, they all must get searching."

"Searching for what, Esau?"

"Searching, for a new place, Miss. Perhaps they doos find a tiny castle."

"That is just a silly children's story, Esau."

"And in that castle, there's perhaps handsome prince waiting for a spidez." Esau sat up and carefully folded his spectacles back into their box.

"Leastways, that's what all the grown-up spidez tell lickle spidez. Now, Miss, could be prince has already been gobbled up by a frog, and right now a frog is sitting 'ere waiting to gobble up all 'e spidez, as they arrive, one be one. Miss, Esau be thinking they be ready now."

"The spiders, ready for what?"

"No, no, Miss, Esau be talking about stubberds, Miss. Give Esau stick here, if 'e please, Miss, so Esau can get pots out of fire."

"What are stubberds?"

"Get the lid off, and 'e can see, Miss. Esau need 'is neckerchief for smaller pot, mind now, lid's hot as old Nick's toes."

"They are apples, Esau."

"Ay, Miss, stubberds Esau calls them. Cut an' cooked in a pot."

"What is this, in the smaller pot, Esau?"

"Honey, Miss. Collected from hive this morning."

"The hives up in the azalea beds, Esau?"

"Gracious no, Miss, not that honey. That be mad honey. Honey, we have today, Miss, be from Cook's kitchen garden. It'll be hot and runny now. Let Esau pour it over stubberds. Not too much, 'cause it be gert strong honey."

"What is mad honey, Esau?"

"Why, honey what makes 'e mad. Bees make it from azaleas."

"Why do you keep the hives in the azalea beds, Esau, if the bees end up making mad honey?"

"Well, her ladyship likes it that way, sometimes Esau put just a smidgling in with tother honey – if I feels like going a lickle mad that day. Someday, perhaps, Esau finds tother use for it."

Eliza watched as Esau took an elder stick and with a pocket knife cut a length of the hollow stick, split it longways, removed the pith and carved out two spoons. He had it all finished in a few moments.

"Miss, Esau be most obliged if 'e would share a lickle luncheon." Side by side, they sat eating mushy, waxy honey covered, apples. To outsiders they would appear an incongruous sight, a weathered old gardener with a voice from Devonshire and a face from Africa and the sea captain's young red-haired gawky daughter.

"Regarding the spiders," Eliza asked, "Do you think they are frightened by their dangerous journey across the water?"

"Well, Miss, maybe a lickle, at first, when they starts, but they's soon getting idea of it, getting the way of the world. And when they find their castle with handsome prince, reckons they be right 'appy, Miss, aye, right 'appy. They probably don't know 'bout dangers of frogs, an' don't 'ave no worrit about 'at, Miss."

"I find it hard to believe that princes are living in castles over the other side of the lake, it sounds a ridiculous idea," said Eliza, and after a few moments added, "But I do like your apples and honey. Your story about the prince in a castle sounds more like a fable than fact, Esau, or maybe it is a metaphor?"

"Well, Miss, Esau wouldn't be able to say. Maybe one, or tother, but who knows what's on tother side of water. Esau not having been over there, Esau's self,

Miss, and no spiders have come back to tell Esau what it be like over there."

"Why have you not been there, Esau, it is part of my father's land?"

"Esau's not wanting to find out – one way or tother, about princes, pigsies and spidez, best leave all as it be."

"So, it was all a story?"

"Maybe, Miss, or, on tother foot, it be a latchet of lies, but it do be a tale, what Esau once heard tell. Truth be, Miss, Esau's not remembering its provenance."

"Why do you concern yourself with it then, if it's only a story?"

"Well, Miss, stories is all us folks 'ave sometimes. Esau be using them to make sense of world, but that's probably cause Esau only got two books, Miss."

"Father has hundreds of books in his library; I am sure he would lend you some."

"Two books be good enough for Esau, Miss. Spidez ain't got no books nor stories; they just floats on air in breeze. Doos it without a thought. But for us folks; we gets up to our waists in muddle-twitching thoughts. Stories be to tell 'e a little of this an' that. Stories be everywhere. Now 'ow do 'e tell which be true stories an' which be a bucket of lies, Miss?"

Eliza walked back to the lake to watch the spiders some more, while Esau packed up his pots and raked the fire out.

"There still are spiders, floating over the lake, but I think not quite as many as when we watched earlier. What are the two books you have, Esau?"

"One book bees 'e Bible, Miss. Lots of stories, in that. Do 'e concern 'e self with Bible stories, Miss?"

"Of course, but the Bible is different."

"Is 'at so, Miss?"

"It was written by God,"

"Esau bees thinking that 'e knows 'e tale of 'e Sower, Miss?"

"Yes, I had to copy it and then learn it by heart, ages ago, to recite to Mother."

"Aye, that be right, Miss, an' 'e did recite it to Esau. Last year back. Esau thank 'e for that, but was that a story, Miss?"

"That is a parable. It has people, not animals in it and it has an application."

"What be that, Miss?"

"An application is a moral to a story."

"And what be moral of that story, Miss. Esau don't rightly member."

She thought for a while, "Farmers should be careful not to sow seeds on rocky ground because seeds need good soil."

"I reckon that be it, Miss. If only spiders had read parables, Miss. Perhaps they wouldn't take to flying over lake."

Eliza looked at Esau and thought that he did muddle everything up so.

"Have you ever seen a spider's castle, Esau?" she asked.

"No, Miss, ain been tother side of water, and anyways Esau heard tell 'at spidez castles bees very lickle."

"How little?"

"As lickle as a midgeman's fimble."

"Are you trying to charm me or trick me? I never know, Esau."

"No Miss, not Esau. Now, let's see if birdez like our stubberds an' honey. Put a smidgen on finger, Miss, an' 'old it out, like this. Aye, 'at's good. Now, we sees what birdez think of the matter, Miss." They both held out their hands with honey and apple on their fingertips. Esau began to whistle, as best he could, like a robin.

"So, what is your other book, Esau?"

"Shush, Miss, here come birdez."

5   Breeches

Sixth of January 1786 – the Purbeck coast, Dorset.

"Miss, you should not stay here. Please, put these clothes on."

"What do you make of my father's gardener, Bethany? I did not notice it when I was younger, doubtless because I had grown up with him, but Esau was singularly out of place in a Sussex house."

Before Bethany could answer, the ship abruptly fell, causing everyone's stomachs to churn over, and the tray of oranges to spill onto the cabin floor. Miss Mansell had ceased to cry, and, apart from a few prayers, sat silently awaiting salvation in whatever manner it should come.

"Make of Esau? What do you mean, Miss? Why do you ask, Miss?"

"When I was young, I thought that he possessed magical powers. I am still not convinced that he is not a wizard. He was always talking about Pixies, as though he believed in such things."

"Well, Miss, lots of folk do believe in Pixies," said Bethany.

"Now please, Miss, the clothes, put them on. I fear there is not much time left."

"Why is that? In these enlightened days, such beliefs would appear out of place."

"Some people like to give the impression that they are acquainted with the ways of the fairies. Perhaps they believe it makes them appear special, knowledgeable or even wise."

"That does not sound like the Esau I know."

"Apart from one conversation about the loan of a pair of shears, I did not have much to do with Esau, Miss. Can we continue this conversation on future occasion – should one be available?"

"Birds ... robins, would come and feed from his hand when he whistled. He would just hold his hand out with a dab of honey and down they would come. I asked him why the birds would sit on his hand and not mine and he told me it was because he could charm them with magical whistling. At the time I did not know what the word 'charm' meant, so I found it in the dictionary in father's study and read that it can have something to do with a bewitching power. I believe that in the same way he grew flowers in the gardens, fed birds from his hands, he could also charm people. Mother always avoided him, and my father never mentioned him, even though he would spend a considerable time with the other servants when he was home from the sea."

"Miss, let's talk about this later; the clothes."

"Clothes, Bethany, what clothes?" Eliza came out of her dream, picked up the breeches and put them to her nose. "Why should I put these on? The breeches are wet and they smell of ... what is that they smell of, Bethany?"

"Sweat, Miss. That is the smell of a man's sweat; Billy Spraggs's sweat, to be exact. He was a very sweaty man, Miss – when I saw him last. Even in these midwinter conditions."

"I have no idea what it is that you are talking about, Bethany. But I will not put these clothes on. I think you have had too much rum."

"Brandy, Miss. I wouldn't drink rum."

"These breeches are soaking. Where did you get them from?"

"I told you, Miss, Billy Spraggs gave them to me; he was a handsome lad. Although, as I said, very sweaty. Mind you that was probably because he had been working on the ship's pumps. Now, Miss, please put them on and save yourself."

"Save myself? Rescue is on the way, Bethany. They will come with boats and get us off in the morning."

"The ship is breaking up; you can hear the timbers cracking, it is sinking and could go down at any moment. You will have a chance to swim in these breeches, Miss. Put them on."

"Where are your breeches and tunic, Bethany? Could not your outfitter, Mr Spriggs …"

"Spraggs, Miss, Billy Spraggs."

"Whatever, could not he supply you with another set?"

"No, Miss, and I doubt I could find any sailors my shape. I'll stay here. All will be good. I will see you in the morning on the shore."

"What's this, there is rescue on its way for you but not for me? Well, I shall stay here with you, if we cannot both go together – Bethany, we are travelling companions – we both go together, or stay here together. I order you to stop suggesting I wear these clothes."

"Order, Miss? There's been a considerable collapse of discipline aboard this ship recently. Few of the crew or soldiers are now following orders. This storm has swept maritime and class rankings away. Nothing is working on the ship. The storm has changed everything. You might say that there has been a sea change. It's time to leave." Bethany finished the last of the bottle and then added,

"But, Miss. I cannot leave. I'm shaped like a barrel. If I jumped into the sea, I would most likely sink in an instant. I have never been in water deeper than the kitchen bath in my childhood home. No, I never have, and I never will swim in the sea, not me, never. And I have never tried to swim. Now, might well be too late to learn."

"I do not understand," said Eliza, "if it is best for me to leave the ship, then why not you, Bethany?"

"You're wiry, young, and strong, you can swim and, most of all, you have a reason to get ashore. With a fine life ahead of you, somewhere. You'll find your cooper, and then the entire world will be yours. Now get these breeches on and go."

"But ... but, I need you, Bethany and ... and I am concerned for you."

"I believe that our pathways are all laid out before us and if mine should lead me to a corner of Heaven; that'll suit me just grand. Now be off with you, Miss."

Again, the ship shifted its position on the rocks, a movement accompanied by a dreadful cracking and splintering of timbers. Some planks, in the roundhouse's deck, sprang up, people screamed and grabbed hold of whatever they could for support. Eliza grabbed hold of Bethany, who gave her mistress a look as much to say, what did I just tell you? Both saw the fear in each other's eyes.

"Miss, please," said Bethany, holding out the clothes. Eliza took them grudgingly, and Bethany began helping her put them on as quickly as possible, before she had time to change her mind. Eliza stood up, a blanket covering the red jacket, her hair tied up and hidden under a sailor's woollen hat. Bethany hesitated and then gave her mistress an embrace,

"Now, go, Miss."

"Thank you, Bethany, I shall always …" But, before she could say anymore, Bethany took her by the arm and led her towards the back of the roundhouse, and to make sure, lifted her up the first few steps of the ladder to the hatchway above.

6   Coop

"It is safest for you to be here, in the roundhouse. Nowhere else on the ship is safe." The captain held out an arm in front of Mary-Ann, his younger daughter.

"But I wish to be excused, Father?"

"Where are you going, Mary-Ann?"

"Please, Sir, I need ..."

"I say again, it is not safe, my child."

"But ... I need to visit the room set aside for ladies' comfort. I need to visit the ... necessary."

"The heads for ladies are now out of use. You cannot get to them, safely. Relieve yourself at the back of the roundhouse or in the corridor there."

"But the crew ..."

"The heads are open to the ravages of the sea. You will have to relieve yourself in a corner."

"But ..."

"Then do it where you stand. In the present situation it is but a paltry thing. Now, no more, my daughter."

Mary-Ann, made her way aft, from handhold-to-handhold until she reached the back of the roundhouse. The ship lurched to one side and she made a grab for the steps to steady herself and someone coming down the narrow stairway stepped upon her hand. She pulled it away, looked up and said, crossly,

"Take care, you oaf, can you not see there is a lady here." Descending the stairs was Eliza, with the blanket still around her shoulders, she looked down, saw her sister and quickly turned her head away.

Her attempt to escape the roundhouse had failed almost immediately. When she had opened the hatchway, a few moments earlier, she had been instantly soaked by freezing seawater, forcing her to turn back. Now her way back to the roundhouse was blocked by her sister. What was Mary-Ann doing here, in the dark, at the back of the roundhouse? How would Eliza explain these clothes? Then Eliza realised that there was no need for concern, Mary-Ann would not look at her, again. She would never willingly look into the eyes of an unknown man, especially a soldier, and certainly not one who was not an officer. Eliza watched her sister struggle to keep her footing while clambering out of the back of the roundhouse. If Mary-Ann recognised her, she would make such a scene, their father would may well have ordered that Eliza be secured, like poor Miss Mansell. Now, there was only one way for her to go, she would have to face the storm again. Her resolve renewed, Eliza climbed the narrow stairway once more, opened the hatch and scrambled out into the icy spray and the deafening roar of the wind. It heaved at the blanket with such force that Eliza thought she would be blown off the ship, so she had to let it go and watch it vanish, instantly, into the night. The storm filled her ears and ripped her breath from her lungs. Walking, holding on, breathing, everything she tried to do was painfully exhausting. On the edge of panic, she tried to hold onto the remains of a safety line, only to find that it was now just a loose piece of rope, and attached to nothing. She got onto her knees but still feared the wind would lift her off the deck at any moment. Lying flat on her stomach, she slithered like an eel across the poop deck, eventually reaching the steps and falling into the well of the ship. Sitting with her back to the roundhouse door, she felt a little better protected from the full force of the wind and tried to stand up. Her breathing became calmer and her eyes, more accustomed to the darkness, but she was still struggling to make sense of what it was before her. All appeared to be devastation. She could not understand what was happening or decide what she should do. On her right, the starboard side of the ship, away from the cliffs, there were glowing shapes in the darkness, which at first, she took to be wild spirits trying to board the ship. Then, as if they were all one, the spirits arose with the ocean, climbing higher and higher. The ship began to groan as it too began to rise. The sea was now towering above her. The spirits looked like they had grown white claws that were curling over the ship to snatch her away. She began to scream but as she could hear nothing above the gale even that seemed useless. Then it became clear; she was not witnessing super-natural spirits but white foam glowing with phosphorescence on the surface of the heaving waves, her father often told a story of one night when he had seen the ocean lit up with phosphorescence. Somehow, she felt better, realising she was not facing the supernatural, but surely, nothing could withstand this fury of nature. Why had she listened to Bethany rather than her father? Her hands scurried over the frozen timber of the doorway, struggling for something to hold onto and prevent the sea from getting her. There was the shattered mizzenmast stump with a rack of wooden belaying pins. She wasted time reaching down to hoist up her non-existent skirts. The wave hit, forcing her to scramble for'ard. She seized the tangled mass of rope. The ship groaned as more timbers bent and snapped from the pressure of the rocks beneath. Everything rose with the ocean, except Eliza, who was abruptly underwater. The shock of the cold screamed throughout her body as the sea, tried to drag her away, straining her grip on the ropes, dragging her across the deck and tugging at her arms until they felt as though they would be pulled from their sockets. She needed air. She kicked and pulled but her left arm had become entangled in the lines. Which way was up? The cold and pressure of the water was crushing her head. She could not breathe. Her feet touched something, she pushed, straightened her knees and broke the surface. The roar of the wind replaced the underwater groaning of timber. Her lungs would not work. She could not breathe. She fought to get air in her lungs, but her chest seemed locked rigid. She could neither breathe in nor out. Was this how it would end? Is this it? Then there came a voice, gentle against the storm,

"Sing, Miss. Sing Eliza."

Silvanus, she thought, you are here. "Sing! You need to sing, Miss." Where was he? Silvanus's voice calmed her, she relaxed, her chest unlocked and air burst into her frozen lungs. She could breathe again. She began to sing the song that she had sang with Silvanus, all those weeks ago,

"Il pleut, il pleut, bergère, Presse tes blancs moutons …"

When the sea drained away from around her, there was no Silvanus. Perhaps he was dead, after all. If so, then was it his ghost, she had heard, come to save her? But she could never think of him as dead. He must be alive; she knew it. Hauling herself upright, as the ship rolled from side to side, it felt as though the wreck was settling back onto the rocks below. Then the vessel seemed to cry out with what sounded like a dying sigh, as trapped air was forced through the hatchways by the decks below flooding. The moon broke through the clouds for a moment. Despite all the chaos the smiling moon was still in the sky. Her hopes lifted. Was the storm ending?

In the moonlight, towards the bows of the ship, Eliza could see the deck sloping away, disappearing into a boiling mass of tangled rigging, broken timbers, casks, bottles and trunks. Amongst all this, there was a flash of red. A soldier, one of the many redcoats on route to Madras. A soldier with a red coat, the same as she was now wearing. A dead body. Was she looking at herself? Her future ghost, washing about in front of her, floating on her back; red and white, dead and lifeless amongst the lolling garbage.

Above that scene, and clinging to the lower part of the foremast, were several more soldiers, and higher up still, there were some sailors, the highest of which continued to climb. Was he hoping to escape and fly away, to be plucked up by passing angels? She looked back at the dead soldier in amongst the heaving wreckage and felt pity for him, and thought of all the other poor men who were trying desperately to save themselves, and get back home to their loved ones. The prow of the ship had almost broken free of the aft section and was now rising and falling separately from the main body. There were men there with ropes, trying to make fast a long spar, which hung out, over the water on the landward side of the ship. Her thoughts snapped back to her own troubles. She needed to do something. It had seemed the answer to her prayers when the ship had struck. It would prevent her from leaving England, but now, all this had happened. Through the darkness, she could make out the shape of a rock. Was this the rock that she had heard the third mate, Mr Reeve, talk about? The moon returned, fleetingly and she saw more than a dozen men clinging onto the big rock. But where was the bridge?

There was only a spar of timber, which was far too short with its end sinking beneath the water with every wave. Even if she could get to the spar, she would not be able cross to the shore without swimming. And she would not be able to swim in this freezing water. When the wave had hit her, she could not breathe and could barely stand upright. Even if she did get onto the big rock, how would she get over that last gap of breaking surf to reach the cliffs? The land might as well be a hundred miles away. She turned, banged with her fists on the roundhouse door. She would have to go back in. Screaming against the wind and pleading to be let back in, she gained no response from inside and sank to her knees crying.

"Soldier, below there. Hey! Lend a hand." It was the third mate, Mr Reeve, hanging over the roof of the roundhouse. He held onto a large crate, which was also hanging half off the poop deck.

"Help me get this coop down onto the deck." Eliza tried to steady it, but it was too heavy and fell on top of her. Mr Reeve climbed down, to be shortly followed by Mr Schwartz,

"Achtung unten," shouted Mr Schwartz, "These very valuable cockerels und must be get ashore safely." Mr Reeve took a rope from over his shoulder and began lashing it around the crate. Another giant wave came over the deck. "Hold on Mr Schwartz, hold onto the crate with all your strength, God willing we will ..."

The wave flooded over the deck and Eliza grabbed hold of the tangle of ropes on the mizzenmast stump again. However, the wave was not as massive as the previous one, and she kept her footing. Mr Reeve and Mr Schwartz did not have the advantage of something to hold onto, apart from the crate, and the wave lifted the two men, washed them up and over the broken gunwale and out into the chaos of the sea. Mr Schwartz soon lost his grip on the coop and thrashed about wildly, trying to get back to the crate. Mr Reeve held out a hand towards him but another wave came, and, although she could still see the coop, Eliza lost sight of both men.

Watching Mr Schwartz, and the strong and capable Mr Reeve's hopeless struggle against the sea, Eliza's fear and despair grew again to such an extent that she could hardly move. Desperately looking about, for something that might be of help to her, Eliza could see nothing but chaos and danger everywhere. Hanging from the top of the broken foremast, now at an angle over the sea and leaning towards the cliffs, one of the sailors was calling out through a cupped hand, but his voice was lost in the storm. He held a coiled rope in the other hand and was making ready to throw it to the men huddled on the rock. He threw it, but the wind whipped it sideways and it fell into the sea. Perhaps, Eliza thought, she could do something similar, if she tied a rope to something. There was rope all over the deck from parts of the disintegrating ship. Most of this seemed too short, too long or too thick. Then, from the front of the ship, out of a broken hatchway, ten or twelve men came stumbling and scrambling. It looked impossible as the hatchway had appeared under water until that moment. This must be the last of the crew, Eliza thought, from the For'ard part of the ship. Most of them were holding something that might float and jumped into the sea, shoreward side. One man had a barrel tied to a coil of rope with which he made ready to jump but before he could, a wave came and he lost his footing. Without his makeshift float, the sea carried him off the deck and away. The barrel with its attached rope remained aboard and rolled across the deck in front of Eliza. This might be her best chance of reaching the shore. Before she could get untangled from the mizzen ropes, Eliza heard a call amid the howling wind, from the poop deck above. Looking up, she could see the tiny figure of her music teacher, Mr Miller,

"Soldier, below, help me down if you would. For pity's sake, help me." She reached up and beckoned him down. He scrambled, headfirst, and fell on top of Eliza, who held onto him as best she could, while a wave came and went, knee-high, over the deck. When it had passed, they were left standing face to face,

"Miss Eliza? It is Miss Eliza, is it not? What are you thinking of, let me help you back into the roundhouse, in the care of your father?"

"I am thinking the same as you, Mr Miller, to make for the shore. Before all is lost."

"Miss Eliza, there was talk of a bridge, but I cannot see one. What are we to do? What are we to do?" As if in an attempt at discovering the answer he knelt, put his hands together and began to pray. Eliza watched Mr Miller, eyes shut, rain-drenched face up to heaven and pleading for help from the Almighty. It seemed as if the Lord answered his prayer almost immediately because a wave came and lifted him up. Still with his eyes shut, he laid back and stretched his arms wide. The gushing water carried him off across the ship, through the gap in the gunwale and out into the sea.

As the ship rocked and pitched, the abandoned barrel with the line, still attached, rolled up to Eliza's feet again, like a dog that wanted a walk. Could it be a sign? She knew now what it was that she had to do and, avoiding any more thought on the matter, she put her arm and head through the noose in the rope. Then pushed the barrel into the gap in the gunwale and waited for a wave to come and take the barrel through the breach. The line streamed out behind the cask, and the forces of water and wind took it towards the shore. The barrel tugged on the rope around her shoulder. She would do it. She stood up, ran as fast as possible across the deck, towards the gap in the gunwale, and jumped ...

Like a child jumping off a jetty into the lake. Like a spidez in the wind,

"Il pleut, il pleut, bergère ..."

7   Jacob

Early Autumn 1784 – The garden of Fiddlesham House.

Over time Miss Kelpwell shrank. Both in formidability and magnitude - or so it seemed to Eliza. The governess, in Eliza's opinion still resembled a member of the crow family but had been demoted from a carrion crow, to a rook, and finally to a jackdaw, which Eliza told herself was a very common and foolish bird. However, Eliza's chances of escaping her overseer did not improve. Kelpwell invariably overhauled her charge and brought her back to the schoolroom by like a self-satisfied jackdaw returning to its nest with a bright shiny pebble. Kelpwell's vigilance always appeared victor over Eliza's escape attempts. Whenever she thought Kelpwell had abandoned the chase, suddenly, there she was, stepping out from behind some wall or bush. Eliza considered that trying to outrun Kelpwell was not going to be sufficient and that it was time to out-fox and out manoeuvre her governess. She needed a plan and it needed to be a good one. An obstacle course, she decided, would be the answer. She would run through various rooms in the house and then out into the grounds. She had worked on the plan for over a week: she hoped to wear her adversary down, by going out of the back door, over to the stables, up into the hayloft, jumping down, running through the back of the kitchen and out across the yard. If Kelpwell was still with her then, she would creep along the hidden path through the azalea beds and close by the bees - the hives with Esau's mad bees and then, lastly, through the woods and down to the lake.

The morning of the escape effort was misty, ideal for the purpose. Kelpwell was keeping up well until she refused to take on the leap from the hayloft. Then, going through the kitchen, Cook shouted to Eliza,

"Mind how ye go in that yard, builders be fixing kitchen roof. Not before time, rain's been getting in since the time of the great flood."

"Careful Miss," shouted the carpenter in the yard, "you'll be having somit on your head." As she ran through the azalea beds Eliza knocked each hive to stir up the bees, and when she came into the open, there was no sign of Kelpwell behind her. Had she done it? To make sure, she ran through the woods and then slowed down to walk down to the lake.

Esau was sitting at the end of the jetty on a box and intently staring at something in the lake. Like a cat after a bird, Eliza crept down to the landing stage and tiptoed out along the jetty. Just before she was about to pounce, Esau turned, put a finger to his mouth and gently patted the post stump by his side.

"Come an' sit 'ere, Miss; here bees shawl for back, it be early in morning, an' there be a chill mist up from sea. Quiet now, Miss, just bees sitting still on this stump, like robin do, an' watch til 'e gets way of world." Eliza sat down beside the old man. The water had a green colour, and reminded Eliza of freshly ladled pea-green soup. Fog drifted out of the woods at one end of the lake, floated over the water and past Esau on the jetty. It brought with it, the smell of the sea and rotten seaweed from the long heaps of bladder wrack thrown up the beach by recent storms. The mist spread a blanket of silence over the lake and added an air of anticipation to the morning's activities, as if they were about to witness some great event.

"I have never seen you fishing before," said Eliza. Esau had propped a long hazel stick with a loop of string tied to the end. Through this, was threaded a fishing line, which snaked out across the lake to a floating swan's feather.

"It is moving. You have a fish. Look a fish. It's taken your bait, Esau."

"Now, 'ush, Miss; 'at bees our bait, what bees moving 'e swan's feather. A lickle rudd fish tied to hook. Caught him yesterday in Esau's net. That bees our bait today."

"A rudd-fish? And your quarry, Esau?"

"Jacob, Miss."

"Jacob? I have never heard of a fish called a Jacob."

"Reckon, 'e ain't, Miss, Esau bees only person what know him an' Jacob be Esau's name for him."

"Well, that is no good having your own names for things. What does everyone else in the world call the fish?"

"As Esau say, Miss, no other living soul knows 'bout this fish, saving 'e now, Miss. But maybe 'e only swims in Esau's head. Perhaps Esau be Jacob's creator. Soon, we'll see. See if Jacob swim in Miss's head too."

"But what sort of fish is it, Esau?"

"Other folk seeing Jacob might call he a luce and some call he a pike, Miss. But Jacob bees a special big pikefish, biggest in the lake. Since Esau bees a young'un, he watch him grow bigger an' bigger, an' eat all manner of critters. A cannonball's what Jacob be, Miss."

"A cannonball, Esau?"

"Aye, he eat his own kin. But Esau reckon Jacob bees best of all predters. It's all he ever doos; eating at night, in morning an' afternoon. What we have to know is what Jacob likes to eat more than anything else."

"And have you found that out, Esau?"

"Aye, Miss. Reckon so."

"Well?"

"Reckon, 'e bees partial to red things, redder 'e better." Eliza pulled a strand of hair, red hair, from beneath her bonnet and wound it around her finger. "Now here bees a thing," said Esau, "a big red thing, sitting here right beside Esau. If Jacob don't like rudd fish, praps Esau'll bees tying 'e to line, Miss. Now, take handful of this muck, Miss, and mix it up. Make it all soft, like a piece of dough. We'll put some smelly bait out by our rudd fish," Eliza did as Esau asked. "Flatten it out, like a griddle cake. Don't go getting it on clothes, mind."

"It smells like old things. What is clay made from, Esau?" Esau smiled to himself, but Eliza spotted the grin on his craggy brown face.

"What are you smiling at, Esau? Are you laughing at me?"

"Oh no, Miss. It bees what I come to respect in 'e, Miss. Other folk would say, clay is clay. Most young ladies, like Miss, wouldn't touch it with a long stick an' its constitution would bees of no concern to them, but to 'e. Miss, clay is matter of great puzzlement. Always asking questions, Esau like that, Miss. Esau always having to find answers, which Esau also fond of. An' that's what make old Esau smile." Esau got his pipe out and let Eliza use the strike-a-light and tinder. The pipe now going, he continued, "Clay. Well, now let Esau think. Ah, Well; Esau have two possible answers for Miss, and not having been to a school or like, they only be guesses. So, Miss will have to choose which Miss prefer, or find Miss's own answer. First, Esau would say clay is what bees left behind after great flood. All the bits of dead and drowned sinners, all rotted and mushed up together. Yes, that be Esau's first guess."

Eliza stopped needing the clay to smell it, and quickly put it down,

"And your second guess, Esau?"

"Clay be all rocks an' stuff of world, worn down by rivers an' dumped on land sometime back. Now, let Esau finish off the makings of bait pudding."

Esau had spotted some time back that when Eliza was comparing alternatives, she would lean her head from one side to the other. As if the two conflicting ideas were bouncing from side-to-side in her skull.

"Of the two, I prefer the Great Flood answer," she said, "but I believe the rivers might wear away the rocks, but I do not believe the world has been here long enough for that. So … Oh dear, I am unsure."

"Being unsure about things, Miss, at Miss's age, is a good thing. 'Less Miss intend being a potter, it probably doos not matter too much what clay be. See 'ere; how Esau mixes 'ese rotten bits of fish into 'e bait pudding. Old Jacob won't be able to resist 'e smell. Watch now; let's see 'ow close Esau can frow bait to quill?"

They both sat there at the end of the jetty. While Eliza looked out over the lake, head cocking from side to side, a canny young fox weighing things up. Esau blew smoke rings and watched them 'get the way of the world' by joining the mist in its sideways journey along the lake and up towards the house.

"If you have known Jacob since you were a boy," asked Eliza, "then why are you trying to catch him now? It would seem that you perhaps ought to be fond of the old fish."

"No, Miss, Esau ain' never been fond of Jacob. Esau always knew that one day Jacob go too far and Esau have to catch him."

"Why, what has he done?"

"Well it's like this, Miss: a while back, Cook, says to Esau, Esau, she says, Mistress will want ducklings soon. Now, Esau's bees feeding those ducklings every day, keeping them friendly so theys won't get flummox when Cook want them. But when Esau goes to get them, they all be gone. All four of them gone, an' Esau have to tell Cook. Says, there ain' any ducklings an' she say, Esau, you told I there were four ducklings, not a week ago now. Have ye eaten all those ducklings ye self? Esau says, No, Cook, vox must have got them, but Esau knows it ain' vox what got them. It bees old Jacob but Esau ain' telling Cook that fish ate her ducklings cause she won't believe Esau. Anyways, Esau must take cart to Chichester and get ducklings from market. So, Esau says to self, Esau, you go and catch old Jacob, tell Cook truth about ducklings an' put fish in one of Cook's big stew pots."

"Poor little ducklings," said Eliza. "I saw them a while ago, Esau."

"Poor ducklings, Miss? Don't bees getting self in no leather over no ducklings, Miss; 'ey can bees right bold at times. Did you ever hear of the Lugworth ducklings? They bees bold as brass."

"I do not think I have, Esau. Is it a story or is it true?"

"That, I cannot say, Miss. Perhaps Miss bees good enough to tell Esau, pinion, when all bees said an' done."

"Certainly, Esau."

"One day ducklings fly up to heaven ..."

"Can ducks fly that high, Esau?"

"Shush, Miss, or Esau bees dropping his thread."

"Are these the ducklings Cook wanted for the pot? No wonder they flew away."

"No, Miss, these bees the Lugworth Ducklings. Praps Miss bees kind enough to listen an' tell Esau, Miss's pinion on that matter, as well."

Eliza got off the jetty post stump and sat closer to Esau, pulling the shawl, snug and cozy around her shoulders and her knees up under her chin. The old man carried on with his tale,

"Ducklings say, 'Lord, we wants a king, like what people has.' Lord say, 'I see what I got in me basket of bits.' Lord finds an old log and frows it down into duck pond. First of all ducklings like 'e log. But it ain't long till they ain' satsfied anymore 'n goes back up an' says, 'Lord, we don't want that old log anymore, we wants a king what does more than sit in lake doing noving, we wants a mighty king?' 'Well,' says Lord, 'let's see what I's got in me favrite bucket here. Ha-ha, here we bees, 'e very thing,' and Lord throws down a lickle fish. It were a fish like Jacob, a luce, what be very tiny at first, but 'e gets bigger and bigger an' soon bees big nough to eat up all those ducklings."

"Was that Jacob the same fish as this Jacob? Or another pike? Are there two Jacobs?"

"Well, Miss …"

"It is very confusing. I think it is a fable, which I have read but I do not think it was about ducks, and I do not think that it is true. In the fable I read, it was frogs, not ducklings. You have muddled things up, Esau."

"Well, Esau bees sorry for 'at, Miss. Esau do muddle up things lots 'ese days. It probly be Esau's natural igronce, or praps his great age, Miss."

Eliza asked, "What is the fable's application, the moral of the story?"

"Well, Esau wouldn't know that. Miss being audience to Esau's story, praps Miss should peg application on it."

"I think it is about children not getting above their station in life."

"Well now, Miss Esau never thought of that. Thought it were a story about some ducks."

"My mother is very concerned that I do not get above my station. She says I will most probably marry a soldier because I am rather plain. My sister, Mary-Ann, Mother says, is far from plain and will most probably marry a baronet."

"Doos that bees so, Miss. Esau wouldn't dare disagree with her ladyship, but Esau always bees thinking of Miss as being far from plain. Esau would say, that Sister doos not know noving about tale of Lugworth ducklings, makings of clay, or what bees bait pudding."

"Well, I do not think that I should like to marry a soldier and I am not sure a baronet would be much better. Perhaps one day I will grow into a lady like my mother, who can choose easily between things." They both sat quietly for a while until Eliza said, "Do you think ducks choose which drakes to marry or do the drakes choose?"

"I would say it be both, Miss. Dare say ducks look for brightest coloured drakes. Bees Miss thinking of marrying a duck?"

"No, Esau, I just meant …"

"Shush! Now. Look, ripples, can Miss see, spreading across lake from feather. Jacob bees having a sniff of lickle rudd fish." Everything went still for a moment.

"He's gone away, Esau, perhaps he is full up with the ducks."

"No, Miss, Jacob be greedy; he bees coming back." The swan quill suddenly sped across the lake for about ten feet and then disappeared beneath the water. At the same time Esau stood up, lifted the rod with a great heave and the it snapped in the middle. However, being a freshly cut sapling, the hazel rod held together. Esau ran back along the jetty, pulling the line behind him, but stumbled and dropped the rod into the water.

"Miss, the line," Esau shouted and Eliza, seeing the hazel rod fast disappearing along the edge of the jetty towards the open lake, tried to reach it, but could not. Then she did something, which surprised herself, as well as Esau, without cocking her head, even once, she took a couple of steps back, then ran and jumped into the water. She was just in time to grab the broken stick as it floated by, but trapped air in her skirts kept her feet off the lake bed and without anything to hold onto Eliza turned upside down as the giant fish began to slowly pull her out into the lake. Running down the jetty, Esau shouted,

"Miss, hold tight," said Esau as he took off his jacket, shouting again, "Swim, Miss." He then sat down on the end of the jetty, feet in the water and slid down up to his chest into the lake. As the young girl floated by, Esau plunged a hand beneath the water, found the scruff of her neck and with his other hand on the line, walked back through the water to the shore, pulling both Eliza and the fish out of the lake.

Eliza could not stop jumping up and down, and spraying water everywhere, like a dog after a swim,

"It's huge, Esau. Look, look how big he is. It's the biggest fish I have ever seen. Is he the biggest fish you have ever seen, Esau?"

"Biggest fish Esau have caught by more than a yard, Miss. Look at rows of needle-sharp teeth. Keep 'e fingers clear of them."

"It is a wonder he has not eaten all of us. Lots of people have swum in the lake."

"Look at cross on Jacob's head, Miss. That be what Devil stole from Jesus. Esau have to kill Jacob now. Don't like to see Jacob suffer, out of water. But before Esau doos, you can make a wish, Miss. Always, when you catch a luce, you makes a wish. 'Cause Jesus be pleased. Close 'e eyes first, mind."

Eliza stopped bouncing for a moment, closed her eyes and wished that one day she would go with her father on his ship to India and ride on an elephant. Esau took a large smooth cobble stone from the water's edge and with one blow, broke Jacob's skull. He then got his sheath knife out, saying, "Let's see about ducklings, now." While Eliza looked on, cut the fish open and out of the big fat sagging belly, pulled the body of the mother duck. Then one by one found the ducklings,

"Look, here be one, and two ... and three ... Aye, three! Only three." said Esau. "So, there bees one duckling what didn't follow mother down Jacob's throat."

"Good for her," said Eliza, "I wonder where the duckling is. Should we search for her?" Eliza gazed out across the lake, searching for the lone duckling.

Esau and Eliza did not go searching. Instead, they lifted Jacob into Esau's wheelbarrow and together took their prize back to the house.

"Jacob be going to frighten Cook, something big."

Back at the house, the cook said,

"I can't be dealing with monster fishes at this time, Esau," said Cook, "not after what I've had to cope with here with Kelpwell, and all." They put the fish in the scullery. Then, Cook sat Esau and Eliza down around the kitchen table, while Eliza's dress hung in front of the fire. With a mug of beer for him and a glass of lemonade for her, Cook told Esau and Eliza the whole story. Kelpwell had run through the kitchen and into the yard, chasing after Eliza. Although the builders had shouted a warning to Miss, they never said a word to Kelpwell. Probably because they were afraid of her, being convinced she was a witch, or the like, on account of her black looks, sinister nature and their overwhelming belief that all women, who were not pretty, nor wealthy, were, most likely, witches. Anyway, the governess was running so fast, she knocked against one of the scaffolding timbers and dislodged a barrel of water from the platform above. It hit her neatly on the head and flattened her black straw bonnet. Then the barrel shed its iron hoops, which fell around Kelpwell's neck. Mucky builders' water went all over her and the wooden staves clattered around in the yard, each bouncing and echoing off the brick walls, like a shattered pile of old bones from the sky.

For a while, Eliza was free to visit and swim in the lake every day. The thought of more monsters, like old Jacob, in the deep looking up at her as she swam, did not stop her from entering the water and added to her sense of excitement. Eliza's mother, in general, disapproved of ladies entering the water, and after mentioning it twice, disdainfully, Eliza had to be careful not to be seen when swimming. Mother even discussed the matter with the captain, who agreed that he could see no reason for a young lady to swim. He added that so much water in contact with a ladies' skin could not be healthy and pointed out that sailors rarely learnt to swim because they believed that such activities would surely be tempting fate.

It was not until a few days after the barrel episode that Kelpwell opened her eyes again. Memories of the incident came back to her, but she felt completely at peace. At last, the Lord's chastisement had come. Punishment for her wicked thoughts had been meted out and she could now forget all about Master Welstan's wandering hands and, more to the point, her tardiness at removing them.

Kelpwell did recover, in a manner, but whereas previously she had worn a face upon which everyone was accustomed to seeing only scowls and a look of disapproval of all things Earthly, now she appeared to always be smiling. She also had developed a strange and distant look in her eyes. Cook said to Esau, that after the matter of the barrel, Kelpwell reminded her of an old macaw her mother's mistress had kept in the kitchen. The bird had terrible cataracts, which had made it blind. It had sounded somewhat like Kelpwell, except the macaw would shout, Aye, aye, Sir! Aye, aye, Sir! Aye, aye, Sir!

The matter which finally broke Mother's resolve to keep Kelpwell, her daughter's inexpensive tutor, was that the governess now had developed a very common accent,

"It's even worse than yours, Esau," Cook had said. Not long after, mother came into the schoolroom to chastise Kelpwell for not keeping Eliza in class. Kelpwell had said,

"Well, my lady, Zat girl, she be a right bugger, not much I's can do, her being runt of e' litter, Misses." Mrs Percy's mouth had fallen open and remained in that position for some time. Much later, the captain said to his wife, "As they say in the East India Company, my dear, "Quality crew cost quality wages."

It was Esau's day to go to Chichester market, and so he took Kelpwell in the cart to meet the Western Mail. That would take her on to Devon and eventually home. She smiled, strangely all the way to Chichester but said not a word for almost the entire journey despite Esau asking about her home in Devon, her family and the weather, which was about the full extent of his polite chatter. Esau waited with her to be sure she caught the mail coach, and once boarded, he said, goodbye and, smiling down upon him, she said,

"The swan shall not speak until the jackdaws finish their chatter." Like many things people said to Esau, he had no idea what it meant, but he replied with a tug of his forelock and,

"Aye, Esau says that's about length of it, Miss.

A week later, Bethany arrived at Fiddlesham.

8   The Ugly Nymph

Fiddlesham House and garden – Morning of Wednesday June 8th 1785

After breakfast, Eliza's mother sat, Chinese porcelain teacup in hand, and delivered instructions to her daughter concerning approaching womanhood. Eliza's duty, mother insisted, was towards her family, but, she declared, for Eliza, this would prove demanding. Why this would be so, her mother never explained, but the young girl was in no doubt as to what it was that mother eluded: Eliza was too tall, too thin and, by far the worst, her hair was too red. In another family, this last feature may have been acceptable, but in the Percy flock; where almost every sibling, parent, aunt, uncle and cousin, once, twice and even, three times removed, had nothing but the blackest hair; Eliza's mother saw her as a very embarrassing child. Mother had initially invited Eliza to her tea parties as a means for her daughter to learn the ways of adulthood and polite society but these invitations stopped when Mother became increasingly vexed by her ladies never appearing to tire of mentioning Eliza's peculiarity; "Your eldest daughter? Such lovely hair, so striking and almost unique in your family?"

Mother reiterated that a woman's first duty was to find a husband - the most satisfactory available. Secondly, to serve and obey her husband, thirdly, to organise the household affairs and, lastly, and most importantly, to supply her husband with many children. Despite Eliza's difficulties, her mother assured her, there was no need for anxiety. Eliza knew that the anxiety referred to was not that of Eliza's but that of her mother's.

"Your father has agreed to your sister, Mary-Ann, following your brother's example and travelling to Madras," her mother had announced. "Although this is very inconvenient, and much against our arrangements, your father has agreed to one last voyage to Asia, on which your sister will accompany him. As for you, Eliza, I fear that even in that corner of Empire your unique assets may still prove an obstacle, although among the Honourable Company's officers there is always a great demand for wives, we cannot encompass the likely shame of a daughter of ours remaining unattached after a year and having to be returned to England. That would be just too much to bear." Eliza had been too stunned to think straight. Was her mother now suggesting that she would not go to India? This change of plan went against everything she had understood. She had never found it easy to speak to her mother. A conversation with her always consisted of listening and reciting, 'yes Mother,' at the appropriate opportunity. All she managed at this time was to stammer, "But …"

"But?" Her mother repeated, interrupting Eliza's faltering words and clattering her teacup onto its saucer, "But, but? Give me no buts, young lady. If that is not the greatest exhibition of insolence that a mother has ever had to endure. Our conversation is now at an end. Please leave this instant."

Out in the garden, her mind was raging. Without thinking where she was going, she wandered through the grounds until she found herself standing by a clump of low trees that Esau was thinning out. Eliza snapped, "Good day to you. What are you doing here?"

"An' good day to 'e too, Miss," said Esau, getting up from his shave horse. "Begging pardon, Miss, but Esau knows from old, that behind Miss's greetings, 'ere be an errand to Miss's visit. Wait a lickle, 'til Esau put billhook away. 'Ere, let Esau turn bucket over an' put coat on top. Now, Miss may sit. Esau thinking this bees longish problem."

Eliza told Esau of her mother's plans for her sister to travel to Madras while she stayed in England.

"Why do Miss believe ladyship picked Miss out to stay, when sister bees going to Madras?" Eliza glared at Esau, "What Miss glowering at Esau for?"

"You know perfectly well, Esau."

"Miss, Esau doos not, less it bees to keep favrit child close by. If it be something Miss done wrong, then in time, Miss may correct things an' Mother may change her mind."

"Yesterday I overheard Mother talking to Aunt Anne at tea. She completely disregarded my presence, and the fact that I could obviously overhear her, and told Anne that I was too tall, too thin and my hair was too red. How would you suggest I go about changing those features, Esau?" Esau said nothing, while Eliza snatched up a cut hazel stick and began peeling off strips of bark as fast as possible. Esau eventually said,

"Well, hardly seems to Esau, Miss, that they bees such an awful bag of burdens. Praps in time, Miss, a wagon of such loads appears easier to shift and Mother may well see the tother side."

"When Mother has spoken her mind, I have never known her to change it," Eliza said.

"The mood Miss bees in remind Esau of early in summer. Shall Esau tell Miss bout it?"

"No," said Eliza, trying to make herself look as angry as anyone might, while sitting on a bucket. The two gazed out over the lake in silence until Eliza said, "Very well then, if you must tell me one of your silly tales."

"Ay, Miss. It were back in May, as Esau said. Looking inside one of hives, up in vegetable garden. Swarm of bees comes from elsewhere. Reckons they comes from hives in azalea beds, cause they were right mad. Probly mad on count they've been eating their own mad honey. Anyways, swarm of bees were monstrus angry. You can tell they be angry because they makes different sounding buzz. They takes to buzzing around Esau's head and a few of critters sting Esau's neck. So, Esau runs away, as quick as old bones will carry Esau down to lake. After a lickle while bees calm down an' fly 'cross water to settle on half-fallen oak tree on tother side of lake. Fallen tree still bees there, see? Propping itself up at water's edge."

"Esau," Eliza said, "I have just told you how upset I am at my mother's plans to keep me in this country against my wishes, and you tell me about bees and trees. I used to think that you were a charmer or even a wizard, but now I am quite convinced that you are a madman." She paused, while she watched Esau smiling and then added, in a gentler manner, "Albeit, an almost harmless madman with a quite uncommon manner."

"Well, Miss, Esau bees sure what Miss says bees true, but when Miss comes down to lake, it was like Miss had a swarm of mad bees in Miss's bonnet. But after sitting a while by the water here, Miss's bees seemed to have calmed down."

Eliza suddenly thought how foolish she must seem, sitting there pouting and being cross with the one friend she had. She thought she should smile and be friendly to Esau. She had been impressed by the mannerisms of her Aunt Anne, and a strange ironic smile Aunt used, when she did not agree with a point but wished to remain cordial. Eliza had been practicing this smile whenever she had an opportunity to see her reflection. She thought this moment would be an ideal occasion to impress Esau with fashionable grown up looks, and so smiled her new ironic smile. Esau, out of years of deference to his superiors, rarely looked at his social betters. Nonetheless, on this occasion, having caught a glimpse of Miss's eyelashes taking on a strange flickering, he took sideways look, and asked, "Excuse Esau Miss, but is there a midge in Miss's eye? After a while with no response from Eliza, he said, "Miss, change places with Esau if 'e would. Come and sit on shaving horse, while Esau use bucket." He took the bucket to the edge of the lake, walked in a couple of steps and then filled the bucket with water. After stirring the water around with a stick for a few moments, he emptied it and filled it again. He repeated this several times until he seemed to find something he had been looking for.

"I tell you my distressing news about me not being able to utter a word to my mother in my defence and you ... and you – if I were a murderer in the dock, at court, I would at least get an opportunity to defend myself – and all you can do to is to splash about in the lake."

"Here she bees, Miss. This what Esau's bees searching for." Esau put the bucket in front of Eliza. "Has Miss ever spied a nymph?"

"A nymph? Why are you talking about Nymphs, Esau?" Esau delved into the bucket, and after a moment lifted something out. Uncapping his hands, he showed Eliza a large writhing insect. She tried for a while to maintain her disinterest but eventually could not help herself and leant closer to inspect the creature.

"It has six legs; it is an insect. I have played and sung the song, Nymphs and Shepherds, on the harpsichord. The music is by Mr Purcell. Nymphs are the pretty and frivolous young girls who dance around playing pipes. It is a rather foolish song. I can play the flute, but not while I am dancing."

"Ay, Miss be right. There bees no way this critter could play pipe an' dance, even with six legs."

"Why are you showing me this now, Esau? Are you trying to divert me?"

"Well maybe so, Miss and maybe no. This nymph be special critter. When God made nymph, he weren't too sure what he were about – maybe God were diverted that day – an' nymph comes out a lickle ugly. So, nymph grumbles about her condition – not wanting to bees ugly, an' live in mud at bottom of lake. God says, 'Well if 'e wants to change, better be doing something about it. So, nymph climbs out of mud, up a reed stalk 'til she be out of water an' then all nymph's scaly ugliness falls away. An' underneath ... well, Miss, come an' watch; out over lake; might take Miss a while, mind."

"What are we watching for, Esau?"

"Shush, Miss." They sat gazing over the lake until Esau whispered,

"Miss, there she bees. Under brambles hanging over water, here. See, Miss?" "It is a little dragonfly."

"Aye, that be crect, Miss. Look at her bootiful; red body an' wings, as thin as snail trails dried in morning sunshine. Devil's darning needle, they doos call her. Tis said they sew up mouths of scolding mothers. That bees what nymphs grow into. What colour would Miss say tis?"

"Red, of course."

"An' what shape?"

"Long and thin."

"Crect again, Miss, some calls her a damselfly. Next year that ugly nymph in your hand, Miss, will crawl up a stalk, an' turn into devil's darning needle, just like that one over the lake. Mind Miss, nymph'll have to do something herself. Have to climb up stalk an' get out of water." Eliza watched the damselfly fly by and followed it along the lake until it disappeared out of sight into the tangle of trees on the other bank.

"Has Miss heard story of Cupid an' the Nymph?"

"I cannot recollect such a story. Is the nymph in this story an insect or one of Mr Purcell's dancing nymphs?"

"Dancing nymph, I reckon, Miss an' she play pipes as well but don't ask Esau how? Oh, Esau forgets; Cupid bees god of love."

Eliza could be nothing other than calm when Esau told a story. Though Esau and Eliza were as different as hare and tortoise, Esau's story brought them together and comforted her. Esau finished his story, and Eliza asked,

"Well, what is the fable's application? What does it mean?"

"Miss, that ain' for Esau to say. No, no."

"Cupid is kind towards the nymph and agrees to her marriage to the shepherd. To marry for nothing other than love," said Eliza.

"That Cupid doos, Miss, that he doos. Well listened."

"I don't understand, though, are you saying that a lady should marry out of respect, or only marry if she is in love? Should I then, not concern myself with travel across the ocean and marriage to a rich Indian officer? Is that what you are telling me, Esau?"

"No, no, Miss. Esau bees telling a tale. Tales be like gardens, full of all manner of flowers. Some folk bees picking roses, tothers pick daisies. No saying what different folk may bees picking. Miss can take what Miss likes from a tale. On their own, they don't mean much. They bees all that folk like Esau have, Miss. If Esau want to know what's right, Esau could look in Bible, an' many folks do that, an' be pleased with what they find in that book. But Esau prefer to look at plants, trees, animals, birds, fishes, insects – see what they do – and also Esau remember his tales. Praps this tale doos mean something, but what that be, Miss, well, that bees the way of tales; different folks see different things."

"I had grown up with the knowledge that one day I would be embarking upon a journey to Madras. The prospect filled me with excitement and I looked forward to the voyage in my father's ship and seeing all the treasures of India, of which I had never stopped hearing about, and remembering with awe, wonderment and – I suppose – a little trepidation. It would have been a great adventure. Did you know, Esau, people ride on the backs of elephants and watch tigers hunting their prey? Why the tigers do not eat the elephants and, for that matter, the riders as well, I could never understand?"

"Maybe Miss, cause tiger knows story about elephant an' greedy tiger what were not satisfied with a fair share."

Eliza lifted her head and briefly they both broke the social conventions of a lifetime and looked directly into one another's eyes. Esau did not see the precocious and prickly young educated girl of class, whom others saw. He saw a young girl on the threshold of womanhood with only an old gardener to share her fears. Eliza saw a mysterious old man; the only other person who would listen to her. But what was he thinking about? She never knew. Did he imagine that she wanted more than her fair share? Did he think that she was a rude young child? Esau had watched her grow up for all these years, listened to her worries about tutors and governesses. She had told him about her life and her family while he had nurtured the trees and plants in the garden. Perhaps, by keeping a watchful eye over Eliza he was trying to cultivate her as if she was part of the garden. How had he learnt all his tales? She had seen him struggle reading a poem, which she had once copied out for Kelpwell. If he had read the fables he told, then he must have laboured long through candlelit nights, struggling over every word. Did he deliberately change the stories to match Eliza's situation or was he unable to remember them accurately? Was the tale about nymphs, Esau's way of saying she was like a damselfly? Would she live long and flourish when she became a damselfly?

They looked out over the lake watching another damselfly flit from place to place along the water's edge. Then Eliza jumped as a pied wagtail swooped down and took the insect out of the air. The bird struggled to fly with the bulky insect in its beak and landed on a branch of a young willow tree, where it bit off the insect's wings, letting them flutter and spin to the lake below. Then the red body in its beak, the bird flew off low across the water. For the second time, in less than an hour, Esau and Eliza caught one another's eyes but again, said nothing.

9   The Devil's Interval

Fiddlesham House – Afternoon of Wednesday 8th June 1785

Visitors to Fiddlesham house often lavished praise upon the captain's charming family. Such compliments always gave the captain a glow of pride. However, in truth, he believed that such compliments were most likely addressed towards his own judgement, rather than the qualities which his family obviously possessed. Such an attitude was derived, not from the captain's conceit but his long years of duty at sea, and his belief that everything aboard a ship was ultimately the master's responsibility. Such seafaring principles, the captain applied to most things in life, whether at sea or on land.

The captain had seen to it, over the years, that Fiddlesham exemplified his own view of the world. The drawing room, for example, featured scientific and artistic wonders of the world and the heavens above. Wonders, which the captain hoped would inspire his visitors to believe in the same values as he did himself and that they were indeed visiting the home of a modern man of excellent taste and accomplishment. The captain hoped that the house and estate, inherited from his father, now illustrated that he was the latest patriarch in a long dynasty of successful and talented men.

The captain's father, Samuel Percy, had acquired the house after successfully building the family's shipping business and amassing a sizable fortune, which included interests in the Americas. Like many other wealthy men, towards the end of his life, the old captain had wished to leave behind something of a tangible nature. This, he believed, would require more than an entry in a bank ledger to summarise its value. So, he began work on enlarging the house. Typical of men of his time and class, he had wished to display, not only his wealth but also his appreciation of a world that had provided such bounty. He was after all living in enlightened times. The house and, in particular, the drawing room, he hoped, showed his grasp of what it was to be a prosperous and civilised man.

Old Samuel Percy had achieved his success on the back of a lucrative slave trade between Africa and the Americas. Subsequently, Eliza's father, the young Richard Percy, had felt this business, although probably necessary, lay uneasily with the nature of being an enlightened man. He therefore sold off his father's interests in cotton, sugar and slaves, along with the family assets in the Western World and invested in the East India Company, which traded predominantly with India, China and the East. Over the years, wealth, travel and a discerning and dutiful wife, had enabled Captain Richard Percy to fill his house with lavish displays of all that he valued in life. There were paintings by Joshua Reynolds and William Hodges, two maritime engravings by the French artist Claude Joseph Vernet, along with numerous other sketches. One of these, which the captain was particularly proud of was a likeness of himself, sketched by the German artist, Johan Zoffany, executed while on route to the Indian coast and China.

Also, in the drawing room there was a spinet and a harpsichord; upon which the captain had arranged instruction for his daughters. Visitors might gaze in wonder at the captain's journeys to Asia using one of his two globes or choose a map to lay out upon the chart table. There was an impressive James Short reflecting telescope, through which, when mounted on the lawn in favourable weather, could be seen the wonders of the moons of Jupiter, the canals of Mars or, a particular favourite of the captain's, the oceans of the moon. To demonstrate his grasp of the universe, he had acquired an orrery, built by the famous clockmaker, George Graham, and showing the mechanism of the planets in the solar system. On the walls of the drawing room there hung turquoise patterned floral wallpaper. Crowning this, was ornate gilded moulded plasterwork, leading the visitor's eyes to the vaulted ceilings of azure with drifting cumulus clouds. To illuminate these wonders, the captain had enlarged the five windows, which ran the length of the outer wall, and rose from floor to ceiling. Any visitors, unaccustomed to such displays of culture would not fail to show their wonder openly.

Nevertheless, when the captain's wife, Mary was showing Anne, her husband's younger sister, around the house, she noticed that Anne was quite capable of restraining her excitement. Anne, who had just returned from India, had seen far greater opulence in Calcutta and had become accustomed to the grand houses of neighbouring officers of the East India Company. In that part of the world, a gentleman might find that an Honourable Company's salary, together with a few additional business ventures, could quickly become lucrative and would lead to the appearance of extreme wealth. Anne had visited the estates and palaces of local native princes, the Nawabs, whose love of extravagance was unrivalled. Her experiences in such places had cast a shadow over every venue she had visited subsequently, particularly the houses she had seen on her return to England. However, she admitted that there was one item, which did impress her. That was a recently acquired painting of Jane, her daughter, which she was delighted to stand back and admire,

"Now, here I can see it, as it should be appreciated, high on the wall and with ample lighting. It is indeed a beautiful painting. When Richard told me of his intentions to ask Jane to sit for the German painter, Zoffany, I must admit I was left rather unimpressed but seeing it now; it is absolutely wonderful."

Noticing a look of sadness spread over Anne's face, Mary said, "You must miss your daughter greatly, Anne."

"Yes, indeed, but her letters are a great comfort, and now this picture … I see Zoffany has included in the work a likeness of dear Samudra. She was my very own beloved Ayah, 'Nanny' or 'governess' you might say. My goodness, how she has aged but …" Anne suddenly turned herself away from the picture. Mary, surprised at her sister-in-law's sudden, and unaccustomed, hesitancy, took her sister-in-law by the arm,

"I agree, Anne," Mary said, "The painting is quite splendid in this situation, and this light, even on a day like today. I am so pleased you approve. I know that when I tell Richard, on his return from London, he will be immensely pleased." Having now composed herself, Anne said,

"I understand that Zoffany is making a remarkable fortune in India. Jane was quite impressed with his talent on the outward journey."

"Yes, indeed Anne. Did you know he even sketched a likeness of Richard, whilst aboard his ship, and during a storm, would you believe? The portrait is here. Come and see." They moved along the wall past numerous pictures and stopped by the likeness of Richard. Mary added,

"It was such a pity that Zoffany lost his royal patronage in this country and had to travel to India. Then I believe that the Royal loss has been the Empire's gain."

"Let us hope, then, that his fabulous wealth and success in India are some small compensations." Anne, smiled, pleased with her own irony.

"Are we to take tea alone, Mary?"

"Not quite, I understand that Miss Dicey and the Signora Medici, and maybe a few others, are to join us very soon. I must apologise, Anne, our room here is rather large. Often, we quite easily accommodate more than a dozen ladies, but I am afraid it is a matter of no small embarrassment that we have such a small number of visitors this morning. I am told our roads are becoming quite treacherous of late and many ladies are quite reluctant to travel on them, unless their journey is of an essential nature."

"I do find it strange, here in England," said Anne, "that the onset of winter arrives every year accompanied by such a surprise for the English. Although the English are always very concerned about the weather – enough to comment upon it endlessly – they rarely think to ask the Almighty to intervene in the matter. In India, the Hindus delegate matters relating to the climate to no lesser deity than Vishnu's sister, Miri. Every year, before the monsoon rains arrive, it is the responsibility of farmers, fishermen and villagers to organise colourful festivals of dancing and costumes all over the country. If performed to an acceptable standard it is believed that these will result in rains that will be sufficient to fill the rivers and underground aquafers but not so mighty as to flood homes and villages."

"And does the goddess often pay heed to these street dances, and restrain the downpours?" asked Mary.

"Some years she does, and when not, then more effort will be put into the following year's dancing and costumes, to ensure the Goddess's attention. At least the Hindus do something about the weather, successful or not; unlike the English whom, it would appear, do nothing but complain to one another. They should thank God that they are not subject to three months of monsoon rains falling on the English mud-filled roads."

"I agree, Anne, but such a biblical downpour might just wash our highways clear of some of the footpads, highwaymen … and now, would you believe it, the labourers are up to mischief, blocking roads and attacking farm buildings and suchlike. One wonders why the army is not in more evidence."

"Labourers, Mary?"

"Oh, I am sure that much of it is exaggerated talk, if not invented talk. I understand that there was recently some destruction of farmers' property in Taunton by rioting labourers."

"What is their quarrel with the farmers?"

"Heaven only knows, Anne. Richard says the new tide mill, built by the harbour, might well prove a target. But then, I cannot understand why. These new contrivances must relieve such arduous labour from the poor. You would think the labourers would embrace such progress. Thank goodness our workers here at Fiddlesham are not of such a frame of mind."

"Do you think I should make new arrangements for my journey home, Mary? When the time comes?"

"No, I am sure there is no cause for concern, and in any case, I shall insist that our man James and several of his strongest men accompany you, Anne, certainly as far as Chichester."

Looking through the windows at the leaves scurrying over the grey lawns, Mary drew Anne close, "I am so pleased to see you, Anne. You bring such warmth to our house."

"And I am pleased to see you too, dear sister, and to be with my family again at long last."

"I have often felt that finding such a gentleman, as my fine upstanding Captain, who possesses such impeccable manners and demonstrates such outstanding attention towards family and duty, was fortunate, but a husband with such an agreeable sister made accomplishment into triumph."

"Is this the famous vase, Mary? Richard has told me so much about it in his letters. He is so very fond of it," said Anne, standing in the alcove, which housed the single blue and white vase.

"See, Anne, the upper section depicts a king - King Wen – with his two daughters, and here, in the lower portion, is a ship. Richard tells me the vase was made over two-hundred years ago. He is very fond of it, seeing a resemblance to members of our own family. He says it was most likely manufactured by a particularly sagacious clairvoyant."

Anne looked closely at the vase and added,

"Albeit," said Anne, "a pot manufacturer who neglected to include Richard's own son in the decoration."

Mary said, "It was one of a set that Richard returned with on his last trip to China, the others proving particularly profitable when auctioned in London."

The two women moved on to gaze out of the windows, across the waterlogged lawns and down the glade between the oak trees, towards the grey lake, the overgrown woodland beyond and the leaden sky above. "I am sure the gardens look absolutely splendid in the sunshine, Mary." Anne said, and then, after a pause, added, whilst brushing off some invisible specks from her bodice, "And the Eyers boy?" Mary looked uncomfortable at the mention of the name, 'Eyers,' "Hardly a boy any longer," she said," Esau must be over sixty years of age. Richard feels it his duty to keep his word to his father; to always provide a roof over his head and employment. But why it must be here, at Fiddlesham, has been a small contention between us for some time. I find having a blackamoor living in the grounds rather disturbing, to tell you the truth, Anne."

"In what manner does he disturb you, Mary?"

"Just his demeaner; and well … his origin; a blackamoor."

Anne smiled, "His colour, Mary? He is hardly a blackamoor, he would pass for a Gora back home in India, Mary, a white man."

"But this is England; Sussex, Anne. Well I suppose that is not the main reason for disquiet; for a considerable time now, Eliza has been enamoured of him. I blame her governess, but cannot seem to find a solution to the problem. I thought all would be well because Eliza was very soon to be journeying to Asia with your two daughters, Anne. But now Richard has decided against the idea and would have her stay here at Fiddlesham."

"I can understand that, Mary. Unless she was to find a husband within a year of arriving in India, she would have to return; at Richard's expense."

"It would seem a reasonable risk, Anne. I cannot believe that there is not a suitable officer in the whole of India who would not take her for a bride. Can they all be so demanding?"

"There might well be such a man, Mary, but on the other hand; the indignation within the East India Company of having one's own daughter returned, I can well imagine would be too much for Richard to endure. The company's officers returning with such ladies aboard their ships are known to refer to such passengers as being, 'returned empty.'" Mary looked shocked, but the conversation had to end when a servant entered the room and announced the arrival of two visitors.

"Miss Dicey and Sin ... Sin ... - begging your pardon, M'Lady ... and Miss Dicey's friend." The maid's face blushed into a deep crimson, which coincidentally matched the colour of the dress of the Signora whose name was the cause of the embarrassment. Lady Percy was quick to control the situation,

"Signora Medici, welcome, and what a pleasure it is to meet you again, and Miss Dicey, I trust your journey was not too disagreeable. Please do come and meet Captain Percy's sister, recently returned from India, for an all too brief visit. This is Mrs John Parks; my sister Anne, may I introduce Miss Dicey and Signora Medici?"

When later, Eliza entered the room, ignored by her mother and guests, she sat at the harpsichord, upright, slender and tall for her age. In her mother's eyes she would have passed for an unobjectionable if unexceptional looking daughter, if it were not for one thing: the colour of her hair.

As early as Eliza could remember her mother had told her that when coming-of-age, she would travel to India. There, she would find a wonderful life full of colour, excitement, riches, beauty and exotic animals such as monkeys, elephants and tigers. Handsome

Indian Army officers would clamour to marry her and, in the cold season she would live in a beautiful house, not far from Madras, full of colourfully clothed servants, and in the heat of the summer she would move further north to a summerhouse on the slopes of the Himalayas. Mother's expectations of fulfilling this colourful vision of Eliza's future had shaped her daughter's early life. She had told her daughter that life in India would be one of which other young ladies could only dream. Eliza's future in India as far as her mother was concerned was not a matter for discussion: childhood and education in England would be followed by a married life in India and then, provided Eliza followed her mother's instruction, a heavenly afterlife.

Eliza looked at her hands on the keyboard. Her fingers also followed that same pattern which her mother had laid down for her life ahead. They must never deviate from the correct path; they should not fidget; touch things unnecessarily or even hold a teacup awkwardly. While at the keyboard, on the cello or playing the flute they should not only never play a wrong note, but always look ladylike and elegant. Mr Miller had taught Eliza musicianship over the past year. Musically gifted and a good student, she had begun playing the cello with the church choir on Sundays but after her first performance she had been hidden behind a screen. Her mother had declared that the cello was not at all suited to ladies. When it came to her own life, Eliza knew that it was her mother who controlled everything. Eliza also knew that she had a privileged life. A willing pupil, from an admirable household, she had a governess and music teacher and parents that were mannered and wealthy. One would have anticipated a smooth passage to womanhood. Eliza had learnt, as her fingers had, to keep time and follow the score but those parts of her that were once quite content, were now no longer so. The girl was becoming a woman and, rather like, as Esau had suggested, the caterpillar changes into a chrysalis, she could not understand the process, could not understand what was happening. She was experiencing not only a transformation in her body, but also a reshaping of her reason. But what was she growing into? A woman, she presumed, but at this moment she had no knowledge of how to be an adult female. All she knew was that, unlike the caterpillar, she was determined to be a mistress of her own destiny.

While Anne, Signora Medici and Miss Dicey finished their tea and listened to mother talk about her husband's recent voyage, Eliza had been joined by her sister and music teacher, Mr Miller. Eliza sat as upright as a Derby porcelain figurine. She had once heard her mother describe her as unexceptional and, except for that red hair, unobjectionable. To the right of Eliza, stood Mary-Ann, shorter than her sister, petite, comely and with – much to her mother's pleasure – hair as black as the burnt cork she used on her eyebrows. Sitting next to Mary-Ann was their music teacher, William Miller. He was not much taller than four feet six inches but made up for his lack of grandeur in stature with a shock of lampblack locks curling down over his shoulders. To those in the room, Eliza's eyes appeared to be fixed on a music manuscript in front of her, but the fact of the matter was that they focussed on nothing. Her mind was toiling over her recent conversation with Esau and the following hour which she had spent in her father's library finding out about metamorphosis. Had Esau been suggesting that there was a similarity between the life changes she was undergoing and the metamorphosis of nymph into damsel fly? Compared to that insect's transmutation, a girl growing into a woman seemed rather a paltry matter. However, how would a damselfly nymph feel if it happened to arrive in a world full of dragonflies? Eliza felt that the she was growing into a role for which she was not prepared but this new world was full of women who were very different from Eliza. Why were Esau's stories so complex? She was sure he was wise, but she could rarely make sense of – or see the relevance in – any of his fables.

In front of Eliza was Mr Miller's handwritten music, which she did not need; once having heard a piece of music, she could remember it by heart. Mother and her 'ladies' were watching but to Eliza she might as well have been alone. At the signal from Mr Miller, her hands began playing the first of a set of variations on a theme by Purcell. This had been arranged by Mr Miller, primarily for her sister, to show off her limited talent upon the violin. After the exposition of the theme, they came to the first variation in which the harpsichord played alone. The music in this section briefly explored other keys before, as customary, returning to the home key, which in this case was C major. At that point, her sister could take up the Purcell's theme again. When initially put before Mary-Ann, Mr Miller had arranged that the violin should also explore these different keys along with her sister's keyboard, but Mary-Ann had displayed such tantrums, complaining that it was ridiculous for her to play in other keys, when she had already mastered C major. Eventually, to restore some peace, Mr Miller had rewritten the variation for Eliza to play as a solo, although this also annoyed Mary-Ann. Eliza, followed Mr Miller's arrangement, venturing from the home key of C major to F major, as written, but then she deviated from Mr Miller's manuscript modulating through the flat keys and ending her variation firmly in the distant key of G♭ with a trill, the usual signal for violin to re-join, and waited for her sister's emphatic note of C to ring out clearly on the violin's highest string. As Eliza knew very well, Mary-Ann's note was now out of tune with the harpsichord, by three whole tones, the musically infamous tritone. The audience collectively winced at the harsh sound. Mary-Ann, although recognising she was out of tune, could not understand why. She stopped playing, and Eliza replayed a few bars and returned to her trill in G♭. The audience relaxed, feeling quite willing to overlook this young player's single error. Again, Mary-Ann tried, and again she failed to find the right note. Aunt Anne smiled, reassuringly, Mother grimaced, Miss Dicey winced again, but Signora Medici leapt to her feet, saying, with her thick Tuscan accent,

"What is this? Why child play La Diavolo Nella Musica? È un insulto a Dio. Is a insulto to the Lord. Fermare! Stop! Stop!"

Anne smiled uncomfortably and Mother's eyebrows took a severe downward turn towards her curling lip. Mr Miller, being a musician with perfect pitch, could tell at once, what had happened and had no choice but to re-join with Eliza to finish the piece in the new key of G♭. Eliza noticed, with great satisfaction, the bright shade of scarlet, which had appeared in her sister's cheeks, clashing with her black as night hair. Eliza's hands stopped playing. There was silence in the drawing room. She stood, turned and made a half-hearted curtsy. Her mother put down her teacup, saying,

"I do believe that at last the rain has stopped. Ladies, shall we walk in the gardens? Mr Miller, would you care to join us? Eliza, you will no doubt wish to remain and practice the art of keyboard accompaniment, especially when performing with your sister."

10   Shears

Late June 1785 – Fiddlesham House

"You wanted to speak to me Madam?" Bethany asked, making a gesture towards a curtsey. Bethany always felt uncomfortable in the presence of Mrs Percy.

"There you are, Bethany. While the ladies explore the rose garden, I would have a word with you concerning my eldest daughter. I understand that she has been spending a considerable proportion of her time wandering the gardens – and even further afield. And what is more, much of this itinerant behaviour appears to be unescorted. Conduct like this we find very vexing, and rather disheartening, because until recently we were forming the opinion that her disposition was improving."

"I beg your pardon, Madam."

"Why is it that when in your charge, she behaves in such a manner?"

"It is difficult, Madam."

"Are you suggesting that I have a difficult daughter, Bethany?"

"No, Miss, I meant to say that it is I who find it difficult to always know her whereabouts. I believe that recently something has disturbed her equilibrium."

"Equilibrium, what nonsense you talk, Bethany. I cannot believe this situation is one of equilibrium and that it should not be beyond your abilities to control. I would like you to instruct my daughter on appropriate behaviour and then ensure that she follows those directions. I never had such conduct from my son,

Welstan, and goodness knows, young gentlemen are notoriously more taxing at that age."

Bethany tensed at the mention of Welstan. She felt herself blushing, and why she should feel embarrassed, she was at a loss to explain to herself. After all it was, he who assaulted her. Since his departure to India, she had been trying, and generally failing, to forget the particular instance. Early one morning, he had entered her bedroom and raped her. Following this attack, he attempted numerous return visits but she had blocked the door with a chair. However, she knew that it was only a matter of time before he got into her bedroom again. At first, she could not think of a way to escape from his advances. Luckily her own mother had come to her help, even though she had been dead for twenty years. Florence Bethany's unmarried mother had seen fit to explain the anatomy of the male, to the point of drawing pictures with chalk on the kitchen floor.

"Flossy," she had said, pointing to an explicit chalked picture on their kitchen floor, "this part of your man causes no end of trouble. But as well as being their greatest provocateur it is their greatest frailty." Mother had then explained, with a list of examples, how even a suggestion of an attack in that area could bring about a change in a man's aggressive mood. Bethany had chosen one of her mother's suggestions, the threat of chopping off the offending organ; castration, she had called it. Until then, Master Welstan had shown a complete lack of imagination, which had suggested to Bethany that she would have to use more than a verbal threat. She had one chance to scare him, and that would have to be enough so that he would never approach her again. It would also have to be such, that he would not want to report the incident to his mother. She had gone to Esau for help and found him outside his cottage. Putting his wheelbarrow down to touch his forelock, he said, "Morning, Miss Bethany."

"Good morning, Esau. I need a particular favour."

"If I can help 'e, Miss."

"I wish to borrow a large pair of scissors, the sort I have seen you use to trim hedges, Esau."

"Is Miss referring to shears?" asked Esau, "Esau doos have several pairs of shears. What do 'e need to cut, Miss? Bring me material an' Esau bees doing cutting for 'e."

"In all likelihood," answered Bethany, "I will cut nothing with them, well hopefully, nothing, but the reason I need the shears, I must keep secret, Esau. So, please tell no one of this business."

"Now, 'e has been here long nough, Miss, to know Esau keeps self to himself. No one, 'cepting Miss Eliza and 'e, take much note of old Esau, let alone ask him favours."

"Alright, I want some shears to scare someone."

"Who's that? I'll not have 'e scaring Miss Eliza with my shears."

"No, no, Esau. I wouldn't do that. I want them to scare a man and persuade him to leave me alone. Especially when I am in my bed chamber."

Having just picked his wheelbarrow up, Esau put it down again and turned to face Bethany. The look on his face told Bethany he knew exactly which man she was referring to,

"If 'e planning to scare fellow Esau be thinking of, Esau can't think of a fellow who deserve it more. Esau 'ave very shears for such an undertaking. Follow Esau, Miss"

They went into Esau's potting shed at the back of his cottage and Esau pulled open a drawer.

"These bees sheep shearing shears. Esau use em for trimming box hedge round front lawn, Miss. Esau would say they be looking mighty fearsome. Mind you, Esau ain't asked any sheep's 'pinion on matter, nor any box edge, for that matter. They bees sprung shears. See how they work: Yous hold them in one hand, like so ..." Esau took a parsnip from an earth box and cut the end of it off in one clean, snip! He wrapped them in a piece of sailcloth and Bethany put them under her shawl. Bethany promised to return them soon. Then, as she left, Esau added, "Take care, Miss, if 'e please. Remember they be scaring shears only, but if 'e find they not be sufficient for 'e purpose, there be a horse castration clamp in ostler's box in lodge."

"Thank you, Esau."

"Bethany, Bethany, my goodness, Bethany, how my despair pullulates. Are you with us? Or are you in another world? I shall ask you again, what are you going to do about my daughter's wandering?"

"Yes, beg your pardon Madam. Yes. I will instruct her as you wish and then do my very best to ensure she does not wander. I will explain the perils that can befall a young lady alone in this world and will make it clear to her – even if I have to draw a picture in chalk."

"Pictures, pictures? This is not an artistic venture, Bethany, it is a simple matter of instruction."

"Yes Madam, instruction."

Bethany understood very well why Eliza had changed her behaviour. Over the years, her mother had led her daughter to believe that she would one day be sailing to India, a land of wonders. Then, without warning, Mrs Percy had upturned Eliza's future. Mother had justified the decision by explaining to her daughter that it was Eliza's own physical shortcomings, which had necessitated the reversal of strategy.

11 Governess

Late June 1785 Fiddlesham House

Bethany found Eliza at the keyboard, trying to make a normally very gentle piece of music, played an a very unresponsive mechanical instrument, sound extremely angry. "Miss, please, it is urgent that we talk."

"I am to practice the keyboard for Mr Miller, Bethany. It appears I am not suited to sea voyages or marriage in India. I must stay here and study to be a harpsichord playing wife of some stammering, pock faced village curate." Bethany removed the sheet of music from the stand on the top of the harpsichord.

Eliza continued playing but shouted angrily, "Bethany, how dare you? Can I remind you, who the mistress is here and who the governess? Replace that music at once."

Looking at the manuscript Bethany asked, "What is this you are playing, Miss? Oh, Nymphs and Shepherds? Your nymphs sound as though they are in dire need of rescue from your shepherds," she gave the music back to Eliza. "Miss, it would be to your advantage to attend to me for a few moments. Please, come and walk with me in the garden."

Eliza got up and, without waiting for Bethany, walked briskly through the open double doors. Bethany ran to try and catch up but quickly became out of breath and called after Eliza,

"Miss, I am sure that if we work together, we can achieve the thing you wish for most. I understand what you are feeling." Eliza stopped and turned to face Bethany, saying,

"Do you believe that you are privy to my innermost thoughts, Bethany? Are you a sorcerer now, as well as a prison guard?"

"I am neither of those, Miss. I am your governess and have been so for some time. Despite what you might feel day to day, I do have your welfare and best prospects at heart. It is my duty ... no, never mind that, it is my wish to help you; believe me when I say, I am fond of you."

"Well, leave me to my own devices then."

"I cannot. Your mother will not allow it and is quite prepared to dismiss me from her service should I fail to follow her instructions."

"Why should that be of concern to me?"

"Because, Miss, it is certain that your mother will replace me with another governess. Better the devil you know – remember Kelpwell?" Bethany could only watch as Eliza ran out of earshot, across the lawns and down towards the lake. There was no way she could keep up with her mistress but she had a pretty good idea where she would find her later: sitting by the Esau's old shed down by the lake. She might as well leave her there to either her solitary musings or a conversation with the gardener.

Nevertheless, an hour later, down by the lake, Bethany found no sign of Eliza. It did not appear that the old boat shed had been open at all that day. Where had Eliza gone? Bethany walked around the lake to the back gate of the gardens. Which way would Eliza have gone? To the left and down to the sea, or to the right along the road towards Chichester? Bethany thought over recent conversations for any indications that may have suggested Eliza's chosen path. Would she have run away – gone to Chichester? That seemed unlikely. No, she felt sure that Eliza would have chosen an isolated place to escape to. Bethany turned left, toward the sea.

13 There was a Crooked Man

Despite his present, and obvious, deformity there was something about Harman Beatcher – his gait, manner of speech and dress – which suggested that he had once been a man of the sea. But now, both in body and soul he gave the overwhelming impression of being the crooked man of the children's rhyme. On the rare occasions he found himself in a crowded street, it was never long before a raggle-taggle of sniggering urchins gathered behind him, calling, "Give us a tanner, Mister" or whistling the crooked man tune. When walking, he had a forward tilt, suggesting to the followers that he was searching for his lost crooked sixpence. To see the proximity of his followers, he would have to stop and turn completely around owing to a permanently locked bones in his neck. This inevitably provoked his disciples to ask whether he was searching for his crooked cat or his crooked mouse. But if they kept their distance, the ragamuffins' antics were of little concern to Beatcher.

In order to counteract his For'ard tilt, when standing still, he had to keep himself upright with the aid of his thick walking stick and, when underway, by almost running and thus pitting his forward momentum against the Earth's gravity. Whilst moving he could use his stick to frighten off any encroaching urchins.

On the track to Fiddlespit Beatcher watched, from beneath his grey crooked eyebrows, as Eliza, Silvanus and the horse turned the bend in the track. Once out of sight, he spun round to face the two young men. He now became surprisingly agile, running forward and threatening the pair with his stick which looked quite a cumbersome weapon. Its shaft was made of oak encased in copper, a covering which over time had turned green with verdigris. At the lower end of the stick, was a short iron spike and at the top, a heavy brass knob. With one twist of this knob Beatcher could get access to a deadly twelve-inch rapier hidden inside. He was never seen without this stick, which meant that few people had ever come close enough to be able to read the faded inscription upon the cane's stock, which read, 'Stoop inglorious from mortal sting are we disarmed.'

The stout young man, called Butt, sat upon the ground, scratching an armpit, while Hap'th, the skinny one of the pair, sat poking the remains of the campfire with his boot.

"What a fine brace of mumpheads ye be," shouted Beatcher. "Of all the critters in the world, I end up with you two; Puff guts and Shag bag, that's what I shall call ye. I couldn't have done worse if I'd left our camp overseen by a couple of bumbarrel tits, even with their necks wrung they'd show more nous than you twins of futility. Leastways they'd not go harrying a sea captain's daughter. What were ye up to? Lallygagging, were ye, baiting her like your dogs bait ducks? Was that it? If you want to chase some mollies, then there be houses in Chichester where for nine-pence an hour you get any fussock of your choice – and a pint of winkles. You could chase them bobtails around the bed all night. No, no, no, come to think of it, reckon that'd be no use to you pair of lobcocks 'cause you'd end up fucking the winkles." The two younger men laughed at the old man's insult and Beatcher took the opportunity to get closer to them and take a sideswipe at Hap'th's back with the knob end of his stick. But he missed and nearly overbalanced into the fire, making the two youngsters laugh even more and enraging Beatcher.

"Reckon ye'll still be gaggling when they strings ye up on a gibbet? But it ain't just you, Hap'th – oh no – things bees worse than that; yes, things bees much worse, ye'll be getting us all done for – all gutted and drawn – like three ducks hanging on a rail outside the butcher's shop. Now: first off, what was your notion, in harassing the copper-topped wench, eh, eh?" Beatcher kept on striking Hap'th to emphasise his words. "Come now, tell I." Hap'th squirmed on the grass in front of the old man, hands over his head, trying to protect himself from more blows. Butt, joined in hoping to avoid getting the same treatment from Beatcher, "I were trying to stop him. He's crazy; I don't know what he were up to. But you always says to keep a watch over him, so that's what I were doing." Beatcher went into a rage and as the Hap'th tried to scramble away, he brought his stick down on his shoulder making him let out a squawk. Hap'th managed to get to his feet but before he could run, Beatcher's stick had struck the side of his leg, sending him sprawling again. Beatcher brought the point of his stick on to Hap'th's back. Hap'th tried to crawl away but Beatcher followed, pressing down into the young man's back. Butt started to come closer but Beatcher turned to face him, threating to draw his rapier. Beatcher continued his attack, only stopping when Hap'th stopped moving and began whimpering. Beatcher stood over Hap'th and whispered, in a patronising voice, "Now, what was your notion, my lad?" Hap'th could hardly speak for sobbing,

"It were her ... she put a spell on I."

"Sorceress, is she, Son?"

"I don't know. She got inside me, stirred me up with her spells. It's what they do, get inside you and find out everything you know."

"What? Who do?"

"Wenches, they all be the same."

"Why not just leave her be, then?"

"'Cause I reckon having seen us here she'll warn Riding Officer Blackmore of our plans, and you wouldn't want that."

"She knows nothing of our business with Blackmore, unless you've told her. She's a wealthy sea captain's daughter. What put it into that pea sized mind of yours that she'd know our plans, Hap'th? And do ye imagine she's a witch? Be collecting newts and frogs to cook in a pot in yonder woods?"

"Look at her hair ..." said Hap'th.

"What about it?"

"It's red. Witches have red hair ..."

"Aye! An' so do squirrels." Beatcher stood up, distracted by a sudden idea, and after a few moments pondering, said,

"All may be well, after all, lads. She'll not be likely to mention this meeting to her family, her being a young girl out wandering all alone with no abigail, governess nor family to oversee her wanderings. She may have well been up to no good. So that's second off: our enterprise – the Blackmore business may be secure yet. Third off: there's this meddling cooper from down the end of the spit. Last off: we also have the business of Master Willow and his meeting of his machine wreckers. They'll be planning to smash and burn farmers and millers' new contrivances and we must learn the 'when and where' of it, because there's a certain gent what's going to pay handsome for such knowledge. Aye, now here's the sweetmeat in the gruel: if on the same night that Master Willow is burning machines, Cooper's wagon catches fire – it looks as though it's built of tinder anyways – and if he were top heavy in gin at same time, all'd go up like a bundle of kindling in the Devil's hearth. And who'd get the blame? Who knows? But not us. Willow and his saplings be meeting at the Red Lodge. You two should go to this gathering and find out which day they be doing their wrecking, and where. Now, get up my fine pair of winkle cockers, there's work to do. Get your minds off the young squirrel-headed wench's hidden money and put your minds to breeching some proper gingerbread, some spankers, boodle for our old age."

"I'll not go to the Red Lodge. It's haunted," said Hap'th, now keeping his distance from Beatcher.

"Not that stuff again, Hap'th," said Butt.

"It's true." Hap'th kept moving further out of reach of the copper stick. But Beatcher was just tapping the pummel with his fingers, "That's to the good. One ugly face is less likely remembered and recognised than a brace of bumbarrelss. Butt, me lad, Hap'th'll take you to the meeting in the punt and leave you there on your lonesome. We must know the watchword and time and place of the wreckers' planned crimes. Let's see they are meeting in three days' time; harbour is full today around midday; if ye go out in punt at two after noon, you'll arrive at the Red Lodge well before anyone else gets there. Leave Butt there and hide ye self in the reeds. Butt, ye will hide away in the roof of the lodge, or some such place, so ye can hear their plans."

12   Sons of Cockcrow

Late June 1785 – Outside Fiddlesham House Gardens, on the path to Fiddlespit

Eliza had walked this way before but never alone and the isolation made her feel unusually nervous. The track ran alongside a grown-out layered hedge, now with tall oak trees making the boundary to an overgrown woodland of tangled elder, hazel and holly trees. She hesitated as she came to a waterlogged patch of land. In front of her was a set of fresh wagon tracks. Who would have brought a wagon down here? Should she turn back? But this was her father's land; she could go wherever she chose. She could smell wood smoke; what was Esau doing right down here almost by the sea? Picking her way carefully between the puddles and ruts, she stopped abruptly. A little way ahead, between two sprawling holly clumps was a tethered horse and nearby two men stood looking into a cooking pot hanging from a tripod over a small fire. Behind them, almost hidden by bushes, was a wagon. Two large liver and white spaniels came running and barking towards her. The men looked up at Eliza, and ran towards her, calling out, "Diber, down! Lady, down!" The dogs stopped almost instantly and lay flat, disappearing in the long grass. The men stopped running and walked hesitantly on. Were they Gypsies, Eliza wondered? But camping here? The two men exchanged nervous glances but said nothing. Eliza walked on, trying to look straight ahead. She had never seen Gypsies camped this close to the house before. If her father's estate manager, Strothman Greedy, knew they were here, he would run them off. He was well known for his loathing of Gypsies. At one time, Eliza had seen a dozen caravans along the road towards Chichester, Gypsy families seeking work on the farms at harvest time. Greedy had raised thirty men, who, along with a pack of dogs, set upon the travellers setting fire to one of their wagons.

Without turning her head and out of the corner of her eye, Eliza could see the two men, now walking parallel to the track which she followed each with a dog by his side. She carefully stayed in the centre of the grassy path. They were twenty yards away now, getting closer to the track all the time and keeping pace with Eliza. Then, the thinner one started to quack like a duck, which seemed to send his dog into a commotion of yelping, howling and jumping. Then the barrel-like man started barking like a dog. What were they up to? Trying to scare her? She thought of turning and staring them down, as her mother might have done, but thought that turning her head might suggest she was feeling nervous at their behaviour and encourage them to be even bolder. She had noticed that they were not dressed in the agricultural clothes of Gypsies. They looked more like they were wearing sailors' slops. When she came level with the cart, she could see it was not like a gypsy's wagon, more in the way of a magistrates' prison van with a barred window on the side. She had once seen one very like it, bringing prisoners to the assizes at Chichester. What was it doing on this road which led to nowhere but a spit of sand and the sea? The tall thin man had peculiarly long arms which he flapped like a bird as he quacked. He was dressed in washed-out blue ill-fitting clothes and had a black rat's tail of hair hanging down his back from under a ragged shapeless cocked hat. The other man was agile considering his barrel-like shape and began running back and forth crossing the track behind Eliza with his dog close by. She could hear his footsteps and now his dog was whining, or was it him? She could not tell. She quickened her pace but it made no difference; the two men easily kept up with her. Perhaps she might be able to run faster than them; she could easily run faster than Bethany but she could not outrun the dogs and if she ran ahead, she would soon have to stop at the sea. Maybe she should call for help but what help might her shouts, or even screams, bring. There was probably not a soul within earshot. Eliza thought how foolish she had been to come this far alone and wished Bethany were with her. Her governess would have known what to do. Why were there such men as these? Eliza should not have to deal with such oafs. Their behaviour, although childlike, was threatening. This is it, she thought, I am to be murdered, or worse. The sudden thought of the 'something worse' and being overcome by these two filthy foolish cutthroats made her feel sick and then enraged her. Without thinking about her actions, she stopped in her tracks, turned around, held her head up and said in a clear loud voice, sounding as much like her mother as possible,

"Just what do you two think you are doing? Come here this instant both of you, stand here where I can speak to you without having to shout and stop behaving so foolishly." To Eliza's surprise, they stopped, looked at one another uncomfortably, lowered their heads and made their way over towards her. Their boldness had faded to timidity. At a few yards distance, Eliza said, "That is far enough." They stood next to one another looking at their feet. Eliza stretched herself as erect as possible, imitating the bravery of a cornered cat she had once seen trapped in the yard by a dog. She now realised how much taller than them she was and said confidently, "Do you not remove your hats in the presence of a lady?" One of the dogs ran up to her and sat expectantly in front of her while the other came sniffing around Eliza's feet. Both dogs now seemed far from vicious.

"Zorry, Miss, we be at dog n ducks, tis only a bit of sport with Diber n Lady," said the thin one.

"Aye, zorry, Miss," said the other. "Wondering, if you might be lost, or zomit? Path ain't going nowhere. Only t' spit. Ain't no place for a …" The thin man stopped and looked beyond Eliza, further down the track from where there came a shout,

"Ahoy!"

The two dogs immediately ran off towards the wagon and disappeared. Turning, Eliza saw another man waving a stick. He was a strange looking man bent double as if inflicted with some awful deformity. He walked with the aid of his stick, when he was not waving it in the air. Despite his stoop, and not being more than four feet six inches tall, he held his head upright. Eliza thought that he was shaped like one of the wrought iron candle holders which she had seen on Cook's kitchen wall.

"Now, my sons of cockcrow, what sport are ye at here. Vexing young lady with dogs, is it?" Then he turned to Eliza, "First off: me lady, regrets at tricks these two witless changelings be playing." Then, hitting the bigger of the two on the shoulder with his stick and making him yelp, said, "Second off: this stout fellow I've known all his life. Looks somewhat like oak tree but rather on the green side of seasoned. Third off: this lad be of similar nature to his cus but as you can see, more of the twig about him than log. They both be apprenticed to I, Miss. As for their dogs; just a pair of English water spaniels, what they be training up to fetch their dinner from the marshes."

"Your trade, and your name, Sir?" asked Eliza.

"Overseer, Miss, mechanical overseer. Which brings me to, fourth off: being that my overseeing is official business to His Majesty's Revenue. These two fools being my mechanicals. Therefore, in a manner, we all be on King's business. I have papers in wagon here, which say as much."

"But what are you doing here on my father's land?"

"Your father's land, you say, and I say, looks to mine eyes like a paradise for fools, unpeopled and untrod and therefore if not fit for all folk then it be in the manner of a King's highway, Miss, and by kindness of His Majesty, it be for the use of all common folk. So, comes my fifth off: the nature of my business."

"Which is, Sir?" asked Eliza.

"Which is to apprehend a wicked gang of cutthroats and smugglers, of whom we have intelligence to effect that they have been seen in these parts."

"You will find no smugglers here, Sir," said Eliza, "I shall now bid you a good day and be on my way," she said, beginning to walk back the way she had come, past the men and along the track back to the house. The hunched-over newcomer was nimble on his feet and skipped in front of her, saying,

"It is in their nature, Miss, cutthroats and smugglers will always be about their business under cover of shadows and darkness, not seeing somit, not proof of its unreality, Miss. Now, sixth off, 'tis not safe for a young lady to be in such unpeopled and untrod places with a bunch of purse-cutters on the loose. Being in the employ of the king, I do insist on taking ye back to your ladyship's home, safe in our carriage here. Now lad, get the nag hitched to wagon, and you there, open the back door of the wagon in order that we may make it comfortable for her ladyship." The two young men ran to their tasks,

"That will not be necessary, I shall return to my house now by myself. It is close by."

She walked on, but the man suddenly gripped her elbow, and began pulling her firmly towards the wagon. Eliza was taken by surprise, but before she could react, the crooked man spun about looking in the direction of the sand spit. Eliza heard hooves, the dull sound of a heavy horse galloping upon the earth. Then from behind some trees on a bend along the grassy track came a young man, head down, standing in his stirrups and galloping upon a grey draught horse. As the rider pulled his horse up, the hunched man let go of Eliza's arm and walked off quickly towards the wagon.

"Good day to you, Miss. Cooper Curtis, at your service. It's Miss Eliza, Captain Percy's daughter is it not?"

"Yes, indeed. But I ..."

"I had the good fortune to meet you at harvest time; the supper on the captain's fields the other side of Fiddlesham. You played some delightful music on your fiddle and after I was introduced to you by your governess, ah ..."

"Bethany. Yes, I do remember it now. You explained to me your trade of cask making."

"And you, to me, the difference between a fiddle and ... a viola was it?"

"Violin, "Eliza corrected. Well, that is indeed correct, so I did," said Eliza.

"How surprising that you should remember, Miss."

"May I enquire, as to your destination, along this back road, Mr Curtis?"

"I rent a small plot of land from your father, down by the lagoon, which I only use in winter time. I make casks and buckets to sell at markets in the summer. Presently, I am on my way to Chichester to purchase some necessities." He glanced at the other men, who were busying themselves hitching their horse to the wagon.

"Perhaps I might walk with you," said the young man, "as far as the path up to your house?"

"Well, I ..."

"I may be poor company, but my horse is very talkative. Dimo, say good day to the lady." The horse lifted its head, nickered and hit the turf three times with his right hoof. Eliza smiled,

"Thank you Dimo, what a courteous horse Mr Curtis has. Your company would be most acceptable, Dimo, and I would be pleased if you might bring your master along with you."

The young man dismounted and joined Eliza walking with the horse between them. Once out of sight of the three suspicious looking men, Eliza felt herself relax a little,

"Your arrival was most timely, Mr Curtis. Those fellows there, were rather disturbing, to tell you the truth of the matter. The hunched man was very strange. He suggested that he was employed on behalf of the revenue service."

"Revenue service? Did he show his papers, Miss?"

"No, Mr Curtis. He did mention papers but I did not see them and I must admit I found the whole encounter rather threatening. The two young men had a pair of English water hounds with them."

"That could be it. Brown, were they?"

"Liver and white."

"That's it. I think I have seen them using the dogs for duck baiting in the mill pond next to the Cat and Fiddle. I visit the inn on occasion with a friend of mine. But we left when a fight broke out about the wagers that were placed upon the dogs. I think it quite unlikely that they have anything to do with the revenue, Miss. I know the revenue officer in these parts, a gentleman by the name of Warren Blackmore, an old friend of mine. Their wagon looks like one once used by the press gangs."

They walked on with the horse still between them. A horse whose head appeared to turn back and forth as if following the exchange of conversation with interest.

"I understand the press-gangs have been largely abandoned," continued the cooper, "since we are no longer at war. However, I have heard that some gangs have turned their hand to kidnapping and extortion. There are also some unscrupulous sea officers who'll pay for their services to procure sailors, pressganging honest folk against the law."

The relief of her rescue had the effect of making Eliza rather more talkative with this stranger, albeit one she had met a while ago. In addition, she found herself smiling, not only at his horse but also because of his easy and confident manner. Very often, she had found talking to working people so tiresome, they became completely tongue-tied in the presence of a lady.

"Mr Curtis, you choose a place to set up camp very far from others, requiring long journeys to obtain your necessities. Why do you not find a situation in town, closer to markets where you might buy your materials and sell your products more easily?"

"Miss, that would be very good, but I need access to the lagoon behind the spit for seasoning timber. And the nearby coppices are ideal to produce charcoal.

Although it is someway from the markets, as you rightly point out, it is the life of my occupation as a cooper to travel and, if needs-must, live in the open air. It suits my nature very well, Miss."

"I too would choose a life of travel, if I had the means. I had been led to believe that I would travel to Asia with my father but it appears now, that will not happen. What is to become of me now, I do not know?" Eliza could feel her temper rising as the thoughts returned that had been so uppermost and distressing of recent. At least the escapade with the three strangers, and her rescue by Mr Curtis, had taken her mind off India for a short time. But now she was falling back into despair. She stopped walking, unable to get her mind off her plight.

"Miss, is everything in order? You seem concerned. I trust it is not I, who has spoken out of place and caused your apprehension."

"Mr Curtis. Would you think it out of place if I were to visit you down by the lagoon on the spit of land at some time, not too far away?"

"It would be an honour Miss Percy, perhaps you and Miss …"

"Bethany? Yes, I would of course bring my governess along."

He seemed taken aback by this suggestion and Eliza thought she had perhaps been far too presumptuous.

"I have no dwelling on the spit, just a wagon, my work tools and a fire."

"Of course, Mr Curtis. That is what I understood you to mean by your mention of a camp."

"Then you would find a master cooper's hearty welcome, a barrel to sit upon, a fire to warm yourself by and perhaps a drink of ale, depending on the situation with my necessities at the time of your visit. I look forward to your visit. Farewell for the time being, Miss Eliza.

May I share your Christian name Mr Curtis?"

"Silvanus, Miss. Silvanus Curtis," he replied. "I bid you good day." He then mounted his horse and continued his way to Chichester. Eliza left the track, through the gate, and followed the path to the house, and her mother's constant censure.

14 Lagoon

July 1785 – The spit of land near Fiddlesham House known as Fiddlespit.

Silvanus spent several months each year at gravel spit of land by the Fiddlesham estate. The lagoon, separated from the sea by the bank of gravel, called Fiddlespit, was useful to Silvanus to soak and season timber used for his barrels. In addition, the spit was an isolated spot where few people found cause to visit. The land was part of the Percy estate, and was administered by the captain's land steward, Strothmann Greedy. Silvanus had arranged with Greedy, a distant cousin of the Percy's, to use the spit each autumn. He would have preferred a straightforward rental agreement, but Greedy had insisted that he could stay at Fiddlespit in return for a few favours. However, sometime later Silvanus heard that Greedy, despite being a Justice of the Peace was turning a blind eye to smuggling operations in the area. If that was the case, then the reasons for this informal tenancy agreement became clear to Silvanus. Greedy would soon be calling in his favours to help with the smuggling activities.

The nature of Silvanus's coopering trade meant that he travelled to various fairs and markets in nearby counties. However, some years earlier this travel had become dangerous and almost impossible, due to Britain going to war with its American colonies. The government had delegated responsibility for providing manpower for its navy to gangs of ruffians. The competition for this lucrative business meant that at every seaport, bridge, turnpike, and outside the doors of many taverns, there were pressgangs lying in wait. Such kidnapping of innocent men at other times would be a breakdown of law and order but these gangs carried government papers rendering their operations legal. At the outbreak of war it was estimated that the Navy needed to recruit sixty-thousand men and the main source of this recruitment was the working men of Britain. Albeit the gangs were only legally entitled to take seafarers between the ages of eighteen and fifty-three, it was up to an aggrieved party to prove that he was too young, too old or that his impressment was in some other way illegal. Such deniel of qualification by an impressed man was usually impossible because pressgangs had a habit of clubbing men to the ground, bundling them away in the dead of night into a locked and barred wagon, taking them to a port and then, either ferrying them straightaway out to a man-o-war or imprisoning them in a holding-hulk. Some days would pass before the, often injured and befuddled, victim was dragged up into the daylight and asked by the officers to produce evidence that he was a man who should not have been impressed. By that stage, defending themselves usually proved impossible. As the war with America went on, and unemployed sailors and labourers became scarce, the gangs turned their attention to tradesmen, most of whom had never been to sea. Some chose to avoid the gangs by taking on the airs and dress of gentry, but that was difficult, not least because the clothes of the wealthy were naturally expensive. Others chose to fend off the pressgangs with a cutlass or pistol, which, of course, was a dangerous path to follow. Still others had families to help them hide away when the pressgangs were about. Silvanus had had no family to assist him, hence he had chosen to keep himself hidden away at Fiddlespit. Eventually the Navy became desperate over the shortage of manpower, and pressgangs began looking even further afield for men in order to fulfil their quota. Paid informers were employed and the pressgangs would be prepared to follow the slightest rumour concerning the whereabouts of a likely man. Often, like foxhunters, they would use foxhounds and beat, flush and even block the hiding places where men might go to earth. A betting man would be wise to lay out on a fox staying free from the hounds longer than an Englishman staying out of the clutches of the pressgang. Although Fiddlespit had the advantage of being remote, it had the disadvantage of being surrounded by sea and marsh. If ever he were cornered at the Spit, Silvanus's escape plan was to hide in the lagoon in an upturned barrel, which he had left ready for that purpose. Silvanus had had no wish to exchange his freedom for life in an English man-of-War. Although the Navy did usually provide regular food and grog, Silvanus preferred a life of freedom on land and in the open air. When the war with America ended, pressgangs were no longer needed and many of their members went back to working on the land, but others, like Beatcher and his minions, decided to use their recently honed skills as a means of illegal revenue.

15   The Red Lodge

21st day of August 1785 – Fiddlesham Harbour

It was Sunday morning and the church bells had just sounded ten o'clock, the tide was on the flood and the harbour nearly full. The wind and rain made those returning from church keep their heads down and skurry home. The few who decided upon a harbourside wander were well cloaked and hooded. All were deaf to the waterborne voices of the two men in the flat-bottomed punt out on the water. If they had noticed them, they may well have queried their business out on the harbour, on a Sunday morning.

    Standing in the rear of the punt with a pole was the sickly and diminutive looking, Hap'th. Sitting in the bow, facing Hap'th, was the skittle shaped, Butt, a robust man, a little older than his partner. Butt was attempting to keep the rain off, by wearing a straw basket on his head.

    "Can you smell that?" asked Hap'th, cocking his nose to the air,

    "Smell, what?" asked Butt, "all I can smell is the rain, the marsh and you."

    "The smell of witches."

    "Oh no, not more bloody witches? Ain't you got anything else to worry about, Hap'th?"

    "We shouldn't be here, not when it's cloudy like this."

    "There ain't no witches here. All you can smell is rotting fish and seaweed. Not witches," said Butt, yawning.

"Did you know that witch's farts don't blow away with the wind," said Hap'th, who had stopped punting while he spoke."

"Watch where you're going, Hap'th, the wind will have us on the mudbank."

Hap'th stretched his pole out to the right to turn the punt away from the mudbank. "Their farts just hang in the air, in the same spot, forever?" He said getting them back on course towards the small island in the harbour.

Strothman Greedy had used the Red Lodge as a hide to shoot ducks but the ever-changing marsh had long since prevented anything other than boats of the shallowest draught reaching the lodge, and then, only at the highest tides of each month.

"Do you know why it's called the Red Lodge," asked Hap'th, "when it's painted green?"

"Maybe the cove who named it couldn't tell his reds from his greens. I met this fellow from Runcton, a year afore last harvest time. A rum cull of a man, Baabaa we called him on account of him having brains like a sheep. He couldn't tell difference between reds and greens and said nearly everyone in Runcton was same, even the lord of manor himself."

"No, no, it ain't nothing to do with Runcton, it's called Red Lodge because of what happened there, some years back."

"Is this going to be one of your Aunt Nana's scary stories what she told littlun's, to stop them wandering on marshes? You see witches everywhere: on Fiddlespit, in trees, ditches and now in the marsh. How's that, Hap'th; witches everywhere?" asked Butt whilst shifting the ladder, which they had brought along to help climb into the roof of the lodge. He tried to make himself more comfortable by putting his feet on the plank seat in front of him but the rain soon began soaking his legs and he huddled up again.

"It's true, I know what happened," said Hap'th, "and it weren't Nana, it were Aunt Winnie told me." Hap'th negotiated the punt into the long narrow creek leading to the lodge while continuing his tale, "She remembered the story from when she were a lass."

"Go on then, what she say?" asked Butt.

"There was this woman – Winnie called her Fustylugs – came to live in village and from day she arrived the winter turned cold with deep snow and freezing nights. Most of cattle died, children went hungry and some babies died too. A witchfinder was staying at Chichester …"

"Witchfinder? How long ago was this?"

"I told you, when Winnie were a lass. Anyways, they asked witchfinder to examine old Fustylugs, and say if she were a witch. But they couldn't agree to witchfinder's fee of a guinea, so they had to make do with a woman who worked for the undertaker, who said she could do it for a crown and sixpence."

"A crown and sixpence? What were sixpence for?"

"For box of needles. Now stick a bung in your gob while I tell Winnie's tale. Betty Bone the woman's name were. But she found no Devil's mark on Fustylugs, but said she was most likely a witch, because she had red hair. So, they pricked her …"

"Pricked her? Ugh, what's that?"

"Pricked her all over with the needles. If there be a place on her what didn't bleed, she must be a witch. But that didn't work, so they tied her to a log and threw her in the village pond. If she were to sink and drown, then she not be a witch, but if she floated, she were a witch."

"Don't tell me, she floated?"

"Aye! She did. How did y'know that?"

"Well she would float, being tied to a fucking log, goose brain"

"I ain't finished yet: they dragged her out of pond and brought her to the harbour and throws her in, without the log this time. But it were dark by that time and she disappeared in the night. All they saw were an owl flying by that very spot."

"An owl? Is that the end?" asked Butt.

"No, not yet. On next day's high tide, Fustylugs were found – on this island by Slimy, who were eel fisherman in these parts. She had given birth to stillborn twins and then cut her wrists with some broken crockery. There were blood everywhere. So, island got called Red Island. When Greedy built the storehouse, to keep cut reed mace for roofs, it were so grand everyone called it a lodge, the Red Lodge. When it came to painting it Greedy wanted it painted green, so ducks wouldn't take fright and he could use place for duck shooting."

"What happened to the owl?" asked Butt, looking over the side of the punt to see why they had stopped. "You'll have to get out, there's not enough water." Hap'th stepped into the mud up to his knees and pushed the punt as far as he could. "I remember hearing about Betty Bone. It were against law to duck witches and Betty Bone were hanged. And that's what'll be happening to you, if you don't stop seeing witches everywhere." Butt got out and helped pull the punt up to the broken landing jetty and they both walked around the outside of the lodge.

"Go get ladder and bring it round back," said Butt. "I can get up through window, and pull ladder up. I'll be well hidden up there." Hap'th got the ladder and Butt climbed up.

"There's a big shelf in the wall here, I can get my head down for a while. Go get the jug of all-nations and pass it up. Need some of that, waiting here all that time." Hap'th fetched the jug and took a swig on the way back,

"Fuck, Butt, what's in this all-nations?"

"Mostly gin and whiskey and a drop of port – I don't know, depends what me Mopsy could get.

"Don't get mauled and sleep through everything," said Hap'th.

"I'll need to get half tinkered to help time pass. Give us a hand to get ladder up here, then you can piss off and hide somewhere till tonight."

Hap'th returned to the punt and pushed off through the rain – sniffing the air as he went.

16   Will O' the Wisp

Sunday 21st day of August 1785 – Fiddlesham Harbour

Around mid-afternoon the rain stopped but towards the sea the clouds were still heavy. Keynor inclosure lay just above the harbour, from there a gentle slope fell away and levelled out by the edge of the marsh. When Silvanus was a boy, this was common land and he and his father would keep watch over their grazing cow and pair of oxen. He knew that coming through here this afternoon would bring memories flooding back. A briar patch now covered the charred wattle and burnt daub, which once had been his house. Through all those years he could still feel the heat of the flames, smell the smoke and hear the crackling of the thatch as the sparks flew on the wind. He could still see the look of panic in his mother's eyes, which the young Silvanus had been confused by and took to be excitement. Every time these fits came upon him, he tried to fight against the memories but tonight they raged and he could not quell them. If he lived for a hundred years, would they ever fade? Eventually Silvanus pulled himself away, pushed through a hedge and walked down the old path, that he had run the night they had come. His father had shouted, "Run, hide in the marsh." When he returned, his home was gone and his father was dead. The next day Greedy had come with teams of oxen and a gang of men to flatten the remains of the gutted cottage.

Much of Fiddlesham Harbour was marshland now, which at low tide was criss-crossed with mud-filled ditches, islets, reed-beds and pools of brackish water. When the water drained at low tide it created a labyrinth of muddy paths enclosed by reedbeds. Only a few fowl hunters and locals, like Silvanus, knew their way through.

The lodge had never been completed; it had a thatched roof but no door. Instead, a sailcloth hung in the doorway, which Silvanus pushed to one side. Inside, a dozen men turned to survey the new arrival. Silvanus touched his forelock in salute. A few nodded in return, while others turned away and continued their whispering.

"Welcome, my friend," said a young man. "You have the watchword?"

"Birth-right," said Silvanus. The man wore a brown frock coat and red and yellow waistcoat over loose black trousers. Shoulder-length hair hung in chestnut curls from beneath a floppy black felt hat, on which was pinned a red, white and blue cockade.

"Evening, to you," said Silvanus, "I am ..." The man held up his hand to cut Silvanus short,

"No names, no homes. That's the rule here. Even if you know folk, keep it up your sleeve. We are like the will o' the wisp: spreading a little light in the darkness but gone by the dawn. Agreed?"

"Aye, sounds wise enough to me."

"Come, join the others. There are a few jugs of ale doing the rounds. Now, if you please, we must begin."

The young man made his way through the crowd. A group of four more men arrived and were asked for the watchword. The young man with the cockade climbed onto a stack of bricks raising himself above the others and began,

"Welcome brothers, to our first meeting of Fiddlesham Wisps. You are here tonight because each of you are known to be trustworthy. Some of you maybe the bearers of grievances for one reason or another. Every one of you here tonight is a brother to each and all. And so, henceforth, I ask that you address all here by no other name than that of, Brother.

It was I who called this meeting tonight and so I will share a name with you. Call me Willow, for tonight I shall play the part of your leader. Like many leaders in our fight, our enemies may cut me down but just like the willow tree, felled by a storm, will root itself where it fell, so shall your leader grow again. On other nights and at other places someone else of our society may take upon themselves the name of Willow.

And now to business: I ask that each of you take a moment to remember an injustice that has been cast upon your family. Think it over and ask yourself this question: were your wrongs ever righted; were these injustices ever redressed."

The men looked at one another and some mumbled out of embarrassment. Willow continued,

"You'll have likely heard the parable of the bundle of sticks. We brothers, must be like a bundle of withies. In unity we have strength; in dissent there is weakness. Think back to your own injustice and consider how you would have felt to have all of us with you on that day? Not only us but all the working men of England by your side. How would you have felt standing for your rights then?

"Now, let us share some of these injustices. Who'll be first? Who'll start then?" Mumbling and shuffling of feet broke out amongst the men. Eventually one man told of his family being evicted by a farmer from a home of three generations. Another spoke of lost employment and the fencing off of common land and the injustice of the inclosures. Yet another told of thefts of livestock. One man complained of witchcraft around the village. Willow interrupted him,

"Brothers, it suits the government for us working men to mistrust and blame our own women-folk for the sufferings brought upon us by that very same government's own brutality and avarice." The men continued telling of more grievances. Silvanus knew that soon they would be looking to him to relate a personal injustice. He recognised a few faces in the crowd and reckoned that they knew him as well. Some would know that his father died trying to save his cottage. After the fire it had been Strothman Greedy who levelled his home, inclosed the common and later sold it to the Percy family. But Silvanus would not be able to talk about that. Although it was the earliest injustice he could remember, it was still too painful. When it came to him, he said,

"Travelling from Portsmouth to Chichester in my wagon, two men hailed me. They said they were on their way back to their ship but being drunk could not tell which direction it was to Portsmouth. I was suspicious, no sailor, no matter how cut they were, could ever be that lost under a sky full of stars. Sure enough, one of the men pulled a pistol from under his jacket. His partner clubbed me from behind, tied my hands and bundled me into the back of my waggon. They turned my horse and waggon around and led my mare back towards Portsmouth. After a while, we came to Nutbourne and stopped outside the George and Dragon." A murmur went around the group of men as they reached the well-known coaching inn. Silvanus continued, "They bound my feet and mouth, left me and went into the tavern. But while they were drinking, I managed to remove my gag. A passing woman heard cries for help, listened to my pleas and said she would get help - but she went without untying me. The two men returned and we set off again. In the centre of Nutbourne, their way was barred by twenty to thirty women brandishing sticks, pots and pans and iron pokers. One of the men tried to fire his pistol but the powder was damp and the two were overrun by the women. I was released and the men thrown into the millpond. Where they were taking me, only they knew but the womenfolk said that since the end of the war they had lost many of their menfolk from the village."

"Sea captains, it appears, "said willow, "are willing to pay good money for illegally pressed men and local magistrates are prepared to turn a blind eye. Well said, Brother. Thank you.

"Soon, the time will come for action and we shall rid this land of corrupt magistrates and clean the seas of crooked ship's masters. And on that day, remember our leader will be named Willow. That might be me, one of you, or another. All will become clear before too long. Remember these words, share them with others but names and faces must be gone – lost in the morning light, as will the night's will o' the wisp vanish from the marshes at the rising of the sun. When this meeting ends, in due course, I shall be asking you one question: who'll join us?

"Well then, my fine fellows, shall we continue?" There was a general mumbling of agreement. The men outstretched their arms, not so much in a spirit of a newfound fraternity, but in the hope that one of the beer jugs would come into their grasp.

"Some here will remember the time when England belonged to the common man. Let's call that man, Jack. He lived in a village with his brothers and neighbours, men who would be there to lend a helping hand at harvest time, lambing or any other hard times.

There was a time when Jack's family could be fed from the bounty of the land, when deer, rabbits, fowl, fish, roots, berries, gleanings of oats and corn would feed his children.

"A time that if Jack's children should become hungry, farmers could be expected to sell their corn at a reasonable price. A time when farmers didn't hoard their grain to artificially raise the price. A time when much of this land belonged to Jack and he could feed his family …"

"And we know who's taken it from him," said a man drinking beer from a jug hanging over his elbow.

"That we do, Brother," agreed Willow. "England belongs to Jack no longer. And who's taken the land from him?" The men looked around to see who would answer, but only the man who had just interrupted, and had rather more than his fair share of beer, was bold enough to take up the challenge, "Papists." he shouted to a surprised murmur from some in the crowd. Willow continued,

"No … Well, yes, maybe you're right, Brother, the Church does the bidding of the thieves but I am not talking tonight of clergyman, Jack's land – our land – was stolen by the government. A government that not one of us here had a say in electing because not one of us here has a vote. This government is made of farmers, businessmen and landowners. A government that claims to govern Jack for his own good, whilst stealing the land from beneath his feet and the bread from the mouths of his children. A government that claims that what once was Jack's now belongs to the rich. Continuing their crime, they force Jack to work like a slave tending the land, which once Jack owned. Society was always a blessing for Jack, but government shows nothing but contempt for him. Government burns his cottages and ..."

"That's true they burnt down the cottage of young cooper's here ..."

"No names, my brothers." Willow interrupted, but the whole group had relaxed on hearing something that most knew about,

"No, that were a lightning strike. My father told me there were thunder about that night," said someone.

"Yes, your father worked for Greedy," said another.

"I heard it were the Papists, from other side of Fiddlesham."

"Revenue men, I were told."

"Probably burnt it down himself or it were some hags. They do that sort of thing all the time."

Silvanus thought that he should tell them that it was men working for Strothman Greedy who had burnt his parent's cottage and that he had seen it burn. But could he control his emotions while recounting that fearful night? Before he could decide, Willow held up his hand to stop the talk, and continued,

"Be that as it may, those who built fences around Jack's land and inclosed it, also claimed the woods for their own and built farmhouses, factories and now, most recently, giant mills, like the tide mill - over the water there - which is taking away all the work from millers for miles around. All the land where once Jack's geese and cattle wandered freely are now out of reach. The self-elected government of the rich have built their palaces on the ruined bowers of Jack's paradise." Willow paused to let the image of his favourite quotation grow in the minds of his audience. One or two nodded in agreement, while some looked at their neighbours wondering where this palace might be.

"Yes, they've built on the ruined bowers of Jack's paradise. And who can Jack turn to for help, in these times of hardship, loss and suffering? The law? In all that is good, it must be a crime to steal Jack's access to land?"

"It's a crime, for sure," shouted someone, while others called out,

"Aye!"

Willow, almost shouting to be heard now, continued,

"Who can Jack turn to for justice? The law, the magistrates? Let us see. Who are these magistrates? These upholders of the law are the very men who have stolen Jack's land - the fat landowners – eleven in every dozen of whom are magistrates. If Jack tries accusing them of theft, he'll end up being whipped or worse. But then these fat magistrates can easily use the law against Jack, accusing him of trespass or poaching. Should Jack ignore the law of the shires and go to London? March to parliament and demand that the lawmakers – his majesty's government – Pitt's government – stand up to the men who are stealing Jack's livelihood? Look, who is sitting on the benches of parliament, wearing Whig, Tory and Liberal colours, it's those very same thieving landowners.

"Who voted these men into their positions of power and government? Why, they elected themselves into government. The land grabbing fat rich farmers are the only men with a vote. And where can Jack go next for justice? The King, his Royal Majesty King George? Will he take up Jack's cause? 'There you are, Jack,' says the king, 'put on this red uniform, take this musket and sail over the sea to my American colonies, there you'll find some people I want you to fight.' And when Jack gets there, I'll tell you what he sees, his

American brothers, and what is their crime: wanting to raise their own taxes and use their own land to feed their own families.

"Where was King George at the siege of Yorktown, while Jack starved and watched his comrades die around him? Was the King at the front when Jack charged from his redoubt? No! I'll tell you where King George was, while his subjects were dying thousands of miles away, he was lying in his bed with his fat queen, speaking German to his English servants and ordering yet another bowl of beef stew.

"So, Jack sails home from the war, back to his village and turns to his last hope, the Church. And what does he hear from the pulpit? Whose voice rings out? I'll tell you my brothers, the voice of the all-consuming landowners.

"And so here we are, who's left that Jack can call upon?" The men looked puzzled, "There are those who'll stand by his side. Those who, when roused, are the strongest in this land, sons of Apollo, daughters of the Moon, they are here tonight, standing next to you. Will they help? They are your brothers, your wives, your sisters, your mothers, your fathers and your children. They are already standing by your side. Brothers, are you now standing by Jack's side? And will you give Jack his liberty?

"Will you follow the call, 'Give us liberty or give us death?'" Everyone clapped, stamped and cheered. Willow held up his hands, "As we stand together in this lodge tonight," Willow continued over the dying cheers of the watery-eyed and drunken crowd of Englishmen, "look around ... you may think that we are few in number. Now, look around." They all looked around. "And look further, look to other lodges. Lodges, just like this one, look to clearings in forests, look to the backrooms of inns, deep down in coal mines, out on the fields and up in the hills. Look on the gundecks of ships, in the hulks, where prisoners lie rotting in chains, and look in every other place where men work, where men sweat, where men bleed and where men suffer while trying to feed their families. The men of Surrey, the men of Southhamptonshire, the men of Kent, the men of Sussex and the men of Fiddlesham. From East to West and North to South, good men of England. They are by your side and in time, and together, we shall take back what is ours." Willow paused as the cheers grew louder and some men argued over the last of the beer. After a while, the group quietened down and Willow continued, "We shall start with something very near here, something that's recently been mentioned tonight but I'll not name it now. You'll soon get the day and the place. And now I shall give you the watchword for our action. That watchword is 'society' and remember our cry is Death to Government! What is our cry?"

"Death to government."

"And death to all governments."

"And death to the King."

"Death to the Papists."

"Death to witches."

"Brothers," said Willow, "we must have a care where we tread. As I said earlier, those who would keep Jack under the government's heel, will happily encourage him to believe that old women are the source of Jack's misfortunes and encourage him to accuse his own women of witchcraft. Be watchful. The gentry spread these tales of witchery to sow seeds of mistrust amongst us. But together we are strong. They'll use their wealth to bribe those amongst us for information, to divide us and set brother upon brother. But together we are strong. Spies will try to search us out. But together we are strong. Gangs of thugs will be set upon us." Everyone was getting the idea of this now and joined in with the chant:

"But together we are strong."

"The courts, the magistrates, the Church and the King himself, all will be against us."

"But together we are strong,"

"They will count for nothing, brothers because we have justice on our side, and ..." Willow conducted his audience:

"BUT TOGETHER WE ARE STRONG."

"So, we end where we began," said Willow, "who'll follow their brothers behind the banner of justice?

"We will," shouted the men.

"We stand united for justice. Let's hear it from everyone what banner shall we follow?" Willow asked, and then again conducted the whole crowd's answer:

"JUSTICE."

Up above, in the loft, Butt had fallen asleep and had been tormented by a repetitive nightmare, in which the hangman had just put a hood over his head, followed by his calming mother's voice whispering, Goodnight Benny, sweet dreams. But then, departing from his usual dream, the gallows crowd unexpectedly shouted "But together we are strong" and then, even louder, "Justice," Butt awoke abruptly and, as he always did when he awoke, he needed a drink but his bottle had fallen from its perch onto the boards beneath, which formed the ceiling to the room below. Butt leant over the edge of his shelf and stretched out his arm to reach the bottle of all-nations; nearly there, just another inch, a fraction more ... suddenly, he was sliding off the shelf. He could not help himself. He tried to land on the boards quietly like a cat might land on all fours, and for a fat man he did quite well, but the joists holding the thin floorboards were riddled with woodworm, and shattered on impact. Some members of the crowd below were quick enough to look up as Butt exploded through the ceiling like a wayward avalanche of worm-eaten timber, reed-mace splinters, rat droppings and flailing arms and legs. Butt landed with an almighty grunt on top of two men, knocking them to the ground. As the dust cleared, the shocked and silent crowd watched as the fat man stumbled around, coughing, spluttering and swearing. "Fuck me," he shouted, wiping lime dust from his eyes and suddenly becoming aware of a crowd of men staring, unbelievingly at him, their mouths hanging open.

"Jesus! I can't see a thing," whimpered Butt, whilst trying to run blinded and winded by the fall.

"After him, lads." Willow shouted, "Stop him." However, Butt was ahead of them and pulled the sail cloth down in the doorway, covering the first few men who fell in a heap and blocked the path of the others. Silvanus was the first of the pursuers out of the lodge and saw Butt standing, hands cupped in front of his mouth, howling like a dog. When he saw Silvanus, he hobbled off, as fast as his winded body would carry him. Willow was next out of the lodge and followed Silvanus through the trampled reeds. Butt was still howling like a dog until an answering howl came from nearby in the reeds. Butt turned towards the sound and after thirty feet, jumped out into the mud, waded out further parting the reeds as he went, until he reached the punt. He climbed into the back while Hap'th got the boat moving. Silvanus and Willow were nearly upon them and saw Butt unwrapping a bundle of rags, took out a pistol and turned it towards his pursuers.

Willow fell to the ground but Silvanus became frozen. Butt pulled the trigger and fired. There was a puff of smoke but no sound of a shot.

"Misfire," shouted Willow. However, Butt's threat had stopped the pursuit sufficiently for the punt to be out of reach.

"I know those men," said Silvanus, "I believe I saw them last on Fiddlespit with the old crippled sailor, they looked like they were trying to kidnap Captain Percy's oldest daughter."

"What are their names? Do you know?"

"I'm afraid not." Others soon caught up with Silvanus and Willow, several said that the man who fell through the ceiling was named Butt. However, all anyone could do was stand and watch, as the punt disappeared out across the harbour, the water mirroring the crimson glow of the clouds in the West.

"Brothers, it seems we have been overheard by spies. We must change the watchword from 'Society' to … 'Grievance'. But for now, get some sleep in the lodge, until the tide is gone and we can all leave."

17   Minnows

August 1785 – The Garden at Fiddlesham House.

"Misbehave, Miss?   'Ave 'e misbehaved?" Esau asked.

"Of course, I have. My mother is furious, and as for my father: having, over my lifetime, spent much less time with him, I can only guess at the level of his fury."

"That be true, Miss, but 'ey be Miss's parents. Ducks and drakes sees things different to ducklings."

"And what of you, Esau, how does an old gander like you see things?" asked Eliza.

"Well, Miss, 'ave Esau told 'e story about minnow an' kingfisher?"

Esau put his sharpening stone down and stood his scythe against the water butt, while Eliza sat down on the stool outside the shed, to face Esau,

"One time 'ere bees a lickle fish swimming in leat that feeds 'e mill. A penk or minnow or such fishy, it bees. Up above sitting on willow branch, hanging over stream is a kingfisher. Bird looks down at penki in 'e stream below an' sees a nice plump lickle minnow, Kingfisher sees 'is dinner. At same moment, fishy looks up and what does 'e see?" Eliza shook her head. "Well, fishy sees 'is destiny." Eliza looked disappointed and Esau picked up his scythe and waited for Eliza's response.

"That is a very short fable, Esau," said Eliza. Esau, continued inspecting his scythe by rubbing his thumb along the blade. After a while Eliza asked,

"Destiny, do you believe in destiny, Esau, that we are all fated? Are our lives all planned? Do you believe that God can see our journeys unfolding before us and that he is guiding every decision we make, everything we do and our every turn? If so, why am I so anxious? Does every other woman of my age see life laid out ahead of her and view it with dread, as I do?"

"Well, Miss, 'at would be different story altogether. Let me think. There bees a bucket full of questions that Miss 'as just tipped out." He got his pipe and tinderbox from his jacket, which was hanging over the half door of his shed. When his pipe was alight, he sat back down,

"Perhaps a story of a different bird. Now, 'ave Esau told 'e about nightingales 'at lived in a golden cage?" He did not wait for any answer but began, "Birds lived in a grand cage, 'ad everything 'ey could want. Plenty of space to hop about. Sun shining through window to warm 'eir feathers. Every day king's own parlourmaid cleans floor with lickle broom 'n gives 'em bowl of insects, an' cup of water. One day, maid forgets an' leaves cage door open. Mrs Nightingale says, 'Look, Mr Nightingale, door bees open and window bees open too, let's fly back to our woodland home.' But Mr Nightingale didn't look 'appy, 'But we got all we need, right 'ere. We're safe from kestrel.' Well, 'ey thought a bit, an' thought a bit more, until maid came back, saw open cage door an' closed it."

"What? Are you saying?" said Eliza, "that I should go away, while I have the opportunity?"

"No, Miss, 'e know Esau'd never say 'at. Who would 'ere be to vex old Esau without, Miss Percy?"

"But what is the story's application? Have you forgotten the ending of your tale? Did one bird fly away and get eaten by the kestrel?"

"Well, maid closed door, so no one knows if nightingales decided anything."

"The fable ends too quickly, are you sure you remembered it correctly, Esau?"

"Praps fable's application is its abrupt end. If 'e were to favour one nightingale's decision 'gainst tother's, which would 'e choose, Miss?"

"Why it is obvious, is it not, Esau? God made the nightingale to live and sing in the woods, to cheer all who may be passing, and not to belong to one person in a cage, albeit a king and the cage be a king's golden cage."

"Not so sure King would agree with 'e, Miss. King might bees thinking God created birds just to sing to 'im. Kings bees bit like 'at, Miss"

"What do you know of kings, Esau?"

"Nothing, Miss, 'e be quite right. Esau, often knows lickle of what 'e's talking 'bout."

"That's a very confusing tale, Esau. How does it help? What am I to do?"

"Well, nightingales didn't rush for open door, cause 'at might of ended with kestrel 'aving a good luncheon. Both birds spoke 'eir minds, 'n if luck 'ad been on 'eir side, an' maid 'ad fallen asleep, 'ey may 'ave weighed 'e decision carefully an' come to wise judgment."

"Why do I bother to pay any attention to your stories, Esau, they are never of any help whatsoever?"

"No, Miss."

18 Porcelain

August 1785 – Fiddlespit

At Silvanus's camp, scores of herring gulls and black-backed gulls squawked into the air. It seemed like an efficient alarm call but there was no one to be seen. All around there were signs of Silvanus: his horse tethered to a stake, sailcloth suspended from one side of the wagon making a shelter and the remains of a fire, which still had a few wisps of smoke and embers glowing brightly in the breeze. This, together with a collection of buckets, a workhorse bench, tools, casks and barrel staves gave the impression that the cooper was not far away. Eliza went over to the horse,

"Where is your master today, Dimo?" The horse nickered softly and nosed her, looking for some titbit. She picked a handful grass for the mare.

"Excuse me for asking so early in our acquaintance, Dimo, but what is your opinion on the situation of young women in these enlightened times?" How easy, she thought, it was to discuss things with a horse. The only human she could ever have a relaxed conversation with was Esau, and he always ended up by confusing her. But she had found it easy to talk to Silvanus after their recent encounter with those ruffians. That was probably because she had been so relieved to be rescued. But he was so unlike her family. Her mother turned everything upside down to suit her own view of the world. In that respect Eliza's sister, Mary-Ann, was proving a fair copy. Here is this horse wanting no more from her than an apple or turnip, and when no such things are forthcoming, is quite content with a handful of grass, which the mare would have been capable of obtaining herself. Eliza thought that perhaps she went too far that morning with the porcelain vase in front of her mother's group of ladies. She thought it over again and her rage began to rise, convincing her that her behaviour, far from being outrageous, had been quite reasonable. Oh, of course, her mother and the rest of the family would never see it that way, but that was the whole point. Neither would the ladies ever view Eliza's conduct as justifiable. Those sorts of people were always the same, pretending compassionate understanding and raising plucked eyebrows in feigned shock at Eliza's behaviour, when all the time, behind their white-lead powdered faces, they were relishing their host's discomfort. Her mother had always strived to dilute her own embarrassment, arising from her lady's comments concerning Eliza's shortcomings, by taking it upon herself to point out her daughter's shortfalls – lavishly and publicly. On each previous occasion Eliza had responded, porcelain faced, and saying nothing. Eliza knew that this lack of reaction from her daughter, infuriated her mother, whose only reaction was to escalate her daughter's humiliation. Eliza always tried to behave implacably, as if her mother was rebuking a statue made of chinaware. Until yesterday, that is.

"And this, of course, is Eliza." Her mother had said, by way of introduction, "As you have seen there is such charm everywhere in my husband's house, due to – if I may be permitted to boast on his behalf – Richard's quest for sophistication. Look at the ships, paintings, scientific apparatus, musical instruments and the house and garden, they all show how fortunate it is to be part of the captain's family. For example, one must look no further than his collection of porcelain, selected and brought back personally from Asia. There are the children: Welstan our son, already making his fortune in India, Mary-Ann, what beauty and talent, a credit to her father and such a delight to us all, and here we have Eliza. Well, it has to be said, and I have said this to Richard, that the beauty and elegance of a whole consignment of porcelain can often be enhanced by the presence of just one slightly cracked pot."

There was laughter amongst the ladies but none of Mrs Percy's audience paid attention to the object of this derision, all being too busy enjoying one another's polite amusement. Eliza took the opportunity to walk slowly over to the alcove. She took hold of the Chinese blue and white vase, brought back by her father on his most recent trip to China. He had been careful to learn by heart its exact description, which he would recite at every opportunity,

"A double-gourd vase, Ming dynasty, you know, and over two-hundred years old. The art-work depicts King Wen and his two daughters in a ship sailing across the ocean." Eliza picked up the precious object and carried it to the centre of the drawing room, directly under the vaulted ceiling. The laughter in the room stopped. Mother, in the rarest of moments, appeared lost for words, but then, on the point of making some sarcastic comment, stopped, as Eliza bent down as if to place the vase on the floor but instead, threw it as high into the air as she could. She did not watch the vase but kept her eyes on the assembled pairs of plucked eyebrows as they followed the porcelain's accent, its apparent motionless moment at the summit of its journey, its accelerating descent towards the marble floor and its spectacular demise into thousands of fragments scudding over the tiles and under the tea tables, almost reaching the ladies' feet. There was a collective gasp, followed by a communal silence, as Eliza, not too hurriedly, left the room, walking carefully through the shattered wreckage of the vase. She had hoped to throw it higher, "despite that," she said, patting the horse, "it was, I believe, the greatest performance of my life."

Her first thought, after walking from the drawing room had been to go to the lake. This had become her retreat, over the years, a place of her own, where even the ever-present Bethany seldom ventured. And down by the old boating shed was where she found Esau. She explained her out-burst, as though she had been watching her own performance. Esau had said nothing, and continued potting up his carnation cuttings. On this, her second retelling of the breaking of the vase, the horse also said nothing.

19 Old Woman Lived in a Shoe

September 1785 – Fiddlespit.

Eliza, hearing a splash, turned around, something was moving in the water. It looked like Mr Curtis, swimming in the middle of the lagoon. How did he get there, and what was he doing? He spotted Eliza and raised a hand in acknowledgement, and then continued with a task involving a floating barrel and rope. Swimming a few more strokes towards Eliza, he stood up and waded ashore. She watched the water run down his buckskin waistcoat and leather breeches. In his hand he held a line, the end of which he carried out of the lagoon and over towards Dimo,

"Good morning, Mistress. Please, I beg your pardon but I must just …"

"And good day to you Mr Curtis, what on Earth are you doing. Some game, or sport that I have not happened upon before?"

"I agree it must seem so, Mistress. But in a few moments, all will be clear." He un-tethered the horse, fetched its collar from the wagon, and harnessing it to the rope from the lagoon, began to lead the horse away heaving something substantial from the depths of the pool. Soon Eliza could make out the sunken treasure was little more than a load of waterlogged timber.

"I purchased this green oak from one of your father's woodlands. It's not far away and makes the need for long trips on the today's unsafe roads, unnecessary. The green oak will season underwater in a short time – six months or so. Not as good as air seasoned timber, but that takes years, and water seasoned timber is good enough for many uses." The bundle was out of the water, and Silvanus detached it from a tangle of chain-shot, which was there, presumably, to weigh the timber down and keep it below the surface of the water.

"I trust you did not reencounter those ruffians on your journey on the road here today, Miss Percy? I have since discovered that the larger of the two men is named Butt."

"Butt. Is he from Fiddlesham, Mr Curtis?"

"I know nothing more of him, except to surmise that he is probably up to no good."

"I did not see anything of Butt, or the other men, today, thank you, Mr Curtis. I had a pleasant walk and saw no one. I believe that I even managed to escape the attention, of Bethany, my ever-present governess. I do believe that my mother values her services as a gaoler over that of a tutor. But I shall leave you now, Mister Curtis, you and Dimo, obviously have much work to do, or perhaps I am delaying you from finding a new set of dry clothes."

"Not at all, Miss, you are a welcome sight in what passes for my estate. All that is left for me to do, to complete my day's work, is another swim, in the sea. This time, to wash the brackish water from my clothes and hair but it is of little matter, this blanket will serve for the moment."

"And how do you find swimming in the sea, is it not dreadfully cold?"

"During the winter months the sea is often warmer than the lagoon here. I am not altogether sure why that should be, maybe the ocean's movement keeps it warm or perhaps the currents bring the water from a warmer place."

"I have swum many times in the estate's lake, starting as a young child but my mother has recently forbidden me to continue. Consequently, I have not swum for some months. Swimming whenever you choose —I must say I do envy you – and in the sea too. My swims in the lake were so enjoyable. I understand that some ladies at various beaches swim with the aid of bathing stations dragged out to sea by horses, doors can be opened for the them to take to the water. It appears a lot of trouble for a swim."

"I could attach Dimo to a suitable cask, in which you could hide yourself and, when out in the sea, you could swim away - all the way to France if you so wish."

"An excellent plan, Mister Curtis, if I were a gentleman or perhaps a cooper's daughter and not servant to my mother's decrees, I would certainly accept your kind offer. I am sure any lady related to your good self would be only too pleased to take part in such a sea swimming adventure. My mother believes that being the daughter of a sea captain makes one delicate to the extreme, only fit for playing the music of long deceased musicians on the almost silent clavichord, or the like. I must say I find it very strange that whilst us females are treated as delicate damselflies and protected from most forms of adventure throughout our lives, we are wholeheartedly encouraged to follow the example of the old woman who lived in the shoe and fill our houses with babies. Compared to giving birth, I should imagine, swimming in the sea a relatively trivial pursuit, just look at the number of women who die whilst giving birth."

"The sea is just the other side of this bank of shingle," said Silvanus. You would not be overseen swimming there. Then afterwards, I could offer you some broth and, unlike your old woman in the shoe, I could also offer you some bread, as well." Without thinking, Eliza could not resist finishing the rhyme,

"Then whip them soundly and put them to bed." Silvanus looked away with an apparent sudden interest in the circling gulls. Eliza, despite herself, felt her cheeks begin to glow red. She turned, looking at the track which led back to her house, as if planning to leave.

"As you can no doubt tell by the sound of the waves hitting the sand spit," Silvanus continued, wishing to dispel his visitor's embarrassment, "there is a considerable sea running today. The waves are far too big and a lady would most definitely be drowned. Also, although that prospect would trouble me greatly, I feel certain that if your mother were to become aware of even a suggestion of such a venture, she would have me hung, drawn and quartered, if not worse, although, I cannot conceive of anything being worse than that particular fate." Eliza smiled, thought for a moment and replied,

"Obviously, you have not heard my sister, Mary-Ann, perform Mr Purcell's Minuet in A minor on the violin. Cats run over water and herring gulls fall from the sky in order to escape her playing." Silvanus laughed easily and said,

"Could I make you a warm drink, before your return journey?"

"I should start back now. Although ... I suppose that I am in no hurry to go home. My mother will have harsh words for me whenever I return. I am afraid I behaved disgracefully before leaving, and in front of her tea ladies. She is probably devising some suitable punishment for me at this very moment."

"I cannot imagine you, Miss, behaving disgracefully. I am sure whatever you did was not that reprehensible."

"I broke a vase."

"A vase? Why, if I possessed vases, I would be tempted to break one every morning, they are so useless and fragile looking. Isn't that what they are designed for?"

"Not this vase. It was my father's favourite. He brought it back from his last trip to China. My mother says it was worth a considerable amount of money."

"Notwithstanding all human precautions, accidents will happen," Silvanus said, trying to calm the young lady, who appeared to him to be growing increasingly distraught at even the mere thought of her recent behaviour.

"It was not an accident, for I definitely meant to do it. Although I did not plan it beforehand, nor think of its repercussions. I stepped forward, picked it up, threw it in the air and watched the faces of my mother's guests as it smashed on the marble floor. The strange thing was, Mr Curtis, I enjoyed it, and have no regret in the slightest. However, I cannot imagine what trouble lies ahead because of my actions."

"But you must have had a motivation."

"Yes, I think so, but whether it was a justifiable motivation is a problem that confounds me."

"I would say, that if a reasonable person, possessed of common sense, and to my belief you are that manner of a person, then any action taken by that person would be reasonable. And in any case, you will be richer for the experience, and the amount of poverty suffered by your family, I am sure will be quite acceptable. I am sure your family are fond of their children more than they are of their vases, even Chinese ones." Eliza did not respond. She appeared to Silvanus to be looking off into the distance. After a few moments, Silvanus said, "I shall put some wood on the fire and warm some water." Eliza appeared to have swiftly come to some decision. She looked directly at Silvanus and asked,

"Mr Curtis. Have you another set of clothes I might change into. I fear that swimming in these skirts would certainly lead to my demise."

"But Miss, your mother?" Asked Silvanus in surprise.

"In my mother's account book, under the column headed: 'Eliza's recent transgressions', the addition of 'swimming in the sea in a set of gentleman's clothes,' would result in very little additions to the column headed, 'Eliza's impending punishments', and in any case, she is not here, and as far as I know, has no way of knowing."

"But Miss …"

"Mr Curtis, I am a strong swimmer, must I recount the day I learnt to swim and captured a monstrous pike?"

20   The Sea from the East

An East Indian Company sea captain preparing for a voyage from London to China and the Far East might well load his ship in the Thames estury with a cargo of trade goods, sign on his officers, find the best crews available – by hook or by crook – and lastly, board his passengers. He would then sail his ship to an anchorage along the East Coast between Ramsgate and Dover, known as the Downs, and there, more often than not, he would be obliged to wait at anchor, his eyes cast to the heavens, not as his early ancestors might have done in prayer and supplication to the Almighty but to observe which way the wind blows. For the most substantial part of the year, westerly winds blow across the southern region of Britain. Even the latest and fastest ships of the East India Company could not, without a great deal of time and effort, sail into the wind. In the Downs there would often be as many as two-hundred ships gathered awaiting a favourable easterly wind to take them down the English Channel and out into the Western Ocean. Some old sea captains would say they could tell, from the temperature, the clouds, and even their aching knee joints, that the wind was soon to change towards the East. Then, in order to steal a march on their fellow mariners, they would up-anchor and make for the Channel. Some days, if the sea captain was an old and well-respected salt, his sudden weighing of anchor and unfurling of mainsail might cause a collective action and a great flotilla of merchant ships would head off, in an abrupt race for the high seas. The air that had recently been dappled with the cries of the gulls, curlews and oystercatchers would now be awash with the calls of boatswains' mates, yardsmen, topmen and the farewell to England refrain of the shanty men. The whole sea would become alive with the sound of sailors and their labours. Ships' captains all racing and attempting to outwit, and out-sail their fellow seafarers. In a time of war, the lookouts would be on the watch for Navy pressgang boats, waiting around the next headland, which might harry them and then, after a show of arms, haul alongside and demand the best share of their crew. It was now, however, a time of peace, and a fresh easterly gale had been blowing overnight and the horizon, off the Sussex coast, was filled with sails, all running down the channel. This day, as well as driving the latest armada of vessels westward, the wind pushed the sea up against the incoming tide and caused a large swell to roll along the Sussex coast to Hampshire, Dorset and beyond.

On the seaward side of Fiddlespit, a steep shingle bank confronted the waves and having no opportunity to curl over and slowly die, the waves rose up, as if taken by surprise, and thundered onto the shingle bank. In anger at their imminent demise, the waves then clawed at the pebble beach, dragging the flints back into the sea.

To Eliza, the scene looked terrifying; the waves would surely drag her under and drown her. "Miss!" Silvanus shouted against the roaring wind and screaming shingle, "If you want to swim, first, you must dive. As you did in the lake. You should dive beneath the wave as it rises but before it curls over. As if you were diving through a doorway. Once through, it will only take a few strokes before you are clear of the turbulent breaking water. Imagine you are a young bird, freshly out of the nest. Perhaps a young tern. You hover for a while over the water and then dive in; imagine it is what you were born to do. It will be like entering a new world, for a few moments, you will be almost overwhelmed by the sudden change and the assault on your senses. Try to overcome this by thinking hard about something you know well. I recite the number of staves for different casks. You are a musician; sing a song. It will occupy your thoughts while you adjust to your new world. Then, soon you will become a different creature, a creature of the sea."

"Are you suggesting I will become a mermaid, Mr Curtis? If so, I am not sure I should continue. I believe that mermaids are harbingers of calamity."

Silvanus sat by her side, "Miss, I cannot imagine that you could bring anything but good fortune to anyone who happens, to cross your path. Except ..."

"Except, Mr Curtis? Please do continue."

"I was about to say, except a person who has recently purchased a Ming vase. But who knows what journey that vase had undertaken before you let it fall? Perhaps it had been fated that it should end, broken on your mother's marble floor."

"Do you believe in fate, Mr Curtis?"

"I do believe that we are destined for certain lives. Although I am sure that on various journeys, we shall reach crossroads and at that point, we have the freedom of will to take any route."

"So, does the Almighty write our lives, Mr Curtis?"

"Maybe he writes yours, Miss, but not a humble cooper like me. He'd be far too busy."

"Why should he ignore you? Surely in the eyes of God, we are all equal."

"Miss," said Silvanus, getting to his feet, "if I may say so, I think this is prevarication on your part. If we are to, let us swim and talk about fate and fortune afterwards – if we be fortunate enough to both survive our encounter with Neptune."

"You are right. The sea looks far too big, Mr Curtis I ..."

"It is only the first step, or two, which will prove difficult. Once out at sea you will just be lifted up and down, as if on a child's swing. I promise that after this, nothing will ever appear the same again."

"I am ashamed to admit that I am too scared, Mr Curtis." Silvanus smiled and gave a wave of the hand as if to dismiss the whole venture,

"No matter, sit here and watch. I will not be long." Silvanus walked to the very edge of the water. The waves washing his feet, he watched for a moment and then, as a large wave rose in front of him, ran a couple of steps, dived with outstretched arms into the wave and was gone – as though the wave had snapped him up. Eliza stood up, trying to see above the crests of the waves for any sign of him. For a moment, she caught a glimpse of him waving, and then he was hidden again. A song, what song might she choose. She could not think. All that came to her was a French children's song. The first song she had ever learnt. She began singing, hesitantly at first and then louder and louder,

"Il pleut, il pleut, bergère ..." Without giving the matter more thought she stood up, ran, jumped towards the wall of water and dived into the sea. It did not help that she had shut her eyes before leaping and had jumped in a rather reluctant, sideways fashion. She landed too late into the breaking wave, which dashed her onto the seabed. She wanted to scream but the cold sea blocked out everything. When she came up, the wave had taken her breath away and she was tumbled back into the next wave. She tried to stand but the cascading stones took her feet from under her and she fell again. Eventually, managing to stand, she found her breath at the very moment a big wave came rising and rolling towards the her. This time she would do it. She would not be defeated.

"Il pleut, il pleut, bergère …" Three steps and she dived through the face of the wave into a white and green turmoil and a strange near silence studded with the ring of cobbles tumbling down the beach. She swam and kicked as the waves crashed above her new and muffled underwater world. On the surface again, in a flood of sound, she swam as hard as she could to escape the breaking waves but she had to stop again because she could not breathe, her lungs seemed to have locked. "Sing, Miss," Silvanus said from by her side, "sing! It will help your breath."

"Il pleut, il pleut, bergère, Presse tes blancs moutons …"

21   Rising Moon

"I will return home now, Mr Curtis. Thank you for ...me to ..." What was the word, Eliza could not think of it? "Helping," that was it, "Helping with the waves in the sea." Turning to take the track back to the house, she was too confused to decide which way.

"Miss Eliza, you should remove the buckskins, dry yourself before returning home and put your clothes back on. You are shivering and I fear the cold has got into your bones."

"Certainly, I mean certainly not, Mr ...what is ... I must apologise ..." Eliza felt faint, began to fall and Silvanus only just managed to catch her before she hit the ground. Eliza's eyes were shut and her shivering had stopped. Perhaps he should let her sleep for a while? Or should he try to warm her up? Should he take her to see the doctor? But all the way to Chichester? How would he get there: six hours in the wagon or two, if he could manage to carry her, on Dimo? Last winter he had swum in the ice-covered lagoon to retrieve some timber. The task had taken longer than he thought and before he had managed to rid himself of his wet clothes, he had become befuddled, as if drunk on beer. He had even wanted to lay outside without his clothes but that day he had managed to convince himself to wrap up in a dry blanket in the wagon with some warm stones from the fire. The best thing for Eliza was to take her to her own house, but what retribution would that bring upon Eliza's head – not to mention his own head? And how would he explain that he had taken the captain's daughter into the sea in this weather - and at this time of the year? He should persuade Eliza to change her clothes but he could not wake her. What was wrong with her? He began to panic. Why had he let her swim in the sea? She was far too frail. He carried her into the rear of the wagon, out of the chill breeze but he could not get the buckskins off. What would she think, waking and finding him trying to undress her? He got a knife and began to cut along the seams of her clothing but soon gave that up because it was taking too long and began cutting the material off. There was still no movement from her – could she be dead already? What should he do? What a fool he had been. Just a young girl and he led her into the cold sea. But she was so confident and such a strong swimmer. Her clothes off, he wrapped her in a woollen blanket and then put another over her so just her nose was visible. He himself was shivering now, almost uncontrollably. Out of the wagon, he collected some hot stones from around the fire, as he did so, he threw some more wood on the glowing embers. In the wagon, he wrapped the stones in some old clothing and placed them under the top blanket, close to Eliza. Did she just move? He leant down close to her lips but could feel no breath coming from her mouth. Perhaps some warm broth might revive her from within. Jumping out of the wagon again, he ran towards the fire to set up the pot on his tripod but in the fading light tripped over an outstretched rope, falling headfirst, hitting his head against one of the remaining fire stones and knocking himself senseless. Dimo, Silvanus's horse, came over to him and whinnied but to no effect. Eliza's arrival had distracted him and he had left the rope still attached between the horse's collar and the timber hauled from the lagoon. The line had become entangled with Silvanus's work bench. Dimo had been trying to pull free to reach some pasture and had, unwittingly, set the ankle height trip line for her master.

Back at the Estate, rather than tell Mrs Percy that her eldest daughter was missing, Bethany had spread the word that her mistress had taken to her bed chamber earlier than usual that afternoon, knowing that everyone would assume that Eliza was hiding away after smashing the vase earlier that day. Bethany had convinced herself that her ward would return home overnight. If not, Bethany would have to raise the alarm in the morning. What was her young mistress thinking of – swimming in the sea with the cooper? Bethany had watched it all from the edge of the woodland as Eliza and the cooper climbed the shingle bank. She had then followed to peer over the top of the bank and saw her mistress swimming in the sea with the cooper. She left her to it and had felt sure that Eliza would return before too long.

The wind had blown the clouds away and then faded to a light breeze. As the stars began to fill the heavens, Silvanus rolled over onto his back, groaning. The heat from the wood he had put on the fire had dried his back and legs. When he eventually opened his eyes, he assumed he had been attacked by some footpads and left for dead. Where were they now? Should he hide in his barrel in the lagoon? But he was too groggy and cold and shivering. Perhaps he could call Dimo over, and escape? He looked at his legs, the one which had been nearest the fire was steaming and the other felt cold and wet ... and then he remembered: the sea ... Eliza! He tried to rise to his feet but quickly fell onto to his knees again. Not only could he not stand, he could not see clearly and it was a dark night; the moon had not risen yet and the fire was low. He added some more logs to the fire and in the light of the rising flames crawled under the wagon to retrieve his dark lantern, candles and a strike-alight. He felt almost too scared to climb back into the wagon to see if Eliza had recovered … or was she … he dare not think of it. His head was spinning but he managed to hang the lantern from the wagon hoops, just above Eliza and put a lit candle in a holder at the back of the wagon … she was breathing. He climbed out again and fetched his cooking pot with the recent remains of some broth from a brace of rabbits he had snared a couple of days previously. He set up the tripod and hung the pot over the fire and then set about untangling Dimo. Once freed, the mare quickly disappeared into the darkness and he left her to wander. When leaving the camp untethered before, she had always returned in the morning, as if reporting for duty.

He could feel the blood, thick and sticky in his hair, and splashed some water from the butt over the cut on his head. The broth had warmed enough, he thought and put some in a bowl. Finding a wooden spoon, he climbed back next to Eliza and propped her up. Now he could see that she was breathing. He fed her a few sips of the warm rabbit stew. But began to feel everything around appear to go into a spin again. Putting the bowl down with the remains of the potage, he laid his head next to Eliza … and knew no more.

When Eliza awoke, she could smell burnt meat. It was the smell of a tallow candle. Cook had used them until Eliza's father had insisted that all the lighting in the house be replaced by sperm-oil lamps and beeswax candles. It was dark outside and she was in the back of a covered wagon lit by the last glow of a tallow candle. Then, in the gloom, she was suddenly aware someone else was in the wagon with her – turning, towards the sound of breathing, almost snoring, Eliza jumped upright out of shock. It was Mr Curtis; eyes closed and face streaked with blood. Who had done this to him? Had those ruffians from the other day returned and attacked him – were they still here? Pulling the top blanket over him she thought to make a bandage for his head and reached down for her petticoat … but … she was naked. Where were her clothes? The warm stones by her side had some rags around them, useful to wipe away the blood from Mr Curtis's face. The blanket needed tucking in around him, the warm stones positioned and, after hesitating for a moment, she lay down next to him. Eliza had never been this close to a man before, or this close to anyone. When Eliza was an infant, Cook had once given her a hug. It had taken her by surprise she had told Cook to leave her alone, being unnecessarily rude to the old retainer.

Calling Mr Curtis by name, she shook him gently but his eyes remained firmly shut. What should she do? Wait until he woke up or … perhaps he was dying. Cold fear made her shiver with that thought and she remembered not being able to speak clearly after coming out of the sea. Seeing the stubble on his chin, about a quarter of an inch long, how strange that must be, she thought. Suddenly his eyes opened and made Eliza start, "Goodness, you're alive, Mr Curtis."

"Why, yes, I do believe so," then after moment or two, holding his head in his hands, he added, "unless this is the afterlife, I still have a mighty painful head?" he groaned. "Thank god that you also appear to be alive, Miss Percy." He smiled. She could smell his sweet breath and see tears glinting at the corners of his brown eyes. Their faces were close and getting closer. Then ... like diving in the sea or throwing a vase into the air ... without thinking, and for the first time in her life, Eliza kissed someone. She pulled away quickly. It was strange sensation, she thought: warm, damp and ... She leant forward to try again and he put his hand on the back of her neck holding her tight. Her red tangled locks fell over his black blood caked hair. How pleasant that was, she thought but did not say so. No, it was much better than that. A while ago, she had read about kissing and could not understand why such a business seemed to be made of it. But now, she could not think of what to say and so remained silent. There was light coming from outside, from the front of the wagon. Then, through the open wagon end she saw a golden moon rising over the gravel bank. Silence seemed strange but pleasant. There appeared no need to say anything and what seemed like forever passed in stillness with his arm around her shoulders.

Eliza would have to say something soon, but what? Her first kiss. She should say something noteworthy. Finally, she remembered a part of a play - which Mother had forbidden her to read but, conversely, Bethany had left a copy with the rest of her work in the schoolroom for Eliza to find. Perhaps it was apt:

"The moon shines bright. In such a night as this. When the sweet wind did gently kiss the trees. And they did make no noise, in such a night."

"A quotation. Why do you choose that one?" asked Silvanus.

"Until I remembered it, I was at a loss as to what to say about my first kiss. All I could think of was, 'You have pleasantly wet lips, Mr Curtis.'" They both laughed.

"The quote is beautiful, Miss, Percy. May I ask what it means?"

"Mr Curtis, do you think that this a suitable point in our relationship when we might dispense with formalities and use our Christian names ... Silvanus?"

"Certainly, Eliza." They kissed again.

"The quotation is about a Trojan soldier called, Troilus. Separated from his beloved Cressida, by an immense wall, one night he climbs the barrier to see her."

"Does it end happily?"

"No, I am afraid that the story does not; Cressida betrays her lover. Perhaps it was a bad choice of quotation. But it is only part of a story, which I think is told to suggest that there is no hope in a world where powerful people can so easily overrule the needs of ordinary people."

"Perhaps, the world seems so at present, at your age" said Silvanus, "but a detested vase has been smashed, the sea has been engaged and all we must do now, is deal with those powerful people ... which might prove easier, as now we are two."

22   Warren Blackmore

A short way outside Fiddlesham, on the road to Chichester, and before coming to the quay, a traveller would pass the Cat and Fiddle. During the day, the landlord and maid of that inn were busy serving the lightermen from the barges and the workers from the

Great Mill, which lay alongside the quay. Most nights, however, the inn was a dark, drab, and empty place.

Tonight, Silvanus stood with his friend, Warren Blackmore, the local riding officer, not in the inn but hiding a short way along the road from the Cat and Fiddle and behind some elder bushes. They were overlooking the quay, which stretched the length of three adjacent buildings that together were known as the Great Mill. Beyond that, the road disappeared into darkness and on towards Chichester.

"When'll they get here, Warren?" asked Silvanus.

"When'll who, get here?"

"Justice of the Peace, Greedy and his men. We need their help, don't we?"

"As soon as these smugglers have loaded their mules with the goods, Justice of the Peace will arrive. Then I'll ride out to arrest the smugglers."

"How many men will Greedy have?"

"Four, maybe five."

"That does not sound many. You're the Riding Officer, Warren, you must know whether it is enough."

"Bloody hell, Si, you have some questions in you tonight. I told you the whole plan the other day. Can you not just let it unfold? All will be well, you'll see. No wonder you live alone; you'd drive any woman mad with your questions. Speaking of which, is it not time you ceased travelling from market to market and settled down? A cooper in this area would surely garner a fair amount of trade, and you'd prove an attractive proposition for any lass."

"Well, I know I can trust you to keep a confidence, Warren," said Silas. "There is a young lady, and things are advancing at an alarming rate."

"What's this Silvanus Curtis has a relationship with a young lady? That's news, why is it not on the tip of every gossip's tongue from here to Midhurst?"

"Well, things never seem to run smoothly, and we have to keep the matter to ourselves."

"Whatever for, Si? I thought you'd have been keen to tell the world your news."

"You are the first to know, Warren."

"Well, come on, who's the mysterious beloved?"

"Ah, but that's just it, if her parents knew they would be set against any such relationship."

"Your secret life is safe with me. Si, you know that. So, her name is?"

"Eliza, Eliza Percy.

Until this moment the two men had been keeping their voices to a whisper but Blackmore's sudden surprise at this news caused him to gasp out loud,

"Captain Percy's daughter, tall and slim with wonderful red hair?"

"Shush, Warren. Voices carry easily at night, in this still air," Silvanus said, looking out to see if there was any movement near the mill.

"Well," asked Warren, "am I thinking of the right young lady?"

"Yes, Warren. She is the one. We plan to elope together soon, before her family ship her off to India and force her to marry some army officer against her will."

"Goodness me, Si, you have chosen a dangerous path. The captain is a gentleman, very wealthy and will not look kindly to you running off with his eldest daughter."

"I know, but what else can I do?"

"Shush, Si, more of this later. Look, the barge is here, coming out of that bank of mist."

Each incoming tide brought all manner of flotsam into Fiddlesham harbour and, of course, some trade. Most of the comings and goings served the Great Mill and this commerce was in the form of sailing barges filled with grain. That night, from out of the darkness a single barge appeared and with an almost complete lack of wind, it slowly drifted into the light from the lanterns hanging from the walls of the mill. A young lad jumped from the bow of the barge onto the quay and looped a line around a bollard bringing the barge to a halt. The Great Mill was not a single mill but three mills in a row, and this night, the crew of the vessel had positioned its hold directly beneath the third mill's sack hoist. This overhanging crane had a gabled roof above it, called a lucam, and reached far enough to span the quay and unload goods from a moored barge. The trap door in the base of the lucam opened with a clatter and the hoist descended. In the barge, an older man along with the young lad filled the hoist's net with sacks of grain.

Meanwhile, at the back of the mill, above the waterwheel, Hap'th put his weight behind a capstan bar. He was so thin and light that it took all his strength to get it moving. The rope began to tighten and slowly raised the sluice gate. Trapped water from the millpond now poured out bringing the waterwheel to life.

Beatcher stood inside the mill, beside the trundling wheel, and pulled a rope bringing axels, cogs and wheels into action ready to hoist the load from the barge. The lighterman whistled twice and Butt, high above in the lucam set the hoist in motion. Hap'th, having started the waterwheel, left it and entered the mill, lowering himself through a hole in the floor into the room with Beatcher who was looking out of a small window in a door at the front of the mill.

"What's happening?" asked Hap'th, against the noise of the waterwheel.

"Shush!"

"Why's it taking so long? And, where are the mules?"

"First off, it will take as long as it takes. Second off, there's a barge load of grain to unload, before we get to our goods. Third off, the mules are not here yet."

"What happens if the mules are late?" asked Hap'th.

"We hold the goods in here, just like we've done before."

"But it's a larger load of goods this time. There ain't enough room."

"Hush! Mules'll are here," Beatcher said.

Meanwhile, Warren held his hand on his horse's muzzle, calming the animal.

"Hush there, Lassie," he whispered.

"Warren, I shouldn't be here," said Silvanus nervously.

"Neither should I Si, but it is my duty and you agreed, because everyone should help their local riding officer. Stop concerning yourself so much. You only have to do something if they should get away from me, and look likely to escape the Justice of Peace's men."

It took another dozen more hoists, for all the grain to be unloaded from the barge to the top of the mill. After which there was a pause, then, from along the Chichester Road, came a string of six mules with two men at the front and one at the rear. The mill hoist was in action again, but this time there were small casks, firkins, in the net, and they were lifted onto the quay, already strung together in pairs ready to load onto the mules' backs, each beast carrying six barrels.

"You have the pistols I gave you, loaded and ready, and the cutlass?"

"Yes," said Silvanus, "but what about Greedy?"

"They're nearly here, coming down the Chichester Road to the quay. Look you can see for yourself, the lights, beyond the mules," Warren said, mounting his horse. He then rode down towards the smugglers on the quay, who did not see him coming at first, being busy loading the mules with the barrels of contraband and who also appeared unaware of Greedy and his men entering the quay from the other end.

Warren Blackmore was a miller since he was a child working with his father. In recent times he had been forced out of business by Strothmann Greedy, who was a landowner, magistrate, Captain Percy's land agent and the local Justice of the Peace. When Greedy constructed the Great Fiddlesham Tide Mill it had put all small millers in the area out of business. Warren, unemployed and seeing starvation approaching had joined the army. It seemed the only way to provide for his wife and daughter but after two months training, and on the verge of going to America, the War ended and the regiment discharged him. Worse off than ever, he considered joining the masses on their long march to seek work in London. He had heard that there was a great shortage of carpenters and masons in that city, who were needed to build houses for the thousands of newcomers and, of course, more millers were required to feed the growing population. However, he then read a notice that His Majesty was seeking a Riding Officer for the area of Fiddlesham and was offering forty pounds per annum, for tracking down smugglers. Warren considered it as a lucrative, and a far less backbreaking alternative to seeking milling in the capital. Also, the thought of being employed by the king appealed to his patriotism. Soon after he had signed up and become the riding officer for the area, he began to receive offers of tea, liquor and money from various sources. All from people he hardly knew. The gifts always came with the same sentiments – 'we approve of the work you're doing to help the local people and would like to show you and your family our appreciation with this gift.' Where the goods or money originated from was never clear, but he felt sure that the gifts were to persuade him to, turn a blind eye, to the neighbourhood's smuggling business. After twelve months of fruitless patrols, one night, he had seen a blue signal lantern near the entrance to the harbour. Following this along the coast, he had surprised three men coming ashore. Gun shots were exchanged, two of the smugglers climbed back into their jolly boat and disappeared out into the darkness, leaving one remaining behind. Desperate to escape Warren, who was on horseback, the smuggler tried to climb the cliff behind the beach. But the top of the cliff had no footholds and the lad was forced down and after some effort, Warren managed to apprehend him. It proved to be a local thirteen-year-old boy named, Davy Moxen. At the trial, the magistrates, spent fifteen minutes considering Davy's case and deciding his fate and six times that length of time over their subsequent luncheon. They, of course, remembered the recent lucrative visit they had received from the treasury officer from London and the splendid meal lavished upon them at the Dolphin Inn in Chichester. After the meal, the magistrates had been reminded of the King's anxiety at the amount of smuggling in East Sussex. Unfortunately for the Moxen lad, his case had appeared less than a fortnight after the treasury officer's visit and the Chichester magistrates, a group which had included Greedy, had, felt it necessary to make an example of him - and sentence him to death. As that might not be a sufficient example to other, would-be smugglers; he was later to hang in chains on Rook's Hill, for the crows to feed upon and all to see.

Moxen had been a well-liked boy from a family that had no father's income to rely upon and his treatment was thought to be unjust by the local agricultural workers. The widespread disgust at the young boy's execution brought Blackmore's stream of 'gifts' to an abrupt end and led to the Riding Officer to fear for his life. If people did not benefit personally from the smuggling trade, they would often know someone who did. It had therefore become difficult for Warren to gather help apprehending smugglers. But Silvanus and Warren had been friends since they were boys and Warren had used that friendship to persuade Silvanus to help in the night's venture.

On the quay, the smugglers had quickly loaded the mules, but Warren could sense something was wrong, the smugglers were not scattering, as expected. Instead, they seemed untroubled by the arrival of Greedy and his men, two of whom, as Warren rode into the light, un-slung their muskets, shouldered their weapons and … fired - not at the smugglers - but at Warren. One of the balls came close, nearly taking Warren's ear off. The sudden noise of musket fire, caused his horse to rear up. Warren, holding a pistol in one hand, could not control her and fell to the ground, dropping his flintlock and hitting the back of his head on the cobbles. There were shouts as Greedy's men came towards him. Warren picked up his pistol, aimed and fired, hitting the young lad from the barge, and knocking him over. The older lighterman stopped to help the young lad back to the barge as the mule drivers led their beasts, now loaded with the firkins, off the quay. However, Greedy with two mounted men and two others on foot, were still coming towards Warren. Why was Greedy not helping him, and rounding on the smugglers? Did Greedy not know it was Warren? He shouted out,

"Stop! It's Blackmore here, His Majesty's Riding Officer." In answer, another two shots rang out. Warren knew he must get away. Against the mill was a fixed ladder leading up to an open loading door. He climbed it, fell inside, closed the door, and slid its two bolts across. Inside he was close to the waterwheel, which was rumbling so much that he could not make out what was happening outside. Standing up, a spoke from the revolving spur-wheel hit him on the head. Why were mills built to accommodate workers no taller than four feet six inches? He would have to remember to keep his head down. The smell of the mill reminded him of his previous life as a miller and being in the mill somehow made him feel safe, but that feeling vanished when another pistol shot came through the timber door, sending splinters of wood into his leg. He shuffled away from the door. Above the noise of the machinery, he could make out the voices of the men outside. Then, what sounded like two of them ran away. No doubt to find another entrance into the mill. How many smugglers would that leave outside the mill, he wondered? Two perhaps? Possibly he could pick them off in the darkness - or frighten them away. There was an opening in the door, but it was close to a lantern hanging on the wall outside. He would make a good target if he looked out through there, and with just one pistol it could prove too dangerous. His leg stung from the splinters of wood and his hands were shaking too much to reload but his eyes were becoming accustomed to the darkness; he could see that there was no other door in the room, but there was a ladder, which led to an open hatch in the roof. He would be better off with another pistol, but he had given Si his pair of flintlocks, why had he let Si have them? Maybe he would come to help, but that was unlikely as Warren had insisted that Silvanus keep his position in the darkness, unless the smugglers tried to escape towards the Cat and Fiddle. He took a deep breath, got his powder horn from his belt and poured a measure of powder into the muzzle of the flintlock, a wad of cloth, lead ball, ramrod it home, prime the pan with powder from his priming horn, click back the frizzen and apart from cocking it, he was ready. Where were the men outside? What were they doing? It was too dangerous to take them on. He needed to find a safer place in the mill where he could face them one at a time. He climbed the ladder into the space above where there was one of the mill's three millstones, which was not revolving, as the mechanism had not been engaged with the rotating spur wheel. Blackmore thought that this was no better a place to make a defence, than the room below. Then a sound from above made him look up. There was a man above him hanging onto the ladder and taking a pistol from his belt. Warren had his flintlock ready, cocked it, aimed, and fired. The man's flintlock fired at the same time, but the ball ricocheted off the millstone. Warren's shot struck home. The man clung there for a moment, with a surprised look on his face, and before Warren could finish reloading, he fell from the ladder onto the top of the crown wheel, which continued rotating carrying the man around until his arm reached the cogs of the hoist's belt-drive. His body jammed into the wheel, and all the mechanisms of the mill, even the waterwheel itself, came to a juddering, groaning, halt. In the sudden silence, the trapped man's cries filled the room. Warren picked up the man's dropped pistol, climbed up to the top of the crown wheel and rummaged through the dying man's belt, pulling it from beneath him. Now he had two pistols and more powder and shot. Having reloaded he stuck the pistols in his belt and slung the spare belt with shot powder over his shoulder. Pulling himself up level with the man's face, Warren realised that he recognised him as one of Greedy's men.

"Get me out of here, have mercy ..." the man groaned. "I have a wife and three children ...have pity on them, if not ..."

"I know you. You're one of Greedy's men and he is a Justice of the Peace. Why did you attack me?" Warren asked.

"It was Greedy. I work for him. We were to frighten you off. I wasn't ..."

"What's your name?" Warren asked, leaning forward to see if he could get the man's arm out from between the cogs of the spur wheel and the hoist drive.

"Austin, Osimond Austin ..." The man's eyes closed and all his pent-up breath seem to leak out of him in one last sigh. Warren knew he was dead. It was the first time Warren had killed a man.

Voices above called out,

"Ossi, is that you?"

"Have you got the bastard?"

Blackmore could see an open door at the rear of the crown wheel room and climbed across making his way over to it. There was a short ladder outside. He could perhaps escape and hide in the woods until daybreak. There came others shouting from above, how many men? He could not tell. Maybe two, no three. He looked outside again. The ladder led into a narrow alleyway along the wall of the mill. For about twenty feet, there were overhanging bushes from the neighbouring woods. Now came more noise from above and shouting,

"Hap'th, where are you?" There was no answer. Warren decided he would make his bid to escape along the alleyway. He looked again. It was clear, he jumped down and ran to the end of the wall. Then, rounding the corner, he ran into an old man, crippled over and resting upon a stick. Twenty-feet further on, behind him, were two others: one weedy stick-like man and the other barrel shaped.

"Thank goodness you're here, Sir," said the cripple, pointing to the pair behind him, "these two cutthroats are threatening an old sailor." Should he retreat or take on the two men behind the old man? Warren pressed on, pushing past the man with the stick, he fired at the front man of the two, but his shot went wide. Before he could fire a second shot, something hit him from behind. All his strength fell away. The old man had stabbed him with a long-bladed knife, pulled from his cane. As he slumped down, Warren's face came level with his attacker. The man held him tight by one arm, stopping him from falling to the ground,

"Thou and Death shall dwell at ease, my friend, and redress rigid satisfaction,"

Warren tried to raise his pistol, but the stiletto twisted in his back and the pain forced him to cry out and drop the weapon. The old man pulled his knife out, and let Warren fall to the ground.

Beatcher wiped his blade on the Riding Officer's coat and, as if he were a preacher saying words over a coffin, said, "Death for death." He then stepped back and let the others in to finish the killing with their hangers.

Silvanus had waited in the woods and watched Greedy on the quay and listened to all the gunfire. Believing that Greedy's men were laying into the smugglers. When Warren did not return, he assumed that his friend had given chase to the gang of smugglers along the Chichester Road with Greedy and his men. Silvanus needed to avoid being seen by locals who would be likely to connect him to this confrontation at the mill and link him to the smugglers. Then again, it might prove as equally dangerous to be associated with Greedy's men. When the barge sailed away and the quay was clear Silvanus made his way quietly back towards Fiddlespit. At the lagoon, the sun was just rising and the herring gulls filled the morning air with their excited cries. He wrapped the pistols in an old cloth and hid them under the seat in the front of his wagon. He disliked carrying pistols, although he had noticed that carrying weapons appeared to empower many men. On him, they eroded his self-confidence. He had surprised himself by agreeing to accompany Warren on last night's mission, but Warren had been persuasive and he had agreed to go along before he knew that he would be issued with a personal arsenal. As soon as he could, he would return the weapons and find out how his friend had made out and how many smugglers were behind bars.

23 London

With an air of apprehension, Mary Percy had described to her husband the events concerning Eliza and the precious vase. However, she was, as Richard would say, taken-aback, by his relative lack of concern, particularly when she had informed him that his daughter had deliberately smashed the vase. Richard had told Mary that far from being unique, the vase was one of a dozen similar objects brought back from his last visit to China.

"Advice from a colleague in the Company," he said, "a gentleman whose wisdom I have come to respect in such matters of commerce, had been to the effect that in order to obtain the best possible return at auction, one should keep the quality and quantity of fine china strictly below decks. Only allowing items to be put up for auction occasionally, every few years or so. In that manner, one would have a reasonable income through the years ahead. 'Flood the market and their value will plummet.' were his words."

Mary looked surprised and then, concerned,

"Richard, the fact remains that our daughter has wilfully destroyed your property for no reason. There must be some sanction placed upon her, or who knows what acts she may perform in the future."

"Let Eliza travel with me to London, my dear. I have some business to conduct and several days away from here may disrupt her behaviour. Also, travelling together will provide an opportunity for me to persuade her of the benefits of living in India and of her duty towards the family." The captain stood up and pulled a chord. When the servant arrived, he said,

"Would you be kind enough to ask my daughter Eliza to meet me in the library?"

24 Threadgate

In the eyes of Daniel Threadgate's many admirers, the young man possessed numerous talents and they could see that he enjoyed showing off his skills in front of an audience - and the larger, the better. He could not only read, but read aloud, and, unlike many from his social background at that time, he could also write. Women, particularly admired his singing voice, which he employed, along with his reading skill, to perform the latest ballads in whatever tavern he thought would have the largest and most profitable gatherings.

To earn his daily bread, Threadgate was a typesetter. But it was his performances in the tavern and market squares, which kept him on the merry side of sober for the best part of every evening. It was, however, his fondness for drink and showmanship, which led to his short-lived fame, premature end, brief notoriety and eternal oblivion.

Threadgate was a compositor. It was his task to compose the lead type in reverse order for printing and on completion pass this to his fellow worker, the pressman. The printer himself, who was a stern master, oversaw all this. The daily routine was for the printer to proofread the copy in the early hours, rant and berate his two employees in the forenoon, then remove himself to the tavern at midday to await his pressman, who would bring the first copy of the broadside to the inn, for the printer to proofread. Then, in the early evening, he would return to his workshop, rant and berate some more before finally dispatching the broadsides for distribution.

It was well known in the printing world that pressmen and compositors were always at one another's throats, and so was the situation in Threadgate's printshop. Over the years animosity had grown between the two, until, fuelled by the efficient errand boy's delivery of liberal quantities of port from the tavern, a fight broke out between the two, resulting in a cracked rib for the pressman and a bloody nose for Threadgate. That alone would not have amounted to much, but the lead type from the trays ended up all over the workshop floor. There was little time to recompose the type and on return, the printer dismissed Threadgate, but retained the pressman, a course of action that Threadgate knew would be taken on account of the latter being the former's nephew.

Apart from the fear that his nose could be broken, which might have a detrimental effect on his relationship with the lovely Lily Hawks, Threadgate knew from experience, having been dismissed three or four times previously from this very same employment, that the printer would find no other compositor to be available in Midhurst. He would, therefore, either have to do all the compositing himself until a suitable replacement was found, which would naturally curtail his afternoon visits to the tavern; on the other hand, he could reinstate Threadgate in the compositor's position. It was therefore almost inevitable that Threadgate would be visited by the errand boy early next day to inform him that he would be given one more opportunity to prove himself and would be expected back at the workshop at the usual hour. Far from being a disaster, his dismissal would give him longer with sweet Lily and, before that, plenty of time to fill his hat with silver coins in payment for his singing. In the tavern the fiddler played and Threadgate sang,

Devil's broth and a sucking pig
Hi Cockalorum Jig jig jig
High on the gallows dance and sings
Handsome Jack O Sixteen Strings
With silver moon on the highest hill
Gold in the sun to take his fill
Lassies in the Inn to fresh his glass
The highway ride for the bold as brass

Although it was early, gradually men and women joined in with the jig, either by banging the tables or getting to their feet and dancing.

Devil's broth and a sucking pig
Hi Cockalorum Jig jig jig ...

Finally, Threadgate sang the last line of the chorus to loud applause and cheering. Customers settled back around their tables and returned to their drinks, food, conversations and self-congratulatory laughter. The room was filling up quickly with men arriving to eat and women visiting to offer the men other pleasures. Threadgate, having shared some coins with the fiddler and pocketed the rest, looked around the tavern and saw a man beckoning him. He looked as though he would have struggled to stand, but when he did, he appeared surprisingly agile and held his head up erect although his body remained almost bent double. Alone at his table, smoking a clay pipe, he asked Threadgate if he would accept a drink in payment for his excellent song. Threadgate sat down, and Lily arrived, poured them both a glass of brandy and kissed Threadgate,
"Don't you go a getting too groggy tonight, Danny now." she said, skipping off to her next customer.

"'Tis a fine song, ye ballad of Jack Rann, eh lad? Twas a bold design; 'at pleased highly this infernal frame. I could see the joy sparkling in thy eyes with full assent!"

Threadgate had no idea what the man was talking about and assumed him a madman. He would make an excuse and leave him to ramble alone,

"I thank you for the ..."

"I heard ye singing same ballad in the market, didn't I Lad? I's been watching a whiles now. Youth, thy strength, thy beauty," since that market day, and I spies somet in thy eye that looks like ambition, when ye sings 'at ballad. Am I right, Lad? Don't get me wrong, cause I's be a man after thine own countenance. Not in any physic way, as ye can see, but in a likewise appetite for the pretentious. 'Youth will change to withered weak and grey, thy senses become obtuse, and in thy blood will reign a melancholy damp of cold and dry to weigh thy spirits down with the balm of life.'"

"Sorry Sir, I ..."

"First off, let me tell ye, tis all good and tight, lad. Things are battened down."

The man took hold of Threadgate's wrist with a powerful grip, preventing him from leaving the table.

"If you'd excuse me, Sir," said Threadgate, but the old man held tight and continued,

"Second off, those what knows will keep it tight below decks. And that brings me to:

Third off: I understand that the old lady in question has not reported the matter, her having been allowed to keep her valuable rings."

Threadgate felt a cold sweat abruptly come upon him. Who was this man and how much did he know so much?

For as long as Threadgate could remember, in every market he had visited, he had sort out the ballad singer, who would also be selling broadsides for a penny a copy. He would mingle with the crowds as they gathered for this free entertainment. It would not have been long before the broadside seller sung the ballad of Sixteen-String-Jack-Rann, which always ended in everybody's favourite crowd pulling verses. In this, our hero of the road danced a jig under Tyburn Tree moments before his execution. This verse would inevitably persuade the bystanders to join the singer, possibly accompanied by a fiddler in larger markets, to dance their own jig. All of which ended in laughter and merriment as the women in the crowd pretended to hang the men with their neckerchiefs. Threadgate had decided that when he had made enough money from compositing and singing, he would follow his chosen profession, become a highwayman and attempt to emulate his hero, the late 'knight of the road', Sixteen-String-Jack-Rann. He purchased similar coloured strings and ribbons which would eventually adorn silk breeches that he would have especially tailored. Before this, and in preparation for his forthcoming career, he had taken part in a single robbery, which had been a far from charismatic affair. It happened late one night on the Portsmouth Road and was all rather shambolic. The victim's carriage, a post-chaise, had, unfortunately, for its elderly occupant, become stuck up to its axles in mud. Threadgate, on foot, and by chance, had come across the carriage leaning precariously to one side and, under the pretext of helping the lady, had seized the opportunity, drawn a pistol and threatened the postilion rider. The postilion rider, elderly like his mistress, raised his hands and straightway fell off his horse into the mud. The terrified lady handed over two rings, seven guineas and thirteen shillings and fourpence ha'penny. But as Threadgate went to make his getaway the coachman, trying to pull himself from the mud, grabbed one of the pair of horse's reins, which, in turn, encouraged the animal to attempt an escape from the mud. Turning to one side, the horse somehow managed to pull itself free and encourage the other horse to escape the mud. But in doing this the team pulled the carriage onto its side, and further into the mire. As the black mud flooded into the carriage, the lady cried out and pleaded for help. Threadgate had dreamt that his highwayman career would spring from the words and sentiments expressed in his favourite ballad. He saw himself as becoming another gallant knight of the road, rather than a ruthless killer, prepared to abandon a recently wealthy old lady to drown in the mud. So, he returned to the carriage to pull the old lady out of the half-submerged post chaise, and left her safely on the grassy verge. Before disappearing through the hedge, however – 'over a hill in the moonlight', as the ballad had suggested he should escape – his thankful victim had persuaded him to return her two rings, which, she said, had belonged to her only daughter, tragically drowned after falling overboard from the Bellarosa, off the coast of the isle of Bermuda, while on route to join her husband in the Americas.

Threadgate's sudden wealth, following this venture had, unsurprisingly, gone hand in glove with a rise in his popularity in the tavern. This convinced him that he was destined for an adventurous life on the road. Beau Dan, to use the sobriquet; which he had recently adopted to introduce himself to his imminent paying customers; unlike his hero, Sixteen String Jack, planned to retire after just sixteen ventures, and then to travel abroad and live out his life in modest luxury.

But now, tonight, there was this man, sat opposite him, who not only knew the lives of famous highwaymen, like Jack Rann, but somehow was aware of Threadgate's own initiation into the world of highway robbery. How did he find out? How was that possible? And who was he, a blackmailer, an informer or justice of the peace? This man did not match Threadgate's pattern for any of them.

"So, we come to it now, lad: Fourth Off: facts are, I'm devising a bit of business and wants a showman to front the venture. A man with proven ability, unafeared, who can ride an horse and handle a pair of pistols. What says ye, my lad?"

"Sir, I thank you for the brandy and the conversation, but I am a printer's apprentice and fully expect to continue in that labour for many years to come."

The older man, put his pipe away and wiped his running nose on his sleeve,

"Quite right Lad. You keep your wind in your breeches and your caution close. I like that in a man. I be at this spot for three more nights, if ye be thinking along a different tack, I'll be here." The man unexpectedly grabbed Threadgate by the arm with a vice-like grip, pulled him close and returned to his gibberish,

"I'll stay not for a reply tonight but in confidence that these waves will eventually find a willing shore."

The next morning the errand boy did not arrive at Threadgate's lodgings as expected. Despite that, Threadgate decided to go to the printing workshop anyway and to arrive at his usual hour, suspecting things would proceed as normal. However, in the morning the printer was at work doing the compositing and told Threadgate that he was no longer needed because an advertisement, placed after Threadgate's last dismissal, had finally been answered and his replacement would be arriving a week hence.

25   Beau Dan

Early in the morning, outside the Spread Eagle inn at Midhurst, stood a yellow bounder with four horses ready to go. For a shilling a mile, it was possible to hire one of these post-chaises along with a postilion rider. The yellow carriages were fast, roads permitting, which usually, they were not. The postilion rider, sat on the left side lead horse, allowing the occupants of the post-chaise to have a panoramic view through the front window unobscured by a coachman.

There were few signs to suggest to a passer-by that this post-chaise in Midhurst was anything out of the ordinary, except for it having four, rather than the usual two, horses. A more observant onlooker may have noticed that there were two particularly smart postilion riders in matching uniforms. The men were sheltering from the rain under the inn's overhanging upper storey. In the inn's courtyard were two more men dressed in the same livery of green breeches, cocked hats, royal blue jackets with gold braid and a fresh pink rose nosegay in their collars. Each carried a weapon, a hanger, in their belt, they also carried an air of superiority, which suggested that these men were private employees and did not come with a hired carriage.

Threadgate rode down South Street wearing a black riding cape covering his silks and ribbons. His collar turned up, and cocked hat pulled down against the rain. All of which made it almost impossible to see his face. Alfred, the post-chaise guard, looked at Threadgate suspiciously, pulling his frock coat to one side and placing a conspicuous hand on the butt of a flintlock pistol. The rider ignored the obvious gesture, and nodded, touching his forelock and calling out, "Good morning, sir," then turned into the inn yard and disappeared from those in the street. Without dismounting, the rider whispered a few words to the stable boy, tossed him a coin and watched him run into the inn. A few moments later one of the inn's maids came out into the courtyard and had a brief conversation with Threadgate, who handed down more coins before turning his mount, leaving the yard and heading off in the Chichester direction, the mare breaking into a frisky brisk canter.

There was soon a flurry of activity around the carriage. Alfred held the foremost two horses while the postilion riders mounted and then he climbed up to his position on the back of the carriage placing his flintlock in a fitted box in front of him. James opened the carriage door and unfolded the passengers' steps. Captain Percy came out of the inn almost at a trot, and Eliza followed a few paces behind. He wore his East India Company uniform but held his sword and belt in his hand, not wishing to wear them during the journey to Fiddlesham. He helped his daughter up the steps and into the carriage but paused before entering himself, saying,

"Good morning, James. Have you had a good breakfast?"

"Ample, thank you, Captain, Sir."

Then up to Alfred,

"Still an easterly blowing, I fear, Alfred. Another wet day ahead." Then remembering the postilion riders, the captain leant back and called, "You two men for'ard there, been fed well this morning?" They both raised their hats and muttered,

"Aye, Aye, Captain."

For Eliza, the journey on the day before had been tedious in the extreme and not much better for her father. Although these modern, and expensive carriages, could reach the highest speeds especially with a team of four, the conditions of the roads meant their journey from Kingston-upon Thames had taken the best part of nine hours. They had not arrived at Midhurst until after sunset. The second part of their journey, today, should prove much shorter and take no more than four hours. Rising from his seat in the carriage, the captain obtained a rug from the shelf at the rear for his daughter, put his feet upon the rail in front, hit the roof with the pommel of his sword, the two postilions dug their heels into the flanks of their mounts, Eliza's head jolted back, her bonnet almost fell off and they got underway.

Despite the rain, his rather silent daughter and the tiresome journey, Captain Percy felt in good spirits that morning having had a successful few days purchasing various goods and arranging their conveyance down the Thames to his ship moored at Gravesend. He was particularly pleased with his recent purchases of harpsichords and spinets. This acquisition had followed the advice of the young Mr Miller who had every expectation that they would make a handsome profit upon sale in Madras. Now, he was looking forward to returning to his beloved home and the rest of his family. Years ago, the captain had looked upon the sea as his home and his officers as family. Recently, however, with marriage, age and a luxurious, not to say, stationary roof over his head, he had begun to prefer the comforts, certainties and rewards of solid brickwork, rather than the vagaries of floating timbers. A life upon the ocean was one that demanded constant decisions. For now, he would be content to sit back and enjoy the last few hours of this ride, comforting himself with a warm glow of pride in his own wealth and good fortune.

For most of the day on yesterday's journey, they had been passing families of the poor,

"Making their way London." Eliza's father had said to her, "It seems that these days all the world is 'making its way to London.' I fear it will do them little good when they get there. The poverty in parts of that city is unbelievable."

Eliza asked, "Why are so many people moving to London?"

"They think they will get rich there. I blame these new charity schools springing up all over the country. They put ideas into the children's heads of the riches and wonders of the big cities. When I was a lad, the poor were content to live in the countryside, upon farms and they were happy that way." Passing a gang of children in a field loading a cart with turnips, or some such vegetable. The captain and Eliza looked on as the children abandoned their work, ran in to the road, trying to keep up with the carriage, and, despite being mud-spattered, wet and cold, cheerily waved their caps, calling out,

"If you please, Sir, a few coins for a crust?"

"Have you a few small coins father, they look so distressed?" asked Eliza. Captain Percy threw a few coins out of the window.

"See how a few coins renew the efforts of the other children. They will always want more, these days, confounded charity schools," said the captain, "they'll never be satisfied, now." One of the children, rather taller than the others, managed to grab on to the open window frame and, by raising his feet, hitch a lift,

"Please, sir …" But James's cut the boy's pleading short with a lash across the lad's back with his coach whip, causing the boy to fall into the mud. Concerned, Eliza leant over her father and looked out of the window, back towards the boy, and saw that he was soon on his feet again. The captain sat back in his seat, "One never ceases to wonder how any man could be content to allow his children to undertake such work as those children. Where are their parents, at home in the dry, around a fire, in some tavern drinking gin, a prison perhaps or have they allowed themselves to fall prey to one of the many illnesses which ravage the lower classes these days?"

They continued their journey in silence for a while, and the captain's thoughts returned to business and a recent conversation with his third mate, Mr Reeve. Who, having just returned from the ship, had suggested that in order to obtain a full complement of crew before their departure to Coast and Bay, they could perhaps press a few men? Although against impressment by nature, Captain Percy had agreed that, if this was indeed the only passage open to them, then they should take it, whilst of course they should keep to the law, wherever that was possible, in spirit at least, if not in letter. Perhaps, the captain thought, the fathers of those child labourers had been pressed, and were aboard one of His Majesty's ships or, indeed, one of the East India Company's vessels at this very moment … But there was still no excuse, in that case, their mothers must stand to face the charge of neglect. Somehow, he had not convinced himself, but decided to end his contemplation and nodded to himself in conclusion. He took out his flask and poured a measure of brandy into the silver flask cap. The flask had been a present from his dear wife, Mary.

The carriage slowed to a halt. Ahead was a flock of sheep filling the full width of the road, which was enclosed by steep embankments on either side. Shepherding the flock was a woman, rather big, manly looking, and not much like the comely shepherdess of the broadsheets. She was dressed in an odd assortment of mud-spattered shawls giving an impression far from bucolic, thought the captain, and quite old for her calling. Perhaps this was the mother of the turnip picking children, greedily working when she should be caring for her family. Soon after the carriage halted, the captain's musings ended abruptly. Interrupted by an outburst of shouting, as two men, one either side, came sliding down the embankment. The captain thought of reaching for his sword, but he was still holding his silver flask and cup and before he could put them down and do anything to arm himself, the door opened, and he had a pistol thrust into his face.

"Get out, or you're a dead man," said a tall, stick-like man with a kerchief, pulled up over the lower part of his face. The captain followed the commands and climbed out. The robber took the flask, tried to drink the remains of the brandy from the silver cup but forgot his kerchief and spilt the brandy over his pistol whilst trying to lift his mask. "Damn it!" he swore and as he struggled to put the flask and cup inside his coat, for a moment he lowered the aim of his pistol enough to make the captain consider taking on the rogue.

"You too Miss, out ya get."

"She is a child," said the captain, "she'll not have anything for you. Stay where you are Eliza."

"Ain't falling for that dodge, your lordship. Dare say, she'll be carrying all your gold n' silver. If 'e know what's good for 'e, miss, 'e won't listen to old Swill-belly, here" he said, poking the captain in the belly with the barrel of his flintlock, "you'll get out and give us the silver, or shall we hang 'e upside-down and give 'e a good shaking to see if 'e rattles?" Eliza climbed down from the carriage and saw approaching on the other side of the road, among sheep, another robber, a barrel of a man, on foot with a pistol pointing at James. As well as two robbers, there was now a horseman, who had arrived from the rear on a black horse. His riding cape pulled to one side, to enable all to see his purple silk breeches and crimson, gold and turquoise ribbons fluttering in the breeze. Riding around the horse and carriage he appeared to be surveying the situation. Until, reaching the captain, he stopped. He too wore a scarf covering his face, but unlike the others it was a woman's thick woollen head scarf, which, as well as making his face unrecognisable, made his words difficult to understand. The captain thought he heard,

"Good morning, sir. May I introduce myself? I am ..." But he could not catch the name, "I have come to relieve you of ..." Then, suddenly, there was a flurry of activity. The big man on foot, being distracted by a press of fleeing sheep around his legs, lifted his pistol to let them pass. James, in the dickie-seat, took the opportunity to reach for his blunderbuss, hidden in front of him for just such eventualities, but the cumbersome weapon took too long to cock and aim and the barrel-like man had time to fire. However, the flint in his pistol failed to ignite the charge and, apart from a puff of smoke, nothing flew James's way. Facing no threat for a moment from that side, James turned his weapon on the captain's stick-like adversary. A shower of lead and iron from the blunderbuss hit the man in the shoulder spinning him around and knocking him to the ground, forcing him to drop his pistol. Until this moment, Threadgate had thought the situation was covered, and not wanting to spoil his cultivated appearance of a gentleman dandy on horseback, had not drawn his pistol. He went for it now, but a gust of wind entangled his ribbons around the flintlock. James turned to Alfred, but he was shaking with fear, hands raised and his pistol still in the compartment in front of him. James grabbed the flintlock, cocked it, took aim and fired, knocking Threadgate off his horse. The horse, being newly acquired by Threadgate, felt no loyalty to its rider and bolted back the way it had come. The two postilions leapt off their mounts and, hangers drawn, ran after the men. The barrel-like man, despite his size, managed to run faster than his pursuers and escaped up and over the embankment. The injured man, holding his shoulder and shouting in pain, climbed up the other embankment. James jumped down and gave chase to the footpad for a few moments, but seeing him disappear into some woods, decided to leave him and return to his master. Meanwhile, Eliza watched as the captain, by the side of the dying man, put on his white gloves and brushed away some mud and sheep droppings from the young man's face.

"I must tell you, young man, you are dying. There being no priest here, I will be willing to hear your confession if you would like to make peace with your maker. Firstly, tell me, what is your name?" The dying man struggled to breath and only managed,

"Beau Dan, highwayman, at your …" The captain shook his head in genuine remorse,

"Bowden? What a dreadful waste of a young life, Mr Bowden. Eliza, please return to the carriage now."

The elderly shepherdess had disappeared, along with the rest of her sheep, in panic, after the gunfire.

As they journeyed on, Eliza could not take her eyes off the highwayman's body draped and secured over the back of one of the rear horses. It was the first dead body she had seen. When they arrived at Chichester, the body of Bowden, the Highwayman with his streaming colourful ribbons gathered a small and curious crowd of onlookers. The incident was reported to the magistrate, an acquaintance of Captain Percy's, James and Alfred arranged for the body to be taken to the undertaker.

The next day by an open pauper's grave in a far corner of the churchyard of St Olav's, the undertaker stood, a black drape over his head and shoulders to keep the rain off, which made him resemble a bedraggled jackdaw. He was trying to remember some suitable lines of verse. Between the undertaker and a mound of soil, the gravedigger leant on his shovel. He was rooted in his favourite diversion: dreaming of digging up King Arthur's golden jewel-encrusted sword.

They were both there for the burial of Tom Thomas, aged one month; Betty Sadley, aged three months; Old Nellie Smith, from Chichester Workhouse, age unknown; and a Mr Bowden, described by the clerk in the parish records as a 'sojourner.' There was a sudden gust of wind and rain fell even heavier. The undertaker began abruptly,

"Hold not thy peace ... at my tears," and then hesitated, trying to recall the psalm. The gravedigger slipped off his shovel and shouted, "Excalibur." Which caused the undertaker to pause, look at the gravedigger and give a reproving shake of the head. The undertaker was tired of waiting in this rain for the vicar, who no doubt was fortifying himself against the weather with liberal glasses of port, and it had reached that time of day for the undertaker's luncheon. He continued,

"For I am a stranger, as my fathers were.

O spare me, that I may recover,

Before I go hence and be no more."

The undertaker walked away towards the inn, eager to eat and drink by way of a small reward for the day's business. For he had been paid twice for the burial of this young man shot on the highway, once by the captain's man and again by the parish.

The rain drummed on the lid of the uppermost coffin, but unlike Handsome Jack O Sixteen Strings, there was no, 'Hi Cockalorum, Jig, jig, jig,' for Daniel Threadgate, alias Beau Dan, alias Mr Bowden. The gravedigger sighed, "What thin pinewood lids this pinchpenny undertaker puts on his coffins." He replaced his hat, spat on his hands picked up his spade and began to refill the grave.

26   Stars

Captain Percy and his daughter's arrival at Fiddlesham coincided with the rain ceasing and the sky clearing.

"It is a fine night, James. I will walk up the drive from here. Eliza, join me, if you please."

After the harrowing journey and the cramped carriage ride, Eliza was pleased to be able to walk up to the house. When the post-chaise had left them, the captain paused for a moment and, looking up, reassured himself of the constancy of the heavens.

"Do you know your constellations, my girl?"

"I have seen their likeness in books but have rarely seen them like this. How beautiful they are," said Eliza.

"That W shaped constellation is always above us at Fiddlesham. It is Cassiopeia?" said the captain.

"Cassiopeia? Was Cassiopeia the mother who sacrificed her daughter to the sea."

"Yes, hmm, I believe so, my girl. It is good you have learnt the constellations. You never know when such knowledge may prove useful."

Eliza said nothing and, after several moments' consideration, could think of no situation that she might find herself in where knowledge of the constellations might prove helpful - unless it was as a metaphor. Did her father pick Cassiopeia deliberately – as a metaphor. She always had problems with metaphors. She could make them up without too much trouble but found it hard to grasp someone else's metaphor. The metaphor for Cassiopeia, in Eliza's situation, was easy. She thought of discussing the subject of constellations and their use as metaphors, but her father had moved onto proving that he could name all the other visible constellations,

"And that red star, there, see that is the top part of Orion, which has not all risen yet, that star is Betelgeuse."

"Should I learn the names of the stars as well, then Father?"

"I should not think so, my girl. I have never seen the need to learn the names of the stars, apart from a handful of the brightest ones. The constellations are enough."

Owing to the lateness of the hour, the customary welcome home by the household was a perfunctory affair. A light meal was served, after which the captain was joined by his wife, and Eliza went to her room. Two glasses of Douro wine were poured and the decanter left behind. Mary stood and the captain sat by the fire and poured a second glass of port. He then told his wife of the day's events on the road from Midhurst.

"So, the flask is lost, Richard."

"I am afraid so, Mary. There is a small chance that it will come to light if the culprit is apprehended, but that is doubtful, and I should think it has been melted down by now."

"To think that some footpad has been drinking from your flask," said Mary.

"I thought it my duty to report the whole affair, of the death of the young man, to the authorities," said the captain, sounding and looking very weary.

"I think it would be more than the wretched man deserved, "said Mary. "Why you did not just leave his body at the side of the road for the crows and rats to feast upon, I do not know. At least, in that case, it would have kept some of the vicious birds and rodents from our gardens and homes, for a few days at least, and the rogue would have achieved something in his life, or rather, his death."

"Yes, Mary but you know my philosophy on matters like that. Notwithstanding, we took the body to the Justice of the Peace in Chichester, Strothmann Greedy. Do you remember him, Mary? I am sure he has been here on at least one of your social occasions, a rather unsavoury looking fellow but well connected. Anyway, he assured me he would investigate the matter and make enquiries, but Greedy is over laden with enquiries at present. Particularly since the recent disappearance of the newly appointed riding officer for the district, I do not recall the fellow's name, but evidently, he had been performing solid service. He had recently disrupted the smuggling gang's operation and brought one of their number to trial and the gallows. He seems to have gone missing now, and foul play is widely expected. Needless to say, all around, men are too fearful to say what they know but Greedy is convinced he can guess the fellow's fate. Greedy said he would send his man to visit the local brokers with a description of the flask, so there is a possibility that it may be found and the robbers apprehended."

"I am still at a loss to imagine what we should do about our errant daughter," Mary said. "May I ask that we discuss the matter tomorrow, I know that my brother, Thomas, should arrive early in the morning and that you will wish to discuss the forthcoming voyage with him but, perhaps before he arrives, we could meet?"

"No matter, Mary. After so long on the road and the matter of Bowden's gang, I am sure sleep will be some way over the horizon. Let us talk about the matter now."

"Matters seem to be worse than I first thought. I have recently discovered that before going with you to London, Eliza did not return home one night. The matter was not reported to me for several days. Bethany and others searched all likely places the girl may have been hiding. Now I have received the most dreadful information. It transpires that Eliza spent the night with the journeyman cooper on Fiddlespit." Mary sat down, her head in her hands, while the captain got up and poured her a glass of port.

"I thought he was a master cooper."

"Goodness gracious alive Richard, what does it matter which rank in his trade he has achieved? The man's a cooper."

"Is this information reliable?" Asked the captain. "Are you confident that these facts are sound? I will say, I find it difficult to believe."

"There would appear to be little doubt. The governess was slow to tell all, being under some absurd notion of loyalty to her charge. I thought of dismissing the governess on the spot but then one wondered if that might lead to a worse situation. I thought we might be able to use her to gain information about our daughter's behaviour." There was silence in the room for a while, until the captain said,

"Sanctions, do you think we should impose sanctions upon the girl?"

"We might keep her confined to her room, or send her away, perhaps?" said Mary. The captain poured himself more port, and after a few moments of staring into the embers of the fire, turned and said,

"Tomorrow, I shall confront her and see what the young woman has to say on the matter."

"Did you discuss the vase incident" said Mary, "during the journey to and from London?"

"Why no. I felt it my duty to build up such a relationship that our daughter would be more agreeable to our decisions. On the occasions when I did venture a question, she responded with her customary implacability, and as I explained the vase is not of great concern to me."

Mary looked confounded, "But her failure to come home overnight? I find that unbelievable. I have never heard of such behaviour, in all my life."

"If I know Eliza, she spent her time in that old gardener's house, down by the lake. It was a favourite haunt of hers as a child, and Esau, despite his looks, I believe to be a trustworthy man," said the captain.

"I think it unlikely she did, all the buildings in the garden were thoroughly searched and, perhaps you are forgetting that Bethany saw her talking to the cooper, down by the sea. I am distraught, thinking what might have happened."

"Calm yourself, my lady, tomorrow, after I have spoken with our daughter, I will go down to see this cooper and get to the heart of the affair, even if I have to open up the man's back."

"Whatever, we discover; I believe that we should reconsider her future," said Mary.

"Perhaps," said the captain, "a sea voyage to India will after all, if not solve the matter altogether, ameliorate it somewhat. I know that this would appear to reward her recalcitrant behaviour but ... to be absolutely straightforward here; I am concerned that Eliza is proving too stressful for you, Mary. None of our other children caused as much concern as Eliza."

"Are you forgetting our son, Welstan?" said Mary.

"Welstan has been uppermost in my mind while considering this matter. Your decision that he should travel to Asia has been proved to be a success. In his case, we responded to his similar youthful behaviour by sending him to India. You have read his latest letter about his successes, 'amounting to a small fortune,' he wrote. I feel that a pragmatic response might prove appropriate, in this instance as well," said the captain.

"Yes, but I do not find Welstan's behaviour similar in the least. He was a young man." Mary paused, then remembered the scripture,

"Our sons may be, as plants grown up in their youth; our daughters as sculptured pillars of the palace."

The captain sighed, out of frustration with his daughter, and returned to the decanter, thinking that the discussion had reached the Bible point; the position in a debate at which logic and rational ideas have been exhausted, and the conversation slips into an exchange of quotes from the scriptures. "Yes, of course," he said, "but one wonders if the parable can be applied to daughters, my dear. Especially in this instance. Can it be used to guide our decisions concerning a reckless daughter?"

"It is surely unthinkable that any respectable gentleman, let alone an officer, would consider marrying her, should they hear mention of this … episode," said Mary. "It seems that the whole household knew of her behaviour before her mother. Now it would appear only a matter of time before our errant daughter's behaviour is discussed behind raised hands following every Sunday church service in Sussex."

"If we deal with this without delay, Mary, it is quite unlikely that anyone in India will learn of anything detrimental about our daughter's behaviour before she has arrived in Madras and is safely married to a respectable officer."

"You are right, husband, as always," said Mary getting up from her seat with a resigned sigh.

"We have a course," said the captain, taking Mary's hand, "and tomorrow morning I shall ride out to Fiddlespit and see this cooper. Accompanied by your brother, Thomas. We need to discuss shipping matters and can do so on the way. What do you say to that proposal, Madam?"

27   Susan

Silvanus was in a predicament; should he get a message to Eliza, concerning their plans to run away together. He had fully intended to complete their venture but as Warren had mentioned, it would be a dangerous task, as it always was when going against the rich and powerful. He had next to no money at this time of year and would need to trade his wagon in for something lighter and faster. If he had some sovereigns in his pocket, things might prove easier. They would need to get far away, Devon, Norfolk, Scotland or France. Planning was complicated because there were so few opportunities to discuss matters with Eliza. Even at church Eliza had been shadowed by her governess who had renewed vigour at chaperoning her charge. He would need to get some money and perhaps after Christmas when the captain had set sail, he might be able to arrange a meeting. That was it then: he would get a message to Eliza by means of Esau – he could be trusted, Eliza had told him; then he would visit Warren to return the weapons; go to the hazel woods, just off the Portsmouth Road; spend a month making hazel hurdles and then sell them at Winchester market. He could be sure of a quick profit with hurdles at Christmas, folk needing new ones to control their livestock in spring. He wrote the letter to Eliza and set off for the Percy house. Leaving the wagon and Dimo spiked and grazing by the side of the road he walked up the back path to the house, trying to keep out of sight. He found the gardener's hut, a little way beyond the lake and looked around for the man himself, but he was nowhere to be seen. There was a timber store by the side of the hut, he would hide in there, if anyone discovered him, he could say he was here to offer hurdles, or trugs for sale and was sheltering out the rain until Esau returned. After an hour he decided, he would have to post the letter under the door and trust in the keen eyesight and good nature of the old gardener. As he bent down, the door opened and the old man was there. He must have returned without Silvanus hearing him, or maybe had been inside all the time.

"Ay, good day to 'e. What can we do for 'e?" he asked.

"Good day to you, too. Curtis is my name, I have been staying temporarily, with permission from Mr Greedy, at Fiddlespit. I am on the move now and was wondering if I could offer you any trugs, hurdles or barrels, before I leave?"

"Well, sorry lad, but 'e captain 'as given no allowance for such things, an' anyways, we's mostly make, or mend goods ourselves."

"Very well," said Silvanus and turned to leave, not being able to think of a manner of introducing the business of the letter to Eliza. He could not believe how nervous he was over the matter but then found himself saying to the old man, still standing on his doorstep,

"I have a letter."

"A letter? Best take 'at up to 'e house, Mister Curtis."

"But my letter is for Miss Percy, Eliza. She told me to trust you in the matter of delivering such messages."

"Miss Eliza did, did she? Well, well."

"Will you see she gets it, Sir?"

"We'll not be sure on 'at matter."

"What causes you to hesitate, Sir?"

"Well, Mister Curtis, please to come in an' take a seat, a while." Silvanus did as Esau asked and sat at the small table in the simple, one room hut. Esau cleared the remains of a bread and honey breakfast and said,

"We dither in saying, aye, to request, as we 'ave known Miss Eliza since she be infant, an' 'ave become very fond of 'er. I will not do anything 'at might 'urt 'er in anyway, an' would do everything in our power, feeble though 'at be, to prevent someone else bringing grief to 'e young girl."

"The fact is I wish to marry Eliza and she wishes to marry me, but her parents have other plans." Silvanus wished he had thought through what he was saying to Esau. He might be telling him too much.

"I do know 'at she bees vexed by mother's plans." Esau paused for a few moments, then slapped the table saying, "Give us 'e letter 'n we'll see Miss Eliza gets 'e, soon as can be." Silvanus thanked the old man, shook hands and left.

By late afternoon Silvanus had reached Warren's home, a small wattle and daub house on the outskirts of Chichester. Warren's wife, Susan opened the door with the little one peeking from behind her skirts.

"Mister Curtis, have you any information about Warren?"

"Information, Susan? What sort of information?"

"Warren has not been home for several days. He was out on a patrol the other night and his horse returned the next day but there has been not a sighting or a word about his whereabouts. I, I …" She turned, and walked back into her house,

"Come in Mr Curtis, I am sorry." Silvanus's mind was racing, what did Susan know of the business the other night? What had happened to Warren? His mind was going through all the pistol shots he had heard, were the shots being fired at Warren and not by him? Is he dead? How can he help Susan? What should he tell her?"

"I am afraid I do not know of his whereabouts; I was expecting him to be here. As I was passing, I thought I would return, em ... some tools he leant me."

"I have been to see the Justice of the Peace, Mr Greedy and he said he will search the neighbourhood. But I have heard nothing."

"I do not know what I can do, I ... I am sorry, Susan, but he is a capable and strong man. I am sure he is safe somewhere and will return home as soon as possible." Silvanus stayed for a while and tried to comfort Warren's distraught wife. He thought telling her what he knew about the situation might not help. He now felt terribly guilty for not looking into the matter of the gunfire. He had been armed with two pistols and a hanger and hat stood around doing nothing. He eventually left Susan and the child, to grieve alone under their terror of not knowing what had happened, but in truth, Silvanus knew little more.

28　　　Ashes

After a good night's sleep in his own bed, followed by breakfast with his brother-in-law, and first mate, Thomas Berrington, the captain felt somewhat revived, and now this morning's fresh easterly and clear blue sky had all but blown yesterday's incident with Bowden, out of his mind. He had been pleased that Mary, despite her initial reservations, had agreed to the plan that Eliza accompany him on the forthcoming voyage to India. Mary's suggestion that Bethany accompany their daughter as a travelling companion was an excellent one. Bethany might well be able to soften the young girl's rage, and they might hope that the governess, once Eliza was married, would easily obtain another position in India; English governesses being a rare commodity in that part of the world. Then, of course, there would be no further expense of a return journey to England. Surrounded by her family and familiar tutors – Mr Miller, Eliza's music teacher will also be aboard – it could be hoped that Eliza might find the trip conducive and arrive in Madras in a settled frame of mind, ready for a future husband. The captain climbed up into his horse's saddle. How often it is that the same troubled waters when viewed in the dark hours of night, can appear so calm in the morning light.

For the short ride to Fiddlespit the captain and his first officer were accompanied by James, the captain's manservant, who was looking unusually fatigued that morning. The captain discussed with Thomas his recent purchases in London, and Mr Reeve's suggestion that they enrol some impressed men for their journey ahead. Like the captain, however, Thomas believed men should not have to be impressed when being offered such an opportunity to travel across the world in one of the world's latest, and most magnificent ships but on the other tack he could see Mr Reeve's point that you cannot plug a leaky ship with fine principles.

They left the shade of the overgrown coppice and by the time they reached the end of the flat spit of land which led to the lagoon they realised that the cooper had left. All that remained were a fabricated workhorse covered with sailcloth and some wagon tracks.

After riding to the top of the gravel spit and looking each way along the shore, the captain rode back saying,

"It appears our bird has flown."

"Though, we cannot be far behind; the tracks look fresh," said Thomas.

"James," said the captain, "be good enough to see if those campfire ashes have any warmth in them."

James dismounted, bent down over the campfire and said, "Drenched by yesterday's rain, sir, and cold."

"Two days in a wagon would be ample for our fellow to make Chichester, or even further," said Thomas, "and who knows which route he may have taken. If we ride to Chichester forthwith, we could surely find someone who would have seen the coming and going of the cooper." However, the thought of spending another day on the road chasing some runaway fellow was just too much for the captain.

"James, what would you say to following this fellow?" If the captain was fatigued by the thought of riding for several hours that day, following his relatively comfortable journey in the post-chaise yesterday, James, after his two days stuck in the wind and rain in a cramped dickey seat, of the same vehicle, was decidedly unhappy. Also, it was James who traipsed around the streets of Chichester with the body of the highway man searching every tavern for the undertaker, and that, whilst the captain quaffed port with his friends.

"Certainly, Sir," said James, "but may I suggest an alternative strategy?"

"Well, go ahead, James, what course have you in mind, my man?"

"This cooper, being a local itinerant, may well prove difficult to locate but there are those who are accustomed to the ways of the bloodhound and for a small fee would sniff out the cooper and carry out whatever instructions, by way of dealing with him, which you see fit to offer."

"Are you suggesting," said Thomas, "that we employ a professional? Where would we find such a person?"

"Well, James, speak up tell us your scheme."

"I know a man who would find the cooper, Sir."

"But would not such activities be against the law?" asked Thomas.

"Not for you, Sir, with your connections. If this person should be apprehended in the pursuit of orders, your name need not be mentioned at all."

"Who is this man, James?"

"His name is Beatcher, Harman Beatcher an old sailor"

"An old sailor, you say; with whom did he sail?"

"The Royal Navy. More than that I cannot say, but for many years he was the captain of the Portsmouth Press, and very successful too. I heard, only last night that he has been seen in the area."

"I am not sure, James. Is he a gentleman?" asked the captain.

"Sir, he is a man following an unsavoury trade, and a gentleman he is not but then …" James struggled to find a way to convince the captain. "If you had a plague of rats aboard a ship, one would not look for a gentleman of refined manners to rid you of the rodents but a rat catcher."

"There are very few rats aboard an East Indiaman ship, James. I have always believed cats to be the answer." Thomas joined the conversation,

"In my humble opinion, it would seem an excellent course to steer, Richard. We do not want to lose valuable time chasing this rogue ourselves."

"Yes, Thomas, I can see your point. Alright, I have decided. James would you be good enough to arrange a meeting between this Beatcher fellow and Mr Berrington here?"

"Me, Richard? Why, yes, of course, Sir, delighted."

"Yes, I shall leave it to the two of you to finalise the arrangements. James let Mr Berrington know the time and place of this meeting as soon as possible. That is settled then. And now, home for luncheon."

29   Punt

If one disregarded the quay, and the three great mills, Fiddlesham harbour amounted to not much more than an inlet from the sea, created by some ancient flood that had washed around the sand spit and rushed inland. On returning to the sea, the great wave must have clawed away trees and soil leaving behind shallow mud flats, suited now to herons, curlews and eel trappers in flat-bottomed punts. It was late afternoon and a black cloud hung over the harbour, like a raven guarding its newly found carrion. A flock of lapwing took off, only to give up almost immediately and flutter down, hiding in the creeks and marshes below. The night was falling and shrouding everything in sea mist. The harbour was empty and smelt of decay. The only water left was a small stream in the mill channel, winding its way down from the mill to the sea, draining the pool above the tide mill dam, which had driven the water wheels. Once this water was exhausted, the wheels went silent and the millstones ceased to grind. Apart from the occasional owls nervously calling to one another, all was now silent. Half a mile below the mill there was a sharp bend in the Mill channel, where, over the years, the coming-and-going of the tides had scoured out a deep hole. There, the water was black and motionless, apart from a few ripples caused by the men moving in their punt. This, they had secured by an anchor thrown onto a mud bank. Any prying eyes on shore, having discovered a break in the mist, would have still seen nothing of the punt, or its occupants, all of which lay hidden below the embankments of mud.

An upright pole, made fast to one side of the punt, held a shaded lantern illuminating the four men in the vessel. In the front was John Butterworth, known as Butt, manoeuvring a plank of wood from beneath the seats. Amidships sat Caleb Sycorax Hepworth, known as Hap'th. Between bouts of searching the shore, mudflats, and water for signs of the malevolence, which he always believed to be not far away. He nursed an injured shoulder. Sitting in the rear was Harman Beatcher originally from Devon and later Portsmouth. A once broken and beaten man, who had come to believe that his continued survival was due to the benevolent and watchful eye of a spiritual being, whom he had named, Fingal, after a doctor who, against all expectations, had kept him alive. Last of the four, lying between Butt and Hap'th was Warren Blackmore, from Chichester, the local King's Treasury riding officer who had, until recently, been in search of smugglers to bring before the local magistrates to face justice. His lifeless eyes stared into the blackness and if their last image had been engraved on their retinas it would have shown the two young men in that punt cutting him to pieces with their cutlasses. Butt had removed Blackmore's coat and boots but had left his shirt and breeches, out of respect, he claimed, but, more likely, because he had seen how badly they were cut through and bloodstained. Butt tied the riding officer's legs to a heavy sack of rocks and then, while Beatcher sat overseeing the work, the two young men set about lifting the dead man on to the plank. Moving the body and rocks proved difficult in the small space of the punt. Hap'th complained of the pain in his shoulder while they struggled to manoeuvre the plank out over the gunwale. All this they did like men performing an everyday duty and when all was ready Beatcher stood up, leaning over his cane.

"First off," he said, "Words for you. You've done good work here, as worthy as any blacksmith at his forge or carpenter at his shave horse. Even better than them, cause you've worked in the shadows and in silence.

Second off: recompense will come your way when recompense comes my way, which will not be long, Fingal willing.

Third off: Words for you to remember, should you awake in the night with some sweating nightmare over today's employment. You are following a trade, a good trade, an honest trade. Unlike 'Revenue' here, dragged from his gawked-up table for snatching up young Davy Moxen and hanging that poor lad in chains for the devil's birds to pick over his poor bones, while his grieving mother quenched the parched ground beneath the gibbet with her tears. This, who was once a man, who we are about to tip into this merry hole, this man who took the pottage from the bowls of honest men, going about their honourable commerce, and all the time filling his own plate to overflowing with the riches of heaven, earth and sea, this man has had justice delivered today. And so, we comes to the final matter,

"Fourth off; some words for the deceased," Beatcher removed his hat and the other two copied, "I say unto him, as we commit his body to the cold water, how unlike the place from whence he fell, now here in hideous ruin and putrefaction you'll lay, vanquished and rolling in perdition. Now say amen, you two."

"Amen," said Hap'th.

"Amen," said Butt, replacing his hat and then tilting the plank so that the bundle slid over the side and was gone. Despite the cloaking fog, Hap'th looked all around nervous that they might be overlooked. He said,

"I don't like it here; it's a witch's hole."

"Here we go, again,"uttered Butt stowing the plank under the seats.

Hap'th was silent for a while, gazing over the side into the depths, then said,

"They hide here when the sun's too bright." Butt peered into the black water beside the boat,

"Bloody witches. I've never seen any witches."

"They steal the eyes of dead men, then, looking through them, they can see the last thing they saw."

"Who told you that?"

"It's true. We should have picked his eyes out." Hap'th said, still looking suspiciously into the black hole.

"Well, if you know about witches," Beatcher said, "you'll know the one thing they can't abide. The one thing what stops their charms."

"What's zat, crucifix?" asked Hap'th.

"No, the smell of piss on a grave," said Beatcher.

"What?"

"Mind you, it has to be a youngster's piss, younger, the better," said Beatcher, "Who's the youngest here?"

"Hap'th, that's you. You're younger than me," said Butt. "There can't be no hag in the whole of England who'd not lose their powers after having a whiff of your piss. Now, go to it." And Hap'th did. Pissing over the side into the witch's hole. Beatcher spat on the spot where Hap'th had pissed, "To finish the spell," he said. Then he took a basket from under the seat, removed a flagon, tankards and food wrapped in a kerchief, and said, "You'll have worked up an hunger after this day's duties and to satisfy that I have roasted duckling with crab-apples for guts and some of King Louie's blood, what just came ashore other night." He took out the long knife from his cane and began cutting the ducklings up. The two men removed their neckerchiefs and handed them over for the food to be shared out. The tankards were filled with brandy and they ate and drank in silence, apart from the sucking of fingers, spitting of bone and feather and the slobbering of grease and skin. To finish off, Hap'th produced a flask and shared out the last of its contents,

"Where'd you get this bit of silver, my bag of sparrow bones?" asked Beatcher.

"Same place I got this shoulder shot full of lead, 'cause Butt dribbled on his powder, when he primed his pistol in the morning, and it didn't fire."

"It were rain got to my powder, but we won't know if your powder were wet or dry," said Butt, "You being too afeard to shoot your pistol, or was the coachman a witch and put a spell on you," said Butt, laughing.

"Witches be women, not men, empty head," said Hap'th.

"Quite now. Pass the light, let's look at this flask, Lad," said Beatcher. He looked it over and found some writing, "'Captain Richard Percy, East India Company,' a pretty engraving of an East Indiaman ship and 'Presented to Richard Percy, my dearest husband. Ever yours, Mary.' No doubting who this belongs to. Aye, anyone seeing this will know where you got it from. Get rid of it, melt it down or, better still, throw it away." Hap'th looked like protesting for a moment but then put the flask back in his coat and waived the matter away.

The boat gave a jolt; the tide was returning. They finished the food, threw the remains overboard, dragged the anchor off the mud-bank and Butt, with the aid of the pole, helped the tide take them back to the mill, while Hap'th nursed his shoulder and Beatcher picked the few teeth he had left.

30   Pottage

Later that night, a carriage came from the Chichester Road, turned into the narrow road and onto Fiddlesham quay where it passed a couple of moored barges, two small waterlogged boats and a punt then halted, tight beside the Cat and Fiddle Inn. Here, there was a blacksmith's forge with an open door, out of which shone a golden light and rang a rhythmic beating of cold iron upon hot iron. The carriage stopped, and an officer stepped out. His blue coat, black velvet lapels, cuffs and collar would have signalled to any seaman watching from the shadows, that this was an officer of the East India Company, the John Company, as it was known. One small gilded crested button glinting from each cuff would have told that sailor that this was a chief mate.

Thomas Berrington was the spirit and image of his recently deceased father, who also had been named Thomas Berrington. The father was a wealthy ship owner who leased his ship to the East India Company on the understanding that his son, serve in her. Thomas Berrington, the Younger, looked at the sign leaning against the open doorway of the inn, a poor representation of a knotted rope and a fiddle. He entered and after a few enquiries made his way through the dimly lit corridors, to the back of the building. He peered through a cracked windowpane into the cramped little room, lit, in part, by a mean oil lamp standing on a small square table set against the wall. More lighting came from a newly lit fire, in front of which, and rather silhouetted against it, was the bent figure of Harman Beatcher, his head upright, above his stooped and hunched body. He gave Berrington the impression of a figure struggling to stand. Smoke from his clay pipe hurried away from him, streaming under the mantle and joined the fresh flames and heat of the crackling and spitting pinewood kindling as it disappeared into the chimney. The bent figure wore dark, shapeless trouser slops, the fashion popular with those who had worked on the sea but were now, by reason of age or rank, not concerned that a seafaring appearance might attract the attention of passing press-gangs. He also wore a brown loose frock coat with folded cuffs, which on someone else, a generation before, might have been a gentleman's coat. The one item of colour about his person was his red and yellow striped waistcoat. This had an overlapping collar, unbuttoned at the neck and almost covered with a large long greasy maroon neckerchief, frayed at the ends and tied in a series of half hitches, which, at a casual glance, might have been taken for a noose, from which he had not quite escaped. On his head he had a black, flat-brimmed felt hat with a grey, but once white, marine officer's feathered cockade.

Berrington, opened the door and asked,

"Beatcher, Harman Beatcher?" The man said nothing, put his clay pipe on the mantle, turned from the fire and, surprising Berrington - for a man of such a crumpled appearance - swiftly skipped around, to sit at the table with his back to the fire. A serving maid entered; more like a gundeck Molly than a country-serving girl, Berrington thought, as he ordered some brandy. Beatcher, without turning, asked for red meat.

"Begging 'e pardon, Sir," said the maid, curtsying in an over-stated manner, and stumbling slightly as she did so.

"But I do believe there be a little pottage of mutton, Sir."

"Be it red meat?" asked Beatcher.

"Begging 'e pardon, Sir, I do believe I have once seen it to be red but the last bowl, I did serve, had more of a greyish manner about it than red – begging 'e pardon, Sir."

Berrington removed his gloves, brushed the seat on the other side of the table from Beatcher and sat down, upright, clean, smart and out of kilter with his companion, whose broken twice-brewed look sat more easily against the tobacco and smoke-stained walls.

"Your, services, Sir, arrive highly recommended, and it is in the matter of those particular travails, which I beg your leave to deliberate upon this evening. I am an emissarial representative at liberty to speak on behalf of a certain, very distinguished, gentleman, whose name I have not the authority to communicate to your good self, Sir, but whom I can pledge lives a life beyond opprobrium. Undoubtedly ..."

"Ye need some cove, sent elsewhere; that be the ragged arse of it, eh?" Beatcher interrupted, not looking up from the flames of the fire.

"That, I agree, Sir, is the ... ah ... substance of my business, but it is with regard to the quotidian specifics, that the distinguished gentleman, to whom I referred earlier, has been most insistent that I bring to your attention here, and tonight."

The maid returned placing a bottle, two glasses and a bowl of pottage on the table between them. She poured a glass of brandy for Berrington. Her gnarled finger joints looking out of place on such a young woman, Berrington thought. He lifted his glass and said, "Your very good health, Sir." Beatcher looked up from his bowl and for a fleeting moment his eyes caught the lamplight and Berrington was shocked by the ruthless look in them. It was an insubordinate and insolent look and struck like a bayonet through a rather unsettled first mate's defences. He reminded himself of the purpose of his rendezvous with this man tonight and the nature of Beatcher's recommendations and said nothing. The moment was soon over as Beatcher lowered his eyes, restoring the gulf in rank between the two. Beatcher took a wooden spoon from an inside coat pocket and began noisily supping his pottage. Berrington settled back and continued, "The matter concerns a certain itinerant journeyman, or as he claims himself to be, a master cooper who …" Berrington stopped abruptly, still unsettled, and placed his hands palm down on the table either side of his glass, ready to move. Beatcher had drawn a long knife from his cane butt. But, to Berrington's immense relief, only used it to split open a knuckle of mutton. He then impaled the boiled joint upon his blade and sucked at it with an almost toothless mouth. Berrington relaxed once again and continued,

"This fellow, for reasons which shall not concern you, has caused such an upset to my gentleman's family, a family whom I would mention is blessed with the utmost courtesy, graces and …"

Beatcher managed the best he could, with gristle, bone and sinew, while only half-listening to the prattling officer, who brought to Beatcher's mind another naval officer - a similar jabbering popinjay - years back. That man had also raised a glass and saluted him with, 'your very good health, Sir.' But that particular bucket of farts' mocking toast had followed a naval court's sentence of, flogging-around-the-fleet. Two-hundred lashes, to be shared between all the ships in port. As good as a death sentence, is what most in the courtroom had believed that day, but the fools had not considered the size of the fleet in harbour, which was seventeen ships. Each batch of twelve lashes had, by navy rules, been followed by recovery of a month or until their squadron was conveniently at anchor. His healing had been supervised by his ship's surgeon, Paddy Fingal, who bathed his wounds with vinegar and then carefully covered them with torn pages from the an old copy of Milton's Paradise Lost. Fingal had taken pride in keeping Beatcher alive and fit enough to take his shirt off for his next batch of lashes. Beatcher had endured. On the very last ship, twelve months after it had all begun, there had been a sickly groan, even from that tub of old tars, brought down by the sight of Beatcher's backbone shining white through his blackened skin. the captain ordered the ship's fiddler to play a jig, to accompany that last flogging, "Capn's joke," whispered the Boson's mate, as he strapped him to the grating. "Hey diddle, diddle, the cat and the fiddle …"

"Give the mutineer something to dance to," had shouted a midshipman.

"And as such," continued Berrington, "I feel you would be sure to see my gentleman's commission is brought about by compassion, rather than any gratuitous intentions towards this … this cooper. And also, if I may add …" Berrington's prepared long list of terms was brought to an abrupt end, as Beatcher's reminiscence, and his mutton, came to a simultaneous conclusion. Wiping his spoon and blade on his neckerchief, he said in a firm voice,

"By the caging of this mischievous Cherub, goodness will guide our task, and resolve will be our sole delight, and weakness our misery."

Berrington paused for a moment, not being able to grasp the relevance of this observation,

"Sir? Well, of course, as you say … Now may we …"

Beatcher interrupted again,

"First off, we need an warrant, signed by an Justice. I's not doing any fake impressments. Have 'e got an warrant?"

"Aye Sir, I have it here," said Berrington, taking a folded document from inside his coat. "All legal and shipshape, signed by the Justice of the Peace but left unnamed, as I believe you requested. Which brings me to the small matter of, but in my humble opinion …"

"Second off." interrupted Beatcher, "We need the name of this Cherub."

"Although not known to me personally, I am informed that his name is Curtis, Silvanus Curtis, he has been known to reside in a temporary camp to the south of Fiddlesham, by a lagoon on a spit of land to the east of Fiddlesham harbour, and known as Fiddlespit by the people of that area. A recent visit to that very location on my part has suggested, however, that he has vacated this camp. I am informed that you have numerous contacts in this part of Sussex and that you might be able to trace his whereabouts. My instructions are that you take him …"

"Fiddlespit, 'e say, I know that cove? So that's Third off, done as well. Next then is Fourth off: the question of boodle. An journeyman? That'll be more boodle. And you don't want him dropped in some hole, so there's some more boodle. Farmer George's war being dead and buried, ships hauled up and all soldiers back to making baskets with their hagriding wenches … even more boodle – and to ease ship's officers, 'at be even more boodle. I'll need an handful of cuff-tossers, men who look like they've the lust for violence but can stand a while before going to it. Also, we'll need a place to hold our Cherub, an rendezvous. So, that's ... fifteen guineas now, and an further twenty guineas when your cherub's wings be trimmed."

"A total not exceeding twenty-five guineas is, I understand, the usual emolument."

"Not understood by me. As I says, in fourth off, an journeymen is more boodle, the war being ended is more, and ship's officers will be in need of good bit of arse-waxing."

Berrington, trying not to wince at the vision Beatcher's phrase, suggested, counted out the fifteen coins and pushed them across the table.

"Not to be excessively pertinacious about the matter but, my gentlemen insists that the warrant be returned at the time of our next rendezvous and the concluding payment. Please be sure ..."

Beatcher finished counting the gold coins for the second time, rose from his seat and, without saying anything further, left the room. Berrington picked up his brandy and raised it to the open door, saying, "And good health to you, Sir."

31   Dogs

October 1785 – Manhoodend Wood

Not far along the road from Chichester to Portsmouth, there was an old drove road heading north. Two miles along that drove road, on the western side, was a large and neglected coppice of oak and hazel which locals call Manhoodend Wood. This coppice was large enough to hide Silvanus's horse and wagon. He had arrived the morning after his visit to Susan Warren and had been worried that if Warren had been murdered that night at the mill, eyes might have fallen upon him and linked him to the business of His Majesty's Riding Officer. His murderers might be searching for him at this moment and with his wagon and horse, it was difficult to hide himself away. But this wood was as good as any place to hide. He was wondering if it was safe enough to light a fire and heat some food, when he heard dogs. The nearest farm was some distance. Perhaps they were a shepherd's dogs, or dogs returning home along the drove road. He was trying to make them out – smaller than foxhounds - not a whole pack - maybe just two or three. Whatever, they were getting nearer, approaching through the woodlands from the southwest. It sounded like the dogs were excited, as if getting close to their quarry. However, if they were returning drovers' dogs, they would surely pass by and ignore him. Before he could take any action, one of the dogs was upon him - knocking him to the ground. It was no more than a large spaniel, he pushed the dog away as best he could and grabbed a lump of wood from his kindling pile. It was not the best of sticks with which to defend himself, and snapped as soon as he struck the dog. But now there was another upon him. The same as the first, a large water spaniel. They were both snapping and barking and looking as though they were very well accustomed to attacking men. He thought of the pistols and the hanger, which he had decided not to return to Susan and which were still hidden in the front of his wagon, but there was no time. He tried to escape by climbing a nearby oak tree. There was nowhere else to go. Where were the huntsmen? They would soon arrive and call the dogs off. Then there was a man, blowing a small hunting horn and the dogs backed off.

"Am I glad to see you, my friend, your hounds here, have mistaken me for a fox."

While saying his, Silvanus realised this was the fat man whom he had seen at fiddlespit worrying Eliza and who he had later come across at the Red Lodge. The man shouted, "Diber, down! Lady, down!" And both dogs backed away lying flat on the ground. Silvanus jumped, down from the tree, saying,

"What are you hunting, out here in the woods with dogs that look more suited to duck chasing than anything else ..." He stopped, as another man came panting up behind him. It was the stick-like fellow, but before he could turn to confront him, everything was cut short, by this new arrival who clubbed Silvanus on the head with something more substantial than his own broken twig that he was still holding.

Much later – he could not tell how much later – he arose from his dreams, like rising out of the sea, but he swiftly fell into the blackness again. He felt like he was in a strange and seemingly never-ending state between rough and smooth; blackness and light; cold and heat.

Was he in Limbo? He floated up and down, between one world and the next, like swimming in the ocean, waves gently rising and falling, but then he was in pain. After what he imagined a considerable time, he awoke again. The pain in his head was so violent now that his only option seemed to be to escape back into his watery world, and then came a raging thirst. The dogs started barking. Were the dogs here and now, or something that his dream was conjuring up? He could hear someone calling, almost inaudible through a roaring wind in his ears. A fire, a house on fire, flames leaping into the night sky. Pieces of thatch flying away like fiery birds in the night sky and then his mother crying. She picked him up, held him tight, Mother, Mother, he shouted. He felt cold, then hot again. Every sensation alternating with its extreme opposite. If only this pain would stop, he might make out who was shouting, and who it was ... he opened his eyes ... smoke filled them, more voices. He tried to move but his arms were bound and something was clamped to his leg.

"You sack of pork, what've ye done now?" Silvanus knew the voice but could not give it a name. "Done for him, that's what I reckons, you've done for him. Secure him tight, I says, not hit him so hard his brains spill out his ears. If we don't get a receipt for him, showing he's alive, we loses all the forthcoming boodle." Then it came to Silvanus, it was the bent-double-man, he recognised his West Country accent and strange way of talking. He had been with the men he had seen on Fiddlespit. Silvanus felt sick. He could not make sense of things and drifted back into the sea, now searching for his red-haired love in the waves. "Eliza, Eliza ..."

When Silvanus eventually awoke again, it took a while for him to realise that he was conscious and no longer dreaming. His hands were indeed bound. He was in a small room with bars at the window. He could see the starlit sky beyond and could hear voices. The bent-double man again,

"Too early and you may be spied upon, too late and you'll miss the tide. Forth off: when you see my blue light from the Spit, it'll be time. Fifth off ..."

"Hang on," interrupted another man, "what happened to Forth off?"

"I told ya; the blue light. Now shut it, Hap'th. Fifth off: put him in the punt and take him to the end of the spit. Don't get the punt grounded."

They were talking about him. Why would they? There must be some mistake. Had they confused him with someone else? The older man must be talking to the two men from Red Lodge, the fat man and the stick-like man, the latter whose name must be Hap'th.

"Now, sixth off: I'll meet you there and we wait for the rendezvous with the lugger."

Silvanus's head was clearing but he remained puzzled. Were these the smugglers who had been mixed up with Warren? The talk of a boat, a lugger, had a pressgang taken him? It did not make sense; he had heard that impressment had ceased since the end of the war. Whatever was going on he must plan and escape before he was aboard some ship. Once there, his fate would be sealed. He struggled to pull himself up into a sitting position, without making any noise. Now he managed to peer out of the barred window and get a better view – get the lay of the land. He was in some sort of carriage. Now he had it, these men had a magistrate's wagon on Fiddlespit, which had been partly hidden by the trees. There were three men outside sitting around a small fire. The older man was eating noisily from a bowl, the fat man drinking from a tankard and Hap'th lying, possibly asleep, against a log. Around Silvanus's left leg there was an iron manacle attached to the floor planks. As his head cleared, he tried to get his mind in order. He needed to think clearly, find a weakness in these men's scheme and be ready to take advantage. Although, there appeared little possibility of escape from his situation. In his favour, he reasoned, the two men from the Red House had not appeared very capable, but then there was older man. Although his appearance was one of a cripple, everything about his actions, suggested otherwise. He was the one he had somehow to outwit and the other two he had to overcome. There might possibly be an opportunity ahead and for that he must be prepared. Most likely he would only get one chance. But he had been fortunate enough to hear some of their plans. He turned a little; trying to get more comfortable and realised, his paring knife was still in his belt; they had not searched him. It only had a blade a few inches long, not much of a weapon against cudgels and pistols but they did not know he had it. Perhaps he might use it as a tool rather than a weapon by cutting himself out of his cage. However, after some time of trying his knife against the floor planks, as best as he could in the dark, he could find no way of getting free of the securing manacle. Poking with his blade into the planks, they felt as though they were made of a hard wood, it would be too long and noisy to cut through them with his knife. At some time, they would have to move him from the carriage to the punt they had talked about; perhaps then, there would be only the underlings. Somehow, he must escape from the punt, but if he were chained there would be little hope.

The next morning, he felt slightly better but pretended to be only partly conscious as the larger of the two men unlocked the carriage door to check his manacle, while the Hap'th, who appeared sickly, pointed a pistol at him. Hap'th struggled with an injured shoulder but brought Silvanus some water. He poured it into a silver flask and left it by Silvanus's side. Silvanus asked what was happening but the fat one told Silvanus to be quiet. "Unless you want to be put to sleep again." He had said. Hap'th was shivering inside a blanket and wore a neckerchief sling to support his arm.

Soon, they left the camp and after journeying all that day, and the following night, the morning of the second day of imprisonment arrived. Silvanus recognised their surroundings, they had entered Keynor Wood, where he had grown up. If he could only get free here, they would never find him. Although he could still see no way of escaping his chains, being on his home ground, his spirits lifted for a while. Silvanus had learnt that the bigger of the two was named Butt. Sometime around midnight, Silvanus guessed, they set up camp in the same area Silvanus had come across the two of them molesting Eliza on the road to Fiddlespit. It rained in the night but Silvanus was warm and slept reasonably well. Apart from being very hungry he was feeling a lot better. With The bent-double man's name was Beatcher, Silvanus had discovered and sometime during the night he must have left the camp. Butt was still there with Hap'th, but the twiglike Hap'th appeared to be suffering with the fever - prospects were looking better, Silvanus thought.

In the morning Butt had to lift Hap'th into the coachman's seat at the front of the wagon. Then, he went to lead the horse, walking with it at the front. Silvanus decided that when Butt entered the carriage to release his chains, to take him to the punt, he would have his knife ready and when the manacle on his leg was undone, he would seize the opportunity to stab Butt in the neck, taking a chance against the sickly Hap'th's pistol fire. But when it came to it, Butt had the better of Silvanus's plans. He released the other end of the chain from the outside of the carriage, then opening the door, Silvanus was told to lift the chain and climb down whilst Butt held the pistol. Silvanus could not get near enough to use his knife. Hap'th was already in the punt at the far end, slumped in a blanket and not moving. Butt held the long chain and threaded it beneath the rear middle seats of the punt and securing his end to an iron ring. He was told to stand and use the pole to punt the craft out into the harbour, while Butt sat in the middle holding the pistol. There was no way Silvanus could see how he might escape. He had underestimated his enemy. He tried to get Butt into a dialogue, but to no avail. It appeared he was following instructions to say nothing.

It was a clear night as they crossed the harbour with the crescent Moon in the east only just outshining Jupiter rising in Orion. The falling tide carried them swiftly out across the harbour towards Fiddlespit and carried Silvanus's mood, to despair. All he could understand was that for some reason he was to be sold off to the Navy as an impressed man. The only cause, for this interest in him, must be related to recent events. What was Beatcher's part in all of this? That, Silvanus could not understand. The punting pole seemed too long to be of any use as a weapon against Butt, even if he could knock him out, he would remain chained to the punt. Silvanus, following Butt's instructions, took the punt almost to the end of the spit. Any further, and the craft would become unstable with the swell coming around the end of the shingle spit from the open sea.

Butt climbed over Hap'th and jumped ashore pulling the punt up the shingle as high as he could and tying the painter to a driftwood log. He then dragged, what now appeared to be an unconscious, Hap'th ashore, then returned with pistol drawn, undid the lock to the chain on the punt, indicating to Silvanus to carry his manacle with him as he climbed ashore. Once there, he could see that the only place for Butt to secure the chain would be around a large trunk of driftwood. Threading the chain beneath the log, Butt would have to get close to Silvanus … and turn his back … this was it. Silvanus pulled his knife and fell upon Butt, knocking him against the log and onto the shingle.

"I have a knife at your neck, Butt. Drop the pistol."

"Damn you, where did you get that from?"

"Where it came from is no matter but where it is about to go, if you don't drop that pistol, should be your concern." Butt did not release his grip on the pistol.

"I don't believe you have a knife, damn your eyes." Silvanus pushed the first half inch of his blade into the back of Butt's neck, making Butt scream out, and throw Silvanus off his back and … drop the pistol. While Butt was crying and holding his bleeding neck, Silvanus rolled over and grabbed the weapon. "Throw the key to the lock over here or I swear I will finish you with your own pistol."

Butt did as he was told and began bandaging his neck with his kerchief. Silvanus removed the shackles and got Butt to chain himself to the driftwood. What next, thought Silvanus. The punt had gone; relieved of its load, it had not been far enough up the beach or tied securely enough, and had drifted out following the falling tide around the spit and out to sea.

He could hear people approaching along the shingle, was it Beatcher? If so, he was not alone, there were horsemen with him. Silvanus ran to the harbour's edge intending to escape by swimming away but the tide had dropped and now there was only mud. The men came over the spit from the seaward side, four on horseback, two on foot with hangers drawn, and a couple of dragoons, muskets at the ready.

"Strothmann Greedy, justice of the peace for Chichester, at your service. Are there any more of you about, young man?"

"No Sir," said Silvanus, "This man here is called Butt, the other Hap'th. They planned to rendezvous with a third but not until the morning."

"And your name is?" asked Greedy from his horse.

"Curtis, Sir. From Fiddlesham."

"Oh yes. Now I know you. The cooper from fiddlespit."

One of the dragoons reported to Greedy, "One manacled, another dead, Sir."

The dragoons brought Butt in front of the Justice of the Peace, pushing him to his knees. Butt said, "Thank God, Sir. Saved from this cutthroat, look at my wounds,"

"He undid the makeshift bandage, to show his wound. "He has kept me prisoner and done for my brother here. Thank God in his Heaven that you arrived when you did and saved me from such a violent man."

"Search them," Ordered Greedy. They did but all they found on Silvanus was the pistol, his knife and the flask with a little water, which Hap'th had given him.

"Let me see that, my man. That's a fine bit of silverware, for a cooper. And with a picture of a sailing ship, from the East India Company, if I am not mistaken. While on the other side we have, 'Presented to Richard Percy, my dearest husband. Ever yours, Mary."

32   Trial

"Silvanus Curtis and John Butterworth, otherwise known as Butt, you are hereby indicted for feloniously assaulting Captain Richard Percy of the East India Company on the King's highway, between Midhurst and Chichester on the twenty-second of September last, and putting him in corporal fear and danger of his life, and feloniously taking from his person and against his will, one silver flask, value two pounds two shillings and sixpence – his property. John Butterworth, how do you plead?"

"Not guilty."

"Silvanus Curtis, how do you plead?"

"Not guilty."

James was called to speak from the witness box,

"I am James Kadam. On the morning of September twenty-second, last, I was travelling on the highway from Midhurst to Chichester. I was in a post-chaise with my master, Captain Richard Percy, of the East India Company, two postilion riders and Alfred Abel, a footman to my master. Captain Percy cannot be here today because he has had to travel to London to prepare for a voyage, on behalf of the East India Company, to Madras. I was riding at the back of the carriage and I was to guard our carriage against robbers. We were approaching the four-mile stone when our way was blocked by a flock of sheep, which appeared not to be under the control of a shepherd. As we waited two men descended the embankment. Both men hid their faces from view and held drawn pistols. The large, man I believe to be Butterworth, the accused, and a thinner man whom I now believe to have been Butterworth's associate, Caleb Hepworth, who has since deceased. Another robber arrived on horseback. Butterworth tried to fire his pistol at me but it misfired. I fired my blunderbuss at Hepworth and he fell to the ground. The mounted robber drew his pistol and pointed it at me, so I took Alfred Abel's pistol – he was sitting beside me in the dickey-box – and I shot the rider off his horse. Later the captain told me that before he died from his wounds, he told the captain that his name was Bowden. At that point Butterworth ran away and Hepworth got to his feet, took the captain's engraved flask and also ran away."

Alfred's evidence was much the same as James's and then Butt told his story.

"I was not there. It were not me that robbed the captain, but Hepworth. As I was walking to Fiddlesham from Chichester, I was violently attacked by Hepworth and Curtis who kept me prisoner. For what reason I do not know. Hepworth died from previously received injuries but before he did, he told me that it was him and Curtis who had robbed Captain Percy on the Highway from Midhurst. He said that Curtis had supplied all the pistols and the horse for Bowden, who had been involved in many violent robberies. I asked Hepworth before he died, 'Did you rob the captain alone?' And he said, 'No, I was with Curtis. I think that Curtis planned to kill me on Fiddlespit but Mr Greedy arrived with some dragoons and stopped him."

It was then time for Silvanus to tell his side of the story. While he had been waiting in prison other prisoners had given him advice on how to give his evidence. Some said he had to make the jury believe in his honesty by being calm and relaxed. They advised him to look jury members straight in the eye, but never the judge. Silvanus could never remember being as nervous as he was at that moment when he stood up. He put his hand on the Bible to repeat the oath but his voice would not come, he pretended to have a cough and that made things worse, the jury got bored waiting and began to talk to one another. The judge banged his gavel several times and Silvanus managed to gasp out his oath. He tried to tell his story, as simply as he could, but without being able to supply an explanation of why he had been taken prisoner, his story sounded implausible.

"I am a cooper. I was apprenticed to a master cooper at the Royal Naval Dock Yards in Portsmouth since I was twelve years old and worked there until the end of the recent war with the American Colonies. At that time, they had too many coopers and I lost my position there and have since sold barrels, buckets and other goods at markets and taken what honest work I can."

The Judge, who had seemed asleep until this moment, banged his gavel and spluttered,

"Get on with it, Man. Luncheon will soon be upon us and we have no desire to hear every detail of your life thus far."

"Yes, m'lord. I was not on the Midhurst Road on the twenty-second of September, last, I was on Fiddlespit but have no one, no witnesses to say that is so. After that I visited Manhoodend wood, near Chichester, to obtain some hazel wood to make hurdles to sell. There, I was attacked by Butterworth, Hepworth and a third man named Beatcher. Hepworth gave me a silver flask with some water in and then the two of them took me in a punt to Fiddlespit with a chain on my leg. There, I fought to save myself with the small knife I carried. Butterworth would not drop his pistol. I therefore stabbed him a little in the neck to make him drop it, which he did, forthwith. I obtained the key for the lock to my chains from Butterworth and removed the chains from my leg, placing them on Butterworth's leg to prevent any further attack from him because I felt sure he would harm me if he could. Then Mr Greedy and others arrived and I learnt that Hepworth had died from his wounds. Butterworth told Mr Greedy the same story that he has just now told the court but he was lying, I did not rob Captain Percy."

Mr Greedy then stood up to tell what had happened.

"My name is Strothmann Greedy, I am justice of the Peace for Chichester. I had received reports and information that there had been suspicious activity on Fiddlespit, namely a blue light appearing. I formed the opinion that this might possible be a signal perpetrated by villains. I had been recently making enquiries about the suspicious disappearance of the Chichester area King's Riding Officer, one, Warren Blackmore. I therefore took a party of armed men to investigate. We found a dying man, who told my man that his name was Hepworth. Another man was in chains and that was Butterworth, who stands in the dock here today. A third man was holding a pistol, a knife and had a silver flask in his jacket pocket, which I later discovered from an engraved inscription upon it, that it belonged to Captain Percy of Fiddlesham. This third man was Curtis, who is also in the dock here today. Hepworth told me that he and a man named Bowden, together with Butterworth, had robbed Captain Percy. Curtis, he said, was nearby on the day, and had supplied the horse, weapons and was to dispose of all stolen goods."

All witnesses, having been heard, the judge directed the jury to decide as to the guilt, or otherwise, of Butterworth and Curtis. They discussed the matter for a few moments and then one juryman stood and indicated to the judge that they had decided upon their verdict.

"And with regard to the prisoner, Butterworth, how do you find?"

"Guilty."

"And with regard to the prisoner, Curtis, how do you find?"

"Guilty, but with a recommendation of clemency." The Judge put on the black cap, banged his gavel and said,

"John Butterworth you are hereby sentenced to death. Silvanus Hepworth, you are also sentenced to death. We shall now break for ... what is it now?" The Clerk to the Court had stood and was looking very agitated.

"Excuse me my lord, may I have discrete word with you before we break for luncheon?"

"What is it now, can it not wait?" said the Judge. The Clerk went close to him and whispered and then the judge replaced his black cap and said,

"Silvanus Curtis, you are hereby sentenced to death. Luncheon."

The whole trial was over in no more than twelve minutes.

33   Lily

Albert Williams, known as Willow, was tall and strong, a labourer who, unusually for his class, was literate. The vicar, who had taught him his letters, saw the makings a theologian in this young man's enquiring mind. Unfortunately, for Willow, early in his education, the vicar's mind and hands had wandered and persuaded Willow, that a life in the Church was not for him. The lecherous priest, however, had planted a seed. One which Willow continued to nurture and grow. Then one day, whilst searching for material to read, other than the Bible, he had found a broadsheet and with the help of a copy of a Dictionary of the English language, which the vicar had loaned him, Willow had become excited that he might educate himself through the written word. This first pamphlet called for volunteers to travel to Paris and join the fight for, justice for all workers in all the countries of the world. It had ended with a rallying call of, 'Liberté, égalité, fraternité.'

Outside Chichester gaol, on the day designated for the hanging, Willow stood watching the crowd gather. He had learnt from his time with the Parisian Sans-Culottes, that a revolutionary should be at the seat of injustice, ready to nurture the anger in men and women and guide them along the road to action. Wherever a crowd gathered to jeer; or a pressgang took a young man away from his family; wherever people gathered to lend a helping hand to an evicted family; wherever men protested at some new machine built to destroy their livelihoods; wherever men were held in a ship against their will to fight their brothers and wherever a crowd gathered to witness an execution; there should be the revolutionary. For generations around Chichester, families had lived in societies which managed their own subsistence; feeding, clothing and housing their families, albeit dependant on the vagaries of local land-owning squires, but all this was changing. Displaced families were now starving and many, would-be, wage-earners had turned to crime. Landowners fought back against protest by flogging, transportation and hanging. Death sentences at Chichester Crown Court had become commonplace, but a counter reaction, by some of the enlightened elite in the area, to this wholesale bloodshed and slaughter of their workers, often for the most trivial of crimes, had led to seven out of every ten men and women's death sentences commuted to some lesser punishment. In many cases, those unfortunate enough not to be spared the hangman's noose by the Chichester Court found themselves transferred to nearby Horsham, where most Sussex death sentences were carried out. In that town, people had become very accustomed to the sight of the gallows and would flock into town, and then onto the Heath, in large numbers on a Saturday morning to witness the hangings. Town gallows were maintained by local merchants and tradesmen who saw the executions, and their accompanying Saturday fairs, as a way of bringing prosperity to the town and thus, filling their own pockets.

This Saturday, in Chichester, the local landowning gentry had seen fit to arrange their own hanging. The town's merchants were hoping to attract something like Horsham's crowds to the town, so broadsheets had been passed around advertising the execution of two prisoners at the fields by the West Gate on Saturday the

8th day of October. Strothmann Greedy, mill owner of Chichester, had generously supplied the gallows.

Willow wandered from group to group, listening to the mood of the crowd. If he felt a gathering to be conducive, he would slip a broadsheet from under his coat. This was headed, 'Stand up to tyranny; join with Will O' the Wisp, and ended with, Liberté, égalité, fraternité.

It was a fine breezy Saturday morning with pleasant autumn sunshine supplying an enjoyable respite in an otherwise wet and dreary autumn, encouraging even more to join the throng. The crowd's excitement grew by the moment, as its members gathered outside East Gate gaol for a sight of the two unfortunate prisoners, who would be paraded along the High Street to West Gate, where the gallows had been erected. As the town clock struck noon the iron studded oak door creaked open and the first of the prisoners immerged after weeks in her dark and filthy cell, blinking and shielding her eyes from the sudden sunlight.

Lily Hawks, weak and faint, was lifted by the prison guards onto the back of a cart and seated on her own coffin, which had been especially built for her by the undertaker, with a thicker than usual lid. Even the hardened guards appeared moved by the tragedy they were overseeing. They were, though, very aware of the volatile sentiments of gallows crowds, who were pressing forward, some cheering, some jeering, and all hoping to gain a better look at this young girl. Only seventeen years old, her tale of woe had begun some months earlier.

Working in the Spread Eagle tavern she had fallen for the charms of the young and dashing Daniel Threadgate, who had explained to Lily that having unexpectedly been bequeathed a considerable amount of money – due to the sad death of a cherished aunt - he now wished to spend some of his fortune on beautiful things; like Lily. He had followed her tirelessly over the ensuing months and, with flattery, silks and fineries, had won her heart. Love's young hearts had consummated their longings in the cellar amid the barrels of the beer to the light of a stubby candle. When, a few months later, with a sparkle in her eyes and joy in her heart, Lily told Threadgate she was expecting their child, he caressed her tenderly, saying that soon they would be married. Before this happened, however, he had explained that he must conclude an important and financially rewarding business transaction. One which he was very committed to. As time went by, he visited Lily less and less. However, she did not feel able to tell anyone else of her plight. Then a few moments after midnight on a hot July night her waters broke. She went down alone to the cellar and upon the cold stone floor, after three hours of pain, stifled cries, for fear of being discovered, she gave birth to a boy and immediately fell into unconsciousness. When she awoke, shortly after first light the baby was gone. She searched the cellar and found her baby on a pile of firewood, covered by her own bloody shawl. The baby's throat had been cut. Not quite grasping the magnitude of the situation, she looked at the slit o the baby's throat and thought, what a shame that is. Without thinking, she carried the baby upstairs into the open tavern room for all to see.

The young girl quite oblivious as to the gravity of her circumstances, and apparently incapable of answering questions on the matter, was examined by a surgeon who confirmed that she had recently given birth. She had been tried in the crown court, found guilty and sentenced to be hanged for the murder of her bastard son.

The second prisoner, John Butterworth, was brought out and his leg irons chained to the cart that carried Lily and her coffin. Found guilty of highway robbery, he would walk behind the cart for the mile journey to the gallows. Sentenced to hang in chains, following his execution, he would not require a coffin. The ballad singer marked his arrival with a verse of Sixteen-String-Jack, to which the crowd gave a great roar of approval and began jigging around the gallows cart. Butt's spirits seemed to lift at all this sudden attention and he waved to the dancers, bringing another whoop of appreciation upon him as well as flowers and rose petals thrown by admiring ladies in the throng. Butt, even more joyous, began dancing his own jig, as far as his chains would allow. Even Willow, jostled along by the masses and cajoled by girls to join their prancing, was surprised at this ardent support for the young highwayman. How the masses cheered for them who robbed from the rich, even if, as in this instance, it was very likely that this man did not intend to give any of his proceeds to the poor. What a happy time the working people of Chichester are having this day dancing an hour on their journey to West Gate, thought Willow, celebrating the agents of the landowning classes hang one of their own working men. Perhaps the people of England, unlike France are just too stupid to start a revolution. Apart from Willow, there was merriment all around. Except, that is, for the prison guards, who feared the crowd were showing such support for the robber they might try to alter the outcome of the day, by releasing him. Then there was poor Lilly, whose fragile resolution of the night before, to face her fate with fortitude, crumbled away in the morning sunshine under this bombardment of sound and chaos. She sat on the cart forsaken, trembling and weeping.

Over in Horsham the gallows catered for as many as six simultaneous executions, although here, in Chichester, Greedy had convinced the court that a single gallows would suffice. This would mean that one prisoner would be forced to watch the other die before their turn came to mount the gallows steps. The executioner, sharing the prison guards' concern for the crowd's enthusiasm for the highwayman, insisted that he should hang first, which of course meant lengthening Lily's torment and suffering. The days of showmen executioners were almost gone. Jonas Box had been hired for the event from Horsham but he would be restrained, efficient and, above all, speedy. The crowd hushed as they reached the foot of the gallows, members of the local guard struggled to keep the crowds behind the rope encircling the scaffold. The Hangman unchained Butterworth and led him up the ladder to the platform and to the trap door beneath the noose. Still smiling and waving, until the very moment when he realised that his time on Earth was at an end, and wishing to say a few words to make his peace with God, said,

"My father, forgive me my sins in this world for I have …" Mr Box pulled the sack over Butterworth's head ending his speech, causing an outbreak of jeering from the crowd, which drowned out the executioner's whispered words to Butterworth,

"Well said lad, soon be able explain all that personally to the Almighty." The priest put a comforting hand on his shoulder, saying,

"Bless you, my son."

Box, crossed the fingers of one hand behind his back, pulled a lever with his other hand and released a huge sigh of relief as the trap door opened and Butterworth fell to his death. There was a gasp from the masses and then stark silence, even more noticeable, following the crowd's recent ferment and frivolity. Jackdaws and starlings circled above cackling at the prospect of ample pickings from such a gathering of untidy people. Now, even those at the rear of the crowd could hear the sobs of poor Lily. Butt's body was cut down, a fresh rope supplied and lily, being unable to walk, through grief, was carried on the shoulder of a guard up onto the platform, where, supported by two men, sobbing and unable to speak, she was held up over the trap door. The hardened old priest had officiated over many comings and goings in this world. Over the years his melancholy had grown and had long since ceased to quelled by gin and wine. He raised his hand to an already hushed crowd. Mr Box whispered to him,

"Please, Sir, if you would, let brevity prevail." The chaplain ignored him and, looking to the heavens above, in his loudest pulpit voice, called out,

"Almighty God, you judge us with infinite mercy and justice, and love everything which you have made …" Then, pausing and realizing that the crowd had heard this many times before, levelled his gaze upon one man in the crowd who was still laughing at another's barracking, thrust forward an accusing finger and screamed,

"You there, yes you, Sir, have mercy in your heart for this child …" now, ranging his hand across the masses, he said,

"If any of ye possesses tears, prepare to shed them now."

The ballad seller thought it an appropriate moment to sing the old gallows favourite, "Fortune's my Foe, why dost though frown on me …" until a man in the crowd, who, having lost his appetite for both his meat pie and the ballad singer's sentiments, threw his pie remains at the songster, cutting his plaintive song short. For the second time that day, Mr Box's crossed fingers proved successful and his work was now completed. The mood had now changed, no one danced, food carts, brought out for the day by butchers and bakers, were now ignored, and the people in the crowd shuffled off back to their work or homes. A few groups remained, gazing at the gallows, pondering the precariousness of their own mortality or listening to the young man, who had a Parisian look about him, reading from a broadsheet about injustices in Britain.

One strange looking man, almost bent double, was talking to the local gravedigger and his wife who had been selling rose petals from a basket.

"And Second Off, it's the matter of the bones. Will you show them grace?"

"Certainly, Mr Beatcher but I will have to be shadowy about the matter, arriving shortly after dark, as the bones become available, I shall collect them in this very same basket, until I have collected them all, or as many as I may find before the foxes … And rest content, Sir, that I shall bury them in the graveyard, in some discrete corner, where you may visit," said the gravedigger.

"Although," added his wife, "it is a goodly walk up to Rook's Hill, where I understand this fellow's body is to be hung but we shall be diligent in this matter and as his bones fall, we shall collect."

"So then, third off: here is one half guinea now for this service and I will provide another half, when 'tis done."

"Thank 'e kindly, Mr Beatcher," said the gravedigger. Who then added, "May I ask 'e a personal question, out of respect for 'e good self, and my own curiosity, which has no import on our transaction?"

"You may ask, cannot say I'll answer, though."

"Is the late Mr Butterworth by way of a relation of yours?"

"I was his overseer, he was in my employ for some time, not in the matter of the highway robbery for which he was unjustly hanged ... also ..." Beatcher stopped and made to walk away as if changing his mind concerning the end of his conversation but then he relented and said,

"Before mine eyes in opposition sits grim Death with my son. And me his parent knows his end as with mine involved, shall be done."

34   Mucking Flats

November 1785 – The Thames estuary.

The first day of travel on the Thames had provided some interest for the travellers. Their journey had taken them close enough to the river bank that they could watch the activity of other travellers and fishermen who lined the banks. Here and there were inns, piers and markets at which they could stop to take refreshment. Their first day's journey had passed quickly enough. Then, after a sleepless night in a noisy lodging house near the Tower of London, the second day on the river was extremely irksome for Eliza. For the journey to India, Eliza's mother had decreed that Bethany would no longer be a governess but a travelling companion. This meant that Bethany could share a room with Eliza. During the night Bethany had become talkative and had told Eliza of her recent visit to Chichester, which had been necessary to buy some clothes for the sea journey. She had heard that James was going there, and asked that she might travel with him. Bethany said that he was going to watch the hanging of the two highwaymen who had tried to rob the captain and Eliza and who had tried to kill James. Bethany, having completed her purchases had joined the crowd following the prisoners but there was only one highwayman the other poor unfortunate soul was a young girl who had murdered her infant bastard son. Bethany had enjoyed telling all the gory details and had made a point of learning the prisoners' names,

"The girl's name was Lily Hawks, a maid at the Spread Eagle tavern," Bethany said, "No older than you, Miss. She had killed her baby – can you imagine such an appalling deed? The strange thing was how everyone's mood changed when the moment came to hang her. All the jeers stopped and people watched in silence, many with tears, even the vicar was crying. Mind you that was probably because he had drunk so much wine – they say he's a terrible drunk. In contrast, the highwayman appeared to be having the time of his life. Well, I do suppose that one could be certain, he has never has had a better time since. His name was Butterworth, John Butterworth. Everyone was disappointed because the other highwayman was not there. James thought he might have been too ill to hang that day. How can someone be too ill to hang? Anyway, they'll hang him at Horsham later, or maybe he has saved the hangman the trouble and died already."

Eliza had not been paying very close attention to Bethany's tale of the hangings and only gradually realised what Bethany was talking about.

"So, who was the other man who was not hanged? Was he the thin man who threatened to turn me upside down to get any money I had hidden? Although their faces were covered, I am certain they were the two men I had come across on Fiddlespit?" Eliza said sitting up in bed.

"It may have been," said Bethany. "I think they said the other highwayman's name was Curtis."

"Curtis?" asked Eliza, a cold shock swept down her spine. "That cannot be. What are you saying, Bethany? No, I find that impossible to believe. You must be muddled; it could not have been Curtis … not Silvanus Curtis."

"Oh, Miss. I never realised," said Bethany, taken aback, "that was the name of the cooper, residing at Fiddlespit - but Curtis is a common enough name," said Bethany. "It seems unlikely, Miss. Did you know him?" Bethany could feel herself blushing as she realised the cooper's name was the same as that of the man who was to be hanged in Chichester. She, of course, knew that Eliza had had a liaison with the cooper, having watched them swim together but had not remembered his name.

"I met him, a few times," said Eliza, "Once after church and once or twice whilst out walking on Fiddlespit? You say he was one of the men that took part in the highway robbery, but I was there. Two of the men were wearing masks, one was thin and the other one fat and the third one who was on horseback, called Bowden, was shot dead and I saw him up close. None of them looked like they could be Mr Curtis."

Bethany looked surprised and added, "Perhaps I got the wrong name, Miss."

There was a moment's silence while they both tried to understand the new situation and what each other had just said.

Bethany eventually said, "Perhaps Mr Curtis was hiding, nearby during the robbery."

Eliza said, "How could he hide living the life of a highwayman?"

"I do believe, Miss, that is the nature of being a highwayman. He would not tell anyone of his true profession, even someone as ... but you are right, it does seem unlikely. I suppose it is possible, just possible, that Curtis was an innocent man. They say that many men and women who face the gallows are in fact, innocent. As he did not hang with the other robber, perhaps evidence has become known to prove his innocence and he was pardoned."

"What happens to pardoned men?" asked Eliza.

"They might be released or get a lesser sentence of gaol, or maybe transportation to the Americas, but I hear that is not possible now, since the end of the war. I am sure they will not hang him," said Bethany concerned at Eliza's growing agitation.

"How would I find out his fate?" asked Eliza.

"I cannot say, but is it of any concern to us now? We are both on our way to another world? What happens to a cooper you once met can be of little concern to you now?"

"Of course, it matters, Bethany. I knew the man, and now you are telling me that he has been lying to me, and that he was a robber. I wish to know the truth of the matter and its outcome."

The second day of travel on the river Thames was aboard a different cutter, bigger and altogether more robust than the first days, and far more suitable to the wider and more open river from the Tower to Gravesend. Whereas yesterday there were two oarsmen, today there were four, together with a waterman on the tiller. The passengers were Eliza's music teacher, Edward Miller, Bethany and Eliza. Her sister and cousins were to follow on, in a few days. The river was on a falling tide, which, together with the four oarsmen meant that they were travelling at a giddy speed. Soon the river was so wide that they were as much as half a mile from the shore, which reduced the passenger's appreciation of their speed. They were to put ashore before joining their ship at a landing on the Essex side of the river at a place called Mucking Flats. There, they would wait at the Crab Inn. Then, when all the passengers had arrived, and the captain had decided that departure was imminent, signals would be sent and the ship's cutter would come to fetch them.

The days went by as drearily as the place's name, Mucking Flats, had suggested they would. Eliza's mood had grown dark since the information about Silvanus. She had said nothing more to Bethany about Silvanus, but she could not stop thinking of that night that she had spent with him, under the stars and talking of their lives to come. She had been able to be so honest and open with him, as she had been with no other person. If he was a highway robber, everything he said must have been lies. She must know the truth behind this affair, but how could she find out?

Day after grey day November slowly dragged itself to an end, and still they waited for news from their ship. The small and cramped inn at Mucking Flats became full of Captain Percy's party, which had grown over the month and each arrival had led to a short-lived rise in spirits. Eliza felt surprisingly relieved after her sister's arrival. For now, with additional young women, she could avoid being the centre of attention around the dining table, all the gentlemen, of course, being quite bedazzled by her sister Mary-Ann's beauty. Mary-Ann, of course, enjoyed every moment, and every ingratiating fragment of attention. From time to time, their uncle, Thomas Berrington, came ashore from the ship, once with letters to send, once to welcome his two nieces and once to bring a violin and violoncello for Mary-Ann and Mr Miller to play. Following this, musical interludes often broke the long winter evenings. At one such event, dismissing the applause, Mr Miller asked,

"Miss Eliza, perhaps you would care to play the violoncello? I am sure everyone would like to hear you play. Miss Eliza is an excellent player of the instrument." Mary-Ann put her instrument down and, scowling, said,

"I am sure my sister will be able to keep the key better, without me."

Thomas said, "Eliza, I did not know you were proficient on such a variety of musical instruments. I never saw you play the bass instrument at Fiddlesham."

"My mother disapproved of my playing the instrument. I occasional played at church but only when hidden away behind a screen."

"Let me assure you Eliza, that if your fortissimo is not too outrageous, your mother shall not come to hear of your playing, certainly from no one present here tonight. If you care not to perform tonight, perhaps tomorrow."

"I'll play now, Mr Miller, have you a suitable manuscript?

"The only pieces I have, Miss Eliza, are some of my copies of the German, Sebastian Bach, I believe you have seen the pieces, but they are rather difficult and strange." Eliza looked through the pieces and chose the saraband[1], as it was the only piece, she thought that she could play well enough, and which would also match her melancholic disposition. She pulled the unwieldy instrument into her skirts and checked the bow and tuning and began.

Among the dining room's audience that night, along with her sister Mary-Ann, were her cousins, Amy and Anabel; uncle Thomas; her music teacher, Mr Miller; the newly arrived fellow passenger, Mr Schwartz; and five fellow stranded travellers, who were awaiting the same Easterly wind that would stir their ships to send cutters for their passengers. None of them had heard

---

[1] Bach – Cello Suite N° 1 iv Sarabande

such music as Eliza played and they all sat in amazed silence watching and listening to the young woman play. She gave the impression, like that of an exhausted rider clinging to a horse. The young men felt quite excited and amazed by Eliza's, so unladylike, performance. As she played, Eliza could not help but think of the time in the sea, when she had watched the clouds rush by, overhead. One section would remind her of the gannet, searching high above, another of terns arriving, hovering, seeing her and darting away and the cormorant she saw approaching low over the water and veering away at the last moment. Silvanus was holding her hand while they were both floating, up and down on the rolling sea … Could he have lied to her? For once in her life, she had trusted another person but could she have been cruelly deceived? She hated him. The violoncello growled under her bow as she took out her anger and turned melancholy into rage. She stopped before the end, and there was silence. Tears flooded down her face and dripped over the music in front of her. She lay down the instrument and bow, stood and walked out of the room to a shocked silence. On the way to her room, she heard Mr Miller calling. He reached her just before she could open the door.

"Miss, please wait. May I please take a moment of your time to talk to you?" Eliza, ignoring him, opened the door and entered her room but could not close the door, Mr Miller was blocking the way."

"Please, Miss. Allow me … What a wonderful performance that was. I have never understood the Bach pieces, just too strange and modern but you … you have understood it and explained it to me. In a few moments, you have taught me more than I have ever been able to teach you in all my time as your tutor. But, Miss, I am concerned, your music does not appear to bring joy to your heart, as it once did, only a few months ago, and as it brings to the hearts of everyone who hears you play. In Madras, your playing will bring you universal admiration, and ... If I may be so bold, I am sure it would also attract many very eligible suitors."

"Mr Miller, I have no desire to play music in Madras or find a suitor, and I would point out that you are in a lady's bed chamber. Please leave. Good night to you, Mr Miller." Bethany arrived and as she stood behind Mr Miller, he could not leave.

"Well, Mr Miller, do come in and join us. I hope you are complimenting my mistress on her performance. Not that I could understand such music, but it did sound very skilful."

"I am indeed Miss. I have never heard such wonderful music played on such a simple instrument as the Violoncello. Your mistress is my mistress as well, and, as I have just explained, she, I believe, can teach us all so much by her musical performances." Mr Miller always felt uncomfortable around Bethany, never quite knowing how, or when, she was teasing. She was far too bold for his liking. Bethany, seeing Eliza's distress, sort to change the subject,

"Come Mr Miller," she said, "let us leave the subject of wondrous music playing. Tell us of your letter from your brother in India, what news is there? Eliza, you must listen I understand that Mr Miller has received a letter from his brother but its contents appear to be a secret. What scandal could it contain, I wonder?"

Mr Miller, who was only a few years older than Eliza, said that there was no secret and that he would indeed relate its contents but not now, or here, in a lady's chamber but tomorrow morning, if the opportunity arose, perhaps, following breakfast.

35 A Letter from India

The following morning, Eliza, having nothing better to fill her time, no other place to sit, and having awoke in a calmer frame of mind than yesterday, joined the others in the only large room in the inn, which served as breakfast, drawing and dining room. As word passed around the assembled, and delayed, travellers that young Miller had a letter from India, and all having a desire to hear as much as possible from their intended destination, the room, now referred to as the withdrawing room, was filled.

Eliza's music teacher, Edward Miller and his older brother, Thomas, were the sons of a well-known organist and music scholar, William Miller of Doncaster. The father had some years earlier written to Captain Percy seeking to purchase a passage to India for his younger son, Thomas, who, after living in London for a year, had fallen into bad company and debt. The organist had hoped that more favourable opportunities might present themselves in India for his son. Thomas had travelled on Captain Percy's previous voyage to India as a midshipman and had shared a cabin with the captain's son, Welstan. On arrival the two young men, one with investment skills and the other musical talent, had gone into business together. Whilst Thomas performed his music at various grand houses, estates and palaces for the Anglo-Indian elite, Welstan Percy would accompany him to the venues and take the opportunity to explore various financial investments. Welstan's talents for business, however, did not reach the heights of his friend's musical prowess and as time went on, in attempts to recoup his numerous financial losses; Welstan's transactions had crossed the frontier between sound investment and reckless gambling.

"Before I read this letter from my brother, I must warn the ladies that it is written as one brother to another and does contain some news that ladies here may find upsetting." This prelude to the main performance intrigued his audience, who fell immediately and completely silent.

My dearest brother Edward,

I write in haste with every hope that I shall find an officer of the Company returning to England, who will be happy to transport this letter home, and that it will reach you before your departure at the end of the year.
What a colourful, exotic, enchanting and extremely hot place this is. I must tell you that a man with any musical talent can make a considerable fortune in this land by performing no more than once a week.
In the first nine months of my time here, it seemed that I was sort out by every house in the land. I would like to tell you that this was because of my musical performing competence, but I fear I should point out to you that, unlike London, where my talent was but a drop in the ocean, here, in India, it is like a flood in a parched land, because there are very few European musicians. You will succeed very well here I am sure my dearest brother, and I look forward to seeing you again as soon as wind and ocean currents permit.
Now for some joyous news: I have been fortunate enough to have been introduced to a young lady by the name Harriet Templar, whose father, George Templar, is a man of note in Madras having amassed a

considerable fortune in the trade of elephants, yes elephants. These animals are ubiquitous in this land and employed, not only as oxen are in England, but often in situations in which horses might be at home. I have fallen in love and hope that marriage will soon follow.

Alas, it is in this matter that my following account has proved so upsetting. On the outward-bound journey with Captain Percy and Mr Berrington, I shared a cabin with, and became a close friend of the captain's son Welstan Percy. I had, on several occasions helped him with introductions to several prosperous people, for whom I had the pleasure to perform, and on one occasion invested a little capital in one of Welstan's business ventures involving the importation of cheese from England. Unfortunately, this made very little profit, as many cheeses proved not to survive the Indian climate. You can imagine, therefore, that I was rather reluctant to invest in another project that Welstan presented. This concerned the purchase of a ship, hiring a sea captain and a merchant, filling the vessel with goods and dispatching it on a cruise of the Coast and Bay trading as it went. Against my initial misgivings, Welstan persuaded me, as a friend, to invest all my money, and some considerable extra, taken out against my good name, in the venture. Welstan had suggested that the only dangers to a ship in such coastal seas were from storms, but if we sent the ship during the summer season, there would only be a minimal risk. The captain and merchant were chosen by Welstan, who felt that owing to his father's seafaring experience he must have inherited some of his maritime judgement. This proved not to be the case and the captain and merchant took their first opportunity to take the ship and its cargo to China where they sold everything, including the ship, and disappeared without trace. We have, only a matter of days ago, learnt about this from a native crewmember, who returned here on another ship to re-join his family and spread the word of his master's deception.

You can imagine how distraught I now am. Not only penniless, but I shall be so for some considerable time to come, but, and by far the worst result of this duplicity, is that the prospect of Mr Templar agreeing to the marriage of his daughter to a near destitute musician, are very small; the love of my life is lost and my life ruined.

Please Edward, tell our father only what you believe will not upset him too greatly.

I wish you a very safe and satisfactory journey,

Your ever-respectful brother,

Thomas Miller

Thomas Berrington approached Mr Miller shortly after he had read his brother's letter and said, in his far from brief manner,

"Rest assured, young man, that at the moment Captain Percy has been made cognoscente of all the relevant facts relating to, and apropos of, this failed venture into which your brother was apparently and reluctantly cajoled, resulting in such a tragic loss, I feel sure he will make every effort to use his considerable influence to rectify the matter."

36   Soup

Eliza's mother had instructed Bethany to always accompany her daughter, especially if she happened to be in a situation where she might wander or get into some mischief. So, when Eliza took advantage in a break in the gloomy weather to take a walk, Bethany accompanied her.

"What a sad story that Mr Miller has unfolded," Eliza said, "Recent events have unsettled my belief in the authenticity of what men say, or do. I cannot believe, however, that my brother, Welstan, would embroil the young man in a financially dubious scheme. I am sure it is not all as it appears from that letter. Welstan is, after all, a Gentlemen."

Bethany had not been surprised by the content of the letter from India; Welstan would remain in her eyes a despicable self-serving young man who saw everything to his own gratification.

"Gentleman, Miss? He may lay claim to the title of 'gentleman', because he is from a family of land and wealth but I wonder if that epithet should not be earned, rather than merely inherited." Eliza stopped walking, although they had not reached the end of the wooden quay, which was their usual turning place. She was surprised and annoyed by Bethany's outburst.

"Why are you being so wicked about my brother, have you fallen prone to the ideas from those American revolutionaries and that man Thomas Payne? What has Welstan ever done to you? Of course, he is a gentleman." Bethany refused to answer Eliza's question and walked on past the little flat-bottomed fishing boat sitting on the mud, and onto the end of the quay, where she lent over the iron railing, looking at the expanse of mud stretching to the horizon, which presumably gave it the name, Mucking Flats.

Eliza caught up, and standing by Bethany's side said,

"Maybe you have some sort of explanation, Bethany. If not, I will accept an apology."

Bethany could not and would not apologise for her views of Eliza's brother. However, she could not come to tell her mistress what had happened, and what her brother was really like. Then she remembered that she was no longer a governess but now a companion, and, had not her travelling companion here, only yesterday, told her how upset she had been that someone had lied to her?

"Very well, Miss. I will tell you the truth about your brother. Before I do, I ask your forgiveness for the upset this will course you, but it is nothing more than the truth of the matter.

There was a seat on the quay sheltered from the breeze by a wooden screen. The two women sat down and Bethany told Eliza, the facts of Welstan's rape. Eliza was shocked and, for a moment it looked like tears might be forming in her eyes. Bethany immediately regretted telling her and decided that she would address the balance, and perhaps teach her recent student a lesson of life. She told Eliza of the incident of the gardener's shears and how, a few weeks after Welstan's attack, she had deliberately not barricaded her bedchamber and when he entered suggested that he should undress and lay naked on the bed. Then she produced the shears, borrowed from Esau, and held them to Welstan's genitals. She told him not to move, while she used the shears to shred his clothes. Then, she sent him naked back to his bedroom, unfortunately he did not arrive at his room before he had been seen by Molly, whose screams brought James with his blunderbuss, racing up the stairs. Following that, he had attempted to pass the blame on to Bethany concerning a missing gold ring belonging to Mrs Percy. Luckily, Bethany had found the ring in her own bedroom box before the searchers came. It had presumably be placed there by Welstan while she was elsewhere. She had had to carry it around in her pocket all that day until she could find a safe place, near Mrs Percy's room, to drop it.

"That is what he was up to," Eliza said, "I overheard the maids discussing the event and assumed that it was some below stairs gossip that Molly had invented. I even scolded her for lying. Poor Molly, I would make it up to her, but then she left the house … after becoming pregnant with a bastard child … Oh, do you think …"

"I am sure Welstan was the father of Molly's bastard child," said Bethany, "and that is why he was sent to India. Your mother considered that her son's 'indiscretions,' as she called them, would go unnoticed in Madras."

"Unfortunately, it's a pity Molly did not have access to your shears, Bethany."

"Maybe I should have lopped off the offending organ when I had the opportunity," said, Bethany.

"On reaching my womanhood," said Eliza, "Mother had supplied me with the keys to the harpsichord. After hearing your woeful tale, I am inclined to think that every mother should supply her daughter with a pair garden shears." The two women walked back to the little fishing boat, where a couple of fishermen were sitting around, and cooking upon, a small iron stove. A warm fishy smell arose,

"What are you cooking, my man?" asked Bethany.

"Crabs, Miss," said the older of the two, who Bethany guessed was the younger one's father.

"Crabs, is it?"

"Crabs and a little flounder, Miss"

"Crabs and a little flounder?"

"Crabs and a little flounder and a few whelks."

"Crabs and a little flounder and a few whelks, is that the sum of it?"

"Yes, Miss, apart from the addition of a small eel. Would you care for a little soup, Miss?"

"Certainly, if you please, now I know that it contains a little eel," said Bethany. The son ladled out two wooden bowlfuls of the steaming fish stew and passed them up to the two women, together with two wooden spoons.

"Leave the bowls anywhere on the path to the inn, Miss, we'll be sure to find 'em."

Bethany, found some coins in her purse and said, "Will fourpence serve for your delicious smelling fish?"

"No, Miss. Begging your pardon but it is the last of the day's catch, we have sold the rest to the inn, where you're lodging. It is custom in these parts for fishermen to share the last of the days catch freely with any hungry person. Thus, bringing luck and good fortune to the morrow's fishing."

The two-woman sat and ate the soup. "Is your faith now restored in the honesty and kindness of some of mankind, Miss?" Bethany asked, pointing with her spoon towards the two men in the boat, before refilling her mouth with more steaming fishy pieces.

"I thought so, Bethany but now I see that this 'crabs, a little flounder and a few whelks ... oh, and a little eel, does, in fact, also contain several oysters. Men, they cannot utter one truthful word but that they follow it with an untruth." They both laughed, and it was not until later, in her wakeful hours of darkness, that Eliza regretted that this friendship had only arisen from their shared experiences of despicable men and that one of them was Eliza's own brother.

37 Sparrows

If Silvanus were to have stretched out his arms, he could have spanned the width of his cell; if he had put his feet against the door, his shoulders would have touched the opposite wall and if he had stood up, his head would have hit the ceiling. He did none of these things, because of the wrist irons and restraining chain that kept him near the floor. In the far wall there was a narrow slit, six inches from the ground, which let some rays of light and a trickle of air into his otherwise dark and filthy cell. If he scraped the filth from the floor, and laid himself on the ground, he could see through the slit into a public courtyard, which led from the street to the prison entrance. Sometimes, a lost breeze, trapped in the courtyard, would swirl around and bring him the faint scent of the countryside or newly fallen rain. Occasionally he saw a couple of sparrows bathing in a puddle in the courtyard. It seemed to Silvanus that sparrows have too much to say, constantly chattering about … what, he wondered? But then, he supposed, they must get through their lifetime's chatter in such a short time because they have such brief lives. His time, he thought, had almost run its course. He usually thought of himself as sanguine by nature but in here, in the gloom of his cell, misery seemed to be the only thing he had in ample supply. He tried to dispel his gloom by conjuring up pleasant memories but then anguish would fill his mind and he would fall into despair, which swirled around inside his mind, like the disturbing and sudden chill breezes in the courtyard. It seemed there was nothing he could do to rid himself of this foreboding. If he had known how short his own life was to be, he might have chattered as much as these little birds. A bowl of water and a lump of bread came through the door hatch once each day. At first, he had used a few crumbs to attract, the sparrows back to his little window but his hunger soon outweighed his longing for company. After ten days, a strange thing happened, he ceased to crave his daily bread supply and the need for company, albeit only tiny chattering sparrows, became paramount.

"Tell me little sparrows, what have I done to bring my life to such an early end and in such a dreadful manner as this?"

He had always carefully planned his life, so as not to insult other souls, and offer no offence but the world had conspired to bring him to this place, and this end. He was beginning to realise that his downfall, and recent liaison with Miss Percy, were most likely connected. John Butterworth had suggested as much, whilst they were waiting in the prison open area before they were locked in their own separate cells. Silvanus asked him,

"What have I done to you to cause you to abuse me so, my friend?"

"Curtis, don't look towards I. Those who offend powerful sea Captains and the likes, must expect swift and dreadful punishment."

They were the last words he had heard from Butterworth and the last words spoken to him directly. Since being in this cell, he had exchanged not a word, except with the sparrows. He sat in a corner of the cell upon some rotten straw that had once been a mattress. He held his knees pressed against his chest, closed his eyes and tried with all his might to think that he was elsewhere; of swimming in the ocean, waves being stirred up by some distant storm arriving and passing him by, lifting him … lifting her. Two swimmers being lifted and lowered gently down again. Eliza singing,

"Il pleut, il pleut, bergère, Presse tes blancs moutons …"

'What are you singing, what does it mean, Miss?'

'I'll attempt to sing it in English, the best I can …

"It is raining, it is raining, shepherdess,

Hurry your white sheep, Let's go to my cottage,

Shepherdess, quickly, come along …"

He had never been as happy as at that moment. It is a fine yardstick of fulfilment, of happiness, he thought, when a person feels as one with another person. For years he had felt contented, but not until that moment had he felt happiness. For that, he had had to escape from the land, float in the sea, in storm-driven waves and risk his life and the life of a young lady. He had been overwhelmed by the moment and taken up by Eliza's openness. Yes, he knew it was dangerous. He had considered the waves and cold sea was as nothing, compared to the dangers he faced by entering that liaison with Eliza, Miss Percy, the daughter of Captain Percy and the powerful estate owning Percy family. Little did he think that it would lead him so swiftly to the gallows. He remembered his mother saying, behave like that and you will end up on the gallows. His mother, there was someone with whom he had been as one. Joined to his mother's hip until the day they came to evict them from their house. His father had protested, and their cottage burnt down. So young and foolish, had Silvanus been, that he laughed and danced as he watched the flames leap from their roof. Then he had looked up at his mother's face in the firelight, and seen her tears of despair. His father had used what little money he had received for his three cattle, to arrange an apprenticeship for him in Portsmouth. Four years later, on a return visit one Christmas, he had learnt that his infant sister and mother had died of the same illness. From then until his moment in the sea with Miss Percy, he been alone in the world. After that swim, they had sat by the fire, warming under a blanket. She taught him the French song. He had roasted a whole duck, which he had caught a few days earlier. They warmed some ale by the fire and drank it by the light of the fire. He had suggested several times that he should escort her home but she had insisted that no one would miss her. Her father being too busy with matters of a forthcoming voyage to India, and her mother having little regard for the whereabouts of her errant daughter. Miss Bethany would know she was not in the house, but she would probably take the opportunity to drink more of her father's port, rather than report her absence. They had stayed huddled together under the blankets, drinking the beer and talking about everything under the sun. They climbed to the top of the shingle spit to watch the orange glow break over the horizon and slowly bring an end to the wonderful night.

Here in the filth of his Chichester prison cell, he heard the town clock strike seven, it would soon be time for food. He felt in his pocket and found a few coins. Perhaps he could pay the prison guard to speak to him, tell him what was happening, how long had he to live, was it hours, weeks or months?

He could hear keys opening the door at the end of a corridor and footsteps approaching, two pairs. He watched the sliding panel at the foot of the door, waiting for it to open. He was ready with his fourpence. But the sliding panel did not open. Instead, a key turned in the cell door lock and the door opened and the diminutive figure of the prison guard entered with another man, whose face Silvanus could not see because of the unaccustomed brightness of the guard's lantern. The stranger's hat, wig, jacket and shining shoe buckles told Silvanus that this must be a gentleman.

"Again, we meet by lantern light Mr Curtis, Strothmann Greedy at your service. I bring you news of an offer which I think you will agree could possibly prove to your advantage, Sir. An initial piece of information, which I am sure you are aware of, Sir, is to the effect that you were not hanged this morning." He paused, wallowing in satisfaction at his platitude, "but I must inform you that your associate, Butterworth was not so fortunate. The timing and place of your execution have been rearranged and were to take place at Horsham on the first Saturday of next month. Notwithstanding this, Captain Percy's representative has approached me to intercede in this matter. The good captain is of an enlightened opinion in matters of the world such as this, and also, his property having been returned, and considering all the relevant intelligence concerning your case, he feels that you might be made an offer that would avoid you bothering the hangman. You will be listed aboard one of His Majesty's Prison ships and transported to a penal colony for a period of fifteen years. In return for this, you will be pardoned for your crimes, after completing the fifteen years. Should you at any time, before being released, attempt to escape, the death sentence will be reinstated and you will be hanged. Do you understand?"

Silvanus signed the papers and two days later was transferred to a larger, shared cell. At the beginning of November, he was taken out of prison to join another man, similarly pardoned in a contract between the mayor of Horsham and the Navy. The escort guards threaded a chain through Silvanus's wrist irons and the two prisoners, with two guards, marched off towards Portsmouth.

38   Muffit

December 1785 – Portsmouth

Silvanus's fellow prisoner looked no older than a boy. He told Silvanus his name was Muffit and swore blind that he had not stolen the linen nightshirts, walnut encased mirror and two silver buckles, for which he had been sentenced. He claimed the maid had taken the goods and sold them to a porn broker who was a friend of the maid.

The journey to Portsmouth took the whole day and most of the night. Much of the journey seemed to be sitting around waiting for one or the other of the guards to come out of an inn. They never passed a single drinking house that they did not enter. By the time it had started to get dark, the two guards could hardly walk and progress was slow. Muffit said that he was desperate to escape and that he would kill the two guards, get the keys to their chains and both could make their escape.

"It's going to be a dark night, no moon. We'll have an advantage but I need your assistance." Silvanus did not believe the risk worth it. If he was caught escaping, he would have his death sentence reinstated.

"If one of these guards gets killed, and we're caught, which is very likely, I am bound to hang. I want to escape but there'll be better chances ahead. Let's bide our time."

"Are you married, Curtis?"
"No."

"Well, I am, five months wed and a little'n on the way. What will 'appen to them if I don't get back?"

One of the guards returned from the inn, the other gripped the chain, pulled the two prisoners to their feet and led them off along the road into the darkness. Muffit was in front of Silvanus and the older man could see the younger man was getting nervous, looking around and nodding in encouragement to Silvanus. He was about to ruin everything. The guards were drunk but they were old hands experienced and would not be easy to overcome by two manacled men. Silvanus would have to stop Muffit. The young man started to pick up the chain between him and the guard in front, which meant he could get close enough to be in striking distance. Silvanus's chain pulled as Muffit made his move but Silvanus pulled back and being bigger and stronger pulled Muffit off his feet. The guard behind shouted a warning to the front guard and had his musket pointing at Silvanus, while the front guard had his cutlass at Muffit's throat."

"Pardon, 'twas my fault, I tripped and pulled the lad over. Sorry, sorry, Sir. Let me help him to his feet."

The guard at the rear relaxed his grip on his musket, in readiness to return the weapon to his shoulder but the one in front was not done with Muffit yet.

"Learn to stay on 'e feet or I'll slice an ear off, do you hear?" To reinforce his threat, he kicked Muffit in the ribs and jumped back with his hanger raised.

At Portsmouth, a cutter took Silvanus and Muffit out to a press-smack, a dismasted ship named Pegasus, used as a holding vessel, which was moored in a quiet backwater. They climbed a steep stairway built onto the side of the ship that led onto the gundeck filled, not with guns, but prison cells and cabins. From there, they climbed down through the orlop deck to the hold below the waterline, which had no headroom to stand up straight in and just a few rays of light filtering through the bars of the grills from the deck above. As Silvanus's eyes became accustomed to this gloom, he realised that there was something like a hundred men crowded into the compartment. Some chained, others apparently free to move about and everywhere it was wet and filthy. The smell was making Silvanus want to retch. He learnt that the shackled men had attempted to escape, offended the guards or just looked as though they might cause trouble. They took one look at Muffit and put chains on his legs, the guards must have recognised something in his manner, but they waved Silvanus through. Each day the guards took the unchained men to the top deck and marched them around the ship for exercise and fresh air. The sky above, even when grey or filled with rain, was a blessed relief for the white-faced and sickly men. Silvanus could see the shore. It was no more than a couple of hundred yards away but there was thick, strong netting from the gunwales up to the rigging completely enclosing the deck. He could see no easy possibility of jumping ship even if he could have managed the swim ashore. Every few days the clerks called out the names of men to be taken off the ship, while at the same time, others arrived. Then, on the sixteenth day the guard read out, Lavender Muffit and Silvanus Curtis's names, together with four others. On the top deck, a couple of midshipmen interrogated them, asking about any skills they might have that would serve the King. Silvanus told them about his coopering. This tallied with the orderly's ledger book and so a blacksmith attached manacles, together with an iron cannon ball, to Silvanus's and Muffit's wrists. The midshipmen led them down the stairway to a waiting cutter, each man carrying their own iron ball. The four pressed men, together with four sailors, a midshipman and two Royal Marines, set out in a cutter across the harbour. It was a misty and wet day but Silvanus was pleased enough to be off the hulk and in the fresh air. It felt almost as good as being free. They all sat three to a seat and crouched as low as they could in the boat to escape the cold wind. Silvanus sat in the middle of the foremost seat. Muffit was sitting to his left. In the light of day, Silvanus realised how young he was, no more than sixteen. He leaned towards Silvanus and whispered,

"I'm gonna swim for it, Curtis. You coming? Two targets; it's a better chance."

"You'll drown; believe me, the chain and shot are too heavy. Don't do it, think of your baby."

"I am, and my pretty, Hattie."

"If we swim on our backs, hold the ball on our stomachs. It'll be fine. Look, the bootnecks are 'alf asleep. Muskets on their backs. By the time they've primed them, we'll be ashore. When the cutter gets to that point over there. See, there's an overhanging tree, good cover for when we get out. It's only twenty yards. Come on man. What 'e got to lose? Do 'e want to spend fifteen years being starved and flogged in some god-forsaken place on other side of the world?"

"Of course not," said Silvanus, "I want to escape as much as you but the chances of success are not good enough. The shot's far too heavy. I know about weighting timber down in ponds. The shot is more than a man can swim with it's crazy."

"You're scared, Curtis, too scared."

"You there," said the midshipman, "no talking, or you'll get a rope's end across your mouth." The midshipman pulled his collar up and his hat down and did not appear very committed to his threat. They reached the overhanging tree, and Muffit nudged Silvanus, winked and suddenly jumped up, pushing one of the oarsmen backwards off his seat and causing confusion in the boat. One startled marine jumped to his feet, causing the boat to rock and tip and water to wash in over the gunwale. The marines could not load their muskets because they were busy grabbing the gunwale to stop falling in. Turning around, Muffit leapt backwards off the boat, holding his iron ball across his chest. The marines, still surprised, did nothing. Silvanus stood up, lifting his iron ball and for a moment thought of following the boy by jumping into the sea, perhaps he could do it but then the midshipman shouted,

"Sit down there. Marines, ready your muskets."

Muffit was doing well, he had put the iron ball in his jacket, so could scull backwards while kicking his legs, as best he could with chains on them. He was making headway towards the tree, not more than a dozen yards away, when the two other prisoners began shouting,

"Swim lad, you can do it." However, the marines' hours of training began to show and they had their muskets loaded, barking their replies,

"Ready to fire, Sir."

"Ready to fire, Sir."

The midshipman, held his hand up but then thought better of this course of action and called out,

"Stop or we'll shoot."

Then a strange thing happened. Muffit stopped kicking … and vanished … without a struggle he was gone from sight. Not even a ripple or bubble left on the surface of the sea where he had been. It was as though he had never been there. The prisoners' shouting stopped and all was silent apart from one oarsman, who muttered,

"Bloody idiot, trying to swim in chains. What'n earth were 'e finking?" The oarsmen manoeuvred the cutter back to where they thought Muffit had sunk but the sea was so murky, no one could see more than an inch below the surface. Two of the sailors tried poking around with their oars but after a few minutes, the midshipman ordered that they continue their journey.

"Perhaps," thought Silvanus, "Muffit deliberately went under the water, turned himself over and came up, out of site, beyond that tree trunk. It was overhanging far enough. Silvanus turned around to look back at the tree but it was now out of sight. The noise of the seashore returned, a dozen nearby gulls began to cry out, probably squabbling over a discarded mullet head. Two oystercatchers flew overhead with a startled cry and somewhere a lone curlew called.

Was this how it was going to be with him? Silvanus thought, every time an opportunity of escape arose, he would choose discretion over valour. Perhaps he was no man of action. He'd have to face it; he'll never see Eliza again. His mood plunged under a press of old memories: the house on fire, sparks, him dancing and his mother crying.

"Oh Eliza, where are you?"

39   Bucket

Boarding Captain Percy's East Indiaman bound for India

After several weeks with nothing to do, other than eat breakfast, walk to the fisherman's pier and enquire as to the contents of the day's soup, there was a sudden bout of activity, which took everyone by surprise. The wind was at last favourable and Captain Percy, having positioned the ship as far easterly as he could, wanted to stay ahead of the fleet of awaiting ships, which might at any time up anchor and be in sight. He had been obliged to tack back and forth across the estuary and then to make headway around Kent to the Downs. The captain would have much preferred a horizon free from other vessels.

It was early on a misty Christmas Eve when they boarded their ship's cutter. Eliza felt in good spirits that day. She had slept little and had instead thought through her situation. Sometime during the night, which she had spent with Silvanus in his camp, they had sworn undying loyalty to one another. It had seemed so important then. She had decided that she would love Silvanus forever, until the sands of time run dry. Then, much to Eliza's shame, as soon as Bethany had mentioned that she thought Silvanus had been arrested, and put on trial, she had forgotten her oath and was quite willing to accept Silvanus as a liar and cheat. How could she? She was ashamed of herself. Now she understood that there was no possible way Silvanus could have been lying to her. He was obviously not a robber and could be guilty of no crime. Eliza must now make recompense, if possible. She must escape from this voyage, return to Sussex and find Silvanus. If it proved to be a fact that he had been hanged, then she would arrange a similar, premature end to her own life. This plan satisfied her. But how she was to execute it, was another matter entirely.

Not long after their cutter cast off, it appeared that they were bounded on all sides by a thick sea mist, which had rolled in from the east.

"Uncle Thomas, how will we find our ship in such weather conditions as these?" asked Eliza.

Berrington replied, "Our coxswain here has a compass, if it should prove necessary and ... Huh ha! Right on time. Did you hear that? The ship's bell. Knowing that we are on the return leg of our journey to collect passengers, and taking note of the changing weather conditions, Mr Congleton, second mate, has ordered that our ship's bell be rung three times every sixth of an hour."

After another hour of rowing, the bell sounded very close. Then out of the mist, and as if from nowhere, the ship appeared. A simultaneous gasp seemed to come from every one of the passengers as they tried to take in the size of the vessel. Eliza had seen many paintings and sketches of large ships, and on a few occasions seen them in the distance at Portsmouth, but she never imagined the reality of their size, now they were close and the ship towering above their tiny cutter, it appeared truly immense. The sailors raised their oars at a command from the coxswain allowing the boat to glide gently up to the floating platform below the stairs. The cutter, having been secured, they were helped onto the platform and then, three at a time, stepped into a large wicker basket. The gate was closed and fastened, and, following some shouted instructions, the whole contraption began to rise. Pulled up from the yardarm. Once high enough, the yard arm swung inboard and the men working the capstan reversed their steps to lower the ladies onto the deck. This was the ship, which would be their home for the next five months. The men working on the capstan sang and looked like they had been doing this work, and living this life, forever.

"Miss, this is Solomon," said Thomas to Eliza, "he plays a fine fiddle. The men call him the shanty-man. Perhaps you and he might play for the officers and passengers one evening?"

Solomon was standing by the capstan and playing a fiddle in time with the men's footsteps around the capstan. Other men were shouting from high above in the rigging and officers and men calling crisp instructions, the former to the latter. The captain stood on the highest part of the deck, looking this way, and that way, and appearing far too busy to acknowledge the arrival of a few passengers, even if they were his close family.

"Miss," said Eliza's uncle Thomas again, "look above, the topmen are ready to unfurl the sails. Lord be praised we are on our way to Madras."

Thomas directed Eliza and Bethany to the far end of the upper deck, where they were told that they may stay to watch the great ship get underway but that they should not move from that part of the upper deck area, which had been allocated for the use of ladies to take the air. The space was no more than six feet by two feet. Uncle Thomas, or Mr Berrington, as he asked to be called, now that he was aboard his ship, said that it would be of some assistance if the ladies would care to look over the stern, to keep watch for the following flotilla of ships rounding the bend in the Thames estuary. Bethany was unaware that Mr Berrington had posted lookouts high in the mainmast, whose keen eyes, and altitude, meant that they would be far more likely to spot approaching sails before any at deck level. But the first mate thought, it might possibly engage the ladies. The anchor was still being weighed and many sails still had to be unfurled, when a cold easterly wind forced the ladies down below.

An hour after sunset, Eliza and her travelling companion felt their whole world lean over as the ship unexpectedly healed over to a starboard tack. The novelty of attempting to walk on a floor, which, although looking perfectly normal, was out of kilter with their sense of balance, entertained them for a while, until it was time to prepare for dinner. Eliza and Bethany had one extremely small cabin, next door was Eliza's sister and two of her cousins. Both cabins were next to the captain's cabin. In fact, they were part of the captain's cabin. The large area, usually assigned to the captain had been partitioned off to accommodate the ladies during the long voyage. For dining, the ladies only needed to move next door to the captain's cabin proper, where the table had been set.

The officers, being much occupied in 'getting underway,' would not be joining them until later. Eliza and Bethany sat at the table with Eliza's sister Mary-Ann, her insufferably silent cousins, a very nervous Miss Anne Mansell and Miss Mary Haggard; both of the latter returning to their families in Madras. There was also, Mr George Schwartz, Mr Miller and several midshipmen, who were passengers but had to be treated as employees to explain their reduced passenger fees. Some were on board to satisfy plans of the captain's, others to fulfil a promise by the captain to an old acquaintance or business partner and some were company employees to whom the captain felt particularly beholding. Much to Eliza's chagrin, Mary-Ann soon became centre of attention for the young men. Eliza thought, they just cannot help themselves from falling under her spell. As Eliza watched her younger sister, coyly answer their questions about her intentions, her opinions on Madras and her view on this and her judgement on that, Eliza tried to imagine what her sister would look like with small pox scars, or an enormous nose or … red hair. It was while studying her thus, she noticed her sister had turned very pale, and was not responding to her table full of young admirers. Unexpectedly, she stood up, quickly followed by all the men around the table rising to their feet as well. The captain's steward had seen the look on Mary-Ann's face and knew exactly what was about to happen. He had been at sea for long enough, and had seen that very same look on other passengers, and even officers' faces, over the years. He rushed forward with an especially reserved bucket. Mary-Ann, in anticipation of this voyage to India had prepared herself for nightly male admiration but had not considered this. She was not accustomed to the feeling of nausea. She looked shocked initially, then surprised and lastly, she tried her best to look angry. It became obvious, to all around the table, that she was about to vomit and all were offering, what became a broadside of suggestions but she refused to place her head in a bucket. Mr Berrington took the situation in hand,

"Begging your pardon, Miss, if you would allow me," and saying that, he put the bucket on the table and with one hand on the back of Mary-Ann's neck, pushed her head into the bucket. The midshipmen, not knowing what to say in such cases, accompanied each of Mary-Ann's heaves with a 'hoorah' or 'well done.'

Bethany said to Eliza, it reminded her of the Chichester harvest fair when the crowds cheer on the young men trying to ride on the back of greased pigs.

Having finished, Mary-Ann's head removed from the bucket, the steward - Tom Fluck - gave his young passenger a cloth to wipe away the peas, pieces of carrot and fresh sole, but Mary-Ann appeared to be in shock. Fluck came to the rescue again and wiped the mess from Mary-Ann's face and an ungainly number of midshipmen offered to help her sit down.

Eliza now appeared in better spirits than she had shown for some time, saying how much she had enjoyed the meal. Bethany agreed it was delicious and added,

"Poor Mary-Ann. I would swear that sole on her face came from the very same bucket we saw this morning on the fisherman's quay at Mucking Flats."

Eliza agreed, "And I do believe she vomited a little eel, as well."

40   Nawab

Dinner, aboard Captain Percy's East Indiaman ship, followed a regular pattern. The ladies, and most of the midshipmen, would dine first and soon after the arrival of the captain and officers, the ladies would leave the dining table by way of a small room, which led to the aft of the roundhouse. They would then make their way around the back of the ship to their own cabins. A couple of days into the voyage, Eliza thought she would attempt to gain more information, in the hope that she might see an opportunity to escape the ship while it was relatively close to the English shore. Accordingly, when they all left the table, she lagged behind. Mary-Ann, ahead of Eliza, paused, turned and said, "Eliza, we are to return to our cabins, do come along, sister."

"I choose to wait here for a while. Run along now little girl." Eliza wanted to listen to her father talking to his officers. She might glean something more of her father's plans and the ship's itinerary. such extra information, she hoped, no matter how small and apparently insignificant, might help in some way to improve her prospects of finding a means of escape.

In the wall of the roundhouse, in a dark corner, there was a small sliding shutter, which Eliza quietly half opened in order to be able to peer through. Her father, with his back to her and reclining on his chair, was beckoning the steward, to fill the gentlemen's glasses,

"Mr Schwartz, you have interests, property and business in Madras, I believe?" The men around the table turned towards the object of the captain's question, Mr Schwartz, who was sitting at the far end of the dining table and facing Eliza's spyhole. Since joining the ship, Mr Schwartz had spoken hardly a word and now that it appeared he would, he gave the impression of being intensely unhappy about the prospect. He raised his bearded chin and pointed nose, squinted through his bloodshot eyes and then added to this disagreeable aspect by preceding his reply with a strange throat clearing affair, which sounded reminded Eliza of a hen, cook had once despatched. Those around the table looked apprehensive and were quickly losing all hope that Mr Schwartz might prove the witty after dinner conversationalist whom they had all wished for to lighten the boredom of such a long journey. It looked to Eliza that this fowl was about to regurgitate something disagreeable before being put out of his misery.

"I have been commissioned by Colonel Mordant, of the East India Company in the court of Nawab Wazir of Oudh." Mr Schwartz spoke with the accent of a man who had stumbled upon the English language late in life, and not as one who had recently acquired the German accent as a fashionable affectation, which had become quite common among the aspiring ranks, who, having learnt of the royal family's Hanoverian accent, thought of it as the height of sophistication rather than a weakness. Mr Berrington joined the conversation,

"I have heard that the courts held by the Nawab of Oudh are amazing affairs, full of music, drinking, gambling and …Err, lechery?"

"Rather like some officer's cabin when this ship is in port, what, Mr Berrington?" the captain jested.

"Indeed, Sir. Although you are always welcome to join us on such occasions."

"I do not know if you are aware, Mr Schwartz, but we were privileged to have Mr Zoffany, the painter, aboard this ship for part of a previous voyage to Madras. I understand that he has been very successful since arriving in India and indeed has been commissioned by the Governor General to produce a likeness of the very prince of whom you speak. As a matter of fact …"

"Asaf-ud-daula is the Nawab Wazir of Oudh , Sir," said Schwartz.

"As you say, Mr Schwartz," agreed Berrington, "Perhaps we may be fortunate enough to see Mr Zoffany's work on arrival in India," Mr Berrington asked,

"The Nawab does not disapprove of gambling then, Mr Schwartz?"

"Not at all. To the contrary, Sir, he relishes and encourages all manner of gaming, especially cock fighting." said Schwartz.

"How interesting, Mr Schwartz, "said the captain with the look of someone with a mouthful of over-ripe pear.

Mr Berrington said, "I have heard that gambling on the outcome of cockerel fights is very popular among the lower orders in London. However,

"Not only London, Mr Berrington," said the captain, "why, I understand that even in Chichester there is a pit at the rear of one of the taverns, and that all manner of footpads and agitators attend the events and so much drink is taken that fights often break out causing the local people to fear for their lives. I heard that just a short while ago the Justice of the Peace in Chichester had to threaten to close the tavern if the practice was not brought to a swift end."

Mr Berrington asked, "Mr Schwartz, I understand that you have on board some special cargo. Livestock, is it not?"

Schwartz cleared his throat,

"Yah, that is, correct."

"Livestock?" asked the captain, "There is more livestock, in addition to Mr Fluck's hens and Mr Congleton's flock of sheep?" Mr Congleton, who had just arrived at the captain's table, said,

"Hardly a flock Sir, at the last count there were one less than half a dozen. Unless Mr Fluck has served one up tonight." the captain continued,

"Mr Schwartz, I was not aware you had livestock on board. We are quickly becoming a vessel that Noah would recognise. Now, if you were to ask me to name the one thing that Madras had a sufficiency of, I would have answered, livestock! Fowl, not to mention cattle are all over the streets and not a herdsman in sight."

There was an uncomfortable silence, for a moment, which Mr Berrington broke with,

"Well, sir, pray help us here, what manner of a beast have you brought on board? Some new breed, I venture?"

Schwartz gave a particularly long rendition of his throat clearance and eventually said,

"Sir, I am having on board my very big cock, to show in the Nawab's court." There was an outbreak of shuffling by the midshipmen

"You understand that in India they have only small cocks. So, I am taking my big cock for the Colonel to wager against the Nawab's cock." Silence fell over the table, as the older men looked at the younger ones, daring them to laugh. The captain, rather bored with the puffed-up silence from the midshipmen decided to test their resolve and with an immaculate straight face, which he prided himself was the result of generations of breeding, said,

"And how big is your cock, Sir?" This brought about the captain's hoped-for outcome, being just too much for one midshipman, whose swollen cheeks burst with a sound like a wheezing pig. The dam broke amongst the men and led to an outbreak of snorting and guffawing all around, which the captain thought to cover by refilling his officer's glasses.

"I also have twelve gamecocks and twenty-four hens," said Mr Schwartz. The German, who never felt able to understand what Englishmen found to laugh about, tried to impress upon his audience the importance of his mission by adding,

"The East India Company is anxious to retain the Nawab's support. The Nawab likes very much the fighting and the gambling with his cock and will often wager thousands of rupees on his, against any other man's cock." This did not help quell the laughter of the group of men, who, although in large part regarded themselves as gentlemen, also saw themselves as sailors.

"Mr Miller, could we ask that you play us some of your steadfast music before these men become uncontrollable?" asked the captain.

"Certainly Sir, I shall fetch my instrument?"

Miller arose and, whilst glasses were refilled, yet again, he went into the anteroom where Eliza was sitting,

"Oh, excuse me, Miss Percy; may I be of assistance in any way?"

"Thank you, Mr Miller, but that will not be necessary."

"My flute," he said, pointing to a case on the table behind Eliza. She moved to one side.

"Mr Miller, I am filled with expectancy at hearing you play but may I ask, that you do not concern the captain with my presence here."

"Certainly, Miss, but I fear for your well-being, Miss. The language of these sailors should not be overheard by a lady and I have every reason to believe that as the evening and the wine flows, the vocabulary may become shoddier."

"Do not concern yourself, Mr Miller. Nothing that I could hear from the mouths of men could shock me." Mr Miller returned to the roundhouse and began playing a lively jig. They were soon joined by two of the captain's band, Solomon the fiddle player, and a soldier drummer boy. As the night went on the songs became louder and bawdier. Eventually, everyone around the table took a turn at inventing new verses for the old song, until Mr Congleton invented the very verse to bring the night's proceedings to a raucous end:

> Up jumps the Cock with spurs on his legs,
> Saying, 'you play the cribbage and I'll stick the pegs.'

And everyone joined in for one last the chorus:

> Singing, blow the wind westerly, let the wind blow
> By a gentle nor'wester now steady she goes.

41   Elishimorta

Thirty-First December 1785 – The Gundeck

Nathanial Mingies was a master at working the uppermost parts of the ship - no matter what the weather. His rank was that of 'topman.' For which he received more pay than an able seaman. At his birth, Mingies' father had smiled proudly and kissed his mother fondly, thanking God and his wife for giving birth to the next in their family's long line of eel fishermen. Thirteen years later and shortly following the birth of his tenth sibling, the family cottage was falling down, their punt had no bottom and Ham creek was an avenue of mugwort waving in the coal smoke from the new factories to the east of London. The Plaistow Levels were now owned, not by those who made their livelihoods from its marshlands, but by those who wanted to drain the marshes and sell the land to house London's ever-growing multitude of factory and dock workers. It was then that Nathanial, kissed his mother and father farewell and left to go to sea.

A well-respected topman aboard several East Indiaman ships, handsome and around thirty, when Mingies called a meeting men took notice. He made his way between the men and boys and hung a second light from the beams above. Pushing his back between two men to lean against one of the big guns, he whispered in a hushed voice,

"Now then, what's to do?" The men looked around at one another and all began muttering at once.

Down below, among these men, the mood was not as light-hearted as it was in the captain's roundhouse. On the gundeck the mess table had been removed, a group of fifty, or so, sailors huddled in the space between two guns, some sitting on the deck, some hanging over the guns and others standing as near as they could. Lookouts stood by the stairwells along the gundeck to keep watch, and ready to signal if any unexpected visitors should arrive. Fiddlers, pipers and drummers held instruments ready prepared, at a moment's notice, to disguise the purpose of their gathering, should it be necessary. All looked nervous, edgy and were wondering how long their meeting might last before they were interrupted.

"What's this new first mate like?" a louder voice asked.

"Berrington's his name. Not as bad, as some."

"Give 'em all Jonah's toss, I says. Why not?" said Michael, continuing, "This ship ain't a lucky ship. It don't look good, all that waiting around at Gravesend, it's a bad sign, I say. And all those, changes, new plugs here, new this, new that, why'd they 'ave to change everything? And did y' know there's a cockerel on board."

"A cockerel?" asked the young boy sitting on top of the gun.

"So, what, Brother?" asked Solomon ready to strike up on his fiddle, should he be needed. "We've had cockerels before."

"No. We've had hens, but not cockerels," said Michael, the twin of the shanty-man, who, despite being born an identical twin, could always be distinguished from his brother, Solomon, by his worried appearance and miserable nature.

"And I ain't told you the half of it yet; it were crowing at midnight. I was up, above, and heard it from the well. It must be somewhere down below."

"I ain't heard no cockerel, are you sure it was a cockerel?" said the boy.

"I were playing in Captain's Roundhouse and heard that the German passenger has brought a cockerel on board," said Solomon. "Mind you, what you heard Brother, I reckon, was the nipper here, getting his nutmegs fouled coming down the ratlines." Solomon said. "They say that can make a lad crow like a cockerel." Everyone laughed, which annoyed the boy, who tried to kick out at Solomon from his sitting position on the gun, but only slipped off his perch, falling with a thud onto the deck and causing more laughter.

"Mingies hushed them, saying, "I saw that German passenger going in and out of one of the cargo lockups, I reckon you're right, Solly, it must be his bird."

"He looks like the Devil," said Michael.

"What's with all this stuff in the hold; all going out to Madras?"

"Ain't they got chickens in Madras?"

"Elephants 'ave eaten them all, suppose."

"And all these passengers; gents in wigs and ladies in silk and lace."

"Well, Mingies, what's it to be? What you got us all here for, tonight." Mingies waved a calming hand and said,

"We need to make the pledge."

"Pledge, not this again, what for?"

"I know I've said it before but it's important ... Solomon read it to us all before we left Gravesend. Bill Douglas was unfairly flogged aboard the ship, the Berry, and his shipmates made a pledge to stand by him if he took his captain to court."

"They didn't though; they didn't stand by him, did they?"

"And why not? Cos it was a stupid idea that would have got them all flogged, or worse."

Mingies ignored this interruption and pushed on, "They did get the captain to trial but the bastard paid off all the witnesses: offered all of them half a guinea each to keep mum."

"And they took the money, bloody rats."

"Judases."

"There's another bad omen; there's not one aboard this ship," said Michael.

"What Judases?" asked Solomon.

"No, rats, you fool."

"That's good, ain't it, no rats?" asked the boy, "I don't like rats.

"No. Ain't you heard that they always get off a ship that's going to go down?"

"Yeh, that's true. I was on the Valentine when it went down off Sark, we all got ashore, and the beach was full of rats."

"Maybe they were there already, local rats."

"No, they were English rats, alright."

"How could you tell?"

"They all had frock coats and powdered wigs." As usual, Mingies thought, the meeting was going to pieces. Soon the music would start up, then the singing, they would get the boy dancing, more grog would come out and another opportunity to get some action on this ship would have been lost.

"Never mind those rats; we've got our own to deal with. The thing is we have a grievance which needs redressing."

"Not that, redressing of grievances mush again. You serve that up more often than cook serves up salt pork."

"But it's true." Mingies knew that unless he got them to agree to a pledge now, it would never happen. "You know we ain't justly rewarded for our labour?" The other men shuffled, shaking their heads. "And if we ask for this or that, or voice a grievance, then what do we get?"

"Backbones laid bare." whispered one of the crew.

"Ay, they say that things be changing but men still don't get a fare share." They had all fell silent, Mingies having got them all listening, went on, "Us sailors don't get a voice. But look, this judge in Captain Johnston's trial, Loughborough was his name, ain't the only one that understands that us sailors are not being treated fairly. There are others ... and soon many judges will be finding in our favour, and getting captains and their officers to pay for a crew's mistreatment. This captain's soft, just like his hands and his officers are the same, and since we have rid ourselves of that bastard Mate, Stone, it's time for us to act. Remember, we are not alone. All the Honourable Company's ships have men like us and all will be taking the same action. Together we are stronger than the officers. You all know that but we must stick together. Who'll pledge, then?"

"What about the Red Coats? There're getting on for a hundred down, t'other end. Are they going to stand by?"

"I'm not talking mutiny, just not being keen to work. We await some, so called, urgent demand and then we just don't turn out. Stay in our hammocks and if anyone asks why, or if they threaten us with the cat, we remind them about Judge Lord Loughborough putting the captain of the Berry on trial for mistreating his crew."

"You're saying, we threaten to take our Captain to court?"

"Will it work?"

"Yes," said Mingies, "I got talking to steward, Tom Fluck - he's a man you can trust - he's always passing down some titbits from the captain's table and I don't only mean food."

"Yeh, in return for a helping of grog."

"Be that as it may, share and share alike," said Mingies, as he tried to hang on to the men's attention. "Fluck overheard Berrington and Congleton discussing the matter of Judge Loughborough. They're running scared, I tell you. Now's the time we should act, by withholding our labour. Who'll pledge?"

"Ay, I will."

"And me." More nodded their agreement, while all looked uneasy.

Mingies took a piece of rolled up parchment from inside his jacket,

"We wrote down some words; an oath. Solomon, come here and read it." Solomon Bevans, the shanty-man was Michael's twin brother and one of the few sailors who could read and write. Their father had reckoned that if they each learnt separate arts, together they would be twice the match for any other. So, whilst Solomon learnt to read, write, play the fiddle and sing, his brother, Michael learnt blacksmithing and carpentry. The crew were always spell bound by Solomon, especially when he put on his pair of delicate looking pince-nez spectacles. Many of them, at one time or another, had asked Solomon to read a letter from their mother, wife or some other family member. These letters had taken months, and in some cases years, to reach them. He could tell that most of the letters he read for sailors, would often be written, not by the senders, but by paid scribes. The difficulty and vagaries of a postal services ensured that receiving a letter was a rare event and it would almost always contain news of the death of a loved one. It was, therefore, quite normal that when Solomon put on his spectacles the crew sat in respectful silence biting their lips in preparation for some tragic news. Solomon read,

"Our cause, is our brothers' cause, together we shall stand,
And, should we not prevail, together we shall fall.
When the cock crows; all the world shall hear it.
Our watch word shall be, Elishimorta"

"Is that it?"
"That bleeding cock again."
"What's Elishimorta?" asked a sailor, not looking happy,
"Shouldn't it end with, 'in the name of God we stand'?"
"What about, 'in the name of the Devil'? Devil's more powerful than God."
"No he ain't, cos God created Heaven and the Earth in seven days."
"Six days."
"It was seven."
"No, the seventh day he rested, so that doesn't count."
"But what does the last bit mean, Elishimorta?" The unhappy sailor asked.
"Human mortality, it's Latin for, human mortality."
"Why don't we say it in English?"
"It sounds better in Latin."

"But he might not understand."

"Who might not understand it?"

"God might not understand it." Solomon ended the long discussion, by proclaiming that, as far as he was aware, God could speak all the languages of the world but, that said, he thought God would be more impressed with the Latin."

"Solly, can you read it again but ending with, 'In the name of God'?" Solomon read it again in solemn tones. Then, one by one, they stood on the cross that Mingies had carved on the deck, held the scroll above their heads, downed half a pint of grog and repeated the last line of their oath,

"Our watch word shall be, Elishimorta. In the name of God."

42   Sampson

Ben Sampson was the only man who didn't take the oath. He never said a word during the meeting of the committee and no one could remember him ever speaking up, or voicing an opinion. He was popular enough with the others, apart from the one or two who did not trust him, for which they had little reason, for he was strong, willing and would help a crew mate when ill or in need of some extra grog. Their dislike may have been derived, unjustly, from him being black and probably an escaped slave. Mingies liked Sam but could not understand his lack of common enterprise. He sat next to him when he returned to his mess area and tipped a drop of his own grog into Sam's tankard.

"Why did you not take the pledge, Sam? You, more than most, I would think that you'd want to pledge with us?"

Being on board this English ship was by far the best part of Sampson's life. Now, this group of sailors wanted him to risk all, just because one or two of them had been whipped.

He had never told Mingies, nor any other soul, his life story, but he did not want to take his history with him, untold, to the grave. So, he thought, this was a good time,

"Mingies, I like you as a brother; I've stood back-to-back with you in a fight, shared my grog with you but now you are asking me to do something that will mean I will most probably hang with you. All because some man, a stranger, on some other ship was flogged? What sense is that?"

"Sam, I beg you, join us. You're not a big mouth, like me and many of the others. The men look to you. If you join us ... I'm not asking that you stand up to the officers, they'll get you for insubordination, and we'll just not do what they ask. Sam?"

Sam slumped down on a bench and seemed to stare off into the distance. Taking a swill of grog, he said,

"When I was a little boy, in Africa, my brother was killed by a lion, I hated the lion and swore that when I grew up, I'd kill all the lions but I was taken away from Africa before I grew up. So, my friend, would you come with me, back to Africa and help me kill all the lions, would any of this crew? I think that is what you want me to do. You are saying to me, Sampson, help us fight all these English lions."

"There aren't any lions in England, only little cats." Mingies replied.

"How would I know, all these years aboard English ships; I ain't, never once, stepped foot on English soil?"

"Come on Sam, you and I, back-to-back, like always?"

"Just not bother to carry out orders, you say?" asked Samson.

"That's it, a day or two and we'll have this bunch of tosspots drinking out of our hands."

Sam sighed, "Alright, on one condition, which is that you listen to my story. I must tell my story to someone before I die."

"Why?"

"When I go to the afterlife my ancestors will ask if I have left my story in this world. I have no children to tell it to, so I would like to tell you."

"That's a deal, I'll be like your son, Sam. I'm listening."

"This is my story, Mingies. The spirits need to know. I am from the Amaxhosa people; the Whites call us Kafirs because they are ignorant. My father called me Ingulule, the Xhosa name for Cheetah and we lived in the mountains, where the Manqondo River meets the Ngqungqu River. We tended our sheep and gathered fruit from the forest. Then came the time when I had to be in the mountains to grow into a man. Down below, in the valley, a lion started taking our sheep. My older brother, and some other boys, went to kill the lion. They cornered the beast and it sprung at them but before the spears could strike home, the lion had killed my brother. When I returned my father told me, and although he loved my brother, he was cross with him for throwing his life away for a few sheep. Not long afterwards, my father told me that some Arab traders had taken a woman from our tribe. He said that he would go and get her back. He tried but he was wounded and the Arab slave traders had dogs, which followed my father's blood trail back to our village and all my family were killed, except for me. I was taken in chains to the big ocean and put in the hold of a ship. After six weeks some of us had to help with the pumps, and our chains were removed. When the crew tried to return us to the hold, we attacked them. But the crew escaped and locked us all in the hold. To punish us they gave us no food nor water for weeks, but I survived by licking rainwater from the timber stanchion next to me and by making a fishing line from strands of rope and tying rotting flesh from a corpse to the end. I used it not to catch fish but rats. There were hordes of them in the bilges below. Nearing shore our ship was damaged and beached. Some others and I broke free and ran away. We came across a band of slaves who had escaped years before. They were called Maroons.

Some of us raided a plantation for pots and pans, but an armed militia captured me and I was put up for sale at a slave auction and bought by an English merchant ship, which had lost a lot of its crew to yellow-fever. Then that ship was stopped by a Royal Navy ship called, Resolution. They took twenty men including me from the merchantman. the captain of that ship was named Cook.

Since sailing around the world with Captain Cook, I have sailed aboard Captain Percy's East Indiaman."

Mingies smiled, 'That's certainly some story. I will remember it for as long as I remember anything, and if I should have children of my own, I shall call the first boy Sampson and tell him your story, when he's old enough." The men shook hands and Sam said,

"Sounds like the winds getting up, out there. Better get busy, refusing to do anything, then."

43   Frumenty

Third of January 1786

During a storm, the most dangerous place on a ship is in the rigging, nonetheless correct setting of the sails is even more necessary in wild weather. Although a storm might be tossing the ship around like a cork on the sea, men must climb up high enough to manage the topsails, whilst desperately clinging on to the ratlines for dear life.

That night the storm hit with squall after squall of cutting hailstones, blinding the men in the rigging and numbing their hands.

However, the busiest place on the ship was not the rigging but the galley. Normally in such a storm the galley fires would be extinguished and all aboard would have to be contented with cold food but the captain had ordered that this day the officers would be served Christmas dinner, although the crew would eat their food cold, and thus leave the galley clear for the captain's steward. Notwithstanding this, the men, on learning that the galley fires were alight, had sent their mess men to the galley, with their skillets and pots, with a view to heating up their day's rations. Tom Fluck, the captain's steward, had given up trying to turn these men away from the galley and was doing his best to work around them, but the men's cooking pots were taking longer than normal. Mr Fluck tried explaining, "Your swinging pot is like a hand in a flame, if he keeps moving, he doesn't get hot."

"Corke! Where is you, lad?"

"Here, Mr Fluck, Sir."

"Stir the frumenty, lad. Make way there, sailor. This is the captain's dinner I 'ave ere."

"What's Captain having, Mr Fluck"

"Captain is 'aving empty fucking bowl, if you don't gets your bony arse out of 'ere, Sailor."

"What in tarnation? Corke! Corke? Open this fucking oven door, Lad."

"Yes, Sir, Mr Fluck."

Stirring his mess pot over fire, the sailor tried again, "Is that roast beef, I can smell there, Mr Fluck? The men'll be so pleased to hear all's well with the captain, up aft."

"Tarnation! Corke, stir that fucking frumenty before it burns. Do I 'ave to tells you every ving fucking twice?"

Up above, Mr Reeve, the third mate, was shouting into Barrington's ear trying to make himself heard above the roar of the wind,

"The crew are absenting themselves from pumping duties, no matter what is said to them, Sir. They keep referring to something about Luffberry."

"Loughborough, did you say, Loughborough, Mr Reeve?"

"Yes, Sir that was the word, Loughborough but with the extra grog today, begging your pardon, Sir, but they're all three parts to the wind,"

"What about the soldiers? Send a messenger to Captain Hawkins; see if you can persuade him to order his men to help on the pumps. If this storm lasts much longer, without efficient pumping, she will be so low in the water she'll never handle - we could founder. Mr Reeve, we'll make one more attempt to go about but the men have not been able to get aloft to clew the topsails.

Therefore, if she'll not answer, we should cut away the topsail masts. I doubt she'll handle well enough otherwise."

"Aye, Aye! Go about, it is, Mr Barrington, Sir."

"Aye, go about, if you would, Mr Reeve?"

The ship turned to larboard to face away from the storm in an attempt to wear – run before the wind - but when she was side onto the storm, the billowing topsails filled and the craft slowly came to a halt. Making no headway, the vessel had no steerage, remained broadside to the storm, heeled over at an alarming angle and continued her headlong journey towards the Dorset coastline of rocks and cliffs.

"Down with the topsail masts, Mr Reeve. Look lively there," shouted Berrington.

"Aye, Aye, Sir. Cut topsail masts it is."

Down below, as the ship heeled over, Corke, who was not holding on to anything more substantial than a wooden spoon, fell and slid across the deck, away from the stoves. Mr Fluck shouted,

"Watch out for the fucking frumenty, there, lad." The pan slid across the hob, tipped over the guardrail and crashed onto the deck, rolling around in a circle on its side and spilling a billowing wave of frumenty, which slopped around the deck. Corke, with terror in his eyes, looked at Mr Fluck unable to say anything. He crouched down to make himself a smaller target for anything that the captain's steward might throw at him. Mr Fluck, like the ship itself, had been struggling to endure the consequences of the onslaught of the storm. It had been a tide of complications for him for well over a week now, and a bowl of frumenty on the deck added little more to the press and toil his day-to-day work was under.

"Lad, lickety-split! Pick it up."

"Shall I throw it away, Mr Fluck?"

"Tar-fucking-nation, no, Lad. It's only for the captain and officers, in weather like this, what's the prospect of the captain, or any other officer in this tub full of fucking tosspots, identifying a few rat droppings amongst a pound of raisins-o-sun?

Ladle it up there, my bacon face. Use that square ladle. What I got blacksmith to make special for ladling stuff off the deck. Get it up, lad."

Eliza was sitting at the end of the table next to her father's place at the head, although the captain was not there at that moment. She thought that the roundhouse cabin must be the most unsettling place in the world, certainly aboard the ship. She had never seen such confusion. What a strange mixture of table guests there were: Mr Miller, she often spoke to but he would always steer the conversation around to his own passion, music. Mr Schwartz was always sitting upright, staring straight ahead. The few times Eliza had engaged him in conversation he had always found it necessary to talk of the fortune he had in Madras, which was awaiting his return. The ship's surgeon, continually attempting to make people laugh, until the night wore-on and he became so drunk, he fell asleep. The purser said very little and looked like the ship's undertaker. The midshipmen were continually alternating between whispers and raucous laughter. Eliza's two cousins, Amy and Anabel, never smiled nor said a word. Miss Mansell talked nervously, even when no one was listening. Eliza's sister, Mary-Ann, constantly tried to impress everyone who she thought might warrant being described as a gentleman and spurned anyone below that rank officers were constantly coming and going wearing outdoor cloaks and hoods dripping with seawater, bringing messages which they whispered in the captain's ear. And men from the galley, bringing heaps of food and drink for a festive dinner that Eliza, and the few others around the table, would be unlikely to look at let alone eat, save, of course for the midshipmen, who approached all eating and drinking as a competitive team sport.

The ship had been underway for over a week and the weather had grown so bad that progress had been extremely slow. As well as trying to become accustomed to constant rolling and pitching of the ship, Eliza, along with the other passengers, had to stay below decks because of dangerous winds, low temperatures, and rough seas. The officers always looked so grave and busy with their duties, and keeping the ship on course, that there was little time for discussions with Eliza or any of the other passengers. The one man who could usually be found in the same place each day and appeared to have time for the passengers was her father, the captain. He had told Eliza that it was his duty to always be on hand when a decision was required. At that very moment he was in a corner of the roundhouse in his small private cabin, where there was a sleeping cot, a small table with sunken basin for washing and a pitcher of water secured by a wooden framework. He was just about to kneel and pray, which he preferred to do with a clear head before dining, when there was a knock at his door,

"Captain, Sir."

"Ah, Mr Fluck What is it?"

"In the matter of the frumenty, Sir."

"Yes, yes, the frumenty, I am full of anticipation, and filled with high expectations, Mr Fluck."

"Concerning of your previous orders, Sir, that the frumenty be served hot. I would be requiring knowing; when you need, that I am to serve it? And will it be with the cods and sole, Sir, or the beef?"

"With the beef, Fluck, always with the beef."

The arrival of Mr Congleton, the second mate, to join Mr Fluck in the captain's doorway brought the steward's conversation to an end.

"Excuse me, Sir, but I have an urgent message from Mr Berrington," said Mr Congleton.

"That'll be all, Fluck … Oh, you have not forgotten the Cock's Wassail have you, Mr Fluck?"

"No, Sir, I have it ready for warming."

The captain turned to his second mate,

"Well, Mr Congleton, out with it, if you please."

"Yes, Sir. The problems with the new hawse plugs have increased, in that both starboard and larboard hawse plugs have been forced inboard, despite the addition of a quantity of hawse-bags to prevent this. Consequently, a good deal of water has been shipped onto the gundeck. Mr Jackson, carpenter's mate, has filled the hawseholes and secured them with hawse-bucklers, but they are forever being washed inboard. As you know Sir, we sailed before Mr Dodds, our contracted carpenter, had arrived on board and therefore we are relying on young Mr Jackson, the carpenter's mate's services. Mr Reeve asked me to ask you if we could enrol the services of the sailor by the name of Michael Beavens, the shanty-man's brother. You may remember, Sir that he was carpenter's mate on our last voyage and proved very competent and speedy. Regrettably, however, he was stripped of his rank and duties owing to persistent drunkenness and insolence, for which he received a dozen lashes."

"Beavens, yes, I remember. Drunkenness is one thing, Mr Congleton, but I'll not forgive insolence. How unlike his twin brother ... Michael Beavens. Now, about Jackson, well, Mr Congleton, his lowly rank is easily resolved; tell Mr Jackson that he is hereby promoted to ship's carpenter for the duration of the voyage."

"Yes Sir, but Mr Reeve was somewhat concerned as to young Jackson's inexperience in carpentry, him being not much more than a boy. I believe him to be aged no more than fourteen years,"

The captain was becoming irritated by Congleton's persistence in this matter, which was also keeping those around the Christmas dinner table waiting for their wassail, not to mention keeping God waiting upon the captain's devotions,

"Mr Congleton, responsibility hangs well on many a pair of young shoulders, I think you will find. I could name you a dozen midshipmen of that age who went on to become successful captains and even admirals."

"Certainly, Sir. Jackson to ship's carpenter it is."

"That will be all Mr Congleton?"

"Beg y' pardon, Sir, but one more matter.

"Well, Mr Congleton?"

"Mr Berrington has ordered that all pumps be manned with a relief pumping crew standing by and a message has been sent to see if captain Hawkins can spare some soldiers to assist on the pumps."

"What is the depth of water in the hold, Mr Congleton, have you measured it, Sir?"

"Not I, Captain but Mr Reeve has overseen that task and informs me that a short while ago there were three feet and four inches of water but that it is still rising."

Captain Percy's personal evening prayers were rather like his log entries, comprehensive but brief and carefully worded so as not to incriminate himself at a later stage. He began,

"Celebrations to mark Christmas day, having unfortunately been delayed owing to the ..." the captain paused; he had been going to say, 'severity of the weather' but then thought that this might be construed as a criticism, on his own part, of what is surely an act of God. He continued cautiously, "Having been delayed due to the grandeur of the weather. Christmas Day festivities will now be going ahead today." the captain, not wanting to appear to renege on a previous decision, which had been recorded in his log, and in his prayers, had ordered that the officers' Christmas dinner should go ahead on a new allotted day, namely today, and that the men's rum ration should be doubled for today. In his prayers that evening, he also felt it necessary to record the recent problems they had been experiencing with the new design of the hawse plugs, which had now been washed away completely, allowing water aboard and causing the pumps to struggle to keep the depth in the bilge to an acceptable level. For a moment, he wondered if he should explain to the Lord the nature of 'hawse plugs' but then admonished himself, for momentarily forgetting the Lord's omniscience.

Prayers concluded, the captain made his way to his place at the head of the dining table, stood up, tapped his glass with a knife and called for silence,

"Welcome ladies and gentlemen, all and everyone, to this rather belated Christmas dinner. For our first course here, Mr Fluck has prepared two cods surrounded by sole with oyster sauce. As custom demands, I shall serve dinner tonight. Now, pass around that wassail bowl and fill your glasses."

The captain began spooning out the fish onto the plates, while cheers of approval roared out from the gaggle of five midshipmen, seated on the right, at the far end of the table; opposite them were three more midshipmen, who tried to shout louder than the first group. The first group responded by flicking pieces of broken bread at the larger group of boys, until the purser said,

"Gentlemen, gentlemen, remember your manners in front of the ladies, not to mention the captain."

Having served the ladies, Mr Miller and Mr Schwartz, the captain, became rather bored by the task and moved the large dish of fish down towards the midshipmen,

"Help yourselves gentlemen." He then returned to his place and raised his glass,

"To the King, the ladies and the East India Company." All repeated the toast,

"To the King, the ladies and the East India Company."

Mr Fluck came through the backdoor, swaying from side to side with the rolling of the ship and trying to keep the silver terrine on an even keel. He placed the terrine onto a flat bag of corn, set on the table to prevent the dish and contents from ending up on the floor, then lifted the lid and, standing as erect as possible, in the circumstances, and with his nose higher in the air than seemed possible, said,

"In the matter of the second course, Sir, we 'ave 'ere the roast leg of a beef, and young Corke, 'ere 'as the bowl of frumenty, piping hot, as ordered. Shall I serve it, Sir?"

"No Fluck, it being Christmas, I shall do that," said the captain, getting to his feet.

Next to the purser, sat the surgeon, who was in conversation across the table with Mr Schwartz,

"You'll find that Mr Fluck is a fine cook, although his raw materials are not always of the best quality but his food is wholesome and satisfying, providing one keeps, one's nose a reasonable distance from one's mouth whilst eating."

"Yes, indeed, Sir," said Schwartz, who took a while to appreciate that the surgeon was joking,

"Ah, so! Yes indeed. Very amusing, Sir. Ha, ha, ha."

"Mr Miller, please tell me," asked Mary-Ann, sniffing her filled glass of wassail, "what is in the wassail bowl?"

"I am afraid I do know, Miss Percy," said Mr Miller, who then waved the steward over, asking,

"Please be kind enough, Mr Fluck, to tell us what is the content of your wassail bowl." Mr Fluck, feeling a sudden surge of importance, stepped forward and in his usual recitation manner, said,

"I am pleased to tell you ladies and gentlemen that the ingredients of the wassail bowl are cock ale." This brought a volley of guffaws from the midshipmen and the end of Mary-Ann's interest. She turned to the surgeon and asked him about the weather prospects. The surgeon explained that it would either get better or it would not. All the while, Mr Fluck continued,

"Which is: three pounds of brown sugar; three pints of hot brandy; three grated nutmegs; a large bit of ginger root, cut up; two bottles of the captain's sherry, which the captain gave me. I do then leave it all 'til it be cold and then add: two more gallons of cold beer, which must be still in the brewing of. Then I must spread some yeast on toasted brown bread and float that on top. Then I's let that stand for a few days; then I's take a freshly killed hen, the older the better – now this of course should have been a cockerel, but we ain't got none, but I did ask if we could 'aver one of Mr Schwartz's cocks, owing to it being bad luck to use an hen in a cock ale, and Mr Schwartz's are the biggest cocks I 'ave ever seen in twenty-years at sea, begging your pardon Miss, but Purser says, no they's not eating cocks but fighting cocks." Mr Fluck continued with his well-memorised recipe, ignoring the fact that Mary-Ann and Mr Miller had completely given up listening, and were now talking to Miss Mansell about Madras. Fluck continued,

"I then parboil the cock, I mean hen, flay him, stamp him in a stone mortar 'til his bones be broken, oh, and I mustn't forget to craw and gut him, when I does flay him; then put the cock … hen into an kilderkin of beer; and put in ten pounds of raisins-o-sun, all stoned; some blades of mace and a few cloves. Put all these into a canvas bag and into the barrel for a week, or maybe nine days; then it be ready to drink." Having finished, Fluck touched his forelock and left the roundhouse to return to the galley, to see to his Figgie pudding.

Miss Mansell was a rather short and homely looking young girl, who in different clothes and other circumstances would have passed easily for a kitchen maid. Talking to Eliza's two silent cousins, Miss Mansell was continuing a very nervous and disturbing account of her embarkation onto this very ship at Madras two years previously,

"Of course, I never understood the reasons why, but we had to get on board this ship without using the ship's own cutters, or any other civilised boats, but were assigned to the native boats, crewed by native men. The journey was most terrifying because one embarked from the beach. We had to stand and wait upon the water and until we were rowed out through the breaking waves. We watched as three previous boats went. Then it was our turn. The native boats were manufactured by stringing pieces of wood together. One cannot imagine how they are expected to survive the journey of a mile or more, through those waves and out to our ship. Reaching the third wave, the prow of our vessel rose into the air and we all just fell into the sea. Luckily it was not cold and there were numerous natives swimming in the sea and I, along with the other passengers, was hooked up from the depths and out into another boat and eventually made it out to our ship, soaked to the very core. I do not know how I managed to live through that, except that God himself must have looked after me. If there was …"

Eliza watched her two cousins looking further and further alarmed at Miss Mansell's account, and the prospect of a similar encounter with the sea.

"My dear cousins," said Eliza wondering if the terror of Miss Mansell's account might have loosened the young girls' tongues, "I am sure my father will arrange for a more civilised disembarkation for us at Madras having learnt of Miss Mansell's experience. Tell me how do you see your prospects in your new home? Will it be to your liking?" However, Eliza's question seemed to raise more fear in the two girls than the prospect of being pitched into the surf at Madras. They both turned, and looked ardently down into their unused and empty wassail cups. Nonetheless, Eliza was impressed by their well-tuned responses which she thought was rather like watching two market fair mime artists. Bethany whispered into Eliza's ear,

"Miss, shall we dare taste a little of Mr Fluck's cock ale?" Eliza glared at Bethany. She had noticed that Bethany had become over familiar since her promotion to, travelling partner, and was growing into the habit of opening conversations.

The captain, was trying to persuade everyone to taste his childhood favourite food,

"Frumenty, the best Christmas food there is, Miss Mansell, will you not try some? Please do. Here you are, try a little. I am sure you will find it to your liking."

After spooning out a portion to the young lady, he filled his own bowl and tucked in with gusto. Between mouthfuls, the captain tried to explain to his younger daughter, Mary-Ann, why, when the wind was so strong, they could not travel faster, which he expanded into an explanation of tacking and wearing of a ship. The captain liked to think of himself a practical man, so he quickly incorporated into his explanation a sauce boat and some cutlery. Mary-Ann, the captain's intended audience soon glazed over, which was an expression that Mr Miller, having been Mary-Ann's music teacher for the past year recognised very well.

A gang of the midshipmen were in a gaggle at the far end of the captain's table,

"Epsom, Yes, let's play Epsom,"

"The Humphries Brothers shall be pudding and pie."

"Yes." The teams were sorted, the game of horseback racing began, to great cheers from the boys and men,

"Half a sovereign on Humphries," shouted the purser.

"Is that your money, or the captain's?" asked the surgeon.

"If I remember correctly, there are more than one Humphries aboard this ship. As usual, Purser, the odds are bent towards you, Sir."

Three of the boys got down on all fours while their partners climbed onto their backs. The race began at the far end of the roundhouse, and continued with numerous collapses and remounting. The purser and surgeon tried to slow the field down by flicking spoonfuls of the captain's Christmas frumenty at various boys. When they reached the table, two runners, and their mounts, crawled beneath it, one went over the top – sending food, drink and cutlery everywhere – and the third pair stopped, because the rider needed to vomit over the head of his mount.

The ship, which had been keeling over to starboard violently straightened up. The pair of boys, riding piggyback across the table, slid towards the captain's end, gathering up bowls of wassail, frumenty and platters of fish and beef, on the way, and delivering themselves, and everything else on the table, into the captain's lap, knocking him over and backwards onto the deck.

Up above, Mr Berrington, Mr Reeve and Mr Congleton were doing their best to save the ship. Conditions had deteriorated alarmingly. The storm had veered to the south bringing ice and snow with it. Despite the help from the army the pumps were not coping and the last report from Mr Reeve to Mr Berrington was that there were seven feet of water in the hold. Berrington had sent a message to the captain that he was going to have to cut away the mizzen mast and possibly the main mast as well, in order to stop the ship being blown onto the English coast. With the foremast alone they might make Plymouth in twelve hours. Mr Reeve returned to the upper deck to tell Mr Berrington that the captain was not to be disturbed, being in his cabin changing his clothes, having been drenched in wassail and frumenty. But Mr Berrington had made the decision, and ordered the mizzen cut down. That had been carried out successfully, but the ship still would not respond to the helm.

"Mr Reeve," said Berrington, "we must cut down the mainmast as well, if we are to gain any steerage in the slightest. Would you arrange that, please?"

"Yes, Sir. Coxswain, a team of men with axes if you would. We shall have the main mast over the side, and while that is being done cut the mainmast stays and ratlines, if you would?"

"Yes, Sir." The Coxswain disappeared below to get the men and equipment, but after a quarter of an hour returned with only three sailors and as many axes.

"Can we have more men on this work, Coxswain? This is not enough."

"I'm sorry, Sir, it was as much as I could do to obtain these men. The crew are being insolent in the upmost and refusing to follow orders. When I threatened to report them to you, Mr Reeve, they said, 'Tell him he can go to Loughborough.' Shall I get some marines, to bring the men by force?"

"No, Sir, time is not on our side. We shall have to set to the task ourselves."

When the mainmast fell, rather than disappearing over the side, as intended, it toppled for'ard, ripping the foremast sail to shreds but leaving the major part of the mast on board in a tangle of timber and rigging. Desperate to get the mast overboard and cut the rigging away, Mr Berrington, along with the Coxswain and four others, took on the work himself, picked up an axe himself and climbed amid the tangle of rope. Abruptly, the mainmast swung away from the foremast and the mass of ratlines began to move.

"Mr Berrington, Sir, get your men out of there, the main is moving, she's going over. As quick as you can, Sir." But Berrington could not hear above the noise of the storm and continued hacking at the ropes. Two of the men saw the danger approaching but could find no escape. In a matter of moments Berrington, the coxswain, four of the crew and the main mast had disappeared overboard. The ship straightened and Mr Reeve ran to look over the gunwale but the tumult had taken the men and the darkness had swallowed them all.

By early next morning the storm had lessened somewhat, some men had erected a temporary sail upon the remains of the foremast and the water in the hold had been reduced to five feet.

"I believe, Mr Reeve, Weymouth to be an obtainable anchorage, rather than Plymouth. Are the crew responding to orders better, Sir, in the light of day and now that the peril we all face must be very evident to all aboard?"

"Somewhat, Sir. I have asked the boatswain to make a list of all the men who are refusing to obey orders, and instructed that they should have pay deducted accordingly."

"Thank you, Mr Reeve."

Fifth of January 1786 – Imprisoned at sea, westward bound, aboard the Martin.

From the one-hundred-and-fifty convicts, mostly in chains, Silvanus wondered, why it was that he, alone, was being taken up above to the open deck? He soon found out; it was his coopering skills that had saved him from being chained up with the others below; he was to help repair and refit the ship's water barrels to store rainwater for use during the voyage. The open air was a short-lived relief, the weather changed, and the sea became so rough that all unnecessary work on deck had to be abandoned. Below decks, and back in chains, he began to hear news, which spread like Chinese whispers: their destination was to be Maryland. But, since the end of the war, the United States had ruled that they would not take any more convicts from Britain's overflowing gaols. The next day more rumours went around to the effect that, should the Martin's captain not be able to convince Maryland buyers that this was a legitimate shipment of white slaves, and not convicts, their ship would be turned around and sent back to Africa, where there would be a ready market for white flesh, albeit not so lucrative.

The fierceness of the storm grew over the next day. Until, in the early hours of the next day, suddenly it felt as if the sea had become a lot calmer and then Silvanus heard the bower anchor chain running out. The first whispers from the prisoners said that they were in the Americas, but that would be impossible in such a short time, either France or Spain was thought to be more likely. The men were becoming desperate to find out more. Then they heard that they had interrupted their voyage to Maryland to seek shelter from the storm, but no one knew where. The storm had been so violent that the ship's crew had not thought it worth putting themselves through the risks of bringing the prisoners any food or water. Some men were eating rats, others found small streams of rain water dribbling down the ship's oak timbers, but often this would abruptly change to seawater.

Silvanus was towards the aft of his row of twelve manacled men, only a few feet from the hatchway. From the darkness of the for'ard part of the ship, came a dozen men, moving as quietly as possible, but made difficult because of their manacles. Somehow, they had broken the single chain which threaded through all the manacles holding the men together.

"Move along, mates. We'll take these places here," said one of the arrivals to Silvanus. "When they bring us some water, we'll get them." Silvanus, and those nearby, moved as far for'ard as they could, while the unchained men sat down and took their places.

"Hush, now lads. We're taking the ship, and you'll all come with us, unless you want to be sold off to Arabs on the Ivory Coast."

"Peck," whispered a voice, "sing out, as agreed and make it sound good, make them believe in you, lad."

Peck called out, "Guard, guard. Water, for mercy's sake. It's been days since we've tasted a drop. Some here will be dead soon, unless we get some water. We're all Christians down here, just like you. In the name of Jesus give a fellow a drop of water."

They all waited but nothing happened. Peck continued,

"There are those of us here, prepared to buy a little water. We have money." A few more moments went by until,

"How much is a firkin of water worth to you, then?" came the voice from above.

"We have five-shillings and sixpence, so far, but maybe we can get a few more of these tight arses down here to part with a little extra money for some ship's biscuits," said Peck.

"Where did you get all that money from?" The answers from above were becoming quite rapid now and Silvanus thought it sounded like the bait might have been taken. They were certainly interested. Peck went on,

"Most men down here have something hidden away."

"One hundred, and more, men should be able to fart out twenty shillings, at least," said the voice from above. There was a pause while, Peck whispered to his fellow mutineers. Then,

"We've got nine shillings and sixpence, and we'll pay more, for water and food tomorrow."

"Twenty shillings or you can go to the Devil." Peck said nothing and apart from the wind above whistling through the ratlines and rustling the furled sails, it was silent. In the darkness of the hold, all eyes were on the trap door.

Around Peck, there was a whispered argument. "If we offer too much, they won't believe us." hissed Peck. But some men still wanted him to up the price. Others said he should plead to their good nature and ask for Christian mercy.

Without warning, the hatch opened, a ladder lowered and a guard climbed down with one hand on the ladder, the other holding a lantern and shouldering a musket. He said, cautiously,

"Show us the money."

"You show us the water, first." Two other guards descended struggling with a cask hanging from a pole between them. They had cutlasses hanging from their belts, but they brought down no more muskets. A fourth man climbed down, nervously rattling chains around his neck and a couple of iron dippers for the water. In one hand he held a flintlock pistol. With the added light from the sailors' lanterns, Silvanus could see Peck for the first time. He was probably just a young lad but due to having been at sea for half a dozen years, looked older. Peck weighed up their chances: twelve manacled men against a couple of cutlasses, one musket and a pistol. "The odds are on our side," Peck whispered to the man next to him, "the guards don't stand much of a chance, if we rush them as one."

"Here's your firkin of water. Now, where's the money?"

"Further down aft," said Peck.

"Well, pass it up here then, else we'll smash this firkin and piss in the puddle and you can lap that up," said the man with the pistol, who was now at the bottom of the ladder. The other three, however, could not wait for their share of the nine and sixpence and began edging aft towards where they thought the money to be. They reached Silvanus's group of huddled convicts, who remained shackled to the deck by their long chain. The sailor in front realised something was wrong but it was too late; they now had their backs to the twelve partially unchained men, who set upon them with a great roar. The ladle carrier fired his pistol but the ball disappeared harmlessly into the oak deck. One of other two guards had no time to draw his hanger before he was grappled to the deck. The guard with the musket must have allowed the rain to get at his powder and become damp because it did not fire. They pulled three of the men towards the fully chained men, who did not take long to take their weapons and overpower them. The man on the ladder tried to flee up above but could not help turning his back upon the desperate men. His cutlass facing the wrong way, his feet slipped on the wet ladder and the men pulled him back down,

"Let me go lads, it was them," nodding towards his fellow guards, "not me. They wanted the money. I agree with you, we're all Christians. Have the water, for nothing. Just let me go. I'll get you some bread as well and how about some rum all round; I know where the captain keeps his key to the rum locker. Have mercy." At the mention of rum some of the convicts began to mutter and lose their resolve.

"Never mind lads, we can help ourselves to that soon enough, and never you mind, Mister," said Peck to the guard, "You're safe with us now. Now, where are the keys to these chains?"

"The key to the long chains is here, on my belt, my friends, but the key for your manacles is kept in the captain's cabin." Peck picked up the guard's cutlass and cut his belt and passed the key to the others. As soon as they were all released, they eagerly drank the water from the barrel, while Peck continued to talk in a friendly manner to the last remaining guard,

"Tell me, my Christian friend, where are we? And what're the captain's plans?"

"I don't know what the captain has planned. He doesn't share that information with us. But the word is we have stopped here because the captain doesn't like being tossed around whilst eating his dinner. It's likely that as soon as the weather eases, we'll up anchor and make way."

"Good," said Peck, "And last of all, where is *here*?"

"Plymouth," said the guard trying to slither away across the deck.

The convicts looked around at one another with grins on their faces. "Plymouth. Thanks, my friend. You have been very helpful." Then, looking like he was about to stand up and leave the guard, Peck whirled around and brought the cutlass down across the guard's face. As the man screamed and fell to the deck, Peck plunged the weapon into the dying man's side.

Having a tankard of port to his lips, the captain was surprised, when he lowered it to see his cabin filling up with convicts. They had, only moments before, relieved the only guard on the upper deck of his musket.

"What do you mean, by this?" the captain growled, standing up and trying to look fearsome, which was difficult for four feet six-inch man, who was shaking with fright and swaying from having just drunk a pint of Madera, almost in one draught. Then, not being able to think of anything more appropriate, he said,

"I am the captain of this ship; this is my cabin and I am dining." Peck, having spent his five years at sea touching his forelock to all manner of, far lower ranked, officers than this captain before him, could not easily forget the gulf between their positions,

"Begging your pardon, Sir, but we would like the key to these manacles." The other mutineers, who had managed to squeeze into the captain's cabin, could not believe their makeshift leader's deference towards the captain, willing to sell them all into slavery. They added to Peck's request, by thrusting their two muskets towards the captain and waving cutlasses across the table, making it clear to the captain that this was not a request but a demand.

The captain handed over the manacle keys and, one by one, the men removed their chains. They left the captain unharmed, apart from chaining him to a ship's stanchion, just out of reach of his Madera.

The ship's two long boats lowered, the men began a furious argument, as to who would go first. After an hour, the men agreed that Peck should lead the first two boats with two dozen men in each. Once ashore, Peck would send the boats back with four rowers in each and bring ashore another four-dozen men. One of the men who Peck picked to be in one of the first boats, was Silvanus.

There was a large surf running, but Peck had not only been a sailor but also a coxswain of a long boat and had experience landing a boat in surf. Notwithstanding, it was lucky that the boats did not capsize. Ashore, Peck eventually managed to persuade some men to row back to the ship with him. After an hour the two boats returned to the beach, but this time, one managed to get broadside on to a wave and tipped over, throwing a couple of dozen men into the freezing water. Some disappeared in the undertow, but most waded ashore, relieved to be free and on land at last. Following the capsize, Peck could only persuade one man to return to the ship with him to collect the last of the convicts. Although most of the men ashore decided that they would be safer in a large group, reasoning that they would be more capable of overcoming any opposition they might chance upon, a half dozen men decided not to wait for the others and make their way inland.

Silvanus thought he would be less likely noticed in a small group and joined the six men ready to leave. They climbed the foreshore and quickly came upon a hamlet, no more than a group of dishevelled fisherman's cottages, which might have been assumed to be abandoned, if it were not for a few dim lights in several of their windows. From there, they made their way up a loose and rocky cliff into some woods beyond. However, the men had made the most of the captain's Madera, brandy and rum before bidding him farewell. Despite drinking from a creek, they had a raging thirst. Arguments broke out; they had not eaten for days and wanted food inside them before disappearing into the wild Cornish countryside. Most men wanted to go back and beg food from the cottagers near the shore, which a few moments earlier they had crept by, but Silvanus put his lot in with two men who had decided to push on away from the sea.

Towards the top of the hill, they halted at the sound of musket shots from below, which was soon followed by a volley of musket fire. Only trained troops fire volleys, Silvanus thought. Perhaps the captain had taken back control of his ship and got word to the authorities ashore that convicts were on the loose.

By the time the sun came up, a storm was raging across Cawsand bay, which was now a refuge for a dozen ships. These were originally sheltering from a south-westerly but, now, since the wind had changed overnight, were relying on their anchors to keep them off Cawsand beach. Two of the ships had already dragged their anchors and were heeling over on the shore, being pounded by the surf. The wind was blowing sleet into Silvanus's face, stinging his skin like glass shards. To escape, he lay down behind a rock and once out of the wind realised that he had lost track of his fellow runaways. The men had gone their own way and he was alone.

He carried on and was soon making his way down through a sheltered wooded hillside. Behind him he thought he heard dogs, and he could make out men shouting, but not what they were saying. They were getting nearer, all the time. He had to find somewhere to hide, safe from the dogs. The shouting increased and he heard a shot. Had the pursuers come across another escaped convict?

At the bottom of the hill there was a muddy brook. Maybe the dogs would not be able to follow a scent in the mud, he thought. They were getting closer. The only thing he could do was to hide in the mud. He found a flat stone, and a few branches, then walked back towards the sound of the hounds, lay down under an undercut bank, put the stone on his stomach, pushing his body into the muddy water and, lastly, he pulled the branches over him to hide his head, as best he could.

If the pursuers did not trip over him, he might be alright. But the water was freezing. His calf muscles began to scream, the pain was almost unbearable. He trembled and tried to sing,

"Il pleut ... il pleut ... bergère ... Presse tes blancs moutons ..."

The dogs and men came along the bank. One hound came over towards Silvanus and started to sniff around, but luckily the other hounds started yelping and the loan dog left Silvanus to himself. The following men did not discover him either and passed on by. When he got up out of the water, the pain had stopped but he could not feel his hands or feet and he was struggling to walk. After a while he saw a light in the gloom ahead. A cottage? He could not make out what he was looking at. His eyes were not seeing things properly. It was as if each eye was seeing different images. He would have to take a chance and plead for help at this cottage or he would freeze and be dead before the morning. The light was from a lantern hanging amid a settlement, not of cottages, but a group of improvised shacks, built from old wagons. The wheels had been removed from three of a group of four carts and sailcloth stretched between them to make the camp. Terrier dogs ran around him, barking, growling and snapping. He fell to his knees and then into the mud; he could go no further. What a kindly state this blackness is, he thought, as his eyes closed.

Three young boys came and stood around him, began poking him with sticks and arguing about whether his shoes were worth any money. He opened his eyes and saw a tall woman standing over him, holding a dark lantern.

"What 'e be at, boys," she said, "don' go a-poking 'e goods, wot 'e wind blows in. Dogs now, git! I says, git!" The dogs yelped as if they had been hit with a stick and ran off into the darkness. The woman, in something like her fifth decade, looked as though she only had a few teeth left, but, thought Silvanus, she remains handsome with her dark skin and one sparkling green eye. Over the other, she wore a black patch, and like a crown upon her head, she wore a wreath of wild plants.

Silvanus's head ached like it had done in the days he had been held captive by Butt and Hap'th.

He asked, "What manner of woman wears mandrake and heather in her hair?" His eyes were working now, and he was slowly drifting out of the blackness, which had kept enveloping him. Perhaps his eyes were playing tricks on him still, and this woman was an apparition. He spoke some more, "Mandrake's a warning to 'keep away' and heather, that's lucky, a sign of welcome."

The woman shone the lantern in Silvanus's eyes,

"Well now, what 'ave we 'ere?"

"My name's Curtis. I'm a cooper by trade."

"A cooper, 'e says? Well, ain't that just custi. My name be Basaba, Basaba Pennell, a name most folk in these 'ere parts squirms at. What manner of woman' I be, 'e will discover in time, if 'e lives long nuff. A cooper, 'e says? And a man what knows his hedgerow plants, excepting it ain't mandrake it be henbane – but I forgives 'e 'at, cause it be common mistake. This be 'e Crown of 'e Moor 'n Bog that I be wearing. The sign of friend 'n foe; 'tis 'e crown of Janus, god of comings 'n goings, beginnings 'n ends and God of 'e gateway. Now me prickly mud-caked hotchi witchi, let's get 'e up. You lads 'ere, 'elp 'im. Put 'im in' Auley McCauley's bender," Basaba said. "Give 'im some broth, wi' a drop or two of killdevil in it. Then wrap up some hot stones to keep 'im warm 'n cover 'im over wi' straw, so ee cook up. Like he be a real prickly hotche witchi. Then when the woodcock coos, we'll see what manner of leftovers 'e storm's blown in. 'A cooper may be of some use to us – worth a few shiners, eh, lads?"

45   Anchors

"Mr Reeve, please, fire distress canons from the larboard guns, and keep them firing at five-minute intervals. Someone ashore will no doubt hear such signals," said the captain.

"Yes Sir, and the anchors?"

"Bower anchor and sea anchors, all lost you say, Mr Reeve? Mr Harrison, the sailmaker, could he not fashion an improvised sea anchor?"

"Yes Sir, but I am not sure there is the time available."

"Well then Mr Reeve, get Mr Congleton to drop the main anchor - together with a prayer or two, I would fancy."

The storm had returned with a fury that none on board had ever seen. They abandoned the destination of Weymouth for the nearer Studland Bay, not a harbour but a sandy beach, where they could reasonably expect to to go aground safely. However, they needed to round St Aldhelm's Head but the storm forced them closer and closer to the shore. If the anchor could hold them for a few hours, their plight may be seen from the shore at daybreak, or if the storm subsided, or the wind changed direction, they might be able to clear the headland and make Studland.

Mr Congleton was in the for'ard hawser locker. The anchor was lowed, and almost immediately it took hold of the seabed.

"Make fast the main anchor hawser." The men amidships received the order and fastened the hawser around the two bollards. The ship swung violently to starboard ... and held. Mr Congleton made his way to the roundhouse to report to the captain.

"The main anchor away and holding, Sir."

"Excellent, Mr Congleton. How far are we from the shore, would you say?"

"Not more than half a mile, Sir. But it is believed that there would be few lights visible along this stretch of the Dorset coast, and in the dark, and this weather ..." The anchor held for an hour. Then, the hawser parted and the ship started swiftly on its way northwards – towards the shore. The captain and officers could tell the moment the hawser parted and Mr Reeve went up above to see what was happening. He hoped that perhaps their position on the charts had been miscalculated and with the tide flooding up the channel from the West, that they might still safely round the St Aldhelm's headland and on towards Studland. His hopes were in vain. The black foreboding shapes of the cliffs loomed out of the darkness, Mr Reeve ran back from his vantage point on the starboard bow, and the ship came to a grinding halt, sending Mr Reeve sliding into the port gunwale.

The bow of the ship, pointing towards the east, rode up between two underwater rocks.

To the shocked people on board, there was, what seemed like, an absolute silence. It appeared that even the fury of the wind and the crashing of the waves had subsided. However, this illusion lasted only a matter of seconds, and then chaos broke out. Below, the soldiers on the pumps were thrown into the water. Their sergeant said,

"Job's done 'ere lads. Get yourselves above and make for shore as best you can, and good luck." Before Billy Spraggs could get to his feet and retrieve his jacket, the water was washing around his neck.

Bethany was thrown from her cot and tumbled across the floor tangled in her blankets. Eliza, on the for'ard side of their cabin, was more fortunate, but even so, she hit her head against the cabin wall.

"What's happening, Miss, have we arrived in port?" asked Bethany.

On the gundeck, the hammocks all swung violently, waking the occupants, who climbed out, dressed, and either ran for the ladders or decided to return to their beds to await orders, which they would probably ignore.

The captain's quill scrawled a long line across his log entry as the ship struck and he fell from his seat.

Kalinda got up, dressed quickly and tried to make out the various barked orders, that she could hear from above. The curtain to her cabin door opened and her husband, a soldier, took her by the arm.

"Have we arrived, husband?"

"No, we have hit some rocks, I fear. We'll go to the captain's roundhouse. It will be safer there, Kalinda."

In the roundhouse, Mr Schwartz and the purser were still discussing possible fortune making ventures, should the purser choose to settle in Madras. The purser fell backwards off his chair, but was quickly on his feet and rapidly realising the situation, said,

"Mr Schwartz, I beg your pardon, follow me, I need your help to bring the strong box here, where it will be safe. It is times like these, that some members of the crew can become uncontrollable."

Mary-Ann was not disturbed when the ship went aground, and was only awoken by her two cousin's screams,

"For pity's sake, be quiet," she said, "what an earth has happened? Have you both had nightmares?"

Mr Miller was in his room, writing to his mother, hoping to get a letter off with the pilot, who was to be dropped off at Plymouth. When the ship hit the rocks, he thought he heard the harpsichord strings all sounding at once.

The surgeon, awoken by shouts and screams, assumed that there was some calamitous situation, which might require his services. He dressed, got his bag and joined the throng outside his cabin, who were all trying to get up the narrow stairs to the captain's roundhouse above.

Miss Mansell, who had not taken any of her clothes off since boarding the ship, because of a dream, in which the whole ship had been left on the sea bed. This had happened when God parted the English Channel, to allow the Huguenots back into France. She had interpreted this as the inevitable biblical end to all aboard. She was ready to walk to France before the waves came crashing back, like the Biblical parting of the Red Sea, and drowned them all.

The cook's mate, Corke, was asleep in his bunk in the galley, while Fluck puzzled over a chess board. He had been studying the same position for an hour, after trying to beat his galley lad at the game since he joined the ship. He could not understand how a boy, so young, could be as good at the game. The moment the ship hit the rocks, the chess pieces were wiped from the board, the cauldron hanging over the fire broke its chain, and water dowsed the fire filling the galley with steam. Corke awoke and screamed out,

"Mr Fluck, what's happening?" And Fluck, trying to retrieve the chess pieces, said,

"I don't fucking know lad. Get out of that fucking bunk and get dressed."

"Dressed for what, Mr Fluck?"

"For fucking everything, lad. Seems like we've gone aground and the ship's going fucking down."

A crowd of soldiers and sailors blocked Spraggs' way, all hurrying and trying to get up a set of broken steps to the gundeck. Trying a different route, he pushed passed them and headed towards the stern. He came to an empty passageway and followed that. In front of him were two sailors with a lantern, looking very much like they were up to some enterprise.

"Well, what have we here? Looks like two lads hiding in a dark corner of the ship and one has an axe. So, Billy's asking himself, will it be worth your time to be giving these lads a helping hand?"

"This is Fluck's brandy store."

"Brandy, you say. Well now there's a bit of fortune, for hasn't old Billy, here, a special party trick, when it comes to brandy, and wouldn't I just love to show you lads how it rolls out. Give us the axe there, mates and I'll find that door's weakness quicker than an alleyway bit of laced mutton can spread her pegs." Armed with three bottles of Mr Fluck's brandy Spraggs went in search of a secluded hideaway where he could drink himself into oblivion and found one on the aft gun deck, under some steps.

On the orlop deck the sheep crashed into the For'ard hurdle that marked their pen. Their combined weight was enough to break the ties and the hurdle fell over, allowing the animals to run off along the deck.

Slowly, as the rocks ground away at the ship's timbers and the water filled the ship, the captain's roundhouse filled with all ranks of men and women, seeking some measure of safety in the sinking ship. Over the next hour, some tried to swim ashore, many drowned; a few knelt and prayed, while others, like Billy Spraggs, attempted to drink themselves into the next world.

It did not take long for Spraggs to empty the first two bottles,

"That's another dead 'n, Billy. Only one left. Will it be enough to get you where you're going? And where exactly are you going, Billy Boy, Billy Boy? And you all the way from County Clare. Your choices appear to have recently narrowed considerably. Narrowed down to just two, but which of them is it to be, Heaven or Hell? Hold fast there, Billy, hold fast. What's this at the top of the ladder, here? Well, I never. Are you dreaming ... or what now, lad? Get yourself into the shadows there. Why, isn't this a fine bit of laced-mutton, if ever saw some? Come on my big beauty, Billy's waiting. Don't be shy, down you come, that's it, all the way. Billy Spraggs, you've just been allocated a destination. A bit overloaded with ballast on the aft end, maybe, but any port in a storm, lad, any port in a storm."

Eventually, Eliza found herself on deck, dressed in Billy Spraggs' clothes, and waiting for signal to jump. The barrel at the end of the rope needed to tighten it. She felt the pull on the line. This is it. She went to lift up her non-existent skirts, then ran towards the gap in the landward gunwale, where, two days earlier, the main mast had fallen and dragged Mr Berrington to his death. Just as she had done as a child, jumping off the jetty into the garden lake at Fiddlesham. Jump and fly, like a spidez in the wind,

"Il pleut, il pleut, bergère ..."

46   Sheep

The rope and barrel pulled Eliza towards the cliff but then snatched her backwards and under water. Her line had snagged some rocks. She slid the noose over her head and, as best she could, swam away from the ship towards the black cliffs. Silvanus's advice to her, about directing her mind towards something else when in the cold sea, did not help. What else was there, apart from blackness, the surf submerging her every minute and preventing her from breathing, and the screaming pain of her freezing limbs? The waves came in great unstoppable ranks, pushing her under their chaotic heaps of white foam and tumbling her over so that she could not easily tell which way was up. Almost as bad as the waves from behind her, were the waves bouncing off the cliff, coming back out to sea, and hitting her in the face. These would have to cross the waves coming in, and the two peaks would lift Eliza high into the air and then plunge her down. After surviving several huge waves, she knew she could not manage many more. It grew darker overhead, and she could see nothing of the cliffs. She must not give up, but which way? Was she swimming in the right direction? She had to keep going. Striking out, her hand hit a rock. She tried to find a handhold in the darkness. If she could get a grip ... but she was being dragged away, out again and pushed under another wave, she could not see how ... then she was back at the rock face again and something gripped her by the wrist,

"Silvanus, you are here."

"That's not me, young soldier. My name's Sampson - but Christian or heathen, here's a hand for you," and he lifted Eliza up far enough out of the swell to rescue her from being drawn out to sea again. She clung to the rocks for a moment, coughing up water and then clawed herself onto the rocky ledge.

"Thank you, Sir," she spluttered, still trying to get her breath.

The man's eyes darted at her, shining brightly out of a black face. He said nothing, just sat on the rocks, knees up and arms around his shoulders. She had seen this man climbing the rigging on the first day.

"You saved my life," Eliza said. Should she explain to him that she was not a soldier? In the dimmest of light beyond the cave, Eliza could just make out the stern half of the ship. It still looked huge, too big to be destroyed, even by this furious sea. Perhaps it will last until the morning when rescue arrives. Then a wave broke over the wreck and rocked it from side to side. After some time, Eliza heard an outburst of shouts and screams from both men and women. The grey dawn was getting lighter all the time, and Eliza could see that there now was no ship. The sea was still rough and tossed about all manner of timber, rope and debris. Eliza could see dozens of men in their shallow cave, but there seemed no way to get out of there and up the cliff. Beyond them, some thirty yards out, a group of men clung to a large rock. Was the tide still rising? If so, it would be harder for them all to cling onto the wet seaweed covered rock. Out in the sea, a dark line marked the face of a great wave approaching. Its crest tipping over here and there and spilling into great white horses. It rose higher when it reached the large, barn size rock and covered it. When it had passed, all the men had gone, and the boulder was empty. A few men were swimming, and one reached the cave.

"Mingies," The black man shouted, making Eliza jump. "Here, over here, swim Mingies, here's my hand." The man made the ledge at the back of the cave and Sampson helped his friend out of the water and onto their ledge, and then tried to squeeze water out of his clothes. He rubbed his feet and hands to try and get feeling back in them. Eliza did the same to her own limbs. She was not sure if it helped, but it was something to keep her mind from thinking about pain. A man, further down the ledge began shouting, screaming out the Lord's Prayer, until, on the second repetition, someone told him to shut up,

"Can't you see, the Almighty is busy whisking up the world's oceans?"

Out near the rock, amongst all the floating wreckage, a man in a soldier's red jacket could be seen swimming towards the cave. He was a strong swimmer and popped up when wave after wave tried to keep him down. Men started shouting,

"Come on, Come on."

"It's Spraggs, you can do it, son. Keep going." But there came wave after wave pushing him under and dragging him back. He was becoming weaker and weaker, until, after one breaker Eliza never saw him come up. Eliza closed her eyes. Is this all happening? She asked herself. Then a face appeared, right in front of her,

"Would you be helping a fellow soldier out of this fucking ocean, mo cara ... my friend?" It was Spraggs with his hand held out towards Eliza. She held onto a rock with one arm and the other she offered to Spraggs, who grasped it and pulled himself up,

"Thank you. You must be one of them what came aboard at Gravesend. Now wasn't that a well-named place to start a fucking voyage like this. How long since you joined?" Eliza decided not to answer. "Not long ago, I'd say by the softness of those hands. Still, it was welcome after that swim." Why can't this Irish soldier just be quiet like everyone else, Eliza thought. She didn't want to have to think of answers to his questioning. He continued with his chatter,

"Well, wasn't that an expensive hour for our much-esteemed Honourable Company. Hey, look, there goes a caora, a fucking sheep swimming in the sea, have you ever seen such a ting? Come on little Miss Mutton Pie, ain't there plenty of room up here for 'e, between me and the boy here. You can keep us warm."

Sampson, seeing the sheep, began to climb down towards it

"What are you doing? Sampson, come back." Mingies held on to Sampson's shoulder, and they both watched as the sheep was drawn back by a receding wave away from the rocks and out of the cave. Sampson sat down again.

Spraggs shouted to him. "What in hell were you doing, my Kaffir friend, intending to ride that sheep to the nearest port, I'd wager? Anyway, now it may well come back with a rescue flock, eh?" Sampson spoke quietly, to Mingies,

"It's my ancestors. They are cross with me and have brought the storm. If I make a sacrifice we will be saved from further disaster."

"Hey, give us a dance, Kaffir, and conjure up some giant whales to save us all.

"Enough, Paddy, give it a rest, or I'll throw you back in the sea," said Mingies.

After that, Spraggs's chattering died away, and the mood in the cave became even grimmer. Men began to sob, and the Lord's-Prayer-man started up again. He seemed only to know the one prayer and was putting all his faith in that. However, no one had the energy now to complain. The pain in Eliza's limbs became less severe, and if she kept perfectly still, she could stop shivering. From the other end of the cave, a familiar voice called out of the gloom,

"I need a volunteer, someone to climb the cliff and get help. We will not be seen here, not from the cliff top, and no boats are going to venture out in this weather." It was Mr Reeves' voice, and Eliza's spirits lifted when she realised that he was here and might be able to assert his calm authority,

"To the east, the left, looks like the easier route." Mr Reeves continued. "Any of the soldiers along there think they might attempt to climb the cliff?" Spraggs looked at Eliza, who lowered her head, and then he shouted back,

"Sorry, Sir, I think I've busted my ankle, and my mate here has delicate hands." No one else answered for a while, until the cook, Mr Fluck, said that he had climbed a lot as a boy, for bird's eggs, and would have a look.

"Oh well," said Fluck, "falling off a cliff can't be worse than fucking freezing to death in this devil's hole." He made his way along the ledge, squeezing past all the men. When Fluck reached the soldier, to make way for him, Spraggs squashed up close to Eliza and he stared hard at her. Did he recognise her? Bethany had said these were Spraggs' clothes, was he going to say something about this? Eliza could not imagine why she was so worried that someone might discover her identity. The situation was so dire, she thought, discovery should be the least of her worries. Fluck disappeared out of the cave and after a while, Mr Reeve called out,

"Mr Fluck, how are you faring, is there a route?" But there was no answer, and then some stones and a few rocks began falling over the lip of the cave into the sea. There was a shout from someone in the cave and Fluck fell into the sea. He must have hit his head before falling into the sea because he floated on his back, being dragged backwards and forwards by the swell.

"We're all going to die here. One by one. What's the point of hanging on here? No one's going to come to our rescue."

"Who's going to try the climb again?" asked someone.

"I'll go," said Mr Reeve. "We should keep trying until someone succeeds."

"Shall I come with you, Mr Reeve, Sir?" asked Corke, the galley boy.

"If you think you can manage the climb, lad."

47   Quarrymen

The first cottage that Mr Reeve, the third mate, and Corke, the cook's mate, came to, was the quarry overseer's house. Only his housemaid was in, but she sent her young son to run and fetch Mr Garland. He rapidly organised a party of men to join Mr Reeve, now re-clothed, to show them the spot where they had climbed up. Young Corke was now too ill and feeble to assist in the rescue and stayed in the cottage. More quarrymen came with ropes, horses, carts, spikes and hammers. Mr Garland, soon devised a means of rescue for those trapped below. Four men would be stationed part way down the slope at the top of the cliff and two more, further down at the very lip of the rock-face. All the men would be secured by ropes, which were secured to spikes driven into the ground. Another rope was thrown over the cliff, down to the trapped survivors.

It had been nearly two hours since Mr Reeve and Corke had left the cave and down below, it had been assumed that they too had fallen. Mr Congleton said, as he was the next in command, he should be the next to attempt the climb. After some difficulty, he climbed eighty feet but the last twenty were more difficult, owing to the loose nature of the rock face. Every handhold crumbled with his touch and every foothold fell away from beneath him, sending stones and rocks cascading down below. This alarmed everyone in the cave, or at least the ones who were healthy enough to be able to be concerned at what was happening, and capable of still being alarmed. They were expecting to see Mr Congleton's body hurtling down at any moment.

Mr Congleton found it impossible to get, even one limb on a rock which might support him and he began to slide down and only saved himself by falling spread-eagle on the sloping cliff. He felt that he was about to fall at any moment.

"God, I beg of you, have mercy. Not to intervene for my sake but all the poor Christian souls below." At that moment the quarrymen's rope appeared by his right hand.

It was an event, which in later life Mr Congleton would describe as his moment of Deus ex Machina. It not only gave Mr Congleton hope of life to come but would define that future life and lead to him exchanging a life at sea for one of spiritual devotion. Not believing what his eyes were seeing, he raised his head with every expectation of seeing the face of God. However, looking up, what faced him was the foremost quarryman. Mr Congleton snatched at the rope. The quarryman shouted back to his mates,

"Take the strain, back there. We got one 'ere," and Mr Congleton was dragged to safety.

At first light, Mingies spirits lifted a little,

"What a mess, Sampson. Is this all that's left of our ship full of souls?"

After a pause, Sampson replied,

"I thought that white men's souls survived such disasters, Mingies. It's their flesh and bone, that struggles."

"I'm not sure, but what I am confident of, is that the officers will be lapping it up in Heaven, while the likes of you and I will be stoking the fires of Hell. Don't look forward to too much, comfort after death. We need to get what we can here and now. Tell me, if you don't believe in souls living in the afterlife, what do you believe in?"

"I believe in the spirits of our ancestors. My father told me a story once."

Come on, let's hear it then, doesn't look like I am going anywhere, for a while."

"A chief had two daughters who went down to the river. They were starving. Out of the river came a spirit who told the girls that the villagers should dig up the few crops they had and slaughter the remaining sheep. They told the chief, who asked the girls to describe the spirit they had seen. The chief said that it was the spirit of their long dead brother, the chief's son. The chief told his people to do as the spirit had said. That night all the spirits of their ancestors returned, bringing with them, lots of food, healthy sheep and new seeds for sowing. After that my villagers always sacrificed a sheep to thank their ancestors."

The vicar, Rev. Morgan Jones, of a village nearby the site of the shipwreck, heard of the shipwreck and wondered how, as well as prayer, he could best assist with the rescue. It seemed that the men from the quarry were already carrying out a splendid operation. He arrived at the cliff top in his pony and trap, together with a crate of brandy to reward the hard working and courageous quarrymen. He had thought that this would be drunk after the rescue had been completed, but the quarrymen felt that the brandy would best ease their work, if they drank it straight away.

After two hour's work, only thirteen men had been rescued. Each time, the rope, with a loop on the end, had to be thrown over the clifftop into the sea. Then all would wait while the rope was blown or washed into the cave. Whoever was the nearest, then took the rope, put it over their shoulders and under their arms, gave it a tug and waited to be hauled up. At the fourteenth occasion it was washed in front of Eliza, who climbed down onto the rocks to retrieve it. About to put it around her head, she noticed Sampson; his eyes half closed and looking feeble.

"Here," she said, "your turn," and she gave him the rope.

"White men first, ain't that the rule in the Honourable Company," shouted Spraggs, "Kaffirs at the back of the line."

Mingies stood up with a struggle and turned towards Spraggs, but Sampson put his hand on his shoulder.

"No matter, Mingies," he said, "Here, take the rope. Your turn. I'll see you, top side in, a while." Mingies knew it would be useless arguing with Sampson. In any case, he told himself, he looks stronger than I feel. Mingies took the rope, put it over his shoulder, pulled and waited. Slowly and jerkily, he was pulled up until he was six feet lower than the lip of the cave then everything stopped, apart from the wind, which spun him around. Hanging in mid-air, and with nothing to hold onto, he continued to swirl around, which made him sick and dizzy. Half an hour went by and there was a pull on the rope and he was moving again. Once he had reached the rock, he tried to walk up holding onto the rope but kept on falling and was dragged over the rocks, ripping his clothes and scraping his knees and hands. Eventually, he came level with the first two men, one of whom was drinking from a bottle,

"Hold up, back there, let's give this fellow a drop of brandy. Here you are my fine friend." Mingies took a swig and was sick almost straight away. At the top, was a cart, which took him up the hill to a cottage. It seemed everyone around him was roaring drunk. Inside a crowded kitchen, a man gave him a pile of blankets, which he wrapped around himself before sitting at a table. A woman brought a bowl of hot broth, some bread and more brandy. After a few spoonfuls of the soup he pushed it to one side, put his head on the table and closed his eyes.

Eliza came up from the cave just before dusk. It was not until daylight that Spraggs was rescued. "Are you the last one, young feller?" Asked a quarryman.

"Just the Kaffir down there, and I am not sure if he's still in this world."

Mingies felt better after a night's sleep and had hitched a lift down to the cliff top, to find Sampson.

"Where's Sampson? He asked Spraggs.

"What, the Kaffir? Dead, at least near to. There's no way he could handle the rope and climb."

"Why didn't you tie him on and send him up?"

"Company rules, was it, white men first?" said Mingies. The quarrymen were beginning to pack up and Mingies said,

"Hold fast there, mates. There's one more below. Give us the rope, I'll go down again and help him.

"No' we're done here, it's only a Kaffir," said the man winding up the rope. Another, younger quarryman, stepped in,

"I'll go down. You been through enough, sailor. Let's finish the job properly." An hour later, the young man returned, dragging an unconscious Sampson. In the cart back to the cottage, Sampson eyes opened,

"Mingies, have we made it? Is this England? Lift me up, let me see. It ain't as green as I thought."

"It's winter."

"Don't forget the story, Mingies." Before Mingies could answer, Sampson closed his eyes and Mingies knew his friend was dead.

48 Antelope

Dorchester

The next day Mingies met the Reverend Morgan Jones and insisted that Ben Sampson was a Christian. Furthermore, Sampson had distinguished himself by sailing around the world with Captain Cooke. The Reverend agreed to arrange for him to have a Christian burial in nearby St Nicholas's churchyard.

"It is the least we can do for such a fine sailor," said the reverend. I will arrange with the mason in the quarry here, to inscribe a stone to mark his grave and thus remind every visitor in years to come that here lies the remains of Ben Sampson, a Christian, who died in the service of his country."

"Thank you, Reverend," said Mingies.

The next day the survivors were taken on the seven-hour journey to the Antelope Inn at Dorchester, some on foot and others by wagon.

Eliza sat on a bench seat opposite Mingies. She felt, as they had shared the trials in the cave next to one another, that he was a man she could trust. But she still dared not reveal her identity. Who knows how these men would react, if they found out who she was? Just as they were setting off, Spraggs climbed over the side of the wagon,

"Room for some skin and bones from County Clare?" he said, pushing in between the sailors who were sitting opposite Eliza. This soldier again, Eliza thought, he is one I cannot trust. What sort of deal had Bethany made with him to get his clothes? How could

Eliza keep herself segregated from the other survivors. There was no way. Unless she revealed her identity. If she walked, she would be better placed to retained her distance from the men. Spraggs was leaning so far forward that his head was almost in Liza's lap, he was close enough for her to smell his breath. She could not tell if he was asleep, or up to some trick. She looked down at the breeches she was wearing. On the right leg, just below her knee, there was a mark, a small patch repair. Was Spraggs looking at that? If Bethany was right and these were his clothes, he would surely recognise his own needle repairs. The wagon hit a bump and Spraggs fell towards Eliza. Putting his arms out to stop himself falling, he held onto Eliza's arms. She could not move.

"Well, aren't I a fine one, dropping off to sleep. Lucky for me there's a strapping young lad to catch me fall. Now, what was it I was dreaming about?"

The landlord, of the Antelope coaching inn, seeing the distressed state of the men, said that they would be fed and cared for at no charge.

As soon as he reached Dorchester, Mr Reeve began organising funds and a mount, on which to set off on the first leg of a journey to London to relay the news of the ship's disaster to the East India Company. The others, the landlord said, would be welcome to stay at the Antelope until they felt fit enough for onward travel, towards which, he would give them each half-a-crown.

During the second night after the wreck, Eliza heard a nearby church clock strike midnight, then one o'clock and still she was awake at three in the morning, by which time the chorus of animal-like grunts, shouts, snores and farts, in her shared room, were almost intolerable. If she closed her eyes and tried to sleep, she awoke to the noise of the three men in the room, or if she did manage to ignore the cacophony and slip into sleep, she would suffer from a sudden sensation of being back underwater and drowning and jump with a start. Finally, she fell asleep, just following the four o'clock chimes. Only to be startled awake by a rough hand over her mouth and being pinned to her mattress. She could feel hot breath in her ear. A voice whispered,

"Now then, Billy boy, I'm asking meself, what 'ave we here? I be pretty sure; all is not as it appears." Spraggs' free hand was under the blankets trying to get between her legs. She twisted her body tried to shout, and get free, but he was too strong. "Well, now Billy me lad, isn't that a fine thing. Our lad here, ain't a lad, he ain't got what it takes to be, lad-like. And wearing your clothes, as well. Mind you, ain't *she* very welcome to them, for the right price." Eliza managed to twist right over so she was lying face down but now her muffled shouts were less likely to awaken anyone else in the room. Spraggs had hold of the belt of her breeches and pulled them down to her knees.

"Well, if you'd prefer it this way, makes no odds to Billy, I like to oblige a lady. She could feel his erect penis pushing between her thighs, what could she do? He was struggling to get his way, at the same time to keep her mouth shut and for a moment his hand slipped, and Eliza got her teeth around a finger and bit so hard, the tip of his little finger came away, bitten clean through. He jumped up, so high that he hit his head and shoulders on the cross boards of the the empty bunk above, sending the bars clattering to the floor.

"Fuck! What the fuck, you've bitten me fucking finger clean off. I'll fucking kill you." He launched himself towards Eliza but became entangled in the fallen bedding and, flying into a rage, began fighting the mattress from the upper bunk. One of the men opposite, who had been sharing the double bed in the room, lit the oil lamp. In the light, Mingies, who was in the other half of the double bed, looked across and saw Eliza desperately trying to pull her breeches up and cover her nakedness. Spraggs was on his feet and went for Eliza, who spat blood and the remains of his little finger at him. He raised his fist, Eliza's back was to the bunks, and she had nowhere to go, but Mingies had an arm around the soldier's neck, pulled him to the ground and sat on him.

"What's going on, here?" Mingies asked.

"I knew from the moment he pulled me out of the sea, he was a she, and in the cart yesterday, I could smell her. I can always smell a woman, no matter what."

Spraggs was still struggling, so Mingies pulled the soldier's belt off and began binding his wrists with it.

"She's bitten me fucking finger off, see." He held up his bound hands and showed Mingies and the other sailors, now out of their bunks and watching the blood, still streaming from his finger.

"So, you're telling us that he, or she, helped save your life in the cave the other night, you found out he was a woman, and thought you'd rape her?"

"She was wearing my trousers."

"Shut your mouth, Paddy." Mingies looked up at Eliza. "What have you to say on the matter?"

Eliza said nothing. She had taken a decision, when in the cave, that the best way to remain incognito was for her to remain calm and silent. But now, Mingies and the other two sailors, was staring at her, and waiting for an answer. She tried to escape by picking up a blanket and wrapping it around her to hide, but Mingies said,

"You've misled us, and that may be for a good reason, or by accident, and this fellow beneath me has got little sympathy going his way, but please …"

There was no way out. She must rely on the help of Mingies. If everyone knew her identity there would be no escaping and soon, maybe tomorrow, officials from the East India Company would arrive from London, and she would be taken back to her mother, who would want to know why she had not chosen to die by the side of her father, sister and cousins. And, worst of all, she could be put on the next ship out to India. If she was ever to find Silvanus again, she needed to keep her identity a secret. She decided she must try to win the secrecy of these three men.

"My name is Eliza Percy,"

"Captain Percy's daughter, of course, I thought I knew the face."

"My travelling companion got me these clothes. I do not know by what means. I needed breeches to stand a chance to swim ashore. I would have perhaps been content to die in my father's arms as, I assume, my sister and cousins have done, but I had fallen in love, for the first time, to a man named Silvanus. The trouble was he was a cooper and in my family's eyes, below my status. So, they put me aboard my father's ship, to send me to Madras to marry an officer out there, against my will."

Mingies needed to think it over, while the other two sat down on the bed and exchanged noncommittal glances.

"What about me fucking finger?"

"Shut up," said Mingies, "you've lost the right to take part in this discussion. Eliza sat down on the lower bunk with the blanket around her shoulders. Then Mingies seemed to come to a decision,

"That's why there were so many ladies aboard, Honourable Company was shipping young English ladies out to India to be married off to Indian officers, and without their say-so?"

"My sister was in favour of the plan, and my cousins, I think. I would not know the wishes of the other ladies on board." The thought of our English ladies being shipped off for marriage in India incensed the other two sailors, and they started, what would appear to have been, a well-practiced rant about the evils of the Honourable Company. After a while, Mingies stood up, tore a strip of cloth off from his shirt and bound up Spraggs finger. Spraggs, still bound, shuffled over to lean against the closed door.

"I have a suggestion," said Mingies. "But all five of us must swear to it, if we are to satisfy everyone here this morning. I say that the three of us men here must swear to keep silent about Miss Percy's identity until she has safely disappeared. Spraggs, those clothes you are wearing, who do they belong to?"

"I don't know his name. It was some fucking idiot, who, rather than face the sea, decided to drink a bottle of brandy and open his veins. He was beyond telling me his name. But sure, as St Patrick, he had no further use for them."

"Good," said Mingies, so now this soldier is not short of a uniform, but she did steal his clothes and should pay for them. Miss, I would say sixpence, of that half-crown that the landlord gave you, would be fair recompense."

"But what about me fucking finger, she bit it off. That's got to be worth a bob or two, cos it ain't going to grow back."

"Well," said Mingies, "if you are going to go around trying to fuck women without their say-so, then you must expect to get something bitten off from time to time. You were lucky it was just your little finger. Mind you, if what I've heard about soldiers is true, a woman would find it hard to discover anything to bight off, as big as a little finger, down there." The sailors laughed, while Spraggs sulked and shrugged his shoulders.

"What do you two say, mates?" The sailors looked at one another and nodded agreement,

"Aye, we'll keep quiet, until the lady's long gone."

"Spraggs? What do you say?" asked Mingies, kicking the soldier's foot.

"Who appointed you, mess deck magistrate?"

"I did," said Mingies, kicking Spraggs's other foot.

"Can you make it a shilling?" asked Spraggs.

"Ninepence," said Mingies.

"Alright, I'll swear to it," said Spraggs.

"Miss?" asked Mingies.

"I agree, I swear," said Eliza looking directly at Mingies, "and thank you."

The money exchanged and the room tidied up, the last thing said on the subject was by Mingies. He came up close to Spraggs holding him by his collar and speaking right into his face,

"If you should renege on your oath, I shall find you, wherever you hide and cut off that little pinkie dangling in your fart crackers."

"Billy Spraggs'll keep his word. I swore, didn't I?"

49   Anfin

"Chichester? One shilling and ninepence will not take you that far, Miss," said Mingies, as they walked down the road, and out of Dorchester. The sun was rising over the low hills in front of them.

"What can I do, Mr Mingies?"

"Walk. You'll have to walk. Keep the money for food, pass yourself off as a working lad and join the crowds heading to London to find work. You'll be safer in a crowd but watch out for pickpockets. I can walk with you as far as Poole, where I should be able to get work aboard a ship. That'll take us two days. Tonight, we'll stop at Bere and find a busy alehouse to get some money. You best stop calling me Mister. Mingies or Nat will do. It's not the fact that you are a woman, which will so easily be discovered, as that you are from the upper classes. Your voice and your confidence give you away. Try not to speak, if you don't want to be caught out, and listen to the voices of those around you and try to copy them. Don't use any of your teeth-breaking words. And you need a new name, What about, Ezekiel. I'll call you, Zekie."

"How can one get money at an inn, Mr Mingies?"

"What did I just say?"

"Sorry," Eliza tried her best at a servant's accent,

"How does we get zome money, Mingies?"

Mingies laughed, "Better."

"Tonight, if there's a good crowd, I'll tell the story of the storm that wrecked our ship. I'll make 'em feel so sorry for us and that might well pay for a night's lodging. But you must keep quiet.

At the Royal Oak that night, Mingies told such a sad and drastic tale of the sinking of their ship; about how the good captain had held his daughters in his arms as the ship plunged beneath the storm-tossed waves; how Mingies and his mate here, Zekie, had escaped; were washed ashore by giant waves and climbed a cliff in the darkness. When his story was over, the landlord gave Mingies and Zeike bowls of stew, bread, cake and ale. They passed a hat around, and when they counted the money, later that night, in one of the inn's rooms, also given them free by the landlord, Mingies had earned eleven-shillings and threepence.

"These fiddlers shiners add up to five shillings and sixpence to you and threepence extra for me because I drink so much more ale than you."

"Is that fair? You must deserve much more than threepence extra. You did all the storytelling. Mingies."

"It's fair enough. You did your part and kept tight lipped. We'll be able to ride in carts most of the way to Poole and then you on to Chichester. Tomorrow, we need to change your coat. Your soldier's claret will get you into trouble before long."

In Bere, they found the house of a tailor who was happy to trade the soldier's red coat for a well mended brown linen jacket with long narrow sleeves and five pewter buttons down the middle.

At Poole they said farewell.

"Mingies, in years to come if you find yourself near Chichester, come to Fiddlesham, and if I am not there, the gardener, Esau, will treat you kindly and reward you for your help to me."

"I need no more reward. I helped you as I would any other honest shipmate. You were a good shipmate. Good luck to you, Zekie."

"And good luck to you, also, Mingies."

The morning was bright and sunny, when Eliza left Poole. There was a breeze from behind her to help her on her way and she had breakfasted well with eggs, oysters, fresh bread and her first ever taste of coffee. Never having been allowed it at Fiddlesham. The strong black liquid made her head spin.

Once out of town, on the Ringwood Road, she did as Mingies had told her and stopped at the first crossroad. Then, when a sturdy cart with a capable looking driver came along, she held a coin in the air and the driver stopped. He said that he could take her to within an hour's walk of Ringwood. The cart itself had a mixture of agricultural tools and machines, for what purpose, Eliza could not tell. Behind the goods, were secured two planks supported from one side to the other, which acted as benches. On one bench sat a woman with a baby in her arms.

"Good morning," said Eliza. The young woman looked shocked, and said nothing. Eliza remembered Mingies advice, don't speak to anyone unless you must, but it was too late, she had forgotten already. The cart rolled on, at not much faster a pace than she could have walked. This, however, was less tiring. After three hours. The cart stopped at an alehouse, crowded with a dozen or so wagons, that had stopped in the muddy unfenced field opposite. While children were running around, women were talking and men were standing around smoking pipes. Eliza bought some bread and cheese a glass of ale, all without having to speak. But the cheese was rotten, the bread was stale and she could not drink because her bladder was full. She looked around, the women were just squatting at the edge of the field allowing their skirts to cover their purposes, but the men? Two men on a bench nearby seemed to be staring at her and then whispering behind their hands. Commenting on her feminine looks, perhaps, or her red ponytail. Some men were going through a backdoor and returning after a few minutes. She watched and waited until she thought that there could be no more men out side, went out and urinated in a gutter at the back of the alehouse.

Returning to the road, four boys were chasing one another around and bumped into Eliza, knocking her to the ground. Before she could get up, the boys had run off. Two men helped her to her feet and with their hands brushed her clothes down. It was the same two men who she had seen whispering in the alehouse. Eliza thanked and assured them that she was uninjured and everything was well. They said, good day, and went back into the inn, which Eliza thought strange as they had only just left the place. Then it struck her. She slapped her palm onto her belt, where she had tied her money in a kerchief. It was gone. She rushed back inside the inn but there was no sign of the men. They must have left by the backdoor. She started to follow but stopped herself, what could she do against two men? The damage had been done; she had no money.

Back outside, there were several wagons, but not Eliza's one. Then she saw her wagon, two-hundred yards further along the road. She would easily be able to catch it at a fast walk. She must continue her journey as best she could. If she could find some shelter that night in Ringwood, she could perhaps make Chichester the following day. She had wished that she had eaten more of the stale bread and mouldy cheese back in the alehouse, but never mind.

The road was more crowded now, mainly with families. Some were smartly dressed and others wore rags. There was a man pushing a hand cart with a child sitting amongst an assortment of, what looked like, their worldly belongings. There were mothers walking side-by-side with their men, some of whom were carrying their babies in a shawl hanging from their shoulders. There were groups of young men, travelling much faster, some with bundles on their backs, and others with all manner of carts and wheelbarrows. Horse riders were quite common, some with their mounts at a trot, causing everyone to clear the road. Then there was a group of nuns in a wagon with a priest driving. Horses were pulling carts of every sort and occasional yellow bounders came dashing along with postilion riders sounding their horns to clear the road. For every one traveller going west there were ten, or a dozen, travelling east - in Eliza's direction.

In a moment the normal commotion of the crowd rose to a roar, as mothers began calling their children and rounding them up out of the road. It was the stage coach – six horses at a gallop, making the most of this flat and dry section of road. Eliza moved to the side but there was still a child sitting in the middle of the road crying. No one seemed to be concerned, despite the stage's horn sounding urgently. Eliza ran out and scooped up the child. The road now being clear, the stage passed safely by. Eliza looked around but everyone was intent on their own journey, or conversation. Whose child did she have? She put him down,

"Where is your mother, young man?" The boy did not answer but offered Eliza the end of a frayed hemp rope, the other end of which was tied around his waist. She took the boy's rope tether. He had a runny nose, which had made streaks through the dirt around his mouth. He wore an adult's jacket with the sleeves rolled back and secured with tied strips of torn cloth.

His boots were likewise too big and he wore a maid's dirty mobcap.

"What is your name, young man?"

"Anfin, Mizter."

"Anfin, your name is Anfin?"

"Anfin."

"Where is your mother, Anfin." The boy did not answer but held up fingers and thumb rubbing them together in front of his mouth.

"Anfin," someone shouted,

"Anfin." And the boy looked around and up the road ahead, where a man was running towards them,

"Anfin, Anfin, there you are. Thank you, Sir, thank you. I hope the boy has not caused problems."

"He was sitting in the road, Sir, when the stage came by ... but all is well now." The man stepped back and looked surprised. Eliza suddenly realised she had forgotten herself and who she was supposed to be, and had said too much. However, the man quickly relaxed and smiled,

"I thank you a thousand times, Sir. Please allow me to help you in some manner, make some part repayment for your kindness." Eliza smiled and shook her head. Then realised that it was too late the genie was out of the bottle, the man had heard her voice.

"It is not necessary, Sir. Any Christian would have done the same."

"That may be so, but I wonder, true Samaritans are very rare, in these days, Sir. Let me introduce myself, Knapman, Genesius Knapman, itinerant player. My friends call me Gen. Which way are you travelling, Mister ...?"

"Ezekiel Percy, Sir, and I am travelling to my home near Chichester via the town of Ringwood tonight, God willing."

"Well, my friend, we travel to Ringwood today. My troupe and family await ahead. Perhaps you would care to join us. We have a cart, which carries amongst other items, food and drink. I'd like to welcome you to travel with our caravan and share what food we have.

The man took the boy's tether and the three of them joined the throng of others on the road to Ringwood.

50   Tom

The three travellers soon caught up with Gen's wife, Sarah, and Eliza accepted their invitation to accompany them on the road to Ringwood; although they seemed a strange family, she felt safe with these travellers. Sarah was a large and strong looking woman of about forty years of age with an open and engaging smile that immediately put Eliza at her ease. However, while Sarah told Eliza about her children and their life on the road, Eliza felt she had nothing to contribute to the conversation because whatever she might say about Ezekiel, would, in essence, be a lie.

They arrived at Ringwood around an hour before sunset. A wintery drizzle hung in the air making everything cold and wet to the touch. They made their way to a field, which they referred to as the Furlong, between the church and the brewery. A large proportion of the field was taken up by stock pens with cattle, sheep, pigs and geese. All of which creatures seemed to be complaining about their confinement. Then there were the camps of the numerous traders, arriving ready for the following day's market. There were groups of men standing around their fires talking and arguing, mostly about money, or so it sounded like to Eliza. There were women with bundles, buckets of water and jugs of ale; several women pushing hand carts, from which they sold firewood at a penny a bundle but most of the encampment appeared to be occupied by children, who seemed to outnumber the adults five to one. All the offspring were engaged in a raucous game of tag, which involved much screaming from the girls and hollering from the boys. Gen and Sarah came to an encampment and were greeted by two old women and half a dozen children, who came screaming around Anfin and ran off with him to take him to join the others.

"Ezekiel, my friend, this is our place. Here is Little Sis. Little Sis, meet a fellow traveller, to whom we owe a great debt of gratitude, of which more later. Little Sis, this is Ezekiel.

"Pleaze to meet, ee, young'n, come and meet Big Sis." As far as Eliza could tell, Big Sis was the same size and shape as Little Sis, and the likeness of the two amazed Eliza,

"Good afternoon," said Eliza, "What a wonderful likeness you two share, how shall I tell you apart?"

"No need," said Gen, "Big Sis or Little Sis, they'll both answer to either. Now, to work, where's Tom? In the inn, would be my wild guess."

"Sarah soon got busy hanging up a pot from a tripod over the fire and the twin sisters finished off erecting a shelter from tarpaulins strung between their wagon and Gen's handcart.

"Big Sis, could I help in anyway?"

"Never 'e be minding that, sit 'e down on the tub 'ere, 'n rest 'e self. Sarah will be getting some nummits in a whiles 'n Gen 'n Tom will be back bi'mby from alehouse when they concluded, their … err."

"Done wiv 'eir tickle-pinching," said Big Sis.

"Aye, done with 'eir irrigation," said the other twin.

The children were fed and then one by one threaded into the rear of the wagon. Each with a hot stone from the fire, wrapped in cloth to keep them warm through the night. Much later, Gen returned to the camp and with him were, what Eliza thought must be the tallest man she had ever seen, over seven-feet in height, Eliza guessed, but as slim as a needle. He seemed a little drunk, but in a jolly mood. Eliza stood to greet him, and Tom held her by the elbows, squeezed them to her waste and then lifted her off her feet.

"Welcums, Welcums. Whot a sharp cat of a lad ee be."

"Tom, put Ezekiel down, you big bull calf. Save those rides for the young'ns," said Gen. Now Ezekiel, this here is Tom, a man of few spoken words, but despite which he do possess the most beautiful singing voice you will ever hear."

Everyone found a place to sit in the dry under the shelter. The sisters brought bread and steaming bowls of pottage around. They ate mostly in silence and having finished their food, fresh wood was put on the fire, woollen blankets brought out and everyone tried to get their feet off the cold ground.

"Now," said Gen, "we must be explaining our business to young Ezekiel, here. Perhaps then, he'll be interested in staying for the market and see us all at work."

"First things first," said Sarah, "Do there be enough ale to see you all through to midnight? I don't wanna be struggling cross field in dark to fetch more."

"Tom an' I be close to topped with it," said Gen, "'n there be 'alf a jug full left 'ere. But Ezekiel, How's 'e for ale?"

"Thank you but I am unused to beer and ale, and feel I have had sufficient," said Eliza, who felt herself glow red in the firelight, as everyone looked at the newcomer with the ladylike words.

"Who's to tell our story then, Gen, so as to inform Master Ezekiel?"

"Well," said Big Sis, "all 'cepting Gen here, be full of the Debbonish 'an will do little more than befuddle the young man."

"You see Master Ezekiel," added Sarah, "Gen, 'e hails from London-way and is the one we puts up to 'splain our ways to new friends, like 'eself. Folks what don't 'ave 'e Debbonish."

"But Tom, 'e be the master of it, 'e be the one what knows it all, it being Tom's own farver what began it all,"

"No,no, no, no, no, no ..." sang Tom, "It were our granfarver an' not our farver!

Little Sis said,

"I never knew 'at. I 'member 'e farver, but not 'e granfarver. When did 'he pass on?"

"I 'member Tom singing one of granfarver's songs, Tom can 'e 'member Old King Rowly."

"Yes," said Gen, "sing it us now, Tom, if 'e remembers it."

Tom sat upright, raised his head to the sky and closed his eyes. After a few moments he began,

'E's making of bastards gert,
And duchessing every whore,
The zurplus and treasury cheat,
'ave made us damnable poor.

Tom waved his arms and everyone, including the children from inside the wagon joined in with the refrain,

Quoth old Rowley the King,
Quoth old Rowley the King,
At council board,

Where every lord
Be led like a dog on a string.

Everyone gave a great cheer and began chatting and laughing and saying how good was Tom at remembering so many of the old songs.

"Quiet, back there," said Sarah to the children, "Go to sleep, now."

Tom said, "But I be thinking it be in the time of Brandy Nan, that granfarver did pass away."

"Brandy Nan," said Gen, "that's what we calls Queen Anne in London. I know that 'cos someone showed me it chiselled on a stone outside the church where she's buried. It says:

Brandy Nan, Brandy Nan,
left in the lurch,
'er face to the gin-shop,
'er back to the church.

"'Nuff said, let's get down to our night's business," said Big Sis.

Eliza listened, amazed, as Gen told, with numerous interruptions and contradictions from everyone else, of the show that had been devised some fifty years previous and which this family of players had been touring around markets and fairs across the South of England ever since. Their performance had been based on the songs of Tom of Bedlam. Gen explained that many years ago the insane asylum in London, called Bedlam, was in the habit of inviting paying guests through its gates to be entertained by the antics of the inmates. So popular and lucrative was this, that the authorities began sending out some of their less dangerous inmates to earn money performing their acts on the streets. Tom's grandfather, and his father saw that this had become hugely popular and attracted large crowds. So, Grandfather had the idea of pretending that they were Bedlamites in order to garner a good crowd and add to their income. Across the South of England other actors began to claim that they were Bedlamites. If a crowd saw through them, they would shout call out that they were, Sham Abrahams. Tom and his family had continued the family tradition ever since.

The troupe of actors told how they had faced a setback last spring when Tom's elder sister, Bess had died of the fever. She had been the troupe's musician and played the fiddle beautifully. When she heard this Eliza said,

"Perhaps I may be of some help. Your life is so different to that of mine, up until recently that is, that I feel at a loss to repay you for your kindness, but I have trained as a musician and have studied the violin for three years, although I must confess that in recent times, I have … well, never mind, suffice to say that if you have a working instrument, and appropriate manuscripts, I could play most music - with a little practice." She stopped. The five faces shone out in the firelight, eyes sparkling and mouth's gaping. Mingies words came crashing into Eliza's mind, 'speak as little as possible and avoid tooth-breaking words.' Would these kind people throw her out? Little Sis spoke first,

I don't reckon we 'ave zo much in the way of manuzcrips, but Tom could zing 'em, if 'e could imitate the tunes on the fiddle?"

"Old on Sis, afore we gets to 'at," said Big Sis, "perhaps Ezekiel 'ere could tell us a little of 'is story. Like 'ow 'e finds 'imself on the road, wiv the likes of us. Be 'e everzo welcum to our company as it be."

This is it, thought Eliza, I must tell them. She took her hat off, removed the leather fastening to her ponytail and shook her hair out. She heard her old friend, Esau say, "tell 'em, Miss, tell 'em, 'n show 'em 'at this 'ere nymph really be a damselfly."

"I have a confession. My name is not Ezekiel … it is Eliza."

51   Bedlamites

Ringwood, Hampshire

Eliza became mesmerised by Tom's strange voice. It was like listening to a choirboy trapped in an adult's body. She had never heard the like of it before. After a while she had to shake herself, so powerful, sweet and sad was his voice, she just wanted to close her eyes and let it carry her away from all the turmoil in her life. But by the end of the morning, she could play two of Tom's melodies on the fiddle. An area was set aside in the market place, the family put on their makeup and costumes and Gen and Sarah started attracting an audience by blowing a horn and banging a drum. The set was an empty cage on a plinth with, what looked like a huge bundle of coloured rags. Anfin skipped and danced around it. The young boy, painted gold, was wearing a turquoise skirt and silver wings. Eliza stood by one of the four glowing braziers, playing one of her new tunes. As she had been instructed, she stopped every now and again to warm her hands near the flames, it being such a cold and crisp morning, even with a fluttering of snow. The crowd, attracted as much by the warmth of the fires as the prospect of entertainment, gathered around. When there were around thirty adults, and as many children collected, Gen and Sarah returned. There followed a growing crescendo of horn blowing, drumming and cheers. Then, the show began with Gen in a loud clear voice,

"Dames and maids, ladies and gentlemen, we bring today, for your amusement, an indisputable inmate of Bedlam ..." The crowd was growing all the time with folk leaving their commerce to come and watch the entertainment. Stall holders and their customers arrived, along with drinkers from the ale houses carrying jugs of ale. Passers-by, visitors, rich and poor, young and old, all looked on, including a tall, amused looking soldier in a red uniform,

"Well, well. And if it isn't our tall, finger eating, red herring of a young lad. Now is she wearing the garbs of a lady? I'd say she was out to impress you, Billy boy. But why not dressed as an East Indiaman Captain's daughter? More like your family of seamstresses. Now isn't this red-headed changeling a wonder, and all for you, Billy Boy. Looks as though she's fallen in with these Bedlamites. And what a tumble that would be from her lofty gilded cage. Not much between her and you now, Billy Spraggs. Just bide your time; just bide your time."

At that moment there was a great puff of smoke from the brazier nearest Gen and a cloud with the distinct smell of gunpowder rose above the crowd. When it drifted away, Tom had appeared sitting in the cage. His hair looked all matted, his beard in tangles and his clothes in rags. There was a great cry of pain from him and Gen began:

> Of thirty bear years have he,
> Twice twenty been enraged,
> And of forty bin three times fifteen
> In durance soundly caged.

Then Tom sang in his eerie falsetto voice:

> But I'll find my merry mad Maudlin
> And seek what'er betides her,
> And I will love beneath or above

The dirty earth that hides her.
While I do sing any food any feeding –
Feeding drink or clothing,
Come dame or maid, be not afraid,
Poor Tom will injure nothing.

That was the cue for Eliza to play the same tune on the fiddle. While she did that, the bundle of rags in the centre, transformed into four goblins and two hags that danced around with streamers and tambourines.

Gen continued:

Hag and hungry goblins
That into rags would rend ye,
The spirit stands by the naked man
In the book of moons defend ye.

The appearance of the hags and goblins, was accompanied by much booing from the crowd, which stopped as Tom shook off his manacles and pushed open his cage. Now everyone could see that his tight-fitting, skin-coloured costume made him appear naked. While Gen continued with the poem, the hags danced around Tom, pulling from an opening in the stomach of his costume blood red streamers which were given to the four goblins and Anfin, all of whom ran around the area making a circle of scarlet. Again, Tom's singing silenced the crowd,

The moon's my constant Mistress,
And the lowly owl my morrow,
The flaming Drake and the Nightcrow make
The music to my sorrow.

And so, the play continued, for the best part of an hour, finishing with Tom returning to his cage and disappearing in another puff of gunpowder.

Alfin, and the other children, ran through the crowd towards the end of the performance with hats to make the collection, and Eliza continued playing, while Gen announced that the hags had access to the Book of Moons and that anyone wishing their fortune told could speak to the sisters in their wagon in the Furlong.

Gen congratulated Eliza and gave her a shilling from the takings. Eliza was amazed by the story of Tom O'Bedlam's search for Mad Maudlin. She said to Gen that the play reminded her of her own search for her Silvanus.

"To that effect," said Gen, "I have been talking to folk, and, of course, there are coopers in the brewery behind the church here, we can make enquiries there, they may have useful information to aid your search."

Later that afternoon Gen and Eliza went to see the coopers. There were some young lads and one elderly man who said he knew of Curtis the cooper. Previous years he had arrived at Christmas time and sold them some roughed out barrel staves but this winter he had not shown. He thought that Silvanus went to Alton at Easter time. That night the family and Eliza agreed to a plan. They would travel around visiting various villages each week and aim to arrive at Alton at Easter time. Eliza could not conceive of a better plan. She did, however, wonder whether Silvanus might return to Fiddlespit, perhaps he was there now, under the impression that Eliza had drowned, along with her sister and father. But if she went there, it would involve revealing to her mother that she was still alive. She was sure that would provoke fury in her mother, as most of Eliza's actions did. Being in disguise she was free to travel around in her search, albeit, dependent on Gen's family for her wellbeing.

52   Bladders

January 1786 – Cawsand Bay, by Plymouth harbour, Cornwall, to Modbury Devon.

Cawsand and Kingsand are two villages separated by no more than fifty yards. Both these hamlets are just above Cawsand Bay's, mostly, rock free and sandy beach. Unless the weather was from the east, this was a safe place to land and launch small boats, during both day or night. When no storm blew it clean, Cawsand reeked of fish guts and fish oil. This stench was a hangover from the enormous catches of pilchards in November by the four Cawsand pilchard boats kept on the beach. Kingsand also had four boats, and the oldest inhabitants can remember the two communities competing, to be the first out to reach the shoals of fish. As many as five thousand hogsheads of fish were landed in a good year. The fish were gutted, layered with salt and placed on the beach in huge piles. After a month, they were put in barrels and pressed to extract the oil, which was used to light homes. However, the primary income, by this time, for the two villages, was not from fishing but smuggling. A ship from France or Spain would rendezvous, some five miles offshore with the eight fishing boats that would take ashore barrels of, tea, wine, brandy and lace, to be sold on, in nearby Plymouth. Overseeing this smuggling operation was Basaba Pennell. Her mother had been an escaped slave from Barbados and her father a fisherman from Gunwalloe in Cornwall. Basaba was respected and feared, from Cremyll ferry at the entrance to Royal

Naval Dockyard to Rame Head, the southernmost tip of Eastern Cornwall. Firstly, because of her ability to wreak violence on those who offended her and secondly, because of the strength in numbers that she could summon. Everyone in the area shared in the lucrative and illegal business, which they helped defend against the regular intrusions from the authorities.

Discovering that an escaped convict had washed up, who claimed to be a cooper by trade, seemed like an answer to Bersaba's wishes. Her cooper had died a year ago, and Basaba had been forced to either purchase barrels, for her tubmen, from Plymouth, which was dangerous because the revenue men would most likely wonder why a Cawsand fishing village might be buying so many manageable sized barrels - these being the very type of casks used to transport illegally landed spirits – or, with a lack of barrels use women to carry brandy into Plymouth in cow's bladders concealed beneath their clothing. This later scheme had been a successful operation, in that, the revenue men were reluctant to put their hands up the women's petticoats. That was until parties of drunken sailors, with no such reluctance towards ladies, began to find it very amusing to split the concealed bladders with their knives and watch the brandy spill over the women's feet.

However, in Basaba's occupation, it paid to be suspicious, was this cooper a spy, or a perhaps a revenue man who might precipitate destruction upon their operation? Silvanus realised he had minimal choice in the matter, because Basaba made it clear she knew he was an escaped convict but if he stayed in Cawsand, she would protect him from the authorities. So, he went along with everything the woman suggested.

After a month, Basaba began to pay Silvanus. It was above what he would normally expect, and as he had free food and lodging, he could save a large proportion of this money for his eventual journey back to search for Eliza. He would have liked to leave as soon as he could, but he saw it as a dangerous situation. Many folk from that part of Cornwall - and a fair number of publicans in Plymouth - were beholding to Basaba and would most likely report back to her, should she put the word about that Silvanus was missing.

Two months went by, and still, there had been no opportunity of escape. He had taken to carrying his money and few belongings with him throughout the day in case an occasion to escape arose.

One morning whilst washing in the tub, outside the camp, Silvanus saw the strangest sight; five women, standing in a group, all of whom appeared grotesquely fat. Or, maybe, they were all pregnant? But if they were, then two of them were extremely aged to be in such a condition. Soon, men began to arrive, fisherman and workers of all sorts from both Cawsand and Kingsand. Basaba stood at the centre of the gathering and said,

"All of 'e knows we've been 'aving a lickle trouble with 'e revenue. They used to leave us alone to do our work, providing cheap goods to everyone. But now, another couple of our women 'ave been attacked by drunken, tars down by 'e dock gates 'n it appears 'ey are mostly 'e same bunch of sailors. It's got to stop. So today we're going to teach 'em a lesson. Every man will go to Plymouth with the bladder-women, some before 'em, and some after, but staying in sight. Spread 'e selves out until 'e get to 'e gate 'en lay into them with clubs and chains. We'll have fifty men to their dozen. It's a lesson they'll not forget in a hurry. Kingsand men, you'll take boats into Plymouth Dock. Cawsand men 'n 'e bladder-women will go on foot with one cart as far as 'e ferry boat. Every man, take a club, hide it in 'e clothes, or bundle, 'n when I give 'e signal, give those sea-crabs the beating of their lives." The men cheered and were excited at the prospect of a fight with the navy - and the extra money Basaba would most likely be sharing around. Silvanus thought it would not end as well as the men hoped. At any one time in Plymouth, there were several thousand sailors, and as many marines, all of whom could be called upon to raid Cawsand. If they found him, he might well end up being taken and put on the next convict ship to drop anchor out in the bay and he would be bound for – who knows where?

"Basaba, shall I go?" said Silvanus, "I have a score to settle with those tars after them starving me for a week on that convict ship?" Basaba, looked into his eyes, the sort of look that elderly women do not usually give to younger men, as if she was judging whether she could trust him,

"Surly, a strong feller like 'e should be able to crack a few skulls, but don't get injured, I need more barrels from 'e."

All the men walked together as far as Kingsand where there was great excitement, children, women and old men coming out to see the Cawsand war party. After a few nips of brandy all around and kisses from girlfriends and wives, the two parties split, some going for their boats and others setting off along the road to Torpoint, the latter being followed by a crowd of children.

Basaba rode the cart, which carried the bladder-women, until they reached a hill where everyone had to walk. The men all took the first three ferry boats and the women the last. By the dock gate, the men filtered into alehouses and shadowy lanes to await the signal. Silvanus thought that this would be his best chance to slip off into the crowded city backstreets. He would have to avoid being followed and watch out for naval patrols, which might ask to see papers that he did not have. The best thing would be to disappear as soon as the fight began, or just before, when all would be occupied, but two men seemed to be keeping close to him, probably at Basaba's instruction. The four bladder-women came waddling down the street towards the gate. They stopped in the centre of the road talking to one another. Young boys and men began gathering around the women, laughing and joking, until a party of six or seven sailors started jostling the women. A sailor drew a knife and a women screamed as one of her bladders was split open. The others held out tankards trying to catch a drink from the flow of liquid from the punctured bladder. The same happened to another woman. Knives were waved so carelessly that Silvanus thought to see blood on the cobbles at any moment, but one of the sailors who had just taken a swig from his tankard yelled,

"The whores, it's fucking piss." A whistle blew and Cawsand men ran in from everywhere. Silvanus ran in as well. His plan being to lose his two guards, who had picked out a young sailor trying escape back through the dock gate. But the sailor's way was blocked by the Kingsand men and he was clubbed to the ground. More sailors came out of the alehouse and set upon Silvanus's watchdogs. This was his chance, he thought, the first sailor, who had been clubbed, was up and running away down the side of the alehouse. Silvanus chased after him. The sailor knew the route, or so it seemed, until they came to a wall blocking the way. The sailor stopped, and so did Silvanus. He was just a young boy, blood covering his face, and he looked scared, as he pulled a knife from his belt. Silvanus dropped his club, held his hands up and said,

"Friend, I have no quarrel with you. I also am trying to escape," he nodded back in the direction they had just come, "I want to escape from them as much as you do."

"Why are you with that gang of smugglers then?"

"I've been held against my will for two months awaiting my chance to get away," said Silvanus.

"Aye, then. You do have the look of an honest man about ye, I suppose. This way," said the sailor, sheathing his knife, climbing over the wall and jumping down onto a muddy beach where there were a couple of wrecked and abandoned boats. Silvanus followed the sailor along the wharf until they came to a ladder, which they climbed.

"This way goes into the dock and that way leads up to Stoke Church and out to the West."

"I thank you, my friend," said Silvanus, "which direction would be safest to flee?"

"They say that to the north is the Great Moor – it's a treacherous place – if you can find your way across it without sinking into some mud hole, or freezing to death, you might escape your pursuers. I'll tell everyone what a fight you put up and how I left you for dead." He winked, and Silvanus tugged his forelock and they went their separate ways. Silvanus walked to the end of a block of warehouses and turned the corner, but Basaba barred his way, standing in front of a row of Cawsand men, all brandishing clubs and hangers. Silvanus turned to run, but there were now two men behind, having that moment stepped out of the warehouse doorway.

"I was trying to catch a sailor; did you see him? I'm sure he was one of those on the convict ship."

"I'm sure you were, my lickle hitchi witchi. Boys, remind Cooper here, where his duty lies, and avoid his hands."

It took three months before Silvanus could get up from sitting, without being reminded of his beating by the pain in his ribs. Other than that, things carried on as usual. Basaba had taken his money from him and promised he could leave when he had made five-hundred barrels. When that was done, she said, she would pay him and he would be free to go. However, Basaba's raid on the sailors had not paid off. The next gang of bladder-women had been stopped by the revenue men who had brought with them an escort of two dozen soldiers. Enough to scare off the women's guardians. Everyone was expecting a raid on Cawsand at any time. Basaba kept a horse saddled, even through the night, ready for a quick escape. To ensure that people like Silvanus did not take a liking to the mount and make their own escape, she had three men in shifts stand guard over it. All the brandy and wine had been hidden away in caves and everyone busied themselves with their fishing apparatus. Basaba told Silvanus to make a large tub to replace the leaky one that held the caramel, which was used in the flavouring of the smuggled French brandy. The French being in favour of a clear spirit whilst the English preferred a golden liquor. But they had no caramel. Silvanus engineered a false bottom in the cask. If they were raided, he planned to hide in the barrel, pull the false bottom over him and then fill the top fifth of the barrel with half rotten pilchards, pushing them up through a hole in the oak above his head. When the barrel had sufficient pilchards, he would plug the hole.

It was early summer when the alarm was raised and word came that all roads to the dock were blocked by soldiers and three launches, full of armed men, were on their way towards the beach. Silvanus followed his plan, but the smell of rotten fish was so vile he was sick and thought he would pass out at any moment. He tried to push the bung out of the side to let some air in, but had forgotten to keep a mallet with him. He hit it with his fist, bruising his hand but on the third attempt it popped out. He could hear voices,

"What was that?"

"What was what?"

"I don't know."

"Check that wagon."

"I've checked it all ready"

"Check it again."

Someone was pushing the barrel. If it tipped over, he would be found.

"Fuck that, it stinks worse than the Devil's shithole."

A whistle blew, there were some shots, he could hear the crackling of a fire and he could see smoke drifting past the bung hole. Then all went quiet. He waited until it was dark, and climbed out. He knew that he must leave the camp that night; by the morning either the soldiers or the smugglers would return. The camp was mostly burnt out but he managed to find some food and a cloak he could sleep under. He would cross the Tamar tomorrow night and travel to the north away from Plymouth. Swimming the river, he would, perhaps, rid himself of the stench of fish and then he would disappear into the Great Moor. He planned that the next town he came to; he would try to get work as a cooper and then, with some coins in his pocket, he might make his way back to Sussex, Fiddlespit and, hopefully, Eliza.

Two weeks later Silvanus was in the town of Modbury and working as a cooper's mate at a brewery and cooperage in the centre of town. After a day's work he would go with the old cooper to the ale house, where the old man had a few pints of beer and Silvanus had his food. Each Friday night they had music, actors or someone reading the broadsides. They were the usual melodramatic ballads but then, something was different, everyone had gone quiet and Silvanus heard a man reading from a broadsheet,

"Ladies were equally distinguished for their beauty and accomplishments; the gentlemen amiable in manners and of high respect. It is hardly possible to conceive a more friendly and happy society than upon Captain Percy's ship ..."

Captain Percy, what was this about? Silvanus stood up, went over to the reader, interrupted him and bought a copy of the broadsheet from him for three ha'pence.

It was about Captain Percy. Eliza's ship had sunk, some survived – but all the ladies had drowned. Eliza dead? There must be a mistake. These broadsheets were full of lies and inventions.

He slept little that night, and when he did drift off, soon awoke with a start and thoughts of Eliza, which made his heart sink and leave him empty. Why was his life so hounded by the death of loved ones? He would leave the next day and make his way back to Fiddlesham, he had only a little money but it was summer, he could sleep in fields and eat what he could. He must find out the truth.

53   Hair

Ringwood

Eliza had stayed with Gen's family for longer than she needed. She had felt safe with them and every new town, market or fair they arrived at, raised her hopes of finding Silvanus. She had grown in confidence and could, without apprehension, converse with people around her without their mouths falling open in surprise. She dressed as a man but did nothing else to hide the fact that she was a woman. Surrounded by a troupe of actors her new personality suited her perfectly and went without question.

They finally arrived at Chichester, only a few miles from her home at Fiddlesham, and she became terrified. Firstly, she might be recognised and thought of as some sort of ghost, and secondly that she was now close to finding out the truth about Silvanus and although she hoped for the best, she feared the worst. She planned to visit the clerk to the magistrates and find out from him the fate of Silvanus. She must do it but she knew what the answer would be. What then? Go back home, to be bullied by her mother? A mother who believed the wrong daughter had survived the shipwreck? Or maybe she should go down to Fiddlespit where she had met her love. She would swim out until the sea took that, which it had failed to take back in January. However, to be listened to at the magistrate's court she needed to become a lady again. She went to the drapers and spent most of her savings on a used dress, bonnet and boots.

The next morning Sarah brought some warm water for Eliza to wash in.

"But before 'e put on 'e new clothes, Ezekiel," said Sarah, "Big Sis and Little Sis 'ere wish to speak with 'e."

"Well, young Ezekiel, Sis and I 'av believed for sum time, it must be providence what brings 'e to us."

"Aye, an' now we can prove it," said the other twin. "'ere, in 'e Holy book, in the very words of Ezekiel, it tells us." Big Sis opened the well-thumbed copy of their Bible, being careful not to drop any of the loose pages. She read,

"And when they go forth into the utter …"

"Now, what be 'utter court' Big Sis?" interrupted Sarah.

"Hush now, Sarah. This doos be the words of God, 'e can't be asking what they mean, Sister."

Eliza joined in,

"I think 'utter' is just an ancient word for 'outside'."

"Well, thank 'e kindly, Ezekiel," said Little Sis.

Big Sis started again,

"And when they go forth into the *utter* court, *even* into the *utter* court to the people, they shall put off their garments wherein they ministered, and lay them in the holy chambers, and they shall put on other garments; and they shall not sanctify the people with their garments."

"That tells us what our own Ezekiel 'ere says, bees true. That 'er old clothes will not stand, and 'at 'er new ones will win people's hearts," said Little Sis.

"So, do 'at mean we take Ezekiel's old breeches and leave 'em in 'e church, 'ere?"

"Aye, probably best to, make sure Ezekiel 'ere, she find her man," said Little Sis.

The children were chased away, and Eliza at last rid herself of Spraggs' boots and breeches. Sarah washed, dried and combed her hair, saying how beautiful it was and how envious she was. Eliza put on the petticoats and dress and Sarah laced it up. Lastly, she put on the boots. How strange she felt, just to be a woman again. Part of her enjoyed the feeling but then that pain returned in the pit of her stomach, because she could not see the way ahead clearly. She was swimming in the dark again.

Outside, it was a glorious summer's day and her newly found family were standing in two lines, like a guard of honour. They were smiling but it was covering a great sadness. She stood in front of Big and Little Sis, they smiled, and curtsied. Eliza had become proficient in imitating their speech and said,

"Ooh, now bless 'e; don't let's be 'aving with any of 'at, give I's a hug." And they did. Sarah gave her a tearful kiss; Gen said that they would be here at this time in twelve months and would like to hear her cello playing and meet her Silvanus. The two girls and two boys joined hands and ran in circles around her and said they would not let her go and Tom grabbed her by the elbows, picked her up and sang,

"Fair lady lay your robes aside,
No longer glory in your pride,
We'll give 'e all our wealth in store,
    If 'e stay and tarry,
Everyone joined in with the chorus,
    "If 'e stay and tarry,
    If 'e stay and tarry , a few days more.

"We'll give 'e gold and jewels so rare,
We'll give 'e costly robes to wear

And now sweet maid, make no delay,

"The time has come, the time has come,
"The time has come and 'e must away."

Lastly, Eliza came to Anfin. She picked him up and held him tight and gave him a kiss.

"Miss, Ezekiel, please may I 'ave a piece of 'e hair. I've a box Tom made for me to keep me memberies in?"

"Of course, my dear friend, and next time we meet I shall give 'e something else to keep in your box."

54   Tuppence

Chichester

The office of the clerk to the magistrates in Chichester was in a corridor, which led to the town gaol. The room was about four yards long and six feet wide. Ledgers were piled from ground to ceiling, in high precarious stacks. There was a high window on one side which, let in shafts of sunlight projecting a latticework of rectangles on the opposite wall. The clerk was a little man with a neatly trimmed beard, rather dirty looking wig and grubby lace collar. He was sitting behind a desk, only two-and-a-half feet wide, which looked far too small for the open ledger, inkwell, quill, small pewter mug and the remains of some sort of pie.

"Good day to you, Sir. I would like to enquire about a recent prisoner held in this goal," said Eliza.

"Yes, yes, Miss, good day to you." he said, excitedly. Then, suddenly remembering his recent pie, he wiped the crumbs from his beard with a green kerchief from his waistcoat pocket. "Yes, yes, now, when was the prisoner in Chichester gaol?"

"I believe it was November last year," said Eliza.

The clerk got up, scraping his chair back and mumbling in a disapproving manner. He put away the volume from his desk and opened a set of wooden steps to stand upon, "November last, you say?"

"Yes Sir."

He reached up and removed one of the top ledgers, placing it on the floor to the right of the other stacks.

He then carried out this same operation for around a half dozen volumes, until he came to one, which he placed upon his small table. It occurred to Eliza that it would be more efficient to keep the current ledgers near the top of the piles, but the clerk did not appear the type of person that might welcome suggestions. So, Eliza kept quiet and waited.

"Name?"

"Curtis"

"Yes, yes. Curtis, you say?" huffed the clerk, whilst scanning down page after page.

"Yes, Sir. Silvanus Curtis."

"Yes, yes. Here we have it." The clerk stopped, covered the entry in the book with a piece of parchment and sat back down in his chair.

"I am afraid that there is a statutory charge, for my services, Miss."

"How much, Sir?"

"Tuppence, Miss. Tuppence-ha'penny, if you would require me to copy it for you. Thrupence, if you want it signed."

Eliza turned her back on the clerk, lifted the front of her dress over her petticoat, undid her makeshift purse from around her waist and took out a silver threepenny bit.

"I do not want it written down, but I will give you threepence for your trouble. Would you read it to me please?"

"Yes, yes. Thank you. Name: Curtis, Silvanus; Age: twenty-two; Crime: murder; Verdict: Guilty: Sentence: Death. CMP …"

Eliza cried out and began to shake. She could not breathe and was about to fall. She swayed, her back leaning against the wall, her legs gave way and she began to slide to the floor. The clerk hurried around, saying,

"Yes, yes, Miss, here, please." He took Eliza by the arm and helped her sit on his chair.

"Well, well. Yes, yes, Miss. Please, may I ask what your interest is in this matter?" he said, in a manner that was likely to be as near to, kindly as he could possibly get. It did not matter anymore to Eliza. What was the point of keeping secrets now?

"He was my betrothed, my loved-one. He was accused falsely, and now … and now he is dead."

"Yes, yes, well, no, Miss. Maybe so, but who knows who might be dead, unless they are in this room with us, but, Miss, I did not finish reading to you and explaining the entry in the ledger. CMP indicates that the prisoner's sentence was commuted by the Mayor's Prerogative. His sentence was changed, at the last moment, to one of transportation, for fifteen years. Eliza paused, trying to make sense of all this.

"Fifteen years? Where did he go?" Eliza asked, standing up and feeling stronger.

"That I cannot say, Miss. I see I did at the time record in the margin the name of the ship, it was the Martin. It may remain at sea, it may have off-loaded its prisoners, or, I am afraid, of course, it may have foundered, ah … sunk, you may not have been aware but there were a lot of storms last winter." If you write to the Royal Navy at Portsmouth, they may be able to enlighten you as to the ship's destiny, and your gentleman's, whereabouts. I will give you the appropriate clerk's name and address, here …" He scribbled the address on a piece of paper, folded it neatly and handed it to Eliza.

"Thank you," she said, "how much is that?"

"Nothing, Miss, and here, please would you take your threepence back. Searches for star-crossed lovers are without charge." He held out the threepenny bit with an embarrassed smile on his face, wished Eliza well and showed her to the door. He then busied himself replacing all the volumes in their original positions and returned to his unfinished pie with the self-satisfied glow that such transactions bring to the years of solitary record keeping of a magistrate's clerk.

55   Asylum

Chichester

"Fiddlesham House? Ain't nobody biding 'ere presently, Miss," said the man standing by the horse and trap at the end of the high street. "Been empty since loss of Captain Percy 'n all 'is family."

"I believe that the captain's lady will be there still, she was not aboard the ill-fated vessel."

"Don't know 'bout 'at, Miss. Shall I ask 'round in 'e inn 'ere. Bound to be someone 'at knows 'bout 'e Percy family."

"No, thank you," said Eliza quickly. She did not want to draw a crowd; she might be recognised. Why had she not bought a bonnet that covered her red hair? It was almost as bad as having a sash with her name embroidered across it. "Please take me there right now, I wish to see for myself. If there is no one there you will bring me back."

It was mid-afternoon when Eliza's pony and trap arrived at Fiddlesham. Everything looked unkempt and overgrown. The grass on the lawn was over a foot tall and looked more like an un-grazed meadow. Where was Esau? Had her mother dismissed him? She made it plain that she did not approve of him. The driver stopped by the front door but nobody came out to meet her. Eliza got down and walked along the front of the house and peered in through the windows to see the furniture, which was covered by sheets. Then she heard voices. The trap driver was talking to someone. Eliza walked back, around the trap and saw that it was the cook talking to the driver.

"Cook," asked Eliza, "where is everyone?" The old women turned around, and her usual scarlet chubby face drained of colour. Her mouth fell open, she screamed and ran down the side of the house and locked herself in the kitchen.

"It's alright, Cook, it is me, it is Eliza."

"Miss Eliza and Miss Marie-Anne died in their father's arms aboard his ship after the gert storm."

"No, I swam ashore, Bethany helped me but I have been all this time getting home."

"Get away, spirit. You can't be Miss Eliza, she has passed on, it was in the 'ampshire Chronicle, the newspaper. I read it meself."

It took some time for Eliza to persuade Cook that she was not a ghost. Eventually she let Eliza into the kitchen and, after more explanation, self-administered smelling sorts, a nip of brandy and a cup of tea, Cook's colour began to return. Eliza discovered that her mother had not wanted to stay at Fiddlesham and had gone to live in their smaller house at Kingston-upon-Thames. Only the cook, housekeeper and a maid remained behind. The housekeeper was at present visiting her daughter in Chichester. Esau had fallen and broken his leg and as there was no one to look after him at the house, he had to go to the workhouse in Chichester but that was full and he had been allocated a bed in the asylum wing of the workhouse.

Cook had given the trap driver some cheese and pickles, and a jug of beer. Eliza paid him and told him to return the next morning to take her back Chichester, when she would visit Esau and bring him back to Fiddlesham. He would have hated being in the workhouse away from the garden and wildlife, and God knows what effect being in an asylum would have had upon him.

"I am very sorry, Miss, but I cannot allow you to enter the asylum. The inmates are extremely dangerous."

"As I have this very moment explained to your assistant," said Eliza, "I do not believe that Esau Eyers could ever be dangerous and certainly not to me. If you will not let me in, will you please bring him here."

"I am afraid that will not be possible, either Miss."

"I understand that he was admitted to the workhouse because of an injury. As he is confined to the asylum, a doctor must have certified him as insane. May I see the doctor's certificate to that effect?"

One hour later, in the back of the trap, Esau looked pale and terrified and after another hour had not said a word or looked at Eliza. It was just after midday when the trap passed the lake on the road up to the house. Eliza stopped the driver,

"Look Esau, it is September and the devil's darning needles are flying over the lake. Look, look."

The old man slowly turned to follow Eliza's pointing finger.

"Autumn? Aye, Autumn bees early 'is year." He turned back and looked at Eliza, as if he had just seen her for the first time in a long while. Surprise gave way to his old wrinkled smile. "Miss, 'e 'ave grown some."

The next day the housekeeper returned. After a similar session, as that with the cook about the newspaper article in the Chronicle, she settled down and agreed that Eliza should take over control of the house finances, admitting to it being an irksome chore. Eliza wrote a letter to the Royal Navy asking about the convict ship named the Martin. Two weeks passed and Esau, apart from using a walking stick had returned to nearer to his old self. Then a letter arrived from Strothmann Greedy, congratulating God on Eliza's miraculous survival. However, he had written that it was with great sadness that he had to inform her that her mother had died three weeks previously after a brief illness, which, no doubt, was brought about due to a weakened heart, following the tragic loss of her honourable husband, Captain Percy and his family. Greedy said that he wished to meet with Eliza to discuss her future. Eliza knew that Greedy was some sort of cousin to her father but what her future had to do with him she did not know, so ignored the letter. She was sorry to hear of the death of her mother, that is what she told the others - and herself - but try, as she may, she could feel no grief. If her mother had held Eliza in her arms just once, after she was born, it would be a surprise to Eliza, and she certainly did not show her anything but distain for as long as Eliza could remember.

Eliza had taken to having meals in the servant's room, feeling more at ease than she could possibly in the huge rooms of the empty house. She invited Esau to come and eat with her. The old gardener was looking better already and could almost manage to walk without a stick,

"But Esau be vexed by 'ee and how 'ee 'ave come back from the dead, but I should not be surprised, 'cos I's always knows that 'ee ave a liking, a passion for life."

Eliza spent that evening telling Esau of her plans to elope with Silvanus and how that had been thwarted by her mother sending her on her father's ship to India. How the storm had wrecked the ship and how her courage had grown by thinking of Silvanus's words and

Esau's words about the spidez. She enjoyed telling him about Gen's family and how, if she could trace them, she would invite them to Fiddlesham to perform. However, sadness flooded back as she reached the end of her tale, because it was not concluded; she had not found out what had happened to Silvanus and waited each day for a reply to her letter from the Royal Navy.

"Esau, my old friend, now it is time for your story. How is it you came to work here so long ago." Before he could start, Cook returned to stoke the fire. Eliza suggested she bring some of her father's port and invite all the household to join them to toast the future of Fiddlesham. This only increased the number by two; a stable boy and young scullery maid.

"Well Esau, will you tell us a tale, or shall I fetch my cello?"

Cook groaned and everyone laughed and then Esau began,

"All of ye know what has just happened to Esau. Strapped to a bed while all mad folk round me yelled and screamed. Esau began to think he'd entered Hell itself and wondered what he had done to offend 'e Almighty so. Esau be shamed to admit now but Esau blamed his mother. For it were 'er what brought 'im into this world without a father – and Vicar says that be a sin. But Esau bees wrong to blame his mother and will try to make amends 'ere and now by telling 'e good folk Esau's story. The only time Esau have told this story, since Miss Eliza's Grandfarver, Captain Samuel, did tell it to Esau.

"Esau's mother, was Rose Percy, no older than Miss Eliza is now when Esau bees born. She bees Miss's Grandfarver's sister. Rose be shipped out to India by her parents, to find husband among the wealthy English army officers. But ship bees wrecked on Indian coast.

All crew and passengers got safely to shore but after two weeks they had not been rescued and were continually attacked by natives. After several more weeks, the crew's black-powder ran out and they were overrun by their attackers. Some of the crew ran into jungle to escape, risking wild beasts while tothers tried to escape into the sea. All but a few of crew be killed. Natives raped my mother, leaving her for dead. But she gets up, when they had gone, and hides in jungle where she meets another survivor from the crew. The two of them walked hundred miles until they came to a town. The son, born of Rose bees named, 'Esau,' after the sailor who had helped her through that long walk. Then, with baby Esau, Rose sailed back to England on a ship captained by Samuel Percy. On the long journey home, my mother became ill. On her death bed, Captain Samuel Percy promised to look after the baby, Esau. The ship docked at Plymouth and grandfarver found a priest who'd found an honest Christian family to adopt baby Esau. So, Esau lived in Debbonshire with Mr and Mrs Eyers for thirteen years. Until outbreak of fever killed many folks all over Debbonshire, including Esau's adopted mother and farver. Priest wrote to Miss Eliza's grandfarver, about young Esau's plight. Asks if Esau should be apprenticed out. But Miss Eliza, your grandfarver, Samuel, says Esau should be apprenticed here, at Fiddlesham, to an old gardener, whose name bees Jacob."

"I thought that were the name of a pike in the lake, Esau?" Eliza interrupted.

"An don't I remember that day," said the cook, "never seen such a fish. And it were same day when old Kelpwell got hit over head with a gert bucket of water and went crazy. Oh, hark at old Cookie, interrupting. Carry on with tale, Esau, if you please."

"Well, that be the long of it," continued Esau, "'cept to say that Esau 'ave lived at Fiddlesham ever since and when 'e old captain died, the young captain, Richard Percy, Miss Eliza's farver, look after Esau, and when 'e died, Esau fell over and broke a leg and got shut up in asylum."

"Miss, shall I fill the glasses again?" asked the housemaid.

After several toasts, to mothers, worldwide, the party broke up and everyone made their way to their own rooms. Eliza walked outside with Esau and down to the lake where his house was. She wanted to make sure he got there safely.

"Thank 'ee, Miss, for 'e company. Housemaid be telling Esau 'ere be a gert pile of unread London newspapers in entrance hall. She were going to burn 'em, but Esau says he'd look at 'em. Shipping reports be in 'em and 'ere maybe mention of young Curtis's ship. Martin, 'e says?"

"Yes, that was the ship's name, thank you, Esau," said Eliza.

"One tother thing Esau must tell 'ee, Miss. About his mother."

"What is that, Esau?"

"Her name."

"Well, you told us all, Esau. It was Rose."

"Yes, Rose, Rose Percy, she was a beauty, your grandfarver told I. Sort after throughout 'e land. But she refused all suitors. She were your grandfarver's sister, your great aunt, Miss. And that Esau wanted to tell 'e was, she had dazzling red hair. Just like 'e, Miss."

"So, we be … you and I, we are cousins, Esau."

"Yes, Miss. Goodnight, to 'e."

56   Greedy

Fiddlesham

"Esau 'ave found it, Miss," Esau called out.

"Silvanus?" asked Eliza, running in from the next room.

Esau read from the newspaper, "'e ship, Miss, 'e Martin, three, three-h …undred 'n …"

"Esau, give it to me," said Eliza taking the newspaper from him.

"The ship, Martin, of three-hundred and thirty-six-tons weight, on the third of January this year, dropped her anchor in Cawsand bay at the entrance to Plymouth harbour. The master of that vessel, Captain Pamp, seeking refuge from the great storm of that time, which led to so many lives being lost along the south of this realm's coastline. This correspondent has recently come to understand that there were over one-hundred-and-fifty convicts aboard the Martin. The intended destination of these felons, mostly sentenced by the Old Bailey at London to transportation, is unclear. The convicts believed their intended destination to be the west coast of Africa, and that, once there, they would be sold into slavery. Notwithstanding, His Majesty's Royal Navy has strenuously denied this, insisting that the convicts' intended destination was Nova Scotia. Whilst the Martin was at anchor and seeking refuge in Cawsand Bay the convicts broke free from their restraints, took over the ship and over fifty of them escaped to the shore. Control of the Martin was soon regained by captain Pamp, his officers and crew. The following day, the vessel, together with its remaining prisoners and crew, continued its way to Nova Scotia. It has now been five months since the Martin's departure from Plymouth and no word of the vessel or its crew has been garnered. It can only be assumed that the Martin came to a tragic end and that all on board perished. Following the Martin's departure from Cawsand Bay, the authorities ashore shot and killed seven of the escaped prisoners and recaptured thirty-four. The whereabouts of the remaining dozen men remains unknown."

"Twelve of 'e men, still bees free, 'e say, Miss?"

"Yes, but thirty-four recaptured."

"What 'e think 'as 'appened to those recaptured, Miss?"

"How should I know, Esau," she said crossly, "Transported to some awful place, locked up, or hanged."

The two of them were quiet for a while.

"Esau shall read 'e papers 'at follow that one, Miss, maybe 'ere's more of the story."

"Thanks, Esau. And sorry to bark at you."

"Never give it mind, Miss. Cousins do 'at sort of fing, like water off coot's back, Miss."

Three days later a reply arrived from the Royal Navy. It said that the ship sank two days out from Plymouth without survivors. There was no mention of any of the escaped prisoners.

As the weeks went by, Esau got back to his normal gardening routine. The horses returned with another stable-hand and ostler. Cook prepared food and the maids did what the maids had always done. All was getting back to a quiet version of normality, except for Eliza, who, apart from answering a few letters, had no real part to play in the life of a country house. Fiddlesham had existed to meet the grand plans of Eliza's father and her mother who had organised her life around the captain. What was a young woman supposed to do in a place like this? She knew that her mother would have insisted upon her finding a husband, preferably an army officer. She wondered about re-joining Gen's troupe again; at least she would have things to fill her day if she lived with them, but where would she find them? Apart from returning to Chichester or maybe Fiddlesham next year, she had no knowledge as to their intended itinerary. She doubted if they ever planned much more than a month ahead. Eliza would have to bide her time and see what she might discover about Silvanus's fate.

The next morning Strothmann Greedy arrived on horseback. Why was he here? Eliza knew him well enough but for as long as she could remember he had ignored her, except for a few occasions when Mother had made some critical remark concerning Eliza's appearance. He had glared at her, disapprovingly and then suddenly exploded with an awful, mocking, hissing laugh, rather like a donkey, Eliza thought, that was trying to bray but could not manage it. It was little wonder that she did not appreciate his visit. Meeting him, in front of the house, she hoped he was just passing and would soon ride off, but the ostler boy came out, took Greedy's horse, and then the housekeeper arrived and asked, "Would Mr Greedy be taking tea," Greedy replied,

"Delightful, I would be very pleased to take tea with you Miss Percy. How kind of you to invite me." Eliza found that she had no way of refusing him now, without making a scene. She sat in the day room at a small table, listening to, and watching the awful man silhouetted with his back against the sunlit window. Eliza could not help assessing the man. No more than five feet three inches in height, he wore clothes that were at least a generation out of fashion. His shoes, scuffed and dirty, had probably at one time been black, and his, once white, silk stockings had, what appeared to be, short lengths of brambles snagged in them. Eliza thought she would not be surprised if, back in Autumn, his legs had borne a substantial crop of mouldy blackberries. Above his stockings, he wore a knee length grey waistcoat, topped by a frock coat, which was also grey, but not cut away at the front, as was the fashion of the day. At his neck, he wore no frills or lace but showed a slightly soiled linen shirt. His grey, shoulder-length periwig had not been tied back and every time he moved his head, a snowfall of powdered ground starch filled the air – apparently, by the smell of the man, thought Eliza, this powder on his wig was not scented with orange flowers, lavender, or orris root, as was the custom, but with some concoction contrived from rotten fish. His face was a bloody battle ground of crater-filled, pockmarked and greasy skin, all surrounding a glowing red nose, so bright and red that it reminded Eliza of the baboon she had once seen in the travelling menagerie at the fair in Chichester and particularly that creature's backside. From within his nostrils, hairs sprouted and Eliza wondered if they were the tell-tale tips of an ashamed moustache, which she had spotted, like two rats, trying to escape the distressing landscape up his nose.

"One must have been devastated at not setting foot in India, what with the opportunities such an endeavour had to offer. May I be so bold as to enquire whether your father had made arrangements for you to meet any particular officers from the Indian army?" Eliza explained that there was not such an arrangement and that she had no intention of attempting another voyage to Asia.

"May one ask if you intend to run Fiddlesham, yourself? It would seem an impossible task for a lady, let alone a young lady, to manage such an estate. As you may remember I am a cousin of your family, albeit a distant relation. When your father and your mother were away from Fiddlesham, the captain was happy to allow me to oversee the management of the estate, which, I must confess, I always felt more of an honour than a chore. I remember the captain saying how comforted he was to know that I would always be here to assist in any way I could, should the need arise, the captain following, as he did, a precarious life upon the ocean." Greedy paused and offered Eliza more tea.

"May one suggest that we fulfil your father's request, and that I assist with the running of the estate. This would leave your good self to lead a more ladylike existence, and who knows what relationship might evolve in time." Eliza wondered if she had heard this man correctly. She had not been paying him a great deal attention, but had he just suggested that he take over the house and in time to come, marry her? She looked over her shoulder and noticed that there was a replacement vase in its niche. Perhaps she could relive the previous vase's demise and throw this one at this atrocious man. How pleasant it would be to drop it on his head. He continued talking about his wealth, from various business successes and how he intended to build more great mills like the one in Fiddlesham.

"Thank you, Mr Greedy"

"Strothmann, please, Miss."

"As I was saying, thank you, but I have no intention other than to manage the estate, and all my families' assets, myself." She stood, but Greedy did not follower her example.

"Good day to you, Sir," Eliza said but still Greedy did not get up from his chair and instead said,

"In that case, Miss, to fulfil your late father's wishes I shall have to seek advice from the law courts. Being under age, I am convinced that your tenure of the estate management is unlawful. I will contest it." Eliza said nothing and walked away. Seeing the housemaid on the way she told her to arrange for Mr Greedy's horse to be brought to the door forthwith and to show him out. She felt sure that Greedy was making idle threats. She remembered her father telling her mother that he was not at all sure that Greedy was in anyway related to him.

By this time, Eliza's hopes of being reunited with Silvanus were getting harder to sustain. She had to keep insisting to herself that he was alive and would one day return. Perhaps he had thought her dead and consequently he had started a new life elsewhere. In that situation how would she ever find him. She talked to Esau about her fears but he was unable to suggest any new strategies and would often smile and say nothing.

57 Honey

Esau had driven the housekeeper to the market in town for their weekly visit. They had left at first light with the intention of returning before sunset, but it was an hour after sunset when the cook reported to Eliza that they had not returned,

"I's a wondering, Miss, if you would like young Peter to ride out and see them home, Esau being old and recently infirm and housekeeper being, rather ... well you know, Miss." Eliza went out to the stable and spoke to the ostler, who agreed to go. He saddled a horse and set off with a lantern. Eliza watched the light sway down by the lake and disappear through the woods onto the Chichester Road. She turned to go back into the house when she saw a movement in the shadows. Someone was standing around the corner to the stable block.

"Miss, a word with you, if you would be so obliging." It was that horrible little man, Beatcher, whom she had met on Fiddlespit.

"What are you doing here? What business have you here?" she asked, keeping well away from him. "If you do not leave, I shall send for my man servant to remove you."

"First off, Miss, I 'ave information which you might find of interest."

She did not know what possible information this man could have, of interest to her. Eliza saw, that as well as his cane, which he rested upon, he was armed with a pistol in his belt.

"Second off, Miss: I understand that, the only staff what is here, is one stable lad and a cook, who is no doubt presently befuddling herself with the late Captain's port."

"You must leave, Sir, this instant," she said, walking away from him and towards the front door. If she could get in quickly enough, she might bolt the door behind her and get to the house's other doors quickly enough to bolt them before he had time to enter.

From inside, and feeling safer with a half-closed oak door between her and the disagreeable man, she said,

"Concerning what matter?"

"Whom, concerning whom, Miss, and my answer is the subject of my third off. I have information concerning a cooper by the name of Curtis." Eliza's heart raced, making her ears ring and her breath falter.

"What is it you know of that man, Sir?"

"Not here, not here, Miss," He pointed up at the stars above, "not under Orion's welkin. Follow me." What does this man know of Silvanus? She followed him, remaining, at what she thought was, a safe distance. He went down to the lake, over to Esau's cottage, opened the door and went inside. Eliza hesitated. A glow grew in the window as he lit the lantern on Esau's table.

"Come in, Miss, come on in. Don't be afeared." She knew that she could not trust this horrid man. It must be some sort of trap, and she was walking into it, but she had to find out what this man knew. "Come along, Miss, and you could hear what happened to Curtis. Because the hangman was saved any work on Curtis's behalf, Miss." Eliza stopped prevaricating and walked in.

"Close the door, Miss. Keep the chill of the night out."

"I insist you tell me what you know of Mr Curtis. It might be information for which I am willing to reward you, Sir."

"Please, sit down, Miss." After a moment's hesitation, she pulled the chair out and sat down at Esau's table. Beatcher stood on the opposite side, took the flintlock out and placed on the table between them.

"Now for my Fourth off: your Mr Curtis was seen in Chichester town only yesterday; my attention being drawn to his presence by an associate of mine. Of course, it was a matter of civic duty that I should report the presence of a convicted highwayman, which of course I did. I believe he is at this moment residing in Chichester town gaol." Eliza could feel tears welling up, she did not want to show a sign of weakness with this man, but what was he after?

"Why have you come all this way to tell me this information, Sir? Is it more of your civic duty?"

"That's my Fifth off, Miss. Some men are all in the eye, some in the ear, some in the arms, some in the entrails, some in the kidneys, some in the pocket, some in the mind, some are even, all in the back, but me, Miss, I be all in the heart. This brings me great suffering from that equivocating worm what always be watching his pocket watch. That worm what burrows into a man's heart. Tick, he deserves to die. Tock, he deserves to live. Tick, he deserves to hang. If only I could rid myself of that worm and his watch, Miss." This man is mad, Eliza thought. I should tip the table over and run out. But then, she supposed, even mad men sometimes tell the truth.

"No doubt you will do what you think best, Sir."

"Very true, Miss, very true, but I have silenced my worm on other occasions by amassing recompense to one side or tother, which matter do bring me to my Sixth off: as things stand the cooper will no doubt hang, bearing in mind his broken contract with the town mayor. But would you be willing to help by donating a substantial amount for me to return to town on the morrow and say that I was mistaken about the identity of Mr Curtis, in the matter of the highway robbery on the Midhurst Road. Curtis would, most likely be released and free to go about his business, and my heart's worm, for one, would leap with joy."

"I have five sovereigns to pay you, when Mr Curtis is here, and a free man."

"Must be on trust, Miss, and in advance."

"Very well, I shall fetch it."

"You might very well do that, Miss, but you might just as well return with a loaded blunderbuss, and deal with my little equivocating worm in an altogether different manner. You stay here, Miss, and tell me the location of this coinage."

He picked up his pistol and took out from beneath his coattails a set of manacles.

"Place your hands in these either side of this oak upright here, what supports the roof. Quickly, now, Miss." She gave him the key to a desk in the library, put the manacles on and he went on his way. The man was obviously lying and would be sure to find more than five sovereigns in the desk, but that would be worth it to rid herself of him.

He had been gone for a few moments, when she heard a horse approaching. The door opened and Esau walked in blinking in the sudden light.

"Miss, what 'as 'appened to 'e. Are 'e injured in some manner?" Eliza explained as quickly as she could about Beatcher, but Esau kept interrupting with questions.

"Esau, there is no time. Have you any way of freeing me from these manacles?"

"An axe, Miss. In my shed. I'll fetch it, now." But before Esau could reach the door it opened and Beatcher came in, holding his pistol. Esau stood motionless for a moment then slowly took his coat off and hung it on the back of the chair and began singing,

"There were three travellers, travellers three,
Wi' a hey down, ho down, fiddlespit hee,
Far and wide they searched for honey,
But found none here for love nor money."

He danced around, as best he could with his injured leg. Beatcher's pistol following him all the time.

"I's must jollowpise to 'e, Miss. 'Aving been carcerated for so long in 'sylum, old Esau got out ov 'e way of drinking zider. Only 'ad a 'ickle drop, but 'e 'as gone to me 'ead, me reason is all watch you might call, unreasonable. But all will be well wi' a 'ickle bit of me special honey, me special azalea honey. Let me get it. Sir, now let me offer 'e a 'ickle honey, food of 'e gods." Esau staggered over to a cupboard with Beatcher following. "Would 'e care for a spoon, Sir?"

"Sit at 'e table, old man. Where I can see 'e." Esau did as he was told, opened the big stone jar of honey and stuck a spoon in. He lifted it slowly out, winding it around and around and watching the light from the lantern shine through the golden liquid.

"Just go now," said Eliza, "You have your money."

"Oh dear, dear, 'scuse I, Miss, Esau don't feel … going to his bed." Esau got up, staggered the few steps to his bunk and collapsed on it, snoring loudly.

Beatcher walked over and poked Esau with the barrel of his pistol. Esau groaned a little but did not wake up.

"Better still," said Beatcher, sitting down at the table and picking up the honey spoon. He dug the spoon into the jar and scooped the honey into his mouth and rolled it around his cheeks. Then the sweetness awoke his greed but did nothing to quell it and Beatcher sat there spooning up the golden honey, until he could eat no more.

Esau woke up and carried on his rambling song,

The female bee do feed
Her 'usband drone 'e best,
With waxy holes 'e honey's stored.
And all 'e rest be numberless.

Beatcher stood up.

"Now, I shall take my leave … Take …" He returned to the spoon, smelt it, took another gulp of honey, thought about it, and then returned his pistol to his belt.

"Sir, you have your money, the key to these chains now, if you please." He ignored her, until he reached the door, where he turned and said,

"Fingal will sort things, by-and-by." Then he appeared to stagger and not be able to support himself with his cane, he tried to prevent himself from falling by running forward but tripped over, and ending by hitting the table with such force that the jar of honey fell to the floor and smashed. Esau stood up and Beatcher pulled out his pistol but could not focus his eyes. He waved the gun in the air, shouting,

"Fingal, Fingal come back. The pistol fired and dust fell from the thatch above. Beatcher's eyes were like fire, as he screamed out,

"Earth's giant sons of bone, in bigness those that now surpass." He stopped, looked down at his feet, and let out a great fart. This was followed by what sounded like a cow emptying her bowels onto a waterlogged field. He then fell to the floor shaking with violent rigors. Esau picked up the pistol and Beatcher's cane and threw them onto the bed.

"Miss, I shall fetch 'e axe, 'n release 'e." He went outside and a moment later Eliza heard a pistol shot. The door opened and Strothmann Greedy stood in the doorway, replacing a smoking pistol into his belt and pulling out a fresh one.

"Beatcher looks about finished to me. What, did the old man poison him?"

"Mr Greedy," said Eliza, "will you please retrieve the key to these manacles. I think it may be in that man's coat pocket?"

"All in good time, Miss. You would not want to miss out on all the fun of the fair. You really should have given my earlier offer due consideration. You might have fared better. What early talent you displayed at escaping from a watery grave, let us now watch how you cope with fire, and then, finely, Earth. Good evening to you, Miss Percy." He left, closing the door behind him. Greedy mounted his horse and headed back along the Chichester road. This was proving better than planned. In one 'accidental' fire he was ridding himself of two witnesses; the troublesome Beatcher, who might have testified against him, and the red headed Percy girl, leaving him free to make a claim on the Percy estate.

Eliza tried to get her hands free from the manacles but failed. From outside came the sound of breaking glass and the crackling sound burning straw. Eliza could see the flickering of flames lighting the window. She was going to burn to death. She stood up and tried to pull the roof support away with the manacles but it would not move. If she stuck her foot out, she might just touch Beatcher, he was still alive and crawling away from her towards the door,

"Beatcher, please the key, I shall save you. Do it now, throw me the key, Sir, before we both perish."

58   Flames

Along with half a dozen Revenue Officers and a dozen soldiers, Silvanus rode towards Fiddlesham. All but Silvanus had come down from London to investigate the disappearance of the King's Riding Officer, Warren Blackmore. Ahead of them, they saw the swaying light of a horseman leaving the Chichester road and disappearing in the heath. It looked like the rider was trying to avoid being seen. The officers went to investigate and arrested Strothmann Greedy. They had received information, which made suspected Greedy of smuggling and involvement in the murder of Blackmore.

This arrest and Silvanus's freedom had followed the huge reward, offered by the king's men, of three-hundred guineas, for information leading to information about the disappearance of Blackmore. Such a sum brought all manner of eyewitnesses to the surface. One of whom had been Harman Beatcher, who, despite being implicated by many witnesses himself, had come forward to report that Silvanus Curtis, a returned transport, had been seen in Chichester. Beatcher was suspected of involvement in several crimes but Silvanus was held by the Revenue for a while and questioned about Greedy. The king's men quickly established that Silvanus was innocent of highway robbery, being falsely implicated in the crime by Greedy and Beatcher. Also, Silvanus's information concerning the events at the Great Mill on the night Blackmore disappeared, confirmed to the Revenue that Greedy was involved with smuggling in the area, and connected to the disappearance and possible murder of Warren Blackmore. Silvanus' original sentence was quashed. Which meant that he would not be tried as a returned transport, for which the penalty would have been hanging. He was now a free man and agreed to help the revenue men with his knowledge of the area.

Having seen Greedy captured, and the work of the night done, Silvanus decided to ride on to Fiddlespit and watch the sunrise. As he approached Fiddlesham house, he saw a glow in the sky. Silvanus rode as fast as possible in the darkness, watching in dread as the flames grew higher. He rode, up the path, past the lake and leapt from his horse. Esau's cottage was on fire. Sparks flew into the air mixing with the stars. Was this real or his persistent recuring dream from his childhood nightmare? He heard his young self shouting with joy, saw him jumping up and down, crying, 'fly sparks, fly sparks, fly.' Someone was on the ground outside the cottage. He had not seen them initially because of the glare of the flames. But it was Esau. Had he been injured in the fire? He was breathing and opened his eyes, saying,

"Miss Eliza, get 'er out, take 'e axe, 'e must take 'e axe, there it be. Hurry now."

Why did he need the axe? Silvanus took it anyway. How could he enter these flames? Had his nightmare been a warning, a premonition and not a recollection? He took off his coat, dowsed it in water from the butt and kicked the door open. There was a rush of flames, which made his coat steam. He held his breath and went in, and there she was on the floor, she was alive. But having just found her, he was about to lose her. He tried to pick her up, but he could not carry her out.

"Let go, Eliza, let go. For God's sake let go, so I can get you out." Then he saw the fetters on her wrists.

She was not holding onto the oak post; her wrists were locked around the roof support. The thatch was well alight now, but cold air sucked in through the open door protected him from the worst of the heat, even so, he was choking with each breath. He did not have long. Picking up the axe, he took a swing at the oak, but the smoke was sapping his energy. Would the roof cave in when he cut through the support? He would have to chance that. With his last gasp of strength, he took a sideways blow at the post - and it splintered and gave way. The thatch fell to the ground sending showers of sparks down upon the two of them. The rush of the fire rose to a great howl, the heat set fire to his coat but Eliza, face down on the floor, had managed to pull Esau's coat over her head and protect herself a little from the worst of the heat. Silvanus dropped his flaming coat, grabbed the fetters and dragged Eliza from around the remains of the post and out into the cool air. There were sparks glowing in her hair, and her skirts were smouldering. He got a bucket of water and threw it over her. She sat upright, coughing and choking. He put his arms around her,

"Eliza ..."

"Silvanus ..."

59   Witness

The following day, the Revenue Officers discovered Beatcher crawling around the woods. He was still quite delirious from the effect of Esau's mad honey. Locked up in Chichester gaol, in the hope of clemency, he offered to tell all of what he knew about highway robberies, smuggling, kidnapping and murder. He claimed that he never knew who had contracted him to kidnap Silvanus as the gentleman remained anonymous. Furthermore, he said although he was witness to the murder of Warren Blackmore, he did not kill him. That act, he believed, was carried out by Caleb Hepworth, known as Hap'th.

Two months later, the jury at Colchester assizes, took one look at Harman Beatcher and decided not to believe a word he said during his trial. They took another look at Strothman Greedy and quickly decided that there was a gentleman whose every word could be trusted. Either that, or they were concerned that Greedy's power of retribution might reach out through his prison bars. Greedy was acquitted, while Beatcher was sentenced to be hanged. However, as reward for him cooperating with the authorities, the part of his sentence, which would normally see a smuggler 'hanging in chains' following his execution, would be waived and after death he would be buried in un-consecrated ground.

Greedy was out of action for two months due to the presence of the Revenue Officers and his resulting imprisonment. This led to his smuggling empire being usurped by the Cuckmere Haven gang, who had moved in and pressed the palms of enough locals to ensure that Greedy found great difficulty rekindling his business.

One evening in June, on the Chichester to Fiddlesham road, Willow sat on a fine white horse, he was at the head of a hundred men and trotting at steady pace while his followers jogged along around him, carrying axes, hammers and sticks. When they reached the Fiddlesham Great Tide Mill, Greedy's four watchmen decided to escape out of the back door, wade across the mill pond and disappear into the woods. The doors were broken open and the mill's machinery smashed. Sacks of flour were looted and then, following a fire being lit in one of the mills, smoke filled the buildings. There were frantic shouts from Willow telling everyone to get out before it went up. All escaped apart from one lad who had run up, instead of down, and was now trapped shouting from the open doors of the lucam. There was a rope hanging from the sack hoist but it did not reach the ground. The boy climbed down and was doing well until the flames from the floors below began to lick around his hands. He fell twenty-feet to the quay below and was lucky that his only injury was a broken ankle.

After the great mill was destroyed, Greedy disappeared. Some said, he had taken his wealth and left Sussex to start a new life elsewhere, others claimed that the Cuckmere Haven gang had murdered him, to ensure a clear path for their captaincy of the Sussex smuggling business and an end to any possible rivalry.

60   Yawning Grave

Chichester

On, what had been, an overcast morning the sun shone briefly as Beatcher climbed the steps to the gallows. His cane with the hidden stiletto had been replaced with a simple hazel stick. Beatcher had known this day would arrive ever since that day when he had stood before the naval court and those months spent in Fingal's cabin. Like all life, death would be its crowning glory. Albeit, the number of years he had endured, after being flogged around the Fleet, would come as a surprise to him. He had wallowed in the personification of death. He had seen Death's shadow where others saw empty corners. He had gloried in reading one book, supplied to him by his doctor named Fingal. Who had been taking pages from Paradise Lost, by Milton, to cover the wounds of whipped sailor's backs. Parchment, being in short supply, Fingal had told Beatcher to wash the leaves and hang them on a line over his cot to dry. Page, upon page, in random order, he had memorised but understood little.

"Any last words?" asked the hangman.

There was only a small number in the maudlin crowd that day. Earlier, the gathering had been quite lively, as it watched a pick pocket and a horse thief meet their end. But now it was lunch time and the square had almost emptied while the nearby inns had filled.

"First off: there be a small recompense in our larboard pocket, for 'e making tidy work of today's business in hand. Second off: we'd like to deliver a few final words, and to that end, 'e'll find further compensation in our starboard pocket. Following which we have a Third off, if 'e would be so obliging."

"A gentleman, ye be sir. I knew it on first sight. Owing to the frequency of these squalls today, perhaps you would allow pithiness to be your chaperon. Now, if ye wouldn't mind Sir, please to position yourself above this fine panel of elm wood. Now, keep 'e elbows close by. That's good. Now I'll take your stick and just secure your hands at the back here." The hangman rummaged in his pocket, hemp for a working man, leather for a gentleman and a silk plaited sash, for the ladies. He chose hemp for Beatcher and tied his wrists behind his back.

"The platform is all yours, Sir."

Beatcher stretched his head as high as his neck would allow him, and began,

"By Sin and Death, a broad way did we pave
To expedite our haggard march along;
We toiled out our uncouth passage,
Forced to ride the intractable abyss;
Plunged into the womb of unoriginal Night,
Swept through that Chaos wild.
Our journey strange with clamorous uproar
And all protesting Fate supreme
Holes, Caves, Lakes, Fens, Bogs, Dens, hide shades of Death,
A universe of Death, which God by curse
Created evil, for evil only good,
Where all life dies, death lives, in nature vast,
Both Sin, and Death, the yawning grave at last."

The dozen drunks and the few curious in the crowd, who had remained and not wandered off to the inn for lunch, looked puzzled or disappointed and a few harked back to that day when a highway robber had performed a song and a jig on his gallows. Beatcher strained his neck around to speak to the hangman behind him,

"Now, to my Third off ..."

But in an instant with the skill and sleight-of-hand of an illusionist, the hangman's right hand slipped the noose over Beatcher's head, pulled it tight, while his left hand operated the lever, springing the catches, opening the trapdoor, bringing a feint-hearted gasp from the crowd of stragglers and sending Beatcher on his way ... to his yawning grave at last.

61   Summer

Fiddlesham

"Early summer be Little Sis's best loved of times. Leaves be bursting with greenness 'n flowers blushing with blooms," said Little Sis.

"And the sky be full of skylarks lost in the sunshine," said Big Sis.

"Seeing the ospreys catch the mullet from the harbour, that's my favourite," said Silvanus.

"Cock blackbird singing from highest tree," added Little Sis.

"Queen bees up, and out of 'er hive, just 'cause she fancy a change, while 'e drones swarm after 'er," said Sarah

"Drones chase 'em out cause of all their nagging," said Gen. Tom began singing gently,

"When birds do sing,
hey ding-a-ding-a-ding,
hey ding-a-ding-a-ding,
sweet lovers love the spring."

"It be summer now, Tom, ain't spring anymore, sing us a summer song." whispered Gen. Tom sang, "Summer is a coming in" and every one joined with, "Loudly sing, Cuckoo!"

Tom continued his own, and louder,

"The cow lows after e calf.
The bullock stirs,

The stag do fart …"

The whole congregation giggled and then went silent as they saw the vicar come out from behind the pulpit.

Esau entered, almost unrecognised in a frock coat, wearing a red rose and on his arm was Eliza, wearing a white dress and daisies in her hair.

After Eliza and Silvanus were married, the family carriage took them back to their house with more than a hundred followers on foot. They all joined in with an afternoon filled with feasting, dancing and music, followed with a magic show from Gen's troupe, of jugglers and tricksters. The banquet was Cook's greatest triumph: haunch of venison with, carrots, turnips, prunes and bowl upon bowl of blood red tracklements. Then the beer and wine began to flow with toasts to the couple from everyone who had drunk enough to overcome their public speaking nerves.

"Esau," asked Silvanus, "shall we have no toast from you, Esau?"

"No, not a toast, from Esau," said Eliza, "but a story, if you can think of an appropriate one for the occasion." Esau thought for a while, then got to his feet, propping himself up with a stick.

"Did 'e see 'e sun rise 'is morning over 'e trees? If 'e did 'e might 'ave seen the sun sparkle through a lickle crystal dewdrop on yesterday's new mown grass below 'e lake. An' see the warmth of 'e sun create a tiny new-hatchling elver in that dew. Not as long as my lickle finger, 'ere. An' with glassiness like 'e finest crystal tear drops. Well, on its way down across the grass, 'is elver met an old an' wily adder.

"Why, for one so newly hatched do you carry such a load of worries into 'is world, young elver?" Asked the snake.

"'Cause us elvers 'ave a long an' perilous journey ahead. Down tumbling streams, through rolling surf, cross a wide and awe-full ocean and all the way there are men with traps, snares, baskets and lines trying to catch us and kill us."

"Why bother?" asked the adder, "Just stay 'ere an' warm 'eself in 'e morning sunshine, like us adders."

"We 'ave to go to find our partners and then swim back 'ere to die alone. But for all our journey there are men, with spears, snares an' nets. We are so much alike, mister snake, us eels an' you adders, that man must make your life a misery too."

"No, man leaves us alone, an' causes as no harm," said the adder, stretching its curls to warm its underside in the sunshine.

"Please, tell me how us eels can stop man from ruining our lives. Is it your venom that scares them off?"

"No, more fearsome than that; it is our reputation that keeps us safe. And that be the end of my tale," said Esau sitting down again.

Sitting at the dining tables were villagers and others, who had come to pay their respects and take some beer to toast the couple. Some were sitting on the lawn while others leaned against trees. Willow was there, looking on and wondering how this new land-owning family would shape up. No doubt the same as all other landed gentry. How Curtis has changed from attending our meetings of Will O' the Wisps, to now looking every part the landowner. Willow could not see him helping towards the revolution. Sitting, surrounded by children, asking questions about fighting savage Cherokees in the war with America, was a soldier. He had managed to get hold of a bottle of brandy by telling the cook how he had saved Miss Percy on the night of the great shipwreck. But no, he did not want Miss, to know he was here. Perhaps he would surprise her tomorrow.

"Now be off with 'e, children." The soldier got up and walked away from the crowd, and stopped at the edge of the woods to turn and watch Eliza and Silvanus wave from the steps of the house.

"Now isn't that a pretty sight, Billy, me boy. Doesn't she look every inch the budding bride and don't us two have some unfinished business to settle. And won't she be pleased to meet you again, Billy? Well, maybe, yes; maybe, no. We shall see."

62   Like two nightingales

Our heroes' lives were filled with happiness and love throughout the long days of that sweet summer. Mingies came to visit and, with the help of some of Eliza's fortune, became the innkeeper of the Cat and Fiddle inn.

Billy Spraggs joined with representatives from the Cuckmere Haven smuggling gang on the understanding that he might add some corporal violence to the gang's growing local presence. And despite everyday imagining that he would realise his vengeful dream of attacking Eliza, he never found the opportunity and settled to quench his feral viciousness by attacking less protected young women. However, in the Spread Eagle one evening his uncontrollable appetite for brandy and young women, led him to get into a fight with the betrothed of a woman whom he had attacked earlier that week. Spraggs pulled a knife and the young man hit him with a coal skuttle and cracked his skull. Three nights later, in Chichester infirmary, Billy Spraggs cried out for his ma, and died.

Gen's troop of Bedlamites, after a stay of a month or so, left Fiddlesham to travel around Southern England with a pledge to return one summer soon.

Then, nine months later, the ostler and the cook discovered that two horses, a cart, Silvanus, his coopering tools, Eliza, her violin and cello had disappeared.

Esau, when asked of the young couple's whereabouts, would look at his interrogator and if they had a little of the collie-bird about them, with a sparkle in their eye, he would tell them the fable of the nightingale. Albeit, his new version was much shorter than the usual tail, in that the two caged birds, confronted with an open door to their gilded cage, just seized the moment and flew away. If, however, Esau's inquirer had the look of the mallard duck, with an unimaginative dullness to their eye, he would say that maybe they had tired of inherited wealth with others working for them and still others feeding them and that they had decided to disappear and make their own way in the world.

Esau looked after the garden and watched as the bees collected nectar and made their honey; damsel flies filled the air in Spring; young pike in the lake grew older and fatter and the sea filled the harbour twice daily. Until one day, whilst weeding the azalea bed, his heart stopped, he died and his body joined the leaf mould in a sunny corner of Fiddlesham graveyard.

Ships sailed the oceans; multitudes continued their journeys from the countryside, filling the cities and travelling the world. Masses slaved and slept, thieved and laboured, fought and loved. Millers ground grain and printers printed broadsheets. At fairs and markets singers sang, musicians played and, if you knew where and when to look, a red-haired women could be seen and heard playing the fiddle, or occasionally the cello, performing an unusual mix of folk tunes, Bach and Purcell. While her handsome husband, the cooper, sold barrels, trugs and hazel hurdles. And the sun, moon and stars journeyed the heavens and the world kept on turning.

List of Characters

Abel, Alfred   Servant to Captain Richard Percy. Accompanies the captain on journeys in the post chaise.

Austin, Osimond   One of Greedy's men who has three children and a wife and is killed by Warren Blackmore in the fight with the smugglers at the Great Mill.

Anfin   Infant son of Gen and Sarah.

Beatcher, Harman   Had been, 'whipped around the fleet' when a sailor and crippled by his injuries. It was at this time that Fingal, the ship's surgeon, introduced him to Paradise Lost, by Milton. He was a pressgang leader, then a smuggler and organiser of highway robbery. He was paid to kidnap Silvanus Curtis.

Berrington, Anne   Married to Thos. Berrington. Has a daughter, Jane, in India.

Berrington, Thomas   Son of Samuel Berrington. First mate. Brother of Mary Percy. Captain Percy's brother-in-law.

Berrington, Samuel   Ship owner and financier.

Basaba (Pennell)   One eyed Cornish/Romany. Leader of the Cawsand smuggling gang.

Bethany, Florence   Eliza's governess and later, travelling companion (Little Flossy, when young).

Beavans, Solomon   Sailor. Twin brother to Michael. Shanty-man,

	Scribe and letter reader.
Beavans, Michael	Twin Brother to Solomon. Ship's blacksmith. Also, a carpenter. Superstitious nature.
Bone, Betty	Witchfinder (popular because of her cheapness).
Blackmore, Warren	Ex-soldier, ex-miller and married to Susan with daughter, Rosie. Horse called Lassie.
Blackmore, Susan	Warren's wife and mother of Rosie.
Box, Jonas	Executioner of Butt & Lilly.
Bowden or Beau Dan	See Threadgate.
Butterworth, John known as Butt.	Beatcher's son and gang member. Always with Hap'th.
Congleton, John	Second mate aged around fifty.
Curtis, Silvanus	Eliza's lover. Lived in Fiddlesham until his cottage was burnt down and his father killed by Greedy's men. His mother arranged for him to be apprenticed to a Royal Navy Cooper in Portsmouth. He is now a journeyman cooper.
Dibber	One of Butt and Hap'th's two duck-baiting water spaniels. The other being, Lady.
Dicey, Agathe	Companion to Medici, Violante.
Dimo	Silvanus' horse (Named after a famous 18th Century racehorse called, Diamond.
Dodds, William	Ship's carpenter – not on board.
Douglas, Bill	Bill Douglas. Unfairly flogged aboard the ship HMS Berry. Took his captain, Johnson, to court before Lord Loughborough.
Eyers, Esau	Gardener to the Percy family. Friend to Eliza. Illegitimate son of Rose, Eliza's great aunt.

	Richard Percy's father was Rose's brother and Samuel Percy, arranged for him to be adopted by a Devonshire family, the Eyers family, but both the Dyers died in an epidemic and Esau was apprenticed to the Fiddlesham estate gardener until Esau became head gardener himself.
Fingal, Paddy	Ship's surgeon to Beatcher. Imagined by Beatcher to be his guiding spirit.
Fluck, Tom	Steward and cook aboard Captain Percy's ship.
Greedy, Strothmann	Captain Percy's land manager and justice of the peace in Chichester. He claimed to be a distant relation of the Percy family. He was owner of the Great Mill and the organiser of local smuggling.
Harrison, John	Sailmaker aboard the ship.
Hawkins, Clement Capt.	Captain of the soldiers aboard Captain Percy's ship.
Hawks, Lily	Bar maid in Spread Eagle. Made pregnant by Threadgate and abandoned. Hanged alongside Butt for the murder of her infant child.
Hepworth, Caleb Sycorax known as Hap'th.	Always with Butt. Works for Beatcher.
Hepworth, Winnie	Hap'th's Aunt.
Jackson, James	Carpenter's mate aged 15 years.
Kadam, James	Percy family coachman and strong arm man.
Kalinda	Soldier's Indian wife. Coming to England for the first time with her English soldier husband.
Kelpwell, Beatrice	Eliza's governess before Bethany. From Devon.

Knapman, Genesis	Known as Gen. Leader of the Bedlamites theatre troupe.
Knapman, Sarah	Bedlamites theatre troupe performer and Gen's wife.
Lady	One of Butt and Hap'th's two duck-baiting water spaniels. The other being, Dibber.
Long, Bess	The Bedlamites' musician who had died before Eliza joined them. She was Tom's sister.
Long, Tom	Bedlamite alto singer and actor with Gen's troupe.
Mansell, Anne	Nervous passenger aboard the ship.
Martin	Convict ship, 14-gun sloop, taking Silvanus to the Americas – or may be Africa.
Medici, Violante	Italian companion to Miss Dicey.
Miller, Edward	Eliza's music teacher and supplier of keyboards to Captain Percy. Born in Doncaster.
Miller, Thomas	Older brother of Edward. Emigrated to India.
Miller, William	Musician of Doncaster and father to Thomas and Edward. Business partner of Captain Percy.
Mingy, Nathaniel	A topman – sailor who works in the uppermost part of the rigging. Born in Plaistow, East London, to a family of eel fishermen.
Mopsy	Suggested girl of Butterworth. She brings Butterworth leftover drinks from the inn, all mixed together, when it's called "All Nations."
Moxen, Davy	A popular young lad who was mixed up in smuggling and caught by Warren Blackmore and hung in chains.
Muffit, Hattie	Wife of Lavender Muffit.

Muffit, Lavender	Boy from prison who accompanies Silvanus from Jail to the prison hulk, HMS Pegasus. Married to Hattie five months and a baby on the way. Whilst being transferred from the hulk to a transportation ship he dives overboard despite wearing a ball and chain and disappears – presumed drowned.
Pamp, Alexander	Captain of ship, the Martin taking convicts to the Americas. Pamp was planning to try and sell them into slavery, although illegal since end of US War of Independence. If not take them back to the coast of Africa.
Parks, Amy	Eliza's cousin – drowned on ship.
Parks, Anabel	Eliza's cousin – drowned on ship.
Parks, Anne	Sister to Captain Richard Percy. She is visiting England. Husband of John Parks.
Parks, Jane	Daughter of John and Anne Parks. Older sister to Amy and Anabel. Went to India on Captain Percy's previous trip.
Parks, John	Father of Amy and Anabel and wife to Anne. He is in India.
Percy, Eliza	Red haired daughter of Captain Richard Percy.
Percy, Ezekiel	Zekie. Pseudonym for Eliza while on the road from Dorchester to Ringwood.
Percy, Mary nee Berrington	Eliza's mother. Captain Richard Percy's wife.
Percy, Mary-Ann	Younger sister to Eliza. Drowned.
Percy, Richard	East India Company Captain. Father of Eliza.
Percy, Samuel	Father to captain Richard Percy. Sister to Rose Percy. Eliza's Grandfather.

Percy, Rose	Aunt to Captain Richard Percy. Raped on the coast of India and gave birth to Esau, later named Eyers.
Percy, Welstan	Older brother to Eliza. Sent to India after raping a servant.
Pegasus	Dismasted ship used as a holding vessel or prison hulk. Moored in a quiet backwater in Portsmouth.
Reeve, Henry	Third mate. Aged around thirty-five.
Sadly, Betty	Aged 3 months. Buried with Daniel Threadgate.
Sampson, Ben	African crew member. African name was Ingulule Manqondo. Last to be rescued from the cave.
Schwartz, George	Passenger returning to India with cockerels.
Smith, Nellie	Aged 75. Buried in a common grave with Daniel Threadgate.
Solomon	See Solomon Beavans.
Spraggs, Billy	Young soldier from County Clair, Ireland.
Templar, George	Father of Harriet Thomas Miller's love. Wife of Jane.
Templar, Harriet	Daughter of George Templar and Jane.
Thomas, Tom	Aged 1 month. Buried in a common grave with Daniel Threadgate.
Threadgate, Daniel named himself Beau Dan – misheard as Bowden.	Printer and highway man. Follower of the famous, Sixteen-String-Jack-Rann.
Tom	See Tom Long.

William, Albert – known as Willow	Would-be revolutionary, distributer of political flyers, follower of Thomas Paine.
Zekie	See Ezekiel Percy.
Zoffany, Johan	German painter who worked in England and India and travelled to India on Captain Percy's previous voyage.

Bibliography

Aesop Fables, Various online collections,
https://www.pagebypagebooks.com/Aesop

Brewer's Dictionary of Phrase & Fable: Adrian Room, Cassell Publishing, 1959

A Circumstantial Narrative of the Loss of the Halsewell (East-Indiaman.) Henry Meriton & John Rogers, William Lane, 1786

The Common Ashodel, Robert Graves, Hamish Hamilton, 1949

An interesting and Authentic Account of the Loss of the Halsewell, East – India – Man, W. Bailey, 1786

Common Sense, Thomas Paine, Will Jonson, 1776

Dictionary of English Folklore, J. Simpson & S. Roud, Oxford, 2000

1811 Dictionary of the Vulgar Tongue: A Dictionary of British Slang, University Whit & Pickpocket Eloquence, Frances Grose, Digest Books, 1785

Feeding Nelson's Navy: The True Story of Food at Sea in the Georgian Era, Janet Macdonald, Chatham Publishing, 2004

The Fishing Fleet: Husband-Hunting in the Raj, Anne de Courcy, Phoenix, 2012

Food in England, Dorothy Hartley, Macdonalds and Jane's

Forgotten English, Jeffrey Kacirk, William Morrow, 1997

The Intolerable Hulks: British Shipboard Confinement 1776-1857, Charles Campbell, Heritage Books Inc., 1993

Jackspeak: A Guide to British Naval Slang, & Usage, Rick Jolly, Fosama Books, 1989

Jack Tar: Life in Nelson's Navy, Roy and Lesley Adkins, Little Brown, 2008

The Great Mutiny, James Dugan, Andre Deutsch, 1966

Henry Mayhew: London Labour & the London Poor, Rosemary O'Day & David Englander, Wordsworth Classics,

Jack Nastyface: Memoirs of an English Seaman, William Robinson, Chatham Publishing 1973, first published 1836

Nelson's Navy, The Ships, Men and Organisation 1793-1815, Brian Lavery, Conway Maritime Press, 1990

Nummits and Crummits: Devonshire Customs Characteristics and Folk-lore, Sarah Hewett, Burliegh, 1900

Old Bailey Records: The Proceedings of the Old Bailey,
 https: www.oldbaileyonline.org, 1674-1913

Paradise Lost, John Milton, Online Text.

The Peasant Speech of Devon: and Other Matters Connected Therewith, Sarah Hewett, Elliot Stock, 1892

A Pocket Guide to the Superstitions of the British Isles, Steve Roud, Penguin Books, 2004

Sea Life in Nelson's Time, John Masefield, Leo Cooper, 1905

Shakespeare's Bawdy, Eric Partridge, Routledge & Kegan Paul Ltd., 1955

Sixty Ribald Songs from Pills to Purge Melancholy, S.A.J.Bradley, Andre Deutsch 1968

Smuggling & Smugglers in Sussex: By 'a gentleman of Chichester', WJ Smith, 1748-9, 1878

The Unfortunate Captain Peirce: and the Wreck of the Halsewell, Phillip Browne, Hobnob Press, 2015

The Universal Etymological English Dictionary, Nathan Bailey, Ulan Press, 1726

The Village Labourer 1769-1832: A study of the government of England before the Reform Bill, J.L. Hammond & Barbera Hammond, Alan Sutton Publishing Ltd., 1987

The Complete Angler. Izaac Walton: Online www.anglicanhistory.org/walton/angler/

Johan Zoffany: Artist and adventurer, Penelope Treadwell, Paul Holberton publishing, 2009

The Percy Family

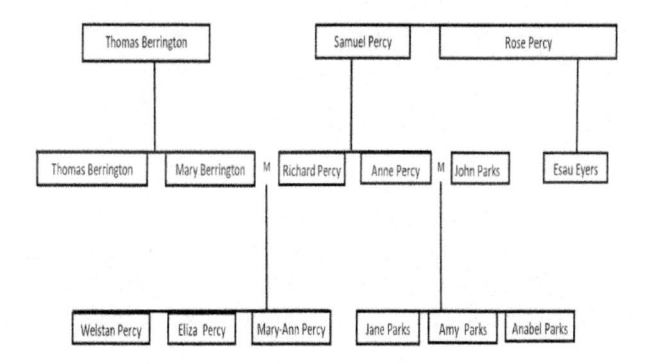

```
        Thomas Berrington              Samuel Percy           Rose Percy
               |                            |_____|
               |                                     |
 Thomas Berrington   Mary Berrington  —M—  Richard Percy   Anne Percy  —M—  John Parks    Esau Eyers
                            |                                                  |
        _____|_____            _____|_____
        |              |              |                    |              |              |
   Welstan Percy   Eliza Percy   Mary-Ann Percy         Jane Parks     Amy Parks     Anabel Parks
```

Printed in Great Britain
by Amazon